True Colours

True Colours

SUE HAASLER

ISIS
LARGE PRINT
Oxford

First published in Great Britain 2004
by
Orion Books, an imprint of The Orion Publishing Group

Published in Large Print 2006 by ISIS Publishing Ltd.,
7 Centremead, Osney Mead, Oxford OX2 0ES
by arrangement with
The Orion Publishing Group

British Library Cataloguing in Publication Data
Haasler, Sue
    True colours. – Large print ed.
    1. Country life – England – Fiction
    2. London (England) – Fiction
    3. Large type books
    I. Title
    823.9'2 [F]

ISBN 0–7531–7475–8 (hb)
ISBN 0–7531–7476–6 (pb)

Printed and bound in Great Britain by
T. J. International Ltd., Padstow, Cornwall

Thanks and love to everyone who helped with the writing of this book, including: Heiko and Mika, Emma Chaplin, Hsin-Yi Cohen, Barbara Henderson, Hilary Johnson, Christina Jones, Kate Mills, Sarah Molloy, Sue Moorcroft, Caroline Praed, Mags Wheeler and Jane Wood.

CHAPTER
ONE

The cliff edge had vanished as cleanly as a stone dropped down a well.

Only a few hours earlier, Beth Jackson had walked outside, into the shrieking wind and rain, and, even though she knew it was a stupid thing to do, she had stood right on the brink of the cliff. The sea was tearing at the rocks deep below in the darkness: she could taste the tang of salt in the air and hear the roar of it. The wind screamed louder, dragging the breath from her mouth and whipping her almost-black hair around her head so that she looked like a sea spirit. She wrapped her arms around herself, burying her cold fingers deep into the wool of the big blue sweater she was wearing — the one that had been Martin's favourite.

Beth knew she was too close to the edge, dangerously close even, but she felt as if she needed to be: that if she didn't look her fears straight in the face sometimes she might be overwhelmed by them. On stormy nights like this it was her habit to go out to that spot; sometimes she cried and sometimes she howled at the wind in anger and if she also felt frightened, so much the better. Afterwards she always felt it had helped.

This night felt different. The storm was more fierce than anything she'd ever known in a whole lifetime of living by the sea, and for a moment it was as if she wasn't standing on the ground at all but was being whirled around in mid-air. She turned to look back at the lighthouse for reassurance. It had stood since 1890, the tallest building for miles around and the brightest, even though the light had been decommissioned and replaced by the automated one out on the rocks. A sudden snatch of moonlight appeared between the filthy black clouds, illuminating the white-painted tower. But on this awful night, instead of looking reassuring it looked like the arm of a drowning man.

Beth pushed a wet hank of hair away from her pale face, her eyes huge and dark and sad. She'd started to shiver, and belatedly realised she was soaked through. Before she turned away to go back to the house, she cast a final look across the black expanse of sea. She did this so automatically she hardly realised she was doing it, and would never have admitted to herself that even after three years she was still looking for the lights of a boat that was never going to come back.

Her feet squelched on the path as she made her way to the largest of the three white-painted cottages that formerly housed the families of the keepers of the Last Reach Point light. The other two were currently unoccupied, their windows unlit.

Beth's father, Bill, was sitting by the fire reading. The table lamp cast deep shadows in his face. Only in his early sixties, he had the deeply lined face of a person who'd spent most of his time outdoors, generally in bad

2

weather. Even with the lines, he somehow managed to look young. It was the spark in his eyes and his resolutely black hair that gave him a Peter Pan look. He looked up, putting his book down on his lap. "There you are, Beth. Nasty old night," he said, with his usual genius for understatement. He didn't comment about Beth going outside in such weather; it was his nature to let people be what they wanted to be and not to worry much about it. Beth thought of her mother, who would have been rushing about getting towels and running hot baths for her when she saw how wet and cold she was. That was the difference between mothers and fathers, and since this particular father had been a lighthouse keeper all of his working life, he wasn't going to get worked up about a bit of bad weather. But this was more than a bit of bad weather: Beth had felt genuine fear and vulnerability out there.

"The waves are slamming at the foot of that cliff so hard you can feel the ground move," she said, holding her frozen fingers out towards the fire.

He nodded. "It's a bad 'un. I've seen worse, mind." Beth knew he was putting on a brave face, and how worried he really was by the ever-crumbling cliff. Their property, which had once been fifty metres from the sea, was now practically falling in — ten metres and counting.

"Where's Danny?" The thought that her son might be outside on such a night really did terrify Beth.

"Skulking in his room as usual." That was no surprise: for Danny to be out would require him to move, and he was currently in the middle of a very prolonged phase of teenage inertia.

"What's he doing?"

"Whatever it is he does up there — your guess is as good as mine. What that lad needs is a hobby. When I was his age —"

"I know," Beth managed a little laugh. "When you were his age you had your amateur radio."

"It's a decent hobby," Bill said. "Did I ever tell you about the time . . ."

"You probably did," she said, knowing that he wouldn't be offended, "and I'd love to hear about it all over again, but I need to change out of these wet clothes first."

In her bedroom, which was small, plain and white walled, like all the other rooms in the cottage apart from Danny's, which he'd painted a delightful shade of blood red, she exchanged one pair of jeans for another, and dragged the soaking woollen jumper off over her head. She held it in her hands for a few moments, reluctant to let it go: wearing Martin's jumper felt like the nearest thing to having his arms around her and she always hated to take it off. She sat down on the bed, still holding it, and gazed out of the window. The storm seemed scarcely less frightening for being behind a pane of glass. It was alive and real and snarling around under the windows. Beth thought about the last time she'd seen Martin, when his boat had rounded the Point and he'd stood on the deck waving at her, as he always did. Except that time, he hadn't come back.

4

The bedroom door opened a crack. Reflected in the window it was as if she was seeing the ghost of Martin as he'd looked when she first met him. They were both fourteen. Beth's mother had recently died. Bill had been appointed as principal keeper at Last Reach Point, and he and his daughter moved up from the Channel Islands which was where his last posting had been.

Lighthouses were so much a part of Beth's life that she was primed to pick out the brightest beacon in any landscape, and in the school playground on that first day it had been the bright chestnut hair of Martin Jackson that had drawn her towards him like a harbour light signalling to a little tugboat. He was so funny and confident, she'd loved him from the day she first saw him, although it was years later before she got him to admit he'd always felt the same about her.

"Mum?" The reflection in the window suddenly spoke, and Beth turned to see her son Danny standing in the doorway. Tall and whip-thin, with his father's red-brown hair and almost turquoise eyes, Danny was looking more handsome every day, if only he hadn't looked so miserable the whole time. At sixteen he was the age and build to carry misery most elegantly, but it tore at Beth's heart that he was always so sad.

"Hi," she smiled at him encouragingly. He carried on simply standing there. "Did you want something?" Sometimes talking to Danny was like talking to a rather taciturn toddler. She patted the bed next to her and was quietly pleased when he came and sat down. He reeked of cigarette smoke, and she was about to say something but let it go. "I was just thinking about your dad," she said.

"Don't." His voice came out cracked, like it used to when it was breaking, and he cleared his throat.

"Don't what? Think about him?"

"*Talk* about him. Don't."

"Oh. Okay." Beth had tried both approaches with Danny since Martin had died: talking about his father, not talking about his father. In three years she still hadn't managed to work out what was best, what would help. All she knew was that talking about Martin helped *her*.

"Is everything okay, Danny?" In the window she watched his reflection, his eyes rolling to the ceiling, his mouth forming a straight, stubborn line. But at least he was sitting there; at least he'd come to find her. Maybe there was hope yet for her beautiful boy.

Before he could speak there was a sound like a long explosion, a bomb going off in slow motion. Beth and Danny jumped up from the bed and ran downstairs. The front door was open, and the wind whipping through it was blowing the pages of Bill's book, abandoned on the hearthrug. They rushed outside to where Bill was already standing. Ashen-faced, he motioned frantically to them to keep back. "A big chunk of the cliff's just fallen," he said.

The ground that Beth had been standing on only a few minutes earlier was now fresh air. They stared at the jagged, broken edge of the cliff and the gaping darkness beyond it.

As if they'd rehearsed it for a scene in a documentary about the doomed Last Reach lighthouse, all three turned and looked at the lighthouse tower. Once so invulnerable and safe-looking, it now looked all too precarious. The distance between its base and the sea was only about half of its height — you didn't need to be an engineer to work out that it wouldn't cope with much more of the ground falling away.

"Now what do we do?" Danny said.

CHAPTER
TWO

Finian Lewis looked up from his laptop computer and out of the train window into the rain-spattered darkness. He thought for a second, then began typing again, a frown of concentration furrowing his otherwise unlined face. Opposite him, Gareth Dakers, former television personality and potential future Member of Parliament, snoozed peacefully, a lock of dark hair curling on his forehead making him look like he was taking time out from filming the latest Jane Austen adaptation. There was something almost narcoleptic about the way Gareth could doze off in the middle of the most stressful situations. Finian envied him — he could never sleep while there was work to be done, and there was always work to be done. The next few months were crucial not only to Gareth's ambitions, but to Fin's as well: steering this man safely into Westminster would give him a lot of kudos in his company: a partnership had even been hinted at, and at thirty-five he was more than ready for it. Not wanting to waste a single moment of preparation time, he carried on working while his employer slept the untroubled sleep of a man confident in the knowledge that his praetorian guard was sorting everything out on his behalf, and all he had to do was to wake up refreshed and ready to smile and kiss babies.

Fin shuffled through a pile of papers and took out a map of the Northlands East constituency. It looked practically barren: the market town of Boldwick where they were now headed was the only town of any size. There were a couple of handfuls of small villages, and a hell of a lot of moorland and farms. This wasn't going to be easy. Both he and Gareth were urban creatures by habit and inclination, and cities were what they did best.

The biggest problem (or rather hurdle, he refused to countenance the word problem), as Fin saw it, was that Gareth Dakers had no local connections with Northlands. Their best option was to make him a born-again northerner: he would appear in his future constituency as much as possible, get involved in local issues, become an indispensable part of the local scene. Fin knew that it was a huge mistake to only go to the constituency when you wanted votes from them. You had to be seen as an advocate, a friend: keep things small-scale and personal.

The first step would be the selection meeting tonight. This would be the first chance that the constituency party in Northlands would have to see and speak to their prospective candidate. It was going to be a formality — word had been handed down from on high that Gareth Dakers was very much the candidate of choice for Northlands East. There was, however, a largish spanner in the works: Mrs Dakers. Or rather, the *lack* of Mrs Dakers. Having the dutiful spouse by his or her side was an enormous asset for a candidate, and since Mrs Dakers was well known herself from her former role as one of the Limit Lovelies from the game show *Take It to the Limit*, it would have been worth several of the committee members' votes just to have her there.

Fin had been furious when she'd announced she wouldn't be making the trip.

"I have commitments," she'd said, in her ludicrously posh accent that still couldn't quite disguise her working-class roots. "I can't just drop everything at a moment's notice."

"What commitments?" he asked her, and she'd given him that look that she reserved for the cleaning woman, the man who did the garden, Gareth's secretary Paul, and for him — they were all the hired help as far as she was concerned. And as far as Fin was concerned, Lorelei Dakers wasn't as grand as she liked to think she was.

"I have an appointment of a personal nature on Tuesday," she said, "and various other things which are none of your business but which I couldn't possibly cancel." Which were all bound to be something to do with enhancing her already over-pampered appearance, Fin thought. Lorelei Dakers appeared to be addicted to therapies of one sort or another.

Gareth was no help whatsoever, as his wife had him totally by the balls. Fin had no option but to make the best of a bad job and go for the sympathy vote: the selection panel were bound to be understanding when they heard that Mrs Dakers had an urgent medical appointment to attend. That the appointment was to get her bikini line waxed, or whatever it might be, needn't be mentioned.

Tomorrow he'd scheduled a press call with the sitting MP and a visit to an outlying coastal village. This was to be the first of many such local meetings, and was part of a programme in which Gareth would show his face in literally every corner of the constituency, no matter how remote. Fin peered at tomorrow's destination on the map. Last Reach. It sounded like something from the Wild West, and with a name like that it made sense to fit in a visit to it at the start of the campaign. They didn't want to hand journalists any "last ditch grab for votes at Last Reach"-type puns.

Boldwick station was announced. Fin clicked his laptop closed, packed it away along with all his papers, and poked his boss's leg with a toe of his shoe.

Gareth started awake, rubbing the back of his hand against his mouth. Fin watched him make the transition from deep sleep to alert wakefulness quicker than the time it took most people to yawn.

"Are we there?" he asked.

"As near to there as the train is willing to take us," Fin replied.

Gareth grimaced. "Why couldn't I have been offered a constituency a bit closer to the hub of things?" he grumbled. "Instead of this God-forsaken dump."

"This provincial treasure," his public relations man corrected him automatically.

Gareth sniffed. "Whatever. Do you know, I don't think I've ever been this far north in my life?"

11

"Not a point you need to emphasise at the selection meeting, I wouldn't have thought."

"Oh — wait, hang on," Gareth scratched his head in an amateur-theatrical attempt to look as if he was thinking. "Is Scunthorpe anywhere near here?"

"At least a hundred miles south."

"Near enough. I did a show once in Scunthorpe."

"I don't think you need to mention that. It's not exactly local." Fin could never tell if Gareth was seriously dim or was just taking the piss. He suspected the latter. He returned to what he'd been thinking about before Gareth woke up. "It would have looked so much better if your wife had been with you, you know."

The would-be politician lowered his voice — at least he had that much discretion. "Oh, please. Can you imagine Lorelei ripping herself away from her precious shiatsu and Pilates to trek all the way up here?"

"She's going to have to start spending plenty of time up here as the election approaches, you know. People find elections so dull because there aren't any real surprises, or real personalities involved. Look at the interest when John Prescott thumped the bloke who threw the egg at him. That's what we need to do."

"Thump people?"

"No — get back to face-to-face politics. Or give every appearance of it anyway. Which means we need Lorelei to do her bit as well."

"Well, the election could be months away. We'll cross those bridges when we get to them, eh?"

The train scraped to a halt in Boldwick station, and the two men started to gather their belongings together.

12

Gareth Dakers yawned. "Find out about flying up, next time, would you, Fin? I feel as though I've been on this bloody train for years."

CHAPTER
THREE

Beth didn't sleep much that night. In the morning she didn't feel at all refreshed and only knew that she had slept because at some point she'd managed to dream, one of those heartbreakingly mundane dreams in which she was sitting on the harbour wall watching the *Jeannie-Beth*, named after Martin's mother and herself, arrive back into the harbour with the morning's catch, trumpeted by seagulls. Danny was a toddler in her arms, squiggling to be free and run down the slipway to meet his father. In the dream she could see Martin, the sun shining on his bright hair; he was holding something up to show Danny, pointing at it and grinning. Beth couldn't see what it was.

Those dreams were the hardest to wake up from, even after three years. She would scrunch her eyes more tightly closed and try to stay in the dream world for a little bit longer. But it never worked, and she was always left with a dragging feeling of loss that would stay with her all day.

After dressing she went straight outside. The autumn sun was directly behind the lighthouse, casting the enclosed yard around the cottages into gloomy shadow, but as she walked by the smooth, white wall of the tower the sun burst over her like a blessing, dazzling silver on the sea. The air smelled wonderful, like cinnamon and lemons, the scrubbed-up smell of after a storm. She walked towards the cliff edge, but this time kept back from it: there was no saying how easily the rest of it might crumble. Which meant she didn't have far to walk at all: the grassy area in front of the lighthouse ended abruptly in a ragged-edged void, like a mouth after the teeth have been knocked out. A shrub had been wrenched up as the land beneath it fell away, and the roots were sticking up, casting long, finger-like shadows back towards her. Beyond, the sea was mockingly flat and calm, apparently satisfied with its latest meal and content to bask in the sun for a while.

Beth fished in her jacket pocket for her bunch of keys, went to the blue-painted door of the lighthouse and unlocked it.

An iron staircase spiralled up the inside of the tower, through rooms which still rumbled from the sound of the generator: even though the lighthouse itself wasn't operational, the generator still provided the electricity to power the three cottages. As Beth climbed the steps, her hands didn't once touch the brass rails: lighthouse keepers never touched the brass fittings, her father had always taught her, as every finger mark only meant more work for them. The lenses and glass of a lighthouse were always kept spotless for the obvious reason that a clean light shines more brightly, but lighthouse keepers generally extended this cleanliness to all areas of the building.

At the top she climbed a short metal ladder through a hole in the roof, and stood beside the light itself for a moment before opening the heavy metal door that led to the gallery.

Up there, even though the air was fairly still, the light breeze was icily cold. The gallery gave her a 360-degree view. To the west, the view was of a broad stretch of scrubby grass intersected by a narrow grey track barely wide enough for a car. Beyond that it was possible to just make out the rooftops of the first couple of houses in the tiny village of Last Reach, a place so small it hardly registered on any maps. To the east was the sea, looking closer than it had ever been, like a grey carpet being rolled out towards her. Even after what had happened to her husband, Beth wasn't afraid of the sea; that would have seemed as irrational to her as being afraid of air, but the thought of what was going to happen to her home and her family filled her with terror. Because it was even clearer from this crow's-nest perspective that it wouldn't take very much more for the cliff to give way again, and then the lighthouse itself, and their little house next to it would be on the very edge.

For perhaps ten minutes she stood there, her mind racing around trying to work out what to do and finding no answers. Finally she turned to come back down, her footsteps echoing in the stairwell. She locked the door and then, out of habit, looked in on the other two keepers' cottages, which were used as self-catering holiday accommodation. They were all immaculately clean, tidy and ordered, a fact which depressed her because tidy bedrooms meant that no paying guests had slept in them last night. Not for many weeks, in fact: business was not exactly booming. Tourism generally had been hit by various world events, which had the added effect of bringing down air fares, so people could afford to go abroad to guaranteed sunshine rather than risk the hit-and-miss Northlands weather. Practically the only visitors they got were dedicated lighthouse enthusiasts.

And after what had happened the night before, Beth couldn't see a way of carrying on. It plainly wasn't safe.

Glancing out of a bedroom window which faced the inland side, she saw a car coming up the track at the back that was the only vehicle access. She hurried outside and emerged into the breezy sunshine.

"Morning, Beth." The visitor was Harry Rushton, wearing his police uniform, though he and Beth had known each other long before he'd been a sergeant or even a constable: he'd been Martin's best friend at school, the three of them practically growing up together. "Bad storm last night," he said. The breeze tugged at his blond hair which was showing no signs of thinning.

"You're not kidding," Beth replied. "We had another cliff fall."

Harry nodded. "One of the boats spotted it. That's why I came up, to see if you were all right."

"You could have phoned," she said, and he missed the teasing flash in her eyes and consequently sounded all flustered when he replied.

"I was coming up this way anyway," he said. Harry Rushton had been finding more and more excuses to visit the lighthouse in recent weeks. Beth sometimes thought that he took his duties as Martin's best friend too seriously, feeling that he had to look after them all in his friend's absence.

"Can I see the damage?" he asked. Beth led him round to the front of the lighthouse, and was amused to notice that he practically kept his back to the wall, as though he was afraid a rogue wave would wash him straight off the cliff top even though the sea was relatively calm this morning. "Bloody hell," he said. "Makes me feel queasy just looking at that." It was part of Harry's charm that he wouldn't hesitate to admit to weaknesses in front of her, even when he was wearing his uniform.

"Maybe we should go in the house," she suggested. "I'll make us some breakfast."

"Well, if you're sure."

"Of course. Bill should be up by now."

"Danny at home?"

"Yes, there's no school today, but we won't see him till lunchtime at least."

"You ought to make him get up for breakfast. It's disrespectful."

"He's a teenager," she said. "Lolloping around is what they do."

"I don't remember doing much lolloping, personally. But then, I had a goal in life. What's Danny's goal? That's what I'd like to know."

18

"I don't think he has one," she said. Harry frowned at her in a way that made her want to defend herself. "I don't want to put pressure on him," she said. "He's been through a lot."

"All the more reason to give him a bit of a shove, I would have thought. I can have a word with him if you want."

"You're taking your duties as his godfather very seriously."

"I promised I would."

Beth paused outside the cottage door, one hand resting on its blue-painted surface, which was warm from the sunshine. "Thanks, Harry," she said, "but I really think he's best left to himself for now."

They went indoors, where Beth cooked a proper breakfast of bacon and eggs, toast made with thickly sliced home-baked bread and a huge pot of tea, all the time making small talk with Harry. They'd known each other for so long that they were comfortable with each other in that cosy domestic setting, and if Beth was being honest with herself she found having him there reassuring.

Her father appeared, with his usual sense of timing, at the precise moment his breakfast was put on the table. "Morning, Harry. Come up to inspect the damage?"

"It's worse than I expected," Harry said, helping himself to some toast. He waited until Bill had settled himself at the table and poured the tea before he came to the point. "Strikes me it's not safe for any of you to stay here any longer," he said, looking anxiously at their faces for a reaction.

Bill set his chin stubbornly, but before he could say anything his daughter said quietly, "I think we know that, Harry, but what are we expected to do? There's no insurance on this place, and we've got nothing in the bank."

"But you can't stay here," the policeman repeated. "The next storm or high tide, that sea's going to be at your back door. It's not safe."

"I've always said I'll be carried out of here horizontal before I go any other way," Bill said.

Beth knew that he was putting on a display of bravado for Harry's benefit, but she wasn't in a mood for it. "There's no use trying to ignore the situation: with the cliff in that state, no one's going to give us public liability insurance, and without that we can't trade."

They all fell silent except for Bill's noisy chewing. Harry, who had finished eating, sipped at his tea, then pushed his chair back. "Thanks for the breakfast, Beth, but I have to be going now. There's a political meeting at the community centre this afternoon, and I've got to go and do my bit in case there's a riot." He chuckled to himself at the thought of such an exciting thing as a riot taking place on his patch, where lost bicycles, lost chickens and lost tourists were about as exciting as things usually got. "Though I don't know what a bloke like Gareth Dakers knows about the likes of us round here. Always struck me as a bit of a namby-pamby city boy."

20

"It's going to be a culture shock for him, all right," Beth said, pleased to have the topic of conversation turned to something outside their current predicament. "It's funny that a television personality would want to run for Parliament at all, never mind wanting to represent Northlands."

"Bloody politicians," Bill grumbled. "It's their fault we're in this state."

Beth ignored him, like she generally did when he was working himself up into a rant, but Harry said, "Are you speaking in the general or the particular, Bill?"

"Don't encourage him," Beth warned, but it was too late. Her father launched into a tirade about everything that had gone wrong since the Second World War, laying it all firmly at the hands of whichever politician had been in charge at the time, no matter what their political colour. He took the scatter-gun approach to political (or any) arguments: if you launch enough missiles, presumably some of them will hit their targets.

"And you can't tell me that something couldn't have been done to shore up the sea defences," he concluded, finally approaching something near relevance.

"They've done it further down the coast, at Carver Bay," Harry chipped in.

"And what's at Carver bloody Bay?" Bill said, waving his fork for emphasis. "Nothing, that's what. No buildings, nothing."

"Linda said she heard a rumour the land was being sold off to a developer," Beth said. Linda was her closest friend, and as proprietor of Last Reach's only shop, she was the best conduit for any news or gossip.

21

"I heard that," Harry agreed. "There was talk of putting a golf course or something down there."

Bill almost choked on his tea. "A bloody golf course? Round here? What do they need a bloody golf course for?"

"Don't knock it," Beth said, trying to be optimistic. "The golfers'd need somewhere to stay, I imagine, so why not a charming nineteenth-century lighthouse? I could do with some extra customers."

"Always supposing there's still a lighthouse to put them in," Harry said. That was the bottom line, and her feeble attempt at cheerfulness was gone.

"I don't know why they couldn't put some sea defences up here as well," her father grumbled on. "If they can do it for a golf course. At one point we were promised they were going to do it, but then apparently the money ran out. Now we know why."

Harry was on his feet now, pulling on his coat. "Speaking as an officer of the law, I've got to remain impartial, you understand," he said. "But if I was you, I'd be going up to that meeting at the village hall and asking your would-be MP what he plans to do about the situation you're in, if he gets elected."

"Wouldn't do any good," Bill muttered.

"It's better than doing nothing," Beth decided. "I'm going to go, even if you aren't. If they can stabilise the sea defences so they can build a golf course, they can damn well do something up here."

"Good woman," Harry said warmly. "I'll give you a lift up to the community centre, if you like. I'll pick you up at about four o'clock."

Bill said, "In that case, if you're having a free ride into the village, I may as well come too." Beth could swear that Harry looked disappointed at the thought of a second passenger.

CHAPTER
FOUR

"You really ought to think about buying a house up here, you know."

"You are joking, I hope?" Gareth Dakers forked scrambled egg into his mouth then dabbed his lips fastidiously with a napkin. "Why do scrambled eggs in these hotels always have the texture of old suede gardening gloves?" he complained.

"If you had a house up here you wouldn't have to put up with hotel food," Fin pointed out. He'd sensibly stuck to coffee and toast. "It would play very well with the electorate. And you should start supporting the local football team."

"But I can't stand soccer!"

"It's not soccer, it's *football*. No one up here would ever call it soccer."

"Are you ever off duty?" Dakers asked his PR man.

"No. So what do you think? About buying a house?"

Dakers put his fork down and refilled his coffee cup. "What I think," he said, "is that I'd rather be kneecapped than live in this dump." Since the "dump" in which the hotel was situated was the administrative hub of the entire constituency and its largest town, this didn't bode well.

"Are you mad?" Fin's grey eyes narrowed slightly, and his voice, with its trace of Yorkshire accent, sank to a whispered hiss.

"What?"

"Never, *ever*, say anything like that in public again. Or in private, come to think of it. All it takes is for one of the waitresses or someone at the next table to hear you and you can kiss your seat goodbye."

"To coin a phrase. Sometimes I suspect you of paranoia, my friend."

"And you'd do well to acquire some paranoia yourself. Your profile might give you a head start in this, but it's fatal to go on thinking you're above the rules of the game."

Gareth Dakers smiled, his patrician lips pursing like delicate sea creatures. "I do not think I'm above the rules of the game where my wife is concerned. And I think you pretty much understand *her* feelings about decamping to the regions."

"I'm sure you can persuade her. Or do you want me to talk to her?"

"I can handle my own wife, thank you. For some things a spin doctor isn't necessary."

Fin privately didn't think this was entirely the case, but he let it go for now. "Pending you becoming a fully fledged Northlands resident, I've had people in London delving into your family tree looking for local connections."

"And?"

"And nothing. Complete blank. You are resolutely southern."

"Thank the lord for that."

"You don't do yourself any favours with this attitude, you know."

"I was just kidding!"

Fin sighed. This was like dealing with a rather dim, albeit very charismatic child. But then, he'd known it wasn't going to be easy.

He liked a challenge. Working for an upcoming PR agency in London, he'd always volunteered for the jobs that no one else would touch, the hard-to-sell things. He could pitch anything to anybody: the proverbial selling condoms to the Pope was what suited him best. It didn't matter if he believed in what he was doing or not, it was all a very enjoyable and very profitable game to him.

Gareth Dakers was his biggest challenge yet. Starting off as a serious stage actor, he'd become better known to a lot of people (but not as many as he liked to think) as the presenter of various television shows, mainly for children. Fin hadn't been able to discern exactly what it was about being a representative of the people that appealed to Gareth — it seemed that it was just another branch of showbusiness to him: he'd loved appearing on television, daytime shows with cosy Irish or Scottish females presenting them had been a particular favourite. He loved being fussed over in make-up, being deferred to by some awe-struck junior floor manager's assistant. Fin could imagine how the charm assault of the fabulous Gareth Dakers smile would play in the *Newsnight* studio, and hoped to be able to prime him with enough political nous to back it up.

26

The party were very keen to have him. He might not have much in the way of a political background, but he had a profile, and that counted for a lot. You could build on a profile.

There were difficulties, though, in that as well as a profile, Gareth Dakers also had a past. When the papers broke the irresistible story of his liaison with a former TV weather girl who was looking for a leg-up (so to speak) into the world of presenting, journalists were all over him like eczema, and it was only the appearance of his wife, stolidly declaring she would stand by her man, that salvaged any of his reputation at all, though even that wasn't enough to keep his career on an even keel.

Dakers had related the full story of what the press invariably referred to as "the Windy Wendy episode" to Finian Lewis not long after they'd met (Fin had known most of it already — he believed in doing his homework — but there was no harm getting it from the horse's mouth). Fin privately thought that, had he been working for Gareth at the time, Gareth could have come out of the whole thing totally unscathed anyway. It was, by anyone's standards, only the misdemeanour of a normal, red-blooded man who was susceptible to a bit of flattery and couldn't say no when it was more prudent to do so.

Fin looked at his watch. "We need to be out of here in five minutes."

"For?"

"Local radio, old people's home — retirement of much-loved matron cum pillar of local community —

visit to an electronics factory, lunch with the incumbent MP."

"Ah! Lunch! What's the incumbent's name again?"

"Michael Armstrong. One of these no-nonsense, bluff northern types."

"As long as he provides a decent lunch." Dakers pushed back his chair, simultaneously flashing a fabulous smile at the prettiest of the waitresses. "Lead on, Horatio."

CHAPTER
FIVE

The waiting room was as plush as a five-star hotel, which was only to be expected considering the prices they charged. The air smelled of lavender blended with a reassuringly masculine whiff of leather and new carpet. The woman picked up a pristine copy of *Vogue* from the marble-topped coffee table and sank back into the comforting embrace of the leather sofa. She crossed her long legs, unable to resist a glance over the top of the magazine at the graceful curve of her calf as she did so. Satisfied that what she saw would bear comparison with anything she was likely to find within the magazine's pages, she settled down to read.

She wasn't paying such vast fees to be kept waiting, however, and two minutes later a young woman in a figure-flattering pale lilac uniform appeared noiselessly at her side. "Mrs Dakers? Would you like to follow me, please?"

Not with that dandruff, Lorelei thought, putting the magazine back on the table and getting to her feet. She was a good six inches taller than the other woman and from that vantage point she had to admit she'd exaggerated the scalp problem. It was merely that for Lorelei Dakers, picking out the physical defects of other people — particularly women — was as much a hobby as a self-protective habit.

The woman led the way down a quiet carpeted corridor to an unmarked door. She opened it and stood back to allow Lorelei to pass before discreetly disappearing.

The large room was furnished with comfy chairs, a long, low cream-coloured sofa and a plethora of potted palms. The wooden blinds were lowered, and the light through them was warm and glowing. Standing in the centre of the room with his back to the window so that he appeared to have an aura of light around him was Dr Harrison Shah, the man with the miracle syringe.

Lorelei giggled, her classically beautiful face creasing into lines of mirth.

"Share the joke?" the doctor said.

"In my head I just called you the man with the miracle syringe," she said.

"It's an apt enough description."

"I know. But it sounded so . . . phallic."

The cosmetic surgeon's eyes twinkled with amusement. "Perhaps you should take that piece of Freudian imagery up in one of your sessions with Mr Goldstein."

Lorelei took off her coat, shrugging the expensive cashmere off and dropping it on to the sofa. "Oh, I'm finished with the therapy, didn't I tell you?" she said. "It was frankly getting too tedious, like one of those interminable autobiographies where the author assumes you give a shit about their grandparents. As soon as Goldstein started getting into what was going on in my life when I was too young to remember, I got bored, and decided my time was better spent on crystal healing or tantric yoga."

She didn't say that the main reason she didn't want to talk about her early life was that she'd only been Lorelei since she was fifteen, and anything from her plain old Lorraine period was not up for discussion, although she might have persisted with Goldstein a bit longer if he'd been as attractive as Dr Harrison Shah.

The surgeon was bending over her now, examining the skin of her forehead. Lorelei could smell his cologne, which was something light but sexy. "You want my opinion?" he said, and she wondered if he was going to wax sceptical about the crystal healing again. He might be handsome but he was sometimes tryingly cynical. "I don't think you really need Botox."

"Oh, for heaven's sake!" she said crossly, and raised her eyebrows so high that her forehead was coaxed into rivulets. "There!" she said.

"Everyone's forehead does that," he pointed out, his own facial expression a mirror of her own.

She laughed. "But yours snaps back." She touched her fingertips to his wonderfully smooth forehead.

"And so does yours." His own fingers on her face were cool and very gentle. They traced a soft line from above the bridge of her nose down to the corners of her lips.

"It's all thanks to you," she said, closing her eyes.

CHAPTER
SIX

"God, you are one handsome bastard," Gareth Dakers muttered, checking his tie yet again in the mirror Fin had procured in the caretaker's office, which had been commandeered for Gareth's own personal use. He smoothed a stray lock of hair into place, then decided it had looked better when it was stray, and fluffed it back out again. Gareth's hair had always been one of his selling points.

He glanced around the room, at the mop and bucket propped in the corner, the battered old table with its surface scarred with paint, glue and cigarette burns, the twisted blind at the tiny window which was too high up the wall to see anything out of. Bit of a comedown from the changing rooms he'd been used to, but the thought made him feel oddly pleased. This was it, then: what Fin would call the "coal face".

The door opened and Fin himself came in, wearing the look of a man who has to think about thirty things at the same time and is rather enjoying it.

"How's the turnout?" Dakers asked him.

"The number of bodies in the hall is immaterial. It's a very scattered population. We've got radio, TV and local papers out there: we'll reach the entire region with that lot. Just be sure you make it count."

"Consider it done," Gareth said. "It's your job to round up the audience and mine to put on the show." He stepped back from the mirror and turned from left to right, admiring himself. "How do I look?"

Fin gave him an appraising look. "Like a filthy rich southerner," he said. "Do you *have* to wear suits that scream Savile Row?"

"Don't you think even the hicks from the sticks might want their representative to the Palace of Westminster to look the part? Always supposing they can spot a bit of bespoke tailoring when they see it."

"I think they'd probably prefer someone who looks more in tune with their concerns."

"Ah, yes, their concerns. And their concerns *are*, again?"

The other man sighed. "Tourism, agriculture, fishing. Haven't you read the notes?"

"Of course I have. I was just testing."

Fin took his tie off and handed it to the other man. "Look, swap ties. You look far too co-ordinated."

"But yours is — oh, good grief."

"Trust me. Have I ever given you wrong advice?"

"I suppose not." Gareth exchanged his flamboyant hand-printed silk tie for the more mundane-looking version offered by his right-hand man, grimacing in the mirror as he did so. "Are you sure about this? It downgrades the entire ensemble."

"Exactly. Now hurry up. The TV people are getting fidgety and we want to make the six o'clock news. Do your visualisation."

"Okay." Gareth addressed the mirror, pulling his shoulders back and pushing forward his chest. He took a deep breath. "I am Nelson Mandela," he said, paused, then tried the phrase again, this time with a pretty unconvincing South African accent. "I im Nilson Mendilla." He turned to Fin. "Nelson Mandela's not doing it for me, I'm afraid."

"Try Kennedy."

Gareth faced the mirror again, squared his shoulders and said, "I am John F Kennedy." His face cracked into a grin. He glanced at Fin in the mirror behind him. "And which one are you? Jackie or Marilyn?"

Fin sighed, exasperated.

Gareth pulled a face. "Couldn't I be someone a bit more *fun*?"

"As long as they have the necessary presence."

This time Gareth intoned, in a heavily nasal Liverpool accent, "I am John-fucking-Lennon."

Fin sighed. "You're not taking this seriously. Visualising being someone you admire, and who has the required charisma, really will help you to come across better. I told you that Bill Clinton learned to walk like JFK by imagining putting on his shoes and walking in them. And when people looked at him they saw someone with the statesmanlike confidence of a Kennedy."

"You come up with some barmy stuff," Gareth muttered. "And I can't imagine what kind of shoes

Nelson Mandela might wear no matter how hard I try. Tell you what . . ." He executed a brief but supremely elegant tap routine ending in the tipping of an imaginary hat. "I am Frank Sinatra. Will that do? I am Frank Sinatra, and it's my planet."

"I would say Frank Sinatra is very suitable for the purpose. Now let's get going."

Gareth followed him out of the room, humming "Come Fly With Me" as they walked.

Beth and Bill walked the last couple of hundred yards to the community centre, Harry having had to go and rendezvous with a couple of his colleagues who'd come up from Boldwick as reinforcements. Half the village seemed to be on their way to the meeting, which said more about the absolute dearth of anything else to do than about the political leanings of the locals.

The community centre hall was perched on a rise in the centre of the village of Last Reach, which itself consisted of a couple of handfuls of houses, a pub and the village shop cum post office, run by Linda and Kenny Morini. It wasn't a picture-postcard village by any means: the houses were plain and functional, built in different eras and different styles, mainly to house fishermen and farm workers and their families. The community centre was shared with several villages but, even so, was woefully under-used most of the time.

On this day it was packed with people, who were behaving in an unusually excited fashion: probably due to the presence of television cameras and reporters with notebooks, tiny tape recorders and big fluffy microphones on long poles. A lot of people were wearing what they'd normally term their Sunday best. Several were passing bags of sweets up and down the rows, and the atmosphere generally was quite festive.

Beth spotted Linda waving at them from the back row. She wasn't much over five feet tall, but seemed to have the energy of fifteen people, and she wasn't difficult to spot. "Beth! I've saved you a seat!" Beth and her father made their way along the row and sat next to her. Other people moved along to make extra room for Bill, and immediately started asking him about the cliff fall of the previous night.

Beth turned to Linda. "How did you know we would come?" she asked her, marvelling that as usual Linda Morini knew what was happening before it *had* happened. Some would call it clairvoyance but really it was because Linda's shop was Last Reach's news hub.

"Harry said he'd seen you," Linda said, pushing her glasses back up her nose and shoving her straight blonde hair behind her ears. Her face was anxious and sympathetic. "Awful storm last night," she said. "How are you all feeling?"

"Not good," Beth said.

"What are you going to do? You can't stay there, surely?"

"I know that, but where can we go?"

Linda patted her friend's forearm comfortingly, as Beth seemed close to tears. When Martin died, Linda was the only person Beth had felt able to cry with. "I wish we could put you up at ours," she said. "But it's chockablock as it is. Ant keeps threatening to join the army and sometimes I wish he would."

"You don't mean it."

"Course I don't. He might be a useless lump, but that doesn't mean I fancy sending him off to get killed somewhere. And can you imagine the state the country would be in if we had to rely on our Ant for defence?" She grinned. "He's sitting over there, look." She pointed to the front of the hall, where Antony Morini's cropped brown hair could be spotted just behind the rows of reporters. "He fancied trying to get his face on telly. Didn't Danny come with you?"

"Are you joking? He's got the house to himself; he'll have his music on at ear-bleeding volume. But I told him if the wind gets up he's got to stay in the house and not go near the tower. I've got this horrible vision of what's going to happen if even more of the cliff comes away."

The noise in the room had been a constant "rhubarb-rhubarb" of excited chattering, but it suddenly dropped to an expectant hush and faces turned towards the stage. The leader of the local council, Ted Bailiss, whom everybody knew because he managed the fish market at the port, stepped up to make a speech introducing Gareth Dakers.

There were two men standing to the side of the stage, both in suits, which wasn't the usual mode of dress around Last Reach, so Beth guessed that one of them must be the star turn. She tried to remember what Gareth Dakers looked like. She didn't watch that much television, and although she knew he was pretty famous, she couldn't quite put a face to the name.

It amused her that one of the men was wearing a very lurid tie, which didn't look right at all with his fairly sober dark grey suit. He was very attractive, though: his face was serious and intelligent, with eyes that seemed to be taking everything in and storing it up for future reference. He had a nice mouth, the kind that looks always on the verge of a smile but never quite smiling. There was something about him that made Beth like him. That tie he was wearing was deeply awful, though.

But it was the other man who was bound to be Gareth Dakers. He was strikingly handsome in a Roman statue sort of way, with a straight, long nose, dark curly hair (which may have been dyed, she thought) and an aristocratic bearing. He stepped up to the microphone, flash bulbs flickered and he launched into his speech.

So this was the man who was hoping to be elected as their MP. No chance, Beth thought: the folks round here would no more vote for that dandy than they would take up ballet. Her fellow villagers filling the room were farmers and fishermen, no-nonsense types with little time for soft southerners. There were a few suppressed chuckles, and a couple of muttered comments that no one was meant to quite catch.

But as Gareth Dakers started speaking, the mood in the hall changed, and so did Beth's opinion of him. His manner became intimate, earnest, as if someone you'd known your whole life had popped in for a talk about something important to you. And the words he used didn't sound like the empty promises of politics. He spoke like he understood their concerns, spoke their language, and had a deeply felt desire to make their lives better. It was an incredible performance. Even Bill looked impressed.

The applause was warm when he'd finished speaking, and he stepped back from the microphone, enjoying the moment, glancing just once at the man in the lurid tie, who was looking quietly pleased.

Councillor Bailiss stepped forward. "Thank you very much, Mr Dakers. Now, ladies and gentlemen, Mr Dakers has agreed to take questions from the floor. From the general public first, then I'll throw him over to the ladies and gentlemen of the press." There were a few chuckles from the front rows where the press people were.

A woman near the front with a blue silk scarf around her shoulders asked Dakers about the transition from showbusiness to politics, and why he'd decided to do it.

Dakers pondered for a second, and said, "More and more, politics is becoming a branch of showbusiness. You've seen all the flashy party broadcasts, the party conferences that are staged like some kind of circus spectacular with all the lights and pop songs. You've heard all the spin. I reckon I'm wise to those games, I know how it works. So I can cut through the nonsense to what's really important, which is representing the true concerns of Northlands, and make sure that the constituency which is on the very edge of England is in the very centre of thinking at Westminster." It was a good answer, if a little trite, and there were nods of approval and even a little ripple of applause. He was wowing the ladies of the morris dancing guild, Linda pointed out to Beth.

The following questions were about local issues (a road-building scheme, farm subsidies), which Dakers expertly dealt with, once again giving every impression that he was a man who cared deeply about his potential constituents and understood their everyday lives.

Despite Beth's earlier scepticism she felt encouraged that here was someone who might be sympathetic to her family's own plight. Her stomach was in knots as she tried to work up the courage to ask him a question. Not naturally extrovert, the thought of standing up in front of all of these people, not to mention the television cameras, was terrifying to her, but she owed it to her family to at least try. A couple of times she stood up to speak, but someone else got in ahead of her. Then she noticed Councillor Bailiss glance at his watch, and realised time was running out. She stood up as tall as she possibly could, thrust her arm into the air, and saw Dakers turn his patrician gaze towards her, his eyebrows raised ever so slightly. She felt rather than saw a camera swivel towards her and the man with the headphones and the furry microphone on a stick moving towards her in a crouching run.

Beth's throat felt as if it had closed up and no words would ever come out, but after a second's struggle they did. ". . . I live, with my father and my son, in the Last Reach Point lighthouse," she said. "It's about half a mile from here, on the coast." She felt her cheeks flush

40

at how stupid that sounded: *obviously* it was on the coast, it was a lighthouse, for heaven's sake — but she forced herself on. "Yesterday a big chunk of land in front of the lighthouse fell into the sea. My home is going to follow it in a few weeks if nothing is done."

"That's very sad to hear," Gareth Dakers said, looking suitably crestfallen. "But I fail to see what even the power of Parliament can do against the might of the sea."

Bill stood up next to his daughter. "The reason our property is being eroded is because the tidal pattern changed when the coastal defences further south were built up, apparently to protect land for a bloody golf course." He pronounced these last words like they were acid drops. Beth had never been so proud of him.

"I'm sorry," Dakers said smoothly, "I'm no expert in marine engineering. But I will promise to look into it." He glanced around the room for the next question.

Beth wasn't going to let him get away with that, not now. "With respect," she said, though respect wasn't what she was feeling at that point, "I don't know if there's *time* to look into it. My family have been told to leave our home by the police," which was stretching the truth slightly, but never mind that. "We can't get insurance any longer. It isn't safe. And we have nowhere else to live."

"If you want to 'look into it'," Bill added, "look *into* why whoever decided there was money to fortify the sea defences at Carver Bay to build a golf course, or whatever it is, didn't feel it was worth saving a lighthouse that's over a hundred years old and is the home and livelihood of this family, a tourist attraction," (if only, Beth thought) "and a landmark for the area."

There were murmurings from the press, and one of them asked whether Dakers would be supporting the proposed golf course. Dakers looked uncomfortable for the first time. "I'll have to look into it," he said, but he sounded less confident and the audience began to react to his uncertainty. The mutterings started up again, with the odd raised voice.

Linda bobbed up like a cork next to her friend, and her supportive presence spurred Beth on to one last effort. "What we need right now," she said above the noise, "is somewhere to live."

"I'd help if I could," Dakers said, but at this there were generalised mutterings in the crowd and, sensing that he was losing the goodwill he'd painstakingly built up, he said, "Believe me, I would offer you my own home if it would help." There were some grunts that this was all flannel and easy enough to say. A couple of people had started walking towards the exit, a fact which the TV cameras were clearly recording, and Dakers couldn't have failed to notice, because what he said next certainly stopped them in their tracks.

He held up his hands for quiet. "Ladies and gentlemen," he said, "I would like to publicly invite this desperate family to live in my own home. For as long as they like."

The crowd fell silent, and a hundred faces turned towards Beth and Bill.

"Thanks," Bill Turnbull said. "We'll take it."

★ ★ ★

After that the flash bulbs went frantic, and this time it was the lighthouse keeper and his daughter who were the centre of attention. One of the journalists at the front of the hall stood up and directed a question at Dakers. "Can you confirm that you've just made this family an offer to come and live at your home?"

Beth had a moment to notice that the man Dakers had been talking to earlier was in earnest conversation with someone on his mobile phone, his back to the meeting. Dakers was facing the assembly with a beatific smile. "Ladies and gentlemen," he said, arms raised in a gesture of magnanimity, "you will find that I am not a man to make promises lightly. When I say I will do something, you can be confident that I will do it. I realise this probably isn't what you're used to from politicians," he paused for a ruffle of laughter to echo around the hall, "but it is my intention — no, my *purpose* — to represent your problems and concerns directly and honestly," he dropped his voice and dropped his hands humbly to his side, "as your servant. And when I see this family of hard-working, honest people in desperate need of accommodation, I am not prepared to turn my back on them."

The crowd erupted into applause, but Beth was mortified. The last thing she'd wanted was to become some kind of charity case, and a way for this man to demonstrate what a man of the people he was.

Linda muttered into her ear, "Cheer up! At least you might get a holiday out of it."

The man in the lurid tie, having put his phone away, signalled to Councillor Bailiss that the meeting was over. Dakers spoke a few valedictory words, including his hope and expectation that he would be seeing a lot more of the assembled throng when he returned as their elected MP, then he left the stage.

Beth and Bill got up to leave, but were immediately accosted by several of their neighbours, asking for their reactions to the politician's offer.

"We're not going!" Beth snapped.

"Yes we are," Bill said.

His daughter glared at him but didn't have time to say anything because reporters began to circle around them, and the last thing she wanted was to talk to them. "Come on, Dad," she said. "Let's see if we can find Harry to give us a lift home."

"We've got to go and see our new friend the politician first," Bill said. "To make arrangements."

"You're not serious?"

"Why not?"

"Oh, for God's sake! He didn't *mean* it! And how would that solve our problems anyway?"

Finian Lewis wasn't a man who was easily flapped. In fact one of the reasons he was enjoying this Gareth Dakers job was that Gareth was apt to throw interesting spanners in the works, which only provided Fin with more of a challenge. When Gareth offered that family the use of his home, Fin had experienced a moment of horror — bringing stroppy examples of the electorate right into the hub of things at such a sensitive time was never going to be the safest plan, but on the other hand nothing like this had ever been done before. It could only add to Dakers's "man of the people" image. As long as it was all carefully stage-managed, it would be an absolute gift. He'd already been on the phone to a couple of editors he'd cultivated to the point where they knew him and trusted him enough to clear space in tomorrow's editions for the story that was about to break. Most of his calls were to local sources: the whole point of this campaign was to get Dakers known locally, as these were the people who would be voting for him.

The worst thing, in terms of publicity, would be if the lighthouse family didn't take up Gareth's offer. It would be seen as a snub, and Gareth would be open to accusations of making hollow gestures. Fin had no doubt at all that it *had* been a hollow gesture, but it was a bloody good one. Now everything hung on how it played to the electorate, and that was Fin's job. He'd need to speak to the lighthouse family immediately, and make sure they were going to take up the offer. He ushered Gareth back into the caretaker's office, assuring the excited press people that they could have photos with the candidate and the lighthouse family in a few minutes if they wouldn't mind being patient and tucking into the snacks he'd had the foresight to organise.

"I expect I'm in the doghouse now," Gareth said as the door closed behind them.

"What? You played a blinder!"

"I didn't mean with you. I meant with my wife."

"Ah. Well, I'll leave that up to you to sort out, but if anyone asks, she'll be honoured and delighted blah blah. I'm going to round up your future house-guests.

Make sure you offer them a lift home after the photo call. While the press are listening."

"What?" but Fin had disappeared. Gareth sank into a chair. "Oh, God, what have I done?" he moaned.

The first thing Beth noticed about Gareth Dakers at close quarters was that he was wearing make-up. Not mascara or lipstick or anything, but there was definitely more than a trace of powder on his cheeks, nose and forehead. No wonder they'd kept the press at the front and everybody else at the back, she thought: men in make-up weren't the norm in those parts.

He greeted Bill and Beth very charmingly, almost as though they were really old friends who were going to stay with him for the weekend.

"Thank you for your kind offer," Beth said. "But we really can't accept."

"Nonsense!" he replied, giving her the most radiant smile she'd ever seen, even more radiant than Tom Cruise, and with utterly perfect, Cruise-like teeth too. "My first responsibility is to my future constituents. It's a tragedy that you're about to lose your home. If I can give you a little breathing space, then at least that's something."

"I don't really understand what it is you're offering us," Beth said.

For a second he didn't look as if he really understood it himself. She wondered if he had a wife and children, and what they would think of her family dropping in on them like this. No, the idea was stupid.

Before Dakers could reply, the man who'd brought Beth and Bill to this room, the man in the lurid tie who'd introduced himself as Finian Lewis, came back in. "If we're all ready," he said, "the newspapers would like some photos."

To Beth's extreme amusement, Gareth Dakers took a powder compact out of his jacket pocket and gave his nose and forehead a little touch-up. He noticed her looking at him and said, "Doesn't do to have a shiny forehead in these circumstances. Don't want people thinking I'm oily." Although this should have made her think of him as more artificial, in fact it was the first glimpse she'd had that he was a real person and not just a celebrity. She wondered if her own face was shiny and whether he'd lend her his powder, but they were already being ushered back out into the hall.

Their friends and acquaintances of Last Reach had gone, but there were plenty of people left, among them half a dozen photographers, and they seemed to all be shouting at once, wanting Beth and her father to smile or not smile or look to this side or that, or for Beth to shake Dakers's hand. A microphone was shoved under her nose and someone asked her for a reaction to the offer.

"We're thinking about it," she said, and before she could say anything else, Finian Lewis told the press people that that was it for now and could they please get in touch with Dakers's office to arrange follow-up interviews. Bill and Beth were ushered back into the caretaker's office and given coffee, while Lewis took down their details so he could contact them to arrange the move.

"I'm not at all sure about it," Beth repeated.

"Don't be silly," Bill said. Beth could tell he was quite taken with his taste of showbiz. He'd taken his glasses off and put them in his pocket (always a bad sign — later on he'd forget he wasn't wearing them and start colliding with things) and he was laughing too much.

"Don't make a decision now," Lewis said, his voice quiet and reassuring. "Sleep on it, think about all your options."

Fin couldn't risk the family turning down Gareth's offer. The story was fantastic — in a political landscape where politicians were so bland it was hard to tell one from the next, this was bound to get saturation coverage. He couldn't have asked for a better start to the campaign — as long as the family didn't back out. Bill, he could see, wasn't going to be a problem, but Beth might well be. She clearly had a healthy scepticism for political people. What he needed was reinforcements.

Excusing himself, Fin left the caretaker's office and returned to the meeting room, where some of the journalists were preparing to leave, and some were waiting to see if they would get anything else from Dakers or the lighthouse family. A few of them were still happily clustered around the snack table: it was amazing how much goodwill you could generate with a couple of plates of mini sausage rolls. Fin observed the

48

pack for a moment or two like a lion at a watering hole watching a herd of zebra, until he had his victim picked out. He knew the exact one he was after — he'd spotted her before the meeting started. It would have been very hard not to spot this particular woman: she was tall and graceful, with the kind of poise and grooming and attitude about her that indicated she was just biding time at the *Northlands Herald* and would very soon be off to better things. Fin discreetly drew her aside and introduced himself.

"Imogen," she said. "Imogen Callow-Creed. *Northlands Herald*." As if she was telling him something he didn't know already: the names of all the journalists present were filed in his head along with their phone numbers, email, fax. "So what's your man up to?" she said. She was very pretty, glossy-haired, pouty lips, nice figure. "What story will I be writing tomorrow? Will it be the 'providing a beacon of hope for this almost-homeless family' angle . . . or 'is he just seeking the spotlight of publicity'?"

Fin decided that Imogen Callow-Creed was the kind of woman he could do business with. "What about glimmer of hope? Calm after the storm? Sea change for lighthouse family?" He was writing the headlines for her and she was laughing. He leaned confidentially towards her. "You'll be needing all of those headlines for the series of exclusives you'll be running."

He thought he saw her pupils dilate a fraction. "Exclusives?" she repeated. "Sounds interesting."

"Privileged access to Gareth Dakers and his family. Interested?"

"I'd jump at it," she said. "But I'd need to speak to my editor."

This was a bit disappointing. Fin preferred people who could think for themselves, not least in this situation because he knew the editor of the *Northlands Herald* was one of the least dynamic people you could ever meet.

"I'll need a yes or no straight away," he said. "I've got other people I can talk to."

"Okay then," she said, flushing a little at her own daring. "Yes. Yes, we'll do it."

"Marvellous. Now, how about we meet for a drink in a little while?"

CHAPTER
SEVEN

"I've just seen you on the news," Danny said as soon as his mother arrived home. Gareth Dakers had very politely offered to give her a lift, but she'd turned it down. She wanted to walk home, to give herself time to think. She'd left Bill in the pub in the village, no doubt regaling all his mates with the story of his imminent removal to live with the famous Gareth Dakers.

Danny was, as usual, slumped on the sofa in a T shirt and boxer shorts that looked well overdue for a wash, clutching a cereal bowl containing a puddle of milk and some soggy, floating Cornflakes. His pale skinny legs were stretched out in front of him and his feet were bare. It was seven o'clock in the evening.

"Danny, you haven't just got out of bed, have you?" He shrugged, lifted the cereal bowl to his lips and slurped the remains of the milk. Resisting the urge to yell at him, because she knew that he was trying to wind her up, she took a deep, cleansing breath instead. "So we were on telly, were we?"

"Is it true that we're going to go and live with that Dakers bloke?"

"No, it is *not* true." Beth went through to the kitchen to put the kettle on. "It's a ridiculous idea. You could tell he didn't mean it."

"He looked like he meant it from where I was sitting."

"Oh, he *looked* like he meant it, but it was obviously a publicity stunt. I wouldn't be surprised if we got a call from him, or one of his minions, to say so, any minute now."

Danny wasn't being put off so easily. "I bet he lives in a mansion," he said. "With servants and everything. He talked really posh. I bet he does."

"Well, we'll never know, will we?" Beth stood looking out of the kitchen window. So much for going to talk to their potential MP. They were in exactly the situation they'd been in that morning: no money, cliff crumbling into the sea, house about to follow it. Suddenly she missed Martin so much, and hated the sea for taking everything that was important to her. What were they going to do?

Not wanting Danny to see her upset, she went upstairs and locked herself in the bathroom for a therapeutic cry. Just lately, any little thing seemed to be setting her off.

Fin walked into a pub that was, to describe it generously, basic. Everything was made of a peculiarly dull wood: floor, chairs, everything, and not a scrap of soft upholstery to be seen. It was the size of someone's front room, which in fact it had once been, with only the addition of a small bar to indicate it had turned into a pub. It was so bare of adornments it looked like a dolls' house waiting to be decorated.

The punters seemed happy enough, though. Most of the customers were men, and the majority of those were gathered in a group by the bar. At the centre of this was the person Fin had come to see: Bill Turnbull, who was obviously holding court about Gareth.

The conversation stopped when Fin appeared. He felt as if he was in a Hammer vampire film and had just stopped off at a coaching inn on his way to Castle Dracula.

Bill introduced him to the others with the air of a man who is getting used to being a minor celebrity, and after Fin offered to buy them all a drink his popularity was assured. As soon as he could tactfully manage it, he drew Bill away to one side for a private chat. They sat down in a corner, on some very hard seats that were ergonomically designed to suit cave dwellers. Actually, a cave dweller was just what Bill Turnbull reminded Fin of, with his small, wiry frame and slight stoop, his messy black hair and lively dark eyes.

"Your daughter isn't keen on leaving the lighthouse?" Fin remarked, as casually as possible.

"None of us is *keen*," Bill said, and drank half his pint in one long gulp. Fin could see this might turn out to be an expensive evening.

"No, I can imagine you wouldn't be. Do you know, I used to dream of being a lighthouse keeper when I was a boy."

"And why was that?" Bill Turnbull asked.

"Oh, you know, the solitude, time to think."

"You must have been a very weird boy," Bill commented, draining the rest of his drink. "Mind you, our Dan is a bit that way himself."

"Solitary? A trip to London might be exactly what he needs."

Bill looked at him like he was mad. "London?"

Fin realised the lighthouse family had assumed Gareth Dakers lived in the constituency. They were expecting nothing more than moving a few miles away. That kind of changed things.

"So you're saying this offer from Dakers involves moving to *London*?" Bill said. "I think I'll need another drink while I get my head round that one." He tilted his glass towards Fin, who obligingly took it and went back to the bar.

When he returned, Bill had apparently *had* time to think. "I've done a lot of travelling in my time," he said. "Only in Britain, mind you, but I reckon I've seen most corners of this country. People don't realise how much moving around you do when you're a lighthouse keeper: you're not assigned to the same light for your whole life, oh no." Fin raised his eyebrows in a plausible display of fascination. "So I'm more used than most to moving around. And Beth, well she would have been used to that life, too. But when I lost my wife, we had to put down an anchor, it wouldn't have been fair on Beth if I hadn't, and Last Reach is where we put it down. And she met Martin — that was her husband — and they had Danny, and this place is all Danny's known."

"So it would be a wrench for all of you?"

54

"Not for me. Like I said, I'm used to moving around. And Dan, I reckon it would do him good to see something more of life. You'll have a hard job persuading my daughter, though."

"Because she's very attached to the lighthouse?"

"Of course she is," the older man said. "It was a little piece of heaven for her, growing up. She had what was basically her own private seaside. Every summer day all through the school holidays she'd be in her bathing costume, collecting shells on the shore. Like a little mermaid, she was. And of course she was very happy there with her husband. He was a lovely lad, Martin. Plus she's as stubborn and proud as they come."

Fin just had to hope she was persuadable, and that, even as they spoke, Imogen was doing her part.

CHAPTER
EIGHT

"Your grandad must have cadged a lift from someone," Beth said, hearing a car approaching the lighthouse and looking over at her son, who was spread right across the sofa like a long pale stain. "Are you planning to get dressed at all today, Danny?" He grunted in reply, and buried his head more deeply in his magazine. There was a knock at the door. "He's forgotten his key again," Beth grumbled, uncurling herself from the armchair.

But the person on the doorstep was about as unlike her father as it was possible to imagine — female, for a start, tall and rather glamorous, in a chilly sort of way.

"Mrs Jackson?" she asked. Beth nodded. "Imogen Callow-Creed," she said. "From the *Herald*. I'd like to talk to you about your move to London."

"London?" Beth repeated, mystified. "What move to London?"

"You've been invited to stay at the home of the election candidate, Mr Dakers, I understand."

"Not in London, though."

"London is where he lives," she said. Beth was thrown: she'd assumed Dakers must live nearby. Didn't MPs have to live in their constituency? The thought of London hadn't even occurred to her. Well, that was it, then. It had been out of the question before, but it was twice as out of the question to move to London. Leaving this house would have been wrench enough, but to leave Northlands altogether was unthinkable.

Danny, overhearing, said, "*London?* Brilliant!" He dumped his magazine on the floor and loped over to join them in the doorway.

"Do you think I might come in?" the journalist said. "If you're not too busy, that is."

Beth's natural impulse was to shut the door in her face, to block out the whole idea of living with Gareth Dakers, or moving to London or the whole stupid business, but her natural sense of hospitality overrode anything else and she led the way inside.

Imogen Callow-Creed (what a name! Beth thought) perched delicately on the sofa, and gazed about her in a way that made Beth feel under scrutiny. Danny had fled upstairs, presumably to put on some jeans now there was a youngish female in the house.

"So you didn't realise Dakers was offering you a move to London?" the journalist asked, sipping at the tea Beth had supplied her with.

Beth shook her head. "I suppose he assumed we knew. But we most certainly didn't."

"But you're going to go, of course?"

"To London?" Even the feel of the word in her mouth was strange. "There's nothing for us in London. Everything we have is based here."

"It would be a big wrench," Imogen agreed, and then started talking about the precipitous state of the lighthouse, concluding, "So you can't stay here, you

57

can't move, what are you going to do?" She let that one hang in the air for a while before getting down to business. "Naturally it's a story with huge resonance for our readers," she said, her eyes enormous now with the sheer *resonance* of it all.

"It might be, but, really we can't just leave here."

"Taking Gareth Dakers up on his offer would have quite a few benefits," the reporter said. "Not least financial."

"How much are you offering?" Danny, who had just reappeared, asked, like he negotiated financial deals all the time.

Imogen laughed, a sound that didn't seem to come very naturally from her, and said, "I'm afraid the *Herald* doesn't have the wherewithal to pay for stories, though naturally we'd love to cover this one. But I can guarantee there'll be cash offers from other publications. We're talking thousands of pounds. Tens of thousands."

Danny and Beth just stared at her.

When Bill came home, slightly the worse for wear, his daughter was sitting at the kitchen table.

"What's up?" he asked. She told him about the journalist's visit, and what she'd said about all the money they would be offered from the press. "Bloody Nora," he whistled. "So he wasn't having me on."

"Who wasn't?"

"Fin — the bloke who's helping Dakers with his campaign. I bumped into him in the pub, and he was saying that was likely to happen. I wasn't sure I believed him, but he seems to know his stuff, and from what you've just said it seems he's right. So tell me all about it."

There wasn't much to tell, really. The bit that concerned Beth most was the idea of moving to London.

Fin had done his work well on Bill, whose face lit up — which in his case meant that a lot of the jowly business that usually hung down had to heave itself upwards, like one of those very wrinkled dogs. "Let's get packing," he said. "London's *great*. Had a whale of a time there in 1968. You were only five. Me and your mother had a month before I had that last posting in Alderney, before we got moved up here." He was quiet for a few moments, and Beth knew he was thinking about her mother. Lighthouse keepers usually had to work wherever they were needed, on a rotational basis, but once Bill had a daughter to look after on his own they were allowed to stay permanently at Last Reach, a land light with accommodation attached, so that he could be a lighthouse keeper and a full-time parent at the same time. So Alderney (and that trip to London) must have been very important to him — the end of his nomadic life, and full of memories of her mother.

"So what was London like then?" she prompted him, wanting to cheer him up again.

"It was fantastic," he said. "London in the sixties, England swinging like a pendulum do. Carnaby Street and the loveable moptops and all that. Your mother couldn't get enough of those bow-tiques. Mind, she wouldn't have anything to do with those tiny mini skirts, try as I might to persuade her. She said that's not what you need when you're maintaining a lighthouse and looking after a kiddy."

Beth remembered her mother always wearing sensible clothes in crumple-free polyester. Not so different to her own wardrobe, which consisted of jeans and T shirts and jumpers, and one skirt suit for weddings. Another reason she couldn't possibly go to London: she would look like the hick from the sticks. Beth wasn't a vain person at all, but it was funny how her mind stuck on that trivial point. "Anyway, we're not going, and that's that," she said, hoping it sounded final enough to rule out all arguments. She didn't know what they *were* going to do, but they'd manage somehow in Last Reach. They had to.

And that might indeed have been that, if Beth hadn't gone and burned her bridges.

CHAPTER
NINE

Imogen Callow-Creed gazed around the lounge bar of the Three Horseshoes Hotel, advertised in the guide books as "Boldwick's Premier Hostelry" and barely managed to suppress a sneer. This was the best Boldwick could do, and it was a total dump. She wouldn't have believed it had she not seen it for herself, but there were actually three horseshoes suspended above the bar — a charming detail, that — and the rest of it was dark wood, parchment-coloured walls with mock-antique maps of Northlands in frames all over them, and the most disgusting mustard and red carpet. Music was provided by a jukebox which, judging by the tunes that she'd heard so far, hadn't had its musical contents replenished in over twenty years. She perched on an uncomfortable banquette wishing she hadn't asked for lemon in her gin and tonic — the lemon was so dried out it was practically a fossil — and directed waves of hatred in the general direction of the Three Horseshoes, Boldwick and Northlands generally.

She couldn't wait to get out of this God-awful place. When she'd been offered the job on the *Northlands Herald*, she'd been on the point of rejecting it, but her friends in her journalism class had said a job was a job, and once you got your foot in the door the sky was the limit. They were dreadful for mixing metaphors in her journalism class. She'd taken their advice, and then noticed that one by one most of them had found jobs in places infinitely more interesting than this shithole.

But all that was about to change. She had this terrific story of Gareth Dakers and his new pets the Lighthouse Family to work on, and she had the ear (and, she didn't doubt, the eye) of Dakers's fabulously good-looking minder. This was a combination, Imogen felt, that signalled her real life as a journalist was about to begin. But, on the subject of Finian Lewis, where the hell was he? She looked at her watch impatiently.

The landlord, who'd been glancing furtively at her for some time, wandered over on a pretext of wiping her table. "We don't get many ladies in here on their own," he remarked.

"I can't say I'm surprised," she replied, then softened her approach. "I mean, it's such a cold night, I expect most people are tucked up in front of the television."

"You waiting for friends, are you?"

She was really tempted to tell him to piss off and mind his own business, but she could at least fill in the time doing a bit of background digging. "I'm from the *Herald*," she said. "I'm covering the people from the lighthouse."

"Oh, yes, Last Reach Point, you mean."

"Yes — do you know them?"

"No," he said. Great start.

"But Mr Dakers is staying at this hotel, I believe," she said.

"He is, but he hasn't been down here yet. Maybe he's not much of a drinker."

"What do local people think of this business about him offering accommodation to the lighthouse family?"

"It's very kind of him," he said. "Everyone knows that coastline has been crumbling for years. The council even talked about putting some kind of sea wall there, or underpinning the cliff, something like that anyway, but all the money's gone to Carver Bay, as I understand it."

"So what's at Carver Bay that's so important?"

"Nothing. Nothing at all. The land used to all belong to some old guy, used to farm it but it's not much use for anything. There was no public access though. Don't know if he's sold up or what, but there's nothing there."

"How interesting."

"Anyway, got to go — customers." He returned to the bar, where a solitary old man with a skinny dog on a lead was awaiting refreshments.

Imogen lit a cigarette and sat back, glancing at her watch. Finian Lewis was now verging on seriously late, but he was no doubt doing that deliberately. He wouldn't want to look too keen. She surreptitiously checked that she was showing just a tantalising hint of cleavage.

When he did arrive, Imogen was surprised at the strength of the pang of lust that swept through her. She could forgive his tardiness now she was reminded how damn good-looking he was.

"Hello, Imogen," he said, smiling sweetly. "Sorry I'm late."

"Oh — are you?" she said. "I just got here myself."

"You must have been thirsty," he said, indicating her empty glass. "Let me get you another one."

"Oh, go on then," she said. "No lemon this time, though."

"You've been introduced to Fred's antique lemon slices, have you?" he grinned. "Perhaps I should have warned you."

"Is there anything else you should have warned me about?"

He gave her a look which made her knees feel all wobbly. "Isn't it more fun if you find things out for yourself?" he said.

CHAPTER
TEN

Beth spent the whole evening stuck in a circular argument with her family. Bill was adamant that they couldn't afford to turn down the move to London, with all the financial rewards that they'd been told about.

"The money would be nice," Beth had to agree. "But we'll be like fish out of water down there. We don't have any friends in London . . ."

"I don't have any friends *here*," Danny pointed out.

"There's Antony Morini." He just snorted. "Well, anyway, apart from not having any friends down there, you'd have to change schools, I'd have to find a job. And I've got no idea how you go about doing either of those things in a place as big as London. It's a stupid idea."

Bill leaned forward in his chair. "So we stay here," he said. "And do what?"

"We'd think of something."

"We haven't thought of anything yet. I vote we give London a go. What's the worst that can happen? We hate it, and we come back, but we come back with a bit of money in our pockets, and having at least tried."

"Grandad's right," Danny said.

Beth would have done anything to make them happy, especially Danny who'd been through so much in his young life, but she didn't see how this was the way — running away from everything that was familiar and reassuring and home, leaving their last bit of security. She thought that maybe she was the only one of them who felt that way about Last Reach. Her father had a gypsy soul, which was why he'd become a lighthouse keeper in the first place: he was happy moving from place to place and happy in his own company. For much of the time since the Last Reach lighthouse was decommissioned and Bill bought the lighthouse building and the cottages with his savings and his redundancy, he'd left Beth (and Martin) to run the bed and breakfast and used it as a base to travel around the country looking up old pals. Being on the move suited him.

And Danny — well, it was true that he didn't really have any friends in Last Reach, he was such a solitary and introverted boy, but Northlands was all he'd ever known and Beth wasn't confident he'd be able to cope with a big city.

As for herself, the main thing that made her want to stay was that she'd been so happy at the lighthouse with Martin. Because his body had never been found and they'd never had a proper burial, it felt as if he was somehow part of the sea and being close to the sea was like being close to him. Something like that, anyway. And she loved the landscape and the people, and had some good friends.

But on top of all that, she admitted to herself, she was terrified to contemplate such a big change, and had no idea how it might work out, this little family from such a remote corner of the country living with these sophisticated Londoners. She couldn't even imagine what they'd do all day, the kind of conversations they might have with a politician and his wife (there *was* a wife, according to Bill. She'd been one of the Limit Lovelies on *Take It to the limit*. This impressed Bill a lot). It was all too weird.

So the argument went round and round and didn't get anywhere. In the end, Danny stamped off to his room and turned on his thunderous music.

"You're not being fair on the boy, you know," Bill said.

His daughter just looked at him. "And what's fair in this life?" She'd had to deal with plenty that wasn't fair in her forty years. Losing your mother when you were still a child wasn't fair. Losing your husband when you were thirty-seven certainly wasn't fair.

"Where's the harm in a free trip to London? Call it a holiday," he cajoled.

"A holiday from reality, that's all it would be. Because when we get back — and this 'holiday' would have to end, we would be coming back — we would still be homeless, that tower out there would still be too close to the cliff edge to be safe, we'd still have no money coming in."

"We could have thousands from newspapers, Dakers's man said. It's better than a slap on the arse."

"I'm not a performing monkey for people who read the tabloids," Beth said. "Not for any amount. And how can you think of leaving the lighthouse? It's been your job and your responsibility and your home."

"Beth, I've lost count of the number of lighthouses that have been my home and my job and my responsibility. That's what being a lighthouse keeper is. I love this place, you know I do, but one thing you learn in my job is there's no arguing with the sea."

"I've learned that, too," Beth said, thinking of Martin again.

"I know you have, love," he said kindly. "But maybe it's time to move on a bit now, eh? Think of Danny, what a fresh start might do for him. Even without what's happening to the cliff, you have to admit there isn't a lot round here for him. Can't see him going into the fishing business, can you?"

"No." She listened to Danny's music thudding through the ceiling. "But there must be some other way."

"Well, if you work out what it is, you let me know. I'm off to bed."

"I don't know how you can sleep with that noise going on."

"I can sleep through a Force 12 storm if I'm tired enough. And frankly, after the day we've had, and trying to argue the toss with you all evening, I'm tired enough."

Beth sat alone by the fire, listening to the noise from Danny's CD player competing with the noise of the wind, which had started to get stronger in the past half hour, whistling in the chimney. It wasn't a cosy sound any longer: every storm meant greater danger.

There was a knock on the door.

Harry Rushton was standing on the step, not in his uniform this time, but in a thick pullover and jeans, looking more like a fisherman than a policeman.

"Twice in one day, Harry?" she teased him out of old habit, glad of the distraction. "You'll be wanting a mug with your name on it next." She stood back to let him come in.

"Funny old do at that meeting," he remarked, sitting down in front of the fire while Beth made a pot of tea. None of the mugs had his name on, but she did always give him the same one, she realised with a smile.

"It certainly was. I must say I was almost convinced by our local candidate. He seemed very caring, until he got asked about something real."

Harry cleared his throat, sounding nervous. "Word around the village is that you're going to London."

She looked at her old friend, his earnest, kind face, and the solid, square-shouldered dependableness of him. Yet another reason for not going to London: not Harry as a person, particularly — though he was very important to her — but what he represented, a connection, roots, somehow. "London?" she said. "Absolutely not. No chance. Let him buy us off like that? No." She told Harry about what Finian Lewis had said to Bill, and how Bill was convinced that moving to London was the best way out for them. "But I really don't want to go," she said.

Harry took a sip of his tea and placed the mug carefully down on the table. He looked awkward. "I'm glad about that, Beth," he said. The tone of his voice was strange and made her glance over at him: her oldest friend, now that Martin was gone: sensible, straightforward Harry. She waited for him to speak again, as he was obviously bursting to say something. "I'm glad you don't want to go to London, because I'd miss you," he said.

"Oh, that's sweet of you to say! I'd miss you, too. If I was going. Which I'm not."

"No, I mean, I'd *really* miss you. You know what I think about you, Beth." He was looking very hot in his jumper — hot and itchy. She decided not to put any more coal on the fire. Harry gestured around the room. "You can't live here any more," he said.

"Is this Sergeant Rushton speaking now?"

"No. Well, in my official capacity obviously you can't stay here either, it's not safe, and someone from the council will be down in the next few days to inspect and I'm pretty sure they'll tell you the same. So you need somewhere to go."

"That's the problem, though, isn't it?"

"There's plenty of room at my place, Beth."

"It would be a bit of a squeeze for four of us."

"We'd manage, to begin with. And Danny'll be flying the nest in a couple of years, so . . ."

"A couple of years?" She'd assumed he was talking about them staying with him for a few days. She hadn't even begun to think years ahead.

70

He misunderstood her. "Of course, Danny's welcome to stay as long as you want, Beth, he's your boy." The music upstairs, which had stopped for a minute now restarted again even louder. "Though I'd have to put a stop to that sort of thing," he added.

"What sort of thing?"

"All that racket. You let him have his own way a bit too much."

"I *what*?" Harry was Danny's godfather, but in the whole of his life Harry had never once offered any kind of opinion as to how Beth and Martin were raising him. Just recently he seemed to be offering opinions quite freely.

Harry sighed. "I'm doing this all wrong." Then, to Beth's absolute horror, he suddenly slid off his perch on the sofa to land rather clumsily on one knee in front of her. "Will you marry me?" he said, his cheeks flushed red and his eyes eager for an answer. She stared at him, lost for words or a way to react. Her silence made him want to say something else, to persuade her. "It's what Martin would have wanted," he said.

In the three years since her husband had been lost at sea, Beth had had so many people telling her what Martin *would have wanted*. How could they know? If *she* didn't know, who'd slept next to him every night for twenty years, who'd washed his clothes and given birth to his son and loved him, how could anyone else? Beth had a quick temper and didn't think what she was saying sometimes, and the first thing that came out of her mouth was, "What Martin would have *wanted* is not to be dead."

Harry sat back on his heels. "Well . . . granted. But failing that, he'd want you to be looked after."

"I *am* looked after," she said stubbornly. "I look after myself. And Bill and Danny. We manage."

"I know you do," he said gently. "I'm so proud of the way you manage, Beth. That's one of the things I love about you."

"You . . . pardon?"

His face flushed again — one of the problems of being so fair. "You must know how I feel about you," he said.

"So . . . it's not just that you're feeling a sense of duty to look after us?" Her voice was more gentle now.

"Not at all. It would make me so happy if you were my wife."

He was still sitting on his heels on the floor, and Beth sat down there beside him, and took his hand. There were tears in her eyes.

"You don't have to give me an answer tonight," he said. "Sleep on it. Talk to Bill about it."

She took a deep breath, and as she did so a tear fell. When she looked at Harry's handsome, sincere and kind face she felt truly sorry she didn't love him. "There isn't anyone for me but Martin," she said.

He looked even sadder than she felt, if such a thing had been possible. "You're worth more than spending the rest of your life alone and in love with a ghost," he said.

"Oh, Harry, if only I'd believed in ghosts it would have been easier to carry on without him."

★ ★ ★

After Harry left, Beth walked out to the lighthouse. The wind howled around the tower, Force 6 she'd guess: her father had taught her how to gauge the wind speed from the feel of the wind on her cheek.

She climbed the steps inside the tower, using only a small torch to light her way. At the top, she switched the torch off, and stood in the gallery. The light from the new, automated lighthouse out on the rocks combed across the sea, which was lifting up into high waves and streaked with spray.

The past three years had been sad, sometimes unbearably sad, but they'd marched on with a kind of reassuring predictability. Nothing new or challenging or controversial had happened, just the living from day to day. Now, in the last twenty-four hours, everything had suddenly changed, and she tried to make sense of it all.

There was Harry's proposal. Why hadn't she seen that coming? When she looked back, he'd been visiting increasingly often recently. She'd just thought he was lonely, and she'd been glad of the company: particularly in the evenings, when Bill was often out, and she didn't feel she could call Linda because Linda had Kenny and her children and it wouldn't be fair. Now she wondered if she'd led him on, and felt horribly sad that she'd made him unhappy. And now everything between them was bound to be different: they wouldn't be able to sit together by the fire and just talk like old friends, there'd always be that feeling that he wanted more. Evenings would be even lonelier now.

Bill and Danny's arguments for accepting the move to London went through her mind next, followed by her own for staying, and she realised that all that was holding her back was fear of leaving the last bit of security she had. But as she looked out across the vast expanse of darkness beyond the lighthouse tower, she realised how small her world had become.

It was time for a change.

CHAPTER
ELEVEN

Danny staggered out of his room yawning, wearing a stretched-looking black T shirt and the most revolting-looking pair of jeans, and almost fell over the vacuum cleaner Beth was trying to clean the hallway with.

"Mum! It's only nine o'clock!" he groaned, as if nine was early.

"We've got Gareth Dakers coming over with a photographer this morning," Beth said. "I did remind you yesterday. I've got to get this place looking reasonable."

"That floor's clean enough to perform surgery on it," he muttered, making his way to the bathroom.

"Don't you dare make a mess in there!" she shouted after him. "Or you'll be needing surgery yourself." She laughed at herself for the way she could produce these mother-clichés. She didn't know where she got them from, not being able to remember her own mother saying them, and Bill certainly didn't. She switched the vacuum cleaner off and surveyed her work. Not perfect, but it would have to do.

With a great deal of cajoling and effort, she managed to persuade Danny to put on a more presentable pair of jeans before the appointed time of ten o'clock. Bill, who'd been experimenting with a goatee beard, had trimmed it neatly, and was sporting a cocoa-brown shirt liberally patterned with large orange and pink flowers. He looked like Abraham Lincoln on acid. Beth didn't think it was the most appropriate look, but she knew how stubborn her father could be and didn't even bother to mention it.

Danny had no such qualms. "Nice shirt," he said, flopping on to the sofa next to his grandfather.

"I bet you're surprised that your old grandad can still be a hep cat."

"A *what*?"

"This is what all the dudes in London are wearing."

"Er : . . . yeah, if you say so."

The doorbell rang, and Beth went to let the visitors in. Her stomach had been in knots all morning, not least over what to wear herself. After a lot of deliberation, she'd decided on a pair of jeans and a cream sweater, as she thought the photographer would want her to look like a lighthouse keeper's daughter.

Running a self-catering business, the family had become used to all sorts of people turning up on their doorstep. They'd once had quite a famous writer staying in one of the cottages. He'd planned to stay for six weeks while he finished the book he was working on, but the lighthouse's generator had a couple of hiccups and the effect on his computer had been less than ideal, so he'd gone off in a bit of a strop to finish the book in Edinburgh. It was only after his departure that Beth had discovered several wigs and a large phallic item in his wardrobe.

But they'd never had anyone like Gareth Dakers. It seemed to Beth as if he was always on stage — not just that he was performing, but he was performing to the back row of the stalls. He greeted her like a long-lost friend, taking her hand in both of his, smiling his devastating smile and exuding charm, gushing praise about the lighthouse, and the landscape and the sea. It would have been loathsome, had it not been for the feeling he gave, as he had at the meeting in the community centre, that he really meant every word he said. Beth couldn't really work him out.

Finian Lewis was with him again, along with a photographer and the female reporter from the *Herald* who'd visited them previously. She was exactly the type Beth hoped that Danny would never have as a girlfriend — she was so pristine Beth would have to spend all her life apologising for the general ramshackle state of her life if he did.

It was all horribly uncomfortable. Bill couldn't have been more obsequious if he'd tried: like a child, Bill couldn't help saying cheese as soon as a camera was present. Danny was being Danny — languid to the point of inert. While the photographer herded them around the garden trying to fit the family and Dakers and the lighthouse into the shot, Beth was thinking about Harry, and how she'd perhaps been a bit hasty in turning him down. Surely a quiet, protected life with Harry had to be better than this circus?

★ ★ ★

Fin hung back from the others. He would only step in if Gareth seemed at risk of losing his grip on the agenda, which was for the local paper to get some shots of the grateful lighthouse family, a quote or two about how much everyone was looking forward to the move to London and then leave as quickly as possible. So he had time to wonder about how it must be to live in such an isolated place. From ground level there was no sign of any other habitation. The only sign of human life was a ship (or was it a boat? Fin couldn't remember if there was a difference) which was making slow and stately progress along the horizon. What must it be like for three people from different generations to be stuck out here in the middle of nowhere? What did they do all day? What did they think about?

He was trying his best not to look at the reporter, Imogen Callow-Creed. He was trying not to even *think* about Imogen, because the previous night had been a bit of an embarrassment.

He'd badly miscalculated there. She was certainly a very attractive, sexy woman, and he'd been going with the flow quite happily until she started attempting to fish in his trouser pockets for his room key. It wasn't that he couldn't cope with assertive women, in fact it was quite a turn-on that she was so obviously keen, but he'd already decided he didn't trust her at all. In fact, he didn't think he even liked her.

"I'm not really a one-night-stand sort of person," he told her, trying to extract himself from the situation gracefully.

"How do you know it would only be the one night?" she murmured. "It might be the first night of many."

"Even so . . ."

"Or it might be the last night of your life. You might die tomorrow." Which wasn't the most seductive line he'd ever heard, even though it had logic in its favour.

"I'm too much of a gentleman to take advantage of a lady," he attempted.

She replied breathily in his ear, while filling almost his entire field of vision with her impressive chest, "I'm no lady."

He was beginning to realise this.

So now, trying not to catch Imogen's eye, he fixed his attention on the lighthouse family: the grandfather rushing about being ingratiating, fetching chairs and moving tables at the photographer's request; the son, sullen and naturally mortified at being the centre of such attention. He didn't look much like his mother, so Fin supposed he must take after his father, who, he'd discovered on questioning some of the villagers after the election meeting, had been a trawler fisherman who'd died in an accident at sea three years earlier. What must it be like for a boy of that age, living out here with no mates, no girls anywhere near? Though a life without girls would at least have simplicity in its favour.

Then Fin looked at Beth. She was standing next to Gareth Dakers, smiling for the camera when instructed, but she looked totally dignified. Not confident, not sure of herself or the situation, but not overwhelmed by it either. And she was quite stunning: her eyes were large and dark, her hair was also dark, and thick, and pulled back into a loose pony tail from which little tendrils had escaped and were curling around her neck. Her sweater and jeans couldn't hide a figure that was rounded and soft, but with a lovely slim waist. He took her all in, the way she moved, her quick, friendly smile, everything was filed away. Fin smiled to himself at the thought of what Lorelei would say when she saw these pictures. Gareth was going to have his work cut out trying to convince her that all this was entirely innocent.

Beth was beginning to feel distinctly cross and foolish. What on earth was she doing, posing around her own home with this bunch of strangers? She almost included her own father in that — with his fawning grin and his outlandish shirt, he looked more like a teenager than Danny did. In the present situation, it was Danny who looked like a beacon of sanity, with his sullen expression. Beth knew that as soon as this was over he would escape to his room and they'd hear Marilyn Manson's noisy attempts at nihilism. At this rate she thought she might join him. Then she caught the eye of the man called Finian Lewis. He was standing well out of the photographer's way, leaning against the garden gate, and from the look on his face he seemed to know exactly what she was thinking, and that given half a chance he'd prefer to be listening to Marilyn Manson too. He smiled at her, and she smiled back.

"Over here, love, to me," the photographer said. "Don't waste that lovely smile. Chin up. That's it.

Smashing." The camera flashed again. "That should do it," the photographer said to his reporter colleague.

They went back into the house, which was blissfully warm after the chilly breeze outside (though it was only a Force 4 this time).

As predicted, Danny immediately bolted to his room, while his mother and grandfather sat down with the politician.

"That wasn't too bad, was it?" Dakers beamed, then to the reporter he said, "Now perhaps you'd like to ask these good people one or two questions only, and we'll leave them in peace."

Imogen pulled a chair forward and sat down facing Bill and Beth, and with Dakers to her left. "You must be grateful to Mr Dakers for giving you a roof over your heads," she said, which wasn't exactly a question.

"Yes," Beth said. "Though . . ."

"And have you ever visited London before?"

"No. But . . ."

"What are you looking forward to seeing the most?"

"Carnaby Street, baby," Bill said. Imogen raised one eyebrow slightly and jotted down his answer.

"Can we presume you'll be returning to Northlands to place your vote for Mr Dakers in the election?" she asked.

Beth wondered how to answer this honestly yet politely. "I don't . . ."

Dakers interrupted. "The exercising of one's franchise," he said, lobbing out one of those shimmering smiles, "is a personal matter between the voter and the ballot box. I'm certainly not doing this as a cynical vote-grabbing exercise."

"It would only grab two votes anyway," Beth said. "My son isn't eighteen yet so he can't vote."

"About your son," the reporter said. "How has he coped with the loss of his father?"

"I don't want to talk about that," Beth said. "Your newspaper had enough about that at the time it happened."

Finian Lewis stepped in at this point, whether out of sensitivity or not Beth couldn't be sure, but she was glad of the intervention. "I'm terribly sorry," he said, "but Mr Dakers is on a tight schedule today, and we have to be somewhere else. Perhaps we could give you some additional comments later?"

The reporter glared at him with more venom than the situation seemed to warrant. "I was just going to ask . . ." she started to say, but he was already steering her out of the door, where Beth heard a muttered discussion going on.

The last one to leave was Dakers, who paused in the hallway and again took Beth's hand in both of his. "It was most charming of you to allow us into your home," he said, and he flashed her that dazzling smile that in his heyday, according to Linda, had had him voted one of Britain's sexiest men by some women's magazine or other.

Finally they'd all gone, and Beth sighed with relief. The relief didn't last long, though, because she realised that there were going to be a lot more days like this before they would be left alone to get on with their lives in London or wherever it happened to be. Again she thought about Harry, and the alternative life he'd offered, and wondered what the next few days would bring.

As Fin drove Dakers away from the house, the press having made their own transport arrangements, the politician was delighted by Beth. "She has these marvellously northern vowels. Just like someone from those costume dramas on the BBC that my wife likes so much. She's charming, absolutely charming."

"I'm going to say this once." Fin drummed his fingers on the steering wheel. "She is a very attractive woman, but don't even *think* about it, unless you want to throw your entire campaign in before it's even got going. In which case I resign right now."

"So it's her or you, is that what you're saying?" Dakers's eyes sparkled wickedly.

Fin sighed. "Why do you always make it sound as though I'm your jealous toyboy? I'm watching out for our respective sodding careers, the good of the party, blah blah. Don't you dare throw it away just because you fancy that woman."

"You're beginning to sound eerily like my darling wife."

"Then I feel sorry for her, too."

"Bloody hell, Fin. Since when did you change your name to Jiminy Cricket? And you've got no room for moralising. When were you going to tell me about you and the lady from the *Herald*?"

"Nothing to tell."

Gareth raised his eyebrows. "I believe you," he said. "Thousands wouldn't. Not if they'd seen the lady from the *Herald* with their own eyes, anyway."

"That went quite well," Bill remarked. He was peeling some potatoes for lunch, letting the strips of peel drop neatly into the open pedal bin at his feet. "Dakers seems all right when you get to know him."

"He's a slimeball," Beth replied. "I can see right through his type."

"With all your experience of the world."

"You don't need experience to know when someone's as false as a plastic Christmas tree."

Bill passed over the colander full of peeled potatoes. "He's a politician, though. They're supposed to be false. So when you think about it that way, his falseness is itself really quite genuine."

"Do you know something?" his daughter said. "I reckon it's because you've lived in so many lighthouses."

"What is?"

"The reason your mind goes round and round in circles. It's all those spiral staircases. You can argue yourself into something and straight back to the place you started."

He looked out of the window at the curved wall of the lighthouse tower. "This is the last lighthouse I'll ever live in," he said quietly, and turned to Beth. "We *are* doing the right thing, aren't we?"

She stood beside him, linking her arm through his. "I have no idea," she said. "I hope so."

84

Privately, she still wasn't absolutely convinced that they *were* doing the right thing. Linda sensed that her friend was wavering and made one final effort to change her mind. "You can't leave your friends, and Danny's school and everything," she said.

"What else can we do?" Beth added a couple of Mars Bars to the basket of groceries on the counter in Linda's shop: she didn't want Danny getting even more grumpy due to low blood sugar on the train.

"We'd sort something out, you know we would. We look after our own in Last Reach."

Beth pulled a face. "That's what Harry said, that I needed looking after."

Linda's eyes were disapproving behind her glasses. "You could do worse than Harry, you know."

"I don't want to marry someone because I could do worse. Do I look desperate?"

"You're not being fair on him. He's lovely, Harry is. I wouldn't shove him out of bed, anyway."

"Kenny might have something to say about that," Beth laughed, and said, "I know it's hard for Harry, but what can I do? How can I love anyone except Martin?"

"You're only forty years old, Beth," Linda said gently. "You can't honestly believe that there won't be anyone else except Martin?"

Beth thought about that for a moment, trying the idea on for size. "I can't say it'll never happen," she decided. "Because you never know when you wake up in the morning what the rest of the day might have in store for you, never mind the rest of your life. That's about the only thing you can really rely on, and you can only decide how you feel and what to do moment by moment."

"So if you stayed in Last Reach, you might find you could let yourself fall in love with Harry."

Linda was mentally trying on wedding hats already, but Beth was quick to stop her. "That wouldn't be fair on anybody, because it might not work out, then we'd all be really unhappy, Harry especially. But maybe I'll write to him when I get to London and get settled in."

"That's better," Linda said, clearly sensing that this was as far as her matchmaking efforts would get her on this occasion. "And I hope you'll be writing to me as well," she said. "I'll definitely be writing to you, keep you up with all the gossip."

Beth laughed. "Oh, I wish you would. I'm going to miss you so much." They hugged.

Linda put the kettle on in the little stockroom at the back of the shop. Beth could never get away with doing the shopping without spending at least half an hour talking with Linda.

The door swung open to admit the wiry form of Tony Jabbocks, who made his living as an odd-job man. Like Linda he was a fairly recent migrant to Last Reach, but although he'd left Yorkshire in the 1980s, Yorkshire had never left him. "Fookin' 'ell, that were a bad storm t'other night. I'm not complainin' mind! It's an ill wind," he said.

"Plenty of work on for you, eh?" Linda said, already putting his favourite brand of cigarettes on the counter.

"Aye, right enough. I've just come back from Betty Cooper's. Half her roof tiles are off. I said I'll have to get one of the lads to help, I'm not ower good wi' heights any more, what with me labyrinthitis." As well as being an odd-job man, Tony was an inveterate hypochondriac who preferred his imagined ailments to end in -itis. "Just as well your place don't want owt doin' to it," he said to Beth. "Can't be doin' wi' lighthouses and such."

"The lighthouse is solid enough," she said. "It's the cliff that wants something doing to it."

"Bit ambitious even for me, that." He peered at her through his not very alert eyes. "Is it right you're moving to London?"

He knew very well that it was true she was moving to London. The whole village knew — the Jackson family had spent the whole of the previous day being interviewed by TV people, radio people, and particularly by newspaper people. Their faces were smiling out from some of the newspapers on Linda's shelves. Beth nodded.

Tony looked incredulous. "Fookin' London? What d'yer wanner move down there for?" Beth gave him the nutshell explanation. "Ooh la la!" he said. "You'll be gerrin' all nobby. Evil fookin' place, London. I'd be no use there, what with the smog and me chronic bronchitis." As if to illustrate this, he produced an enormous and none-too-clean handkerchief and coughed theatrically into it. "And you want to watch your Danny," he added. "It's a hotbed of drugs and vice down there."

"I don't think Danny . . ."

"Keep 'im away from that King's Cross Station. Meat rack, that's what they call it. The streets are slippery wi' used condoms, they say."

"For heaven's sake, Tony," Linda said. "You don't have to believe everything you hear, and you certainly don't have to repeat it. You make it sound like Sodom and Gomorrah."

"I speak as I find."

"Have you ever physically been to London?"

"I've gorrer cousin in Romford."

"That's not London."

"If you think any family of mine'd be stupid enough to live any nearer to fookin' London than Romford you're thicker than you look."

Linda had been known to throw people out of the shop (literally throwing — she might have been five feet hardly anything but she was powerful) for less than that, but the whole village had become skilled at ignoring Tony Jabbocks over the years.

But Beth couldn't help wishing he hadn't made King's Cross sound so horrible. That was the destination printed on the train tickets that were propped up on their mantelpiece at home.

CHAPTER
TWELVE

There was something about this house that made it a joy to come back to, Lorelei Dakers thought, as she slipped one glove off and rummaged in her glossy black Prada bag for the front-door key. The autumn sunshine lit up the front of the house, which was long, low and painted a very subtle shade (she'd chosen it herself) of pink, which chimed perfectly with the climbing roses around the door. She'd always wanted masses of roses in her garden, and since the house and grounds were her responsibility, she got her way. The gardener was doing a good job: there were still quite a lot of blooms, despite the lateness of the year.

Inside, it was warm and peaceful. Lorelei slipped out of her shoes and poured herself a drink, walking through the house to the conservatory at the back which overlooked a sloping lawn and yet more rose bushes. Lawns were a bit pointless, she thought. All that mowing — not that she'd ever touched a lawnmower herself, but the buzzing sound was positively migraine-inducing on a sunny afternoon. She wondered if it might be feasible to have it all dug up and have a swimming pool instead. It would be good for Gareth to get some exercise, and she couldn't help thinking her own upper arms were beginning to show slight signs of wear and tear, but more than that, think of the cachet of having a swimming pool. She'd be the envy of her friends.

She sat down on a sofa piled high with cushions, sipping at her drink, thinking about friends, and how she had a bit of a dearth of same. This was partly as a result of being very competitive herself, partly because she preferred to steer Gareth well clear of any temptation after the Windy Wendy episode. It was a policy that had succeeded in preserving her marriage, but as a result she had to admit that she was often very lonely.

Admittedly, they were both moving into a new phase of their lives now. She thought perhaps her task might be easier when the biggest temptations surrounding Gareth would be all those dreary lady politicians with their misguided attempts at power-dressing, or even more ludicrous, the ones who thought a leather jacket and a pair of kitten heels qualified them as sexy.

What politics needed was a touch of proper glamour, and she and her husband were the ideal people to provide it. There was nothing to stop Gareth going all the way to Number Ten: there'd never been a good-looking prime minister, she thought, thinking back over all the portly, baggy-eyed men who'd been in office during her childhood, and then the dreadful Mrs Thatcher, a man in drag if ever there was one, and the flaccid members who'd followed her. She allowed herself a little chuckle at that. As a *double entendre* it was even better than Dr Shah and his magic syringe.

She was getting good at this: perhaps she could ask Fin about the possibility of her writing a satirical column for one of the better dailies.

Her nose wrinkled at the thought of her husband's PR guru. That man had far too much influence, in her opinion — here she was herself thinking of asking his permission to do something! There was no denying he was bloody clever, but the world was full of men who were too clever, and in her experience they wasted all their time trying to outmanoeuvre each other. It was all very tedious, particularly as Gareth seemed to spend far more time with Fin than he did with her these days. Lorelei might almost suspect there was something between them if she hadn't been totally convinced of her husband's heterosexuality. She wasn't entirely sure what team Fin batted for, though. He gave every appearance of heterosexuality, but his ability to find her totally resistible made him deeply suspect in her eyes.

Then there was this business of the family of northerners who were about to be dumped on her. Lorelei was sure that was all Fin's doing as well. As if it wasn't bad enough to have him lurking about the place all the time, as well as that spotty secretary boy they'd hired, now she was going to have an old lighthouse keeper, a tragic widow and a teenager who was bound to be a drug addict. She'd seen the first third of *Trainspotting* on television and knew what the north was like in terms of drugs.

She stood up abruptly and stamped off to the kitchen, her good mood evaporating fast. She plonked the glass beside the sink and went into the lounge, where the cleaning woman had left the newspapers in a beautifully ordered pile

Lorelei didn't usually bother with newspapers — she got enough of politics and stuff from her husband — but she thought she might glance through and see which of them might be most amenable to a well-written satirical column by a high-placed society wife. She would call the editors direct — it would deprive Finian Lewis of the satisfaction of making any sarcastic comments. Picking up the top one, she started to flick through the pages, ignoring the news with a practised deftness and picking out features. But one feature caught her eye more than the others, because it was accompanied by a photograph of her husband, looking very handsome as usual. The headline was RAY OF HOPE FOR LIGHTHOUSE FAMILY. Lorelei saw that in the picture Gareth was standing in very close proximity to a rather stunning-looking woman. Surely this couldn't be . . .? She read on, and found that indeed it was the woman whom her husband had described to her as "a middle-aged mother". Lorelei attempted to pull a face, but the Botox had worked perfectly and her skin remained as smooth as the surface of a new jar of cold cream. For Gareth to have deliberately tried to mislead her regarding the woman he was bringing to live with them meant one of two things: he was either shagging her or hoping to.

The all-too familiar feelings of hurt and betrayal ripped through her. He'd promised faithfully (hah! That was a laugh) that he'd mended his ways. His dalliance with that weather girl, Windy Wendy — who had, let's face it, nothing going for her except a rather prominent frontal system — had caused enough turbulence and depression to last a lifetime. Later, Lorelei had had no option but to check herself into the Priory to recover from the trauma, at Gareth's expense, of course.

But the woman in the picture looked an altogether more alarming proposition than Windy Wendy. Lorelei hurled the newspaper on to the table, and picked up the phone. The number she dialled was that of Finian Lewis.

The day had gone beautifully. A campaign launch that most would-be MPs would kill for, with Dakers's face gazing confidently out of the pages of every newspaper in the country. Admittedly many of the reports were cynical in their attitude, accusing Dakers of making political capital out of a family's plight, suggesting this might all be a stunt. They'd wheeled out various opposition spokespeople, but none had anything really damaging to say. Fin had pre-empted the only possible criticism — that this was a token gesture and what was really needed was a whole raft of policies to benefit the entire community rather than simply a quick fix for one family — and had made sure that these were the very words with which Gareth opened his main speech of the day, at a local agricultural college.

A moment of madness had been spun into pure gold, and Fin was more than satisfied with his work. Then his phone rang.

"Lorelei? Sorry, Gareth's busy at the moment, he's chatting to . . ."

"The lighthouse family, I suppose." Her voice had a strangled quality, as though she'd prefer to be yelling at someone but was making a determined effort not to.

"To the president of the local pig farmers' guild, as it happens."

She snorted. "Hmm. One and the same."

"Pardon?"

"Look, there's no way I'm having that woman in my house."

"Which woman?"

"That lighthouse creature!"

"But she seems very nice," Fin said, guessing correctly that Lorelei had seen the pictures.

"She's not coming here, and that's final. Get it sorted."

"Lorelei, I realise that having impromptu house-guests is not ideal, but it's doing wonders for his profile up here. This could really make the difference between him winning the election and not. You do want him to win the election, I take it?"

Her response was more of a choked yelp than words, but he took it as affirmative. Then she said, "What about Dogwood Avenue? You could put them in there. They don't have to live with us."

Dogwood Avenue was a house in a rather seedy part of London that Dakers had had converted into flats. The ground floor was let to tenants, but the first was currently empty. Fin had stayed there for a few weeks himself while he was looking for somewhere else, and he suspected that Gareth used it as a love nest at other times.

"Then we really *would* be open to accusations of tokenism and doing this as a stunt," he objected. "Gareth has offered them the use of his *home*, and I'm afraid only his home will do." His voice dropped to its kindest, most confiding note. "Tell you what, though — after a week or two, I expect you could shunt them off to Dogwood Avenue. So you'd only be inconvenienced for a short while."

"So what does she look like, this lighthouse woman? In the flesh, I mean?"

Fin wasn't going to ruin her newly acquired outward calm by telling her that Beth was beautiful, in an elemental sort of way, with hair like a raven's wing, dark intelligent eyes and skin like warm milk, so he said, "You know the sort. Sturdy, country type." He hoped his voice was conveying armpit hair, washday hands, and flabby upper arms. Not that Beth had any of these things, but Lorelei would be better disposed to her if she thought they existed.

At that point, Gareth's discussion with the president of the pig farmers' guild ended, and Gareth himself appeared, flanked by several journalists with whom he was chatting most amiably.

"I can hear my husband," Lorelei said. "Put him on."

"I don't think . . ."

"Who's that?" Gareth asked.

"Your wife." Fin handed him the phone, hoping that he'd softened Lorelei up sufficiently.

"Darling! How are you?" Gareth gushed, fully aware that the journalists were paying attention to every word.

"More than a little pissed off that you're about to fill my home with a load of inbreeds from the constituency, my love."

"And they're very much looking forward to it too!"

Silence from Lorelei.

"Added to which, darling, it'll give you a chance to try out that goose recipe you've been dying to have a go at." She'd never cooked in her life, and he knew it.

She said, "You mean the recipe where you're plucked, stuffed and roasted? Because that's what I'd like to do to you for this."

"Sounds marvellous, darling. I'll talk to you later. Mwah mwah."

CHAPTER
THIRTEEN

"Told you it'd be a mansion," Danny's predictions about the Dakers' showbiz lifestyle were clearly accurate: the taxi had stopped outside a high iron security gate, behind which the family could see a huge house, painted a queasy shade of pale pink.

"I want to run away right now," Beth muttered, but Bill patted her arm and said, "We're as good as any of these people, and don't you ever forget it."

"Yeah," Danny said. "We're doing *him* a favour, remember? All that publicity."

Bill paid the taxi driver, who was throwing their bags into a heap on the pavement, then they were alone, abandoned in a leafy lane in who-knew-where. There were more trees than Beth had expected: the roadside was lined with them, and there were more behind the high walls surrounding the houses. What was absent was any sign of people: there was no one walking a dog, no one pushing a child in a buggy, no one on their way to or from work, nothing.

Bill gave the iron gate an experimental rattle, but it was locked tight shut. "Maybe we're supposed to shout," he said, and hollered, "Helloooooo." There was no sign of life from the pink house.

"It doesn't look as if we're expected," Beth said, and felt ready to burst into tears.

They'd spent the previous days packing up everything they owned. Some of it had been sold, some of it was being stored in Linda's garage and attic. And the rest was in the cases and bags around them. Beth looked at the heap of mismatched suitcases and holdalls: not much to show for all those years of work and marriage and life.

On their last night in Last Reach the weather had been so calm and beautiful that it seemed ridiculous that they were having to leave because their home was under attack by the sea. Beth climbed to the lighthouse gallery — as they all had at some point during that day, she suspected, each member of the family wanting to be alone with his or her own thoughts and memories of this isolated and lovely home. Gazing out across the sea, she had one of her silent dialogues with Martin. She'd sometimes had a fantasy that Martin hadn't drowned at all. Instead, he'd been washed up on a shore in Norway and had amnesia and was living with a nice, kind, Norwegian woman. Maybe they even had kids. Perhaps occasionally he had a fleeting feeling that he'd had a life somewhere else, and a vague picture of her might have formed in his mind, but she wouldn't have wanted him to leave that nice Norwegian woman who'd been so kind to him and loved him, because she would have hated anyone else to have to go through the pain that she'd suffered. She was just glad he was alive and happy and loved.

And she knew, with absolute confidence, that he'd want the same for her. So she told him that she was leaving the lighthouse, to try to make life better for Danny, but that part of her would always be there, in the home they'd shared together.

Even as she was descending the steps, she was already trying to push down the flutter of excitement in her chest, though. It was easier to think that she was all regrets and misgivings about going, and deny that part of her was really looking forward to it.

Linda had driven them to Boldwick station, and as the car drove away from the lighthouse Bill and Danny both looked back at it, but Beth kept her eyes fixed on the road ahead. Linda guessed how her friend was feeling, and kept up a non-stop stream of gossip, partly to take Beth's mind off it and partly because if she kept talking, Beth wouldn't have to say anything herself. For Beth, leaving Linda had been as hard as leaving home, and she missed her badly now.

Danny was examining the gate. "Hang on," he said. "There's a doorbell." And there was, embedded into the wall in a way that was so discreet it was ridiculous. Danny pressed it, and after a second or two the gate slid noiselessly inwards, "Like in a horror film," he said, clearly approving of this gothic detail. Laden with luggage, the three of them staggered up the driveway, past a very expensive-looking car the colour of rain, to the front door of the pink house. It was exactly the colour of the icing on Linda's daughter Cait's christening cake, a proper Barbie-pink. There were roses in gaudy shades of pink and red all around the door.

The front door opened. Beth expected Mrs Dakers to come out, or perhaps a housekeeper, given that the house looked so posh. She was nervous of the reception they would get, anyway, so she was quite relieved when the figure who appeared was the apparently ubiquitous Finian Lewis.

"Beth!" he said, as if he was greeting an old friend. "Bill! Danny! You got here all right, then?" Beth nodded. "That's great, but . . . I'm afraid you're a touch early," he frowned. "Would you mind getting into the car?"

"What?" Had they come to the wrong place? The train journey had been horrible, and Beth wanted nothing more than to put her feet up with a nice cup of tea. But tea wasn't on the cards just yet.

"What we'd really like is for the press to get a nice shot of you arriving and being welcomed. But unfortunately you're a bit ahead of schedule."

"We got an earlier train."

"I wish you'd let me know," he said. "Now, if you wouldn't mind getting in the car, we can make sure there's a proper welcome for you when you arrive." He picked up some of their luggage, which was apparently allowed to enter the house even though its owners weren't.

They got into the car, which had leather seats more comfortable than most armchairs Beth had experienced. She sat back, feeling as though she'd entered some strange *Alice in Wonderland* world. A skinny youth in

100

an overly roomy suit came out of the house and got into the driver's seat. He looked too young to have a driving licence, never mind be in charge of such a swanky car, but Lewis seemed confident. "Give it about half an hour, Paul," he said. "I'll ring you when we're all set up. Sorry about this," he smiled at Beth.

As they drove off, Bill observed that it was like Beth and Martin's wedding day, when Beth and Bill had to make an extra circuit of the village because she'd been so eager to get to the church that she'd insisted on leaving the house far too early. Bill had been concerned that they'd get there before Martin, but they needn't have worried, because he'd already been at the church for half an hour himself. Beth smiled to herself at the memory of him standing at the altar, and how handsome he'd looked.

She didn't want to say much in front of Paul, whoever he turned out to be, so she concentrated on having a good look at her new neighbourhood. It wasn't how she'd expected London to be at all, but probably this was the very posh part where all the famous people lived. The houses were invariably huge, beautifully maintained and obviously occupied by the filthy rich, but at the same time there was something unwelcoming about it. A total lack of shops, for a start, not even a pub (Bill wasn't going to settle in well here, she predicted) and not even a bus stop to get to anywhere else. She supposed all the people who lived here had cars.

"What do you think, Dan?" Bill asked.

"Looks boring."

"Danny!" Beth was aghast at his rudeness, even though he was only putting into words exactly what she'd been thinking.

"Wait till I show you Carnaby Street and the King's Road, and Soho. That's where it's all happening," Bill said. Beth thought she noticed a muscle twitch in the driver's completely stubble-free cheek. He probably thinks we're thick northerners, she thought. They all will. It's going to be awful. She was beginning to feel very depressed.

A phone rang, and Paul answered, speaking apparently into thin air but there must have been a microphone somewhere around.

"Okay, I'll approach from the south then. I'll let them know." He turned to them. "If anyone asks," he said, "you've just arrived. I picked you up at the station."

"Thinly disguised as a black cab driver," Bill muttered.

"I *would* have been there if you'd let us know when to expect you." So that meant it wasn't a lie at all then. Was that what they meant by "spin"?

This time, as they approached the pink house, the gate was surrounded by people. Beth had seen this sort of thing on television, crowds of press waiting outside a court for the verdict, or outside a celebrity's house when there was a scandal. It was unbelievable that this was all for them: cameras all set up, photographers up on stepladders. There was even a policeman — when she saw the uniform for half a second she thought

Harry had come to take them back to Last Reach, and she might well have gone with him if he had.

The cameras were flashing even before Paul had stopped the car. This time the gates were already open, and as the car slid through them the gang of photographers charged inside along with them. Beth noticed the front door of the pink house opening, and Gareth Dakers came out, accompanied by a very glamorous-looking woman of around her own age.

Paul opened the door to let her out of the car, and Mrs Dakers stepped forward and gave her one of those showbiz greetings, a quite stiff and formal "air kiss" in the vague vicinity of each cheek. She looked friendly enough, and was very pretty, with smooth skin and honey-blonde hair, though her face was oddly serene — Beth wondered if she might be on tranquillisers, and couldn't have blamed her if she was, with all this insanity going on around her all the time. Dakers stood right next to his wife, and greeted Beth with a more formal handshake, clasping her hand in both of his as seemed to be his habit. This was repeated with Bill and Danny, though Beth noticed Mrs Dakers keeping her distance from Danny. She'd told him he shouldn't be wearing his Cradle of Filth T shirt, but he'd refused to get changed.

Reporters thrust microphones at them from every direction, but Dakers spoke on their behalf. "Ladies and gentlemen," he said, "I'd just like to say how thrilled my wife and I are that this family of my future constituents are able to honour us with their presence, and we look forward to doing our very best to make their stay as comfortable as possible."

"Mrs Jackson!" people were shouting. "Do you have anything to say? How do you feel about leaving your home behind?"

Beth was speechless, but Dakers said, "I'm sure Mrs Jackson will be happy to talk to you tomorrow, but having spent the foregoing several hours on a railway service which has suffered horrendously from the short-sighted policies of the previous administration, I expect she's direly in need of a rest. So if you'd like to come this way, Paul will bring in your bags." Which was going to be an easy task for Paul, since most of the bags were already inside the house. The press people continued to yell at the family and the cameras were still in their faces, but Dakers propelled them into the house, and the door closed.

They'd arrived.

CHAPTER
FOURTEEN

What an ill-assorted band they made for supper that night. Beth and Danny Jackson, Bill Turnbull, the ever-present Finian Lewis, and Dakers and his wife, who was apparently called Lorelei. Her name sounded foreign to Beth even if she didn't (Beth thought she could detect the tiniest touch of *EastEnders* when she spoke). Nor did she seem overtly friendly, though she was very well mannered and always asking them if they were comfortable and was there anything they needed, to the point where it grated a bit. Beth couldn't blame her: she imagined what it would have been like if the situation was reversed and she'd been forced to take a strange family into her home. Not the holiday cottages — she was used to strange people staying there — but in their cottage itself. She decided she'd try to speak to Lorelei Dakers on her own as soon as possible, to try and smooth things over with her a bit.

For now, Beth was so tired and felt so disconnected from anything real and normal that she could hardly take in any details about what anyone talked about, or what they ate, or anything about the meal except that she was on constant watch to make sure Danny or Bill didn't drink too much wine and make fools of themselves. She was aware of Finian Lewis being quite kind, and mediating between the Dakers and their guests. For the first time she realised that he had a faint northern accent himself and asked him where he was from.

"South Yorkshire," he said. "Near Sheffield."

"A bloody southerner!" Bill grunted. The Dakers looked confused.

"Sheffield *is* south, when you live in Northlands," Fin explained.

"Lorelei gets palpitations anywhere north of the M25, don't you, darling?" Dakers said.

"Nonsense," she replied. "More asparagus, Danny?"

"Erm, no thanks," he said, amazing his mother with his sudden grasp of manners. He didn't mention that he'd never had asparagus before. Neither had Beth, come to that.

"Fantastic asparagus," Bill said. "Lovely sauce. Is it a German recipe?"

"I've no idea," Lorelei said.

"Only I thought your name must be German, or Austrian."

"It isn't."

"My wife was named after Lorelei Lee, in *Gentlemen Prefer Blondes*, weren't you, darling?"

"Yes." She looked quite cross for some reason.

"So diamonds'll be your best friends then," Bill said.

"Aren't they everyone's?" she laughed. Everyone else laughed too, out of politeness rather than amusement.

It was that kind of conversation — trivial, awkward, no one really wanting to be there. More than once Beth found herself thinking wistfully of evenings sitting round the kitchen table at her home in the keeper's cottage, or at Linda's, and wishing she was back in Northlands.

Beth was used to rising early, and she laid in bed for a while the next morning straining to hear any indications that anyone else was up. She thought it would be very rude to start walking around the house before her host and hostess were out of bed. But there were no sounds at all. Eventually she ventured downstairs at eight o'clock.

Every aspect of the house fascinated her: the plush, deep stair carpet, the works of art hanging on the wall down the staircase (squiggly abstract things like Danny used to bring home from infant school, but she'd bet they were worth a bit), even a chandelier. Beth wondered how they managed to dust it. None of it was exactly what she would call tasteful, in some ways too showy, but it was very comfortable and rich-looking and completely different to anything she'd been used to.

The dining room where they'd eaten the night before was empty, and looked so tidy that it seemed as if no one had eaten there ever. The long rectangular table gleamed like a mirror. But there was a smell of coffee somewhere around, and by following her nose Beth found the kitchen. Lorelei Dakers was sitting at a huge oak table, dressed and fully made-up, with a cup of coffee and a glass of water in front of her.

"Good morning!" she said, with a brightness Beth could tell she didn't feel, even though her face, as Beth had noticed the night before, wore an expression of unblemished serenity. "Did you sleep well?"

"Beautifully, thanks." Beth had hardly slept at all, in fact, but it would have been rude to say so.

Lorelei got up and poured her guest a cup of coffee, which she placed on the table. She didn't offer any milk or sugar, or any breakfast either, and although Beth was quite hungry she didn't dare say anything.

The two women sat down at opposite sides of the table, and exchanged awkward little smiles for a moment or two. Beth, deciding to deal with the problem directly, said, "It must be very annoying for you to have us descending on you like this."

"Not at all," Lorelei replied. She was giving Beth a very weird look. "I'm used to my husband's passing whims." Which was a strange thing to say, Beth thought.

"Is he at home today?"

Lorelei laughed. "Are you joking? I'm lucky if I see him once a week. You were very honoured yesterday to actually sit down and have a meal with him."

"You must miss him, when he's away campaigning." No reply. "Do you ever go with him?"

She shrugged. "Sometimes. But, frankly, it's very tedious."

Beth was getting nowhere with the topic of Lorelei's husband, so she cast around in search of other subjects. She noticed that the kitchen was full of domestic appliances: she'd never seen so many items of gleaming

108

chrome machinery in one place. She made a few complimentary remarks and pointed at one of the appliances. "What's that one for?"

Lorelei looked at it uncomprehendingly. "It's . . . I don't know, some kitchen gadget thingy. Is it for roasting garlic? No, that's a smaller one. It's a bread maker, I think."

"Oh! I've heard of those. How does it work?"

"I wouldn't know."

"Don't you use it?"

"Are you kidding? When do I ever have time to make bread?"

"Do you work long hours, then?" Finally this was something Beth could relate to.

Apparently Lorelei couldn't, however. "Work? No, I don't go out to work," she said.

Beth wondered exactly what she *did* with her time, if she didn't work and she didn't cook, and she didn't go on the campaign trail with her husband because it was too tedious. Maybe she had hobbies, but apparently nothing she was so enthusiastic about that she would tell you all about it at the drop of a hat, like Bill and his precious amateur radio.

"It's very good of you to let us stay here," Beth said. Again no reply. "I wondered if we could do anything to help, while we're here. I could help you in the kitchen, and maybe Danny could cut the grass or something."

Lorelei practically shuddered. "We have *people* for that," she said.

Beth was getting nowhere, and she still hadn't been offered any breakfast.

CHAPTER
FIFTEEN

Loathed him, despised him, hated him, detested him. *Almost* pitied him. To describe how Imogen Callow-Creed felt about her editor would require a Thesaurus entry all on its own. Nigel Packman was a nice enough man, if you'd met him in a pub or playing darts or something — not that Imogen would ever have lowered herself to play darts: the gym was more her idea of fun, and you'd never have found the corpulent Nigel at a gym. But as an editor he had no vision, no ambition, and no drive. He ran the *Northlands Herald* as if it was a cosy service to the community, steering it generally away from controversy and unpleasantness. "There's too much nastiness in the world," he would say. "What our readers want is to read pleasant things about the region, all the good stuff that happens here."

Imogen couldn't believe his attitude — it was so retro! When she arrived at the *Northlands Herald*, fresh out of college, she had high hopes that it wouldn't be long before she could move on to something infinitely better, but as things stood, she was never going to get any nationals or even the better regionals to notice her when all she was doing was churning out nice, cosy, regional stories. She'd hoped Nigel would change his approach, but to her utter bafflement, niceness seemed to have acquired a bit of a following and cosy was actually selling.

It was infuriating.

Nigel Packman had been particularly pleased with her story on the lighthouse family moving to live with Dakers. It had all the elements he appreciated in a story — regionality, human interest (subsection: family in peril), a knight in shining armour, a bit of glamour in the form of Beth Jackson and Lorelei Dakers, celebrities. But Imogen wasn't satisfied with that. A story like this didn't come along every day (or even once a decade, in a dump like Northlands), and she was going to milk it for all it was worth.

There was an added angle now. Fin Lewis. She'd never been so humiliated in her life. That man had spent an entire evening flirting with her as if his life depended on it, oozing charm, till she was at the point of wanting to tear his clothes off with her teeth. Then he dropped her like a hot brick from a great height (she really was going to have to watch those metaphors). Well, he wouldn't get away with behaving like that.

A couple of mornings after the family had moved south, Imogen marched into her boss's office, her eyebrows set to stun.

"Morning, Imogen." Nigel Packman's soft, large girth spilled through the sides of his adjustable office chair, like porridge in a string bag. His chubby neck strained against a tie in busy shades of lilacs and purples, clashing admirably with a pale peach shirt. Topping all this was a head of unruly sandy hair which

111

had no discernible parting but was making several independent attempts to part, like a species of fancy guinea pig. He was smiling warmly at the young, eager reporter whom he privately thought of as his protégée.

"What's happening with the lighthouse family story?" she demanded.

"Great story," he smiled. "You did a lovely job there."

Imogen couldn't believe this. Cover all the bases, she'd been taught at journalism school. Get every angle. Never let a good story go until you've wrung every last drop out of it. And so on. "So is that *it*?" she said.

"What more is there?" he shrugged.

"What more? We're talking about Gareth Dakers here. Gareth Dakers of the Windy Wendy scandal. Gareth Dakers who's just adopted a whole family into his house, which includes a very eligible widow."

"And you're saying?"

"I'm talking leopards and spots. There's more to this than meets the eye. When you look at his track record . . ."

Packman interrupted her. "Everybody's entitled to one or two mistakes in their life. We have no evidence that he's up to anything at all dodgy, and the readers won't like it if you start harassing the poor man."

Imogen was practically boiling over. "Just let me pursue it a bit longer. Do you really believe Gareth Dakers invited them to live with him purely out of the goodness of his heart?"

"Why else do it then?"

112

Imogen sighed: she didn't really know, she just had a feeling there was something. "For the publicity," she offered, a bit lamely.

"So if we don't give him any publicity, he'll have failed."

As a piece of logic it was flawless. As a piece of journalistic advice it sucked.

"I was thinking about ringing Michael Armstrong for his opinion."

"The sitting MP? We already ran a comment from him. What's he going to say? Dakers is in the same party."

"Well, what about the opposition, then? I'm telling you, Nigel, this story's got more legs than a millipede."

"We're not *Tonight With Trevor McDonald*, you know, or *Pano*-blooming-*rama*."

"But . . ."

"But nothing. Look, love, you're young, enthusiastic, you want to be the latest newshound, but we don't do that at the *Herald*. We leave all that dirty stuff to the nasty papers. Now, if you're not too busy being scoop of the year, we need someone at the magistrates' court, and Brian's had to take little Sasha to the dentist."

Imogen took the utmost care not to slam the door as she left. She didn't particularly care what Nigel Packman thought. She would pursue the story anyway, and when she had it, if Nigel couldn't see what a great story it was, she'd easily find someone who did. It would be her ticket out of this dump.

And while she was pursuing Gareth Dakers, she could also pursue his spin doctor. What fun.

CHAPTER
SIXTEEN

While Beth was attempting to foster some sort of communication with Lorelei, Gareth Dakers and Finian Lewis were in a car on the way to the studios of *The Morning Show*. Gareth was delighted to have been invited to snuggle up on the sofa of one of his favourite daytime presenters, the lovely Cara Chadwick. She had precisely the right combination of flirtatiousness and attitude to present him in his best light — serious yet sexy.

"How do you think Lorelei's getting on with your new lodgers?" Fin asked him, grinning, because he already knew what *he* thought about it.

"She'll be fine," Gareth said, without thinking about it at all, because he was reminiscing about a night at a showbiz awards bash a few years before when things could have become very interesting between him and Cara Chadwick.

"You know, that lighthouse family could be useful to you in all sorts of ways," Fin observed. "Being seen out with the old dad might be a good move. Take him to the pub or something."

"You *are* joking, I assume?"

"No, it'd be great for your man-of-the-people image."

"Couldn't I take Beth out for a drink instead? Far easier on the eye than the patriarch." Fin didn't say anything. The car swept past the security barrier and into the studio car park.

Cara Chadwick dropped by to say hello while Gareth was in make-up.

"How are you, dear heart?" she greeted him, bestowing a quick peck on his newly powdered cheek. The make-up woman tutted and retouched.

"All the better for seeing you," he smiled. Cara Chadwick really was lovely — soft and almost plump (as near as TV presenters ever got to it, anyway) yet glamorous, with a sexy hint of Scottish accent.

"Marvellous. I've got the running order here for you. It's been a little revised since the one we faxed to you earlier." Fin's hand plucked the piece of paper out of her hand before Gareth could even reach for it, and his eyes skimmed over the list of makeovers, recipes, a sob-piece about a pensioner who'd been beaten up. The name Karl Baron leapt out at him as if it had been written in red: Karl Baron, the opposition's candidate for Northlands East.

"Why weren't we told that Karl Baron was coming on?" he asked the presenter. "We were expecting a one to one."

"It'll be so much more fun this way, don't you think?" she smiled.

Fin didn't share his boss's fond opinion of Cara Chadwick — to his mind she was more than a mite cleverer and therefore far more dangerous than she let on. But at the moment Dakers needed all the publicity he could get. They were just going to have to front it out, and the first step was to not appear rattled. "It'll be good to see old Karl again," he said, his voice like honey poured over a razorblade.

"He's dying to discuss your lighthouse family stunt," Cara purred, with a little too much emphasis on the final word. "Shame the family themselves were unwilling to appear."

Fin knew that they weren't so much unwilling as unaware — he hadn't bothered mentioning it to them. He preferred them to settle in and be a bit more under control and predictable before they were thrown into this kind of situation. Live TV would be a bit dodgy right now.

"They're very tired after the move and everything," Fin explained. "But a couple of days of Lorelei's TLC should sort them out, then I'm sure they'd be thrilled if you invited them on."

"I'm sure they would be," she said, with a knowing smile. "And it keeps your man in the public eye a tad longer. Anyway, must dash — got to meet and greet this baby pop star who thinks he's the new David Cassidy just because his dreary little single is at number one."

"David Cassidy?" Gareth said. "You're showing your age there, Cara darling." The look she gave him indicated that that hadn't been the most tactful thing in the world to say.

Fin waited till the door had closed behind her and the makeup woman had gone in search of another tardy

116

guest, and he and Gareth began to once again go through precisely what could and couldn't be said regarding the lighthouse family.

CHAPTER
SEVENTEEN

Lorelei Dakers's life was obviously very busy, because she left the house not long after Bill appeared in her kitchen. Or maybe it was the hideous acid-green op-art shirt he was wearing that repelled her.

"Where did you get that?" Beth asked him.

"Granny Takes A Trip," he grinned.

"Sorry?"

"It was a clothes shop in the King's Road in the sixties. The sign over the door used to say 'One should either be a work of art or wear a work of art.'"

"Did they really mean it *that* literally?" Lorelei muttered, before making her excuses and leaving.

Like his daughter, Bill had obviously been hoping for breakfast, but like Beth he was to be disappointed. Beth had resolved that she would have to say something about the breakfast situation to Mrs Dakers when Danny got up — a teenage boy needs regular supplies of food, what with all that growing and raging hormones to feed, but there was no chance before she disappeared.

Bill started poking around in the kitchen cupboards.

"Don't!" Beth said.

"Why not?"

"Well, it seems so rude!"

"*She's* the one who's rude. My stomach feels as if my throat's been cut. We'd never treat anyone like that who came to stay with us." Which thought only reminded Beth of her own cosy little kitchen, such a contrast to this sterile, appliance-heavy, food-light establishment. It was a kitchen like you see on television sometimes, with acres of marbled counter top, and one of those huge American-style fridges that looks as if it was built to house a month's supply of Elvis Presley's snack needs. But even the fridge didn't admit ready evidence of any real food, at least not bread or butter or eggs or bacon.

Luckily, help was at hand. They heard a key turn in the kitchen door, and a tiny woman in huge glasses that magnified her eyes to a degree that made her look like a baby owl, practically blew through. She smiled in a friendly way and began to unroll yards of woollen scarf from round her neck. "It's physical out there," she said. "I wouldn't bother chancing it if I was you. And if I was you I'd be called . . .?"

"Beth Jackson," Beth said, amused. "And this is my father, Bill Turnbull."

"Of course. The northerners. Lovely to meet you. I'm Jessie, Jessie Wade. I do a bit of cooking and cleaning for Mrs Dakers. Have you had breakfast yet?" They shook their heads, and Bill's stomach growled right on cue. "Thought not. She doesn't eat breakfast herself, and I expect it didn't occur to her that anyone else might. Scrambled eggs on toast do you?"

★ ★ ★

After breakfast, which Beth had made Danny get up for, reasoning that they might not be offered another meal for some hours so he'd better get nourished while he had the chance, Jessie disappeared upstairs with a very high-tech-looking vacuum cleaner that was almost taller than she was. Before she went she mentioned that her "lord and master" was appearing on a daytime TV show, and suggested the family might like to watch it. One of the kitchen cupboards was opened by some secret mechanism to reveal a small television, which she switched on before departing.

"Don't you want to watch it?" Bill asked her.

"No time," she said. "And when you've rinsed someone's pubic hairs down the plughole on a daily basis over several years they lose their mystique." She laughed. "That's why I'd never clean for Pierce Brosnan, no matter how much he offered me in the way of money or sexual favours."

Beth turned her attention to the television so she didn't have to think about the myopic Mrs Wade getting to grips with 007.

She'd seen this show a couple of times when Danny was off school and slumping around. He always had the television on: it was as if he needed the stimulus of something moving in front of his eyes to convince his body that he was still alive. Beth liked the woman who presented it, because she wasn't too skinny like some of them and seemed to have a bit of intelligence. The first person to be interviewed was a boy of around Danny's age who was apparently at number one in the charts. Danny uttered a stream of semi-audible expletives.

"Don't you like him?" Beth asked.

"He's a talentless wanker," was the reply. "Manufactured pop shit."

"You're only jealous," Bill said, winding him up.

"I wouldn't be heard dead singing this kind of crap," Danny replied.

"I wish you wouldn't use such horrible language," Beth said, sincerely glad that Dakers and his wife weren't around to hear it. "And you only encourage him," she said to her father. "You wouldn't have let *me* swear like that."

"It's different for boys," Bill said.

"No, it isn't."

After the reviled singing teen (who Beth privately thought was quite sweet, very polite to the presenter and he sang like an angel, though she wouldn't have said so in case her son never spoke to her again), there was a commercial break, then the presenter began to introduce Gareth Dakers. Before he came on, they ran a piece of film. It was them, arriving at the Dakers' house the day before, getting out of the car to be met by a rapturously welcoming Lorelei and Gareth Dakers. That's how it appeared, anyway.

"Oh, what do we look like?" Beth muttered.

"You look great," Bill said. "Dead photogenic."

"They didn't show the bit where we had to drive round the block like lemons," Danny observed.

"Or that our luggage had already gone inside."

"Or that Mrs Dakers had a face on her like a slapped arse as soon as the cameras were gone."

"Danny!"

121

Then there was a shot of their lighthouse, with a DANGER: KEEP OUT sign on the gate that hadn't been there before. Beth wondered if they'd just put it on for the cameras. The lighthouse looked so beautiful, and it was a lovely sunny, cold-looking day in Northlands. Beth knew just how the air would feel on her face on a morning like that. Her throat ached, wanting to be back there. She felt that all three of them went a bit still, like they couldn't trust themselves to speak or even look at each other.

The programme returned to the presenter, and now she had Gareth sitting on the sofa opposite her, next to a man Beth didn't recognise. Gareth looked very dashing, and the presenter woman was quite obviously flirting with him.

The topic of conversation was Beth and her family. The main thrust of the other man's argument (he was going to be opposing Gareth in the election, apparently, and he was a born-and-bred Northlander) was that Gareth had invited them to London merely as a stunt to boost his popularity. Beth thought that could hardly come as news to anyone watching — did they really think he'd acted out of pure altruism? But Gareth "vigorously refuted" the suggestion. He was sincere, he said sincerely, and Beth was impressed by the way he kept calm while the other man was clearly having a go at him, accusing him of being a carpetbagger and not having the interests of the people of Northlands anywhere on his agenda. Gareth responded to that by calmly dissecting selected policies of the other man's party. Then the presenter said that, unfortunately, the

122

lighthouse family had been asked to appear but had declined.

"I didn't decline — did you?" Bill asked his daughter.

"I wasn't asked. Didn't know anything about it till just now." She was puzzled. "Maybe I ought to ask Mr Dakers about this when he gets back."

"You should," Bill said. "I would have loved to sit on the sofa with Cara Chadwick."

Jessie had reappeared, her face red from hefting the vacuum cleaner down the stairs. Bill sprang up to help her.

"Thanks, sweetheart," she said. "Himself still on, is he?" she peered at the television screen, where Cara Chadwick was thanking her guests and moving them to the other side of the studio to sample the work of the morning's celebrity chef.

"They said we'd been invited to appear," Bill said. "And we weren't."

"Mum's going to have a go at Mr Dakers about it," Danny added, clearly very amused by the idea.

Jessie sniffed. "Wouldn't do any good, love. He's probably as much in the dark about it as you are. It's that Finian Lewis who organises all that sort of stuff for him; it's him you want to be having a word with."

"What exactly does Finian Lewis do?" Beth asked. "I mean, what's his job?"

"His job is to get Mr Dakers into the House of Commons. And he'll do it too, they reckon. But any journalist, anybody, who wants to talk to Mr D they have to go through Mr Lewis first. *Mrs* D's got no time for him at all. She says the reason he's called Fin is he's like a shark — and there's only a bit of him shows on the surface."

"Isn't that more like an iceberg?" Danny said and Beth glared at him for being rude.

"Oh, he's like an iceberg, all right. Can't say I know him, really, but in a way I even feel as if I work for him, too, as if we all do. Even you do."

"We certainly don't!" Beth was indignant.

Jessie sniffed again. "You're here, aren't you? It's all part of the window dressing."

It was what they'd known all along, but it didn't stop Beth feeling used and ashamed. It felt like a betrayal of Martin and all he'd done for his family. He'd worked so hard to give them everything they needed, he'd been proud of his family, of their independence and strength. Beth didn't think he'd be very proud of her now. Maybe she should have fought harder to stay in Last Reach, kept exploring all the possibilities until there was absolutely no choice, instead of allowing herself to be cajoled and flattered into being what Jessie had called "window dressing" for the political ambitions of a man who had far more than they ever would.

She stopped herself, before her anger turned into self pity. Whatever choices she'd made, she'd made them with the best interests of her family at heart. Of course Martin would be proud of her — he'd always been proud of her.

124

CHAPTER
EIGHTEEN

Lorelei hoped her yoga class would work its usual magic. She might have time afterwards for an aromatherapy massage, or a reflexology session — something to restore her badly rocked equilibrium. She was feeling so irritated at life in general and her husband in particular that there seemed every danger she might start grinding her teeth again. Perhaps a quick visit to the orthodontist while she was at it.

That was the great advantage of the Haven: it combined spa, retreat, clinic and — aptly enough — haven, under one handy roof. There was even a shopping service, so that while you were busy having your chakras realigned you could send someone out to do the Christmas shopping for you, or pick up your dry-cleaning.

Lorelei swung her long and shapely legs out of the taxi, reflecting on all the wonderful uses of money. They said it couldn't buy you love, but it could certainly purchase everything else that was needed for a happy and comfortable life. Which wasn't strictly true, when she stopped to think about it. She wasn't very happy at all. She had a husband she hardly saw, and then there was that dreadful family who were even now, she imagined, disporting themselves in all kinds of nihilistic northern ways across the expensive upholstery of her lovely home. That skinny boy in his dreadful T shirts, the old man who thought he was incredibly amusing and charming, not to even mention his dreadful daughter. Though Beth, it had to be said, was a lot less loathsome than she might have been. Lorelei had never liked any woman who was better looking than she was. Going out on the pull in her teenage years had been much easier with a mate who was a bit of a dog. It wasn't fair on the mate, she knew, but again that was the way the world worked. You had beauty, then you had money, and if you had enough money you could hang on to the beauty a bit longer. It was a simple equation. Except there was Beth Jackson, exuding a kind of homespun glamour with nothing more than a pot of supermarket own-brand moisturiser in her toilet bag (Lorelei had looked) — and yet there was something warm and approachable about her.

Lorelei mentally gave herself a shake. It wouldn't do to start getting friendly with her — it was too risky having temptation like that in Gareth's way. Charity was supposed to begin at home, but did that really literally have to mean in *her* home? She decided to raise the subject of moving the family out to Dogwood Avenue with her husband that evening.

Sighing deeply, she pushed open the door of the Haven. The first person she saw was the almost criminally attractive Dr Harrison Shah. He was leaning against the reception desk, a cup of coffee in one hand

and a pile of papers in the other. He glanced up and smiled radiantly at her.

"Too soon for a top-up, surely?" he said, his eyes professionally assessing her paralysed frown lines.

"Yoga," she said. "I need to de-stress after one bugger of a day."

"It's only ten a.m."

"I meant yesterday. And how the rest of the day is going to be."

"Sounds serious. Are you sure yoga will do the trick?"

She shrugged prettily. "I thought I might try a massage if it doesn't. Or perhaps something brutal like Tae-Bo would be better."

"I have a better suggestion." He led her away from earshot of the receptionist. "What about a nice, civilised spot of lunch and some rather good wine?"

"No one to lunch with," she had to admit.

"I'm grateful for that, because I was suggesting that you do me the honour of being my lunch guest," he said. "How about if I meet you after your yoga class and my morning appointments are over?"

"I'm de-stressing as we speak," she said.

CHAPTER
NINETEEN

"I'll be back later on to cook dinner," Jessie said, stuffing her stick-like arms into an oversized coat — the kind of coat Linda would have described as a "shoplifting special".

"Couldn't I do dinner?" Beth suggested. "It'll give me something to do, and be a way of saying thank you to Mr and Mrs Dakers for their kindness."

The housekeeper looked at Beth doubtfully. "Could be tricky," she said. "Mrs D is into food combining this week. She just has pure proteins in the evening, no carbohydrates."

This sounded mysteriously more like separating than combining, but Mrs Dakers was clearly a lot more sophisticated than Beth. She wasn't going to be put off, though. "Maybe if you jot down what you were planning to cook, I can rustle it up. I'm used to cooking for faddy eaters at the lighthouse."

"You don't know the meaning of faddy till you get to know Mrs D. But if you're sure, I wouldn't say no to an evening off. I'll be back later to load the dishwasher."

"I'm sure I can manage that," Beth said, even though she'd never used a dishwasher before. She glanced around the enormous kitchen and the rows of gleaming appliances. "If you could perhaps show me which one it is . . ."

Preparing the food wasn't difficult. Beth loved to cook, and it made the place feel more homely to have cooking smells wafting around. She sent Bill and Danny out to try and find an off licence to get a bottle of wine and perhaps some flowers, wishing she'd thought to ask Jessie where they should try first.

Gareth Dakers was expected back around seven o'clock, but Jessie had said his wife might appear any time after five. Beth felt a little nervous of how Lorelei Dakers would react when she saw another woman had taken over her kitchen, but she hoped she'd be happy with the results. Stirring at the sauce for the chicken, she felt quite content.

By seven everything was ready, but Beth was still completely alone in the house. Mrs Dakers hadn't returned at five, and Bill and Danny were presumably lost somewhere in their pursuit of retail outlets. Or, more likely, they'd found a pub, and Bill was sampling the wares while Danny tried to make a case that sixteen was practically eighteen for the purposes of being served alcohol before settling for a Coke.

Beth put everything in the oven on a low heat and sat down.

At last she heard a car in the drive, and a moment later footsteps in the hallway.

"Something smells nice," she heard Gareth Dakers say, and then the sound of his footsteps going upstairs. Eventually he appeared in the kitchen.

"Oh — hello," he said. "All alone?"

"Mrs Dakers isn't home yet," Beth said.

"You really must call us Gareth and Lorelei, you know. All this Mrs Dakers stuff makes you sound like the hired help."

Beth didn't tell him that's exactly how she felt, she just smiled. "I've cooked dinner."

He looked taken aback. "Have you really?" he said. "How marvellous. When will it be ready?"

"It's ready now, I'm just waiting for . . ."

"Don't bother waiting for Lorelei. She's probably dining with one of her chums in town. Where are your nearest and dearest?"

She told him they were probably in a pub somewhere.

"Just us then. Pity to let the food spoil."

Beth had to agree, and it was his house after all, so she started to serve up the chicken. It wasn't anything fancy at all — she'd simplified Mrs Wade's recipes — but he seemed pleased. They sat down to eat at the table in the kitchen rather than the dining room, and Beth had a very strange feeling, as if she was watching herself on television, eating dinner with this celebrity who'd been on television himself only that morning. Things like that didn't happen in her world.

Gareth Dakers was charming. He kept her amused with a constant flow of showbiz anecdotes, and laughed easily and often. It seemed he couldn't resist putting on a show for whatever audience happened to be around, but there was no doubting that he was excellent

130

company, and really quite nice. At one point he mentioned Cara Chadwick.

"We saw you on her show this morning," Beth said, recalling that she'd promised to tackle him about the family allegedly being asked to appear on it themselves.

"How did I come across?" he said. "No forehead shine, I trust?" He was alluding to the time at the Last Reach Community Centre when she'd seen him powdering his face.

"No, you were perfectly matte," she said. "But there was one thing that bothered me. Cara Chadwick said we'd been invited on to the show and we'd declined."

He smiled that fabulous, bandbox-fresh smile. "I hope that wasn't a presumption on Fin's part," he said. "He thought that you'd be tired after all your travelling yesterday."

"It would have been nice to have been asked."

"That's what I said to him, but he does like to get his own way." So it *was* Finian Lewis's doing, as Jessie had said.

Suddenly Lorelei Dakers was in the doorway. "This is cosy," she said. Neither of them had heard her come in.

"Hello, darling," Gareth said.

"Have you eaten?" Beth asked her.

"Have you eaten?" Lorelei mimicked. "Sitting there — in *my* kitchen, may I remind you? As if you own the place."

Oh-oh. Beth had wondered if she might get territorial about it, but given her obvious lack of interest in the culinary arts had hoped she wouldn't.

"I'm sorry," she said. "I thought it would be nice to cook dinner for you."

"And dine tête-à-tête with my husband." Lorelei stepped forward into the kitchen and pulled out a chair with exaggerated precision.

"Have you been drinking?" Gareth said, to which his wife replied,

"So what if I have? You do what you want, I do what I want, and we're both marvellously bloody happy. In fact what I want is to go to bed." She stamped off, and Gareth sat there looking at Beth, who was mortified.

"Shouldn't you go and see if she's all right?" she said.

"She's drunk, she'll get over it."

They continued eating in silence. Beth wondered if Lorelei had a drink problem — you did hear about these rich women with nothing to do all day except drink sherry. Gareth didn't seem to be feeling anything about it except mildly embarrassed. If it had been Bill or Danny putting on a display like that, Beth would have been mortified — and given that they weren't back yet, the possibility was still there.

She realised that although she'd thought cooking dinner would be a nice gesture, it had been a big mistake. Lorelei was clearly not happy to have them in her house at all, and now in her eyes Beth was taking over her kitchen, and it probably looked as though she was trying to steal her husband too. It was all a dreadful mess, and Beth wished with all her heart that they'd never left Last Reach.

132

The phone rang, and Gareth excused himself and went off to another room to take the call. Beth sat looking forlornly at the scraps of food still left on the plates, and after a minute or two got up and started clearing away.

When Danny and Bill got back she was so pleased to see them that she almost hugged the air out of her son's lungs.

"Mother!" he protested. "Give up!"

As predicted, Bill was much more drunk than Lorelei Dakers had been, but Bill had always been what you'd call a "happy drunk".

"We've had a brilliant time," he said. "Loads of people recognised us from the telly, and kept buying us drinks. I was surprised, because I thought southerners were meant to be tight. You should see the prices though."

"What's for dinner?" Danny wanted to know. Beth took their food out of the oven, and they stuck into it ravenously, and things seemed a bit more normal for a while. If she closed her eyes she could almost pretend they were on holiday. Not that they'd ever had a holiday in the whole of Danny's life, but she had a great imagination sometimes.

"Where are the lord and lady of the house?" Bill asked after his first wave of hunger had been satisfied. Beth told them about what had happened. Her father laughed. "So she's a boozer, is she? She should have come out with us, eh Dan?"

"I doubt she'd have enjoyed herself," Beth said.

Neither Gareth nor Lorelei Dakers reappeared that evening, so the Jacksons took themselves off to bed early, Bill to read, Danny to listen to his Walkman and Beth to try and work out what their next step should be.

She hung up her cheap-looking clothes on the scented, padded hangers that the wardrobe in her room was provided with. It was a very flouncy, frilly room, with bits of lacy trimming everywhere. It all looked a bit grandmotherly, to Beth's eye, from the pink flowered curtains to the mother-of-pearl-trimmed hairbrush and mirror on the dressing table. It seemed as though Lorelei Dakers (because it had to be a woman who'd chosen the furnishings for this room) hankered after a kind of old-style grandeur.

Beth sighed deeply, and got into bed, pulling the old-fashioned quilt up to her chin but not closing her eyes. This was unbearable. The previous evening, when they'd first arrived, had been difficult, but that was to be expected considering it was their first night. But now she'd made things so much worse, causing an argument between Dakers and his wife, and they were clearly not welcome at all. If they stayed here Lorelei Dakers would only get more unhappy, and Beth hated to be the source of such trouble. So there was only one thing to do: she'd done as Bill and Danny wanted, and given London a go, but it hadn't worked. They would have to go home.

CHAPTER
TWENTY

"We've got a problem, Fin." Finian Lewis had just stepped on to the down escalator at Holborn tube station, close to his company's office, but he managed to back-pedal and jump off before the phone's signal disappeared, much to the annoyance of the other travellers.

"We don't talk about problems, remember?" he said into the phone. "They're *issues*."

"This is one hell of a big issue, then. Lorelei wants the lighthouse family out."

"Well, I knew she wasn't happy but . . ."

"I mean she wants them gone — now. She's threatening to talk to the press if they're still there this evening."

"What happened?" Oh, typical Gareth. Couldn't even handle that one small thing.

"She came back yesterday evening totally smashed, accusing me of all sorts of things vis-à-vis Beth Jackson."

Fin sighed. "You haven't, have you?"

"What? No! I was just having dinner with her — which she cooked, by the way. She's a fantastic cook."

"This is slightly problematic."

"I thought we didn't use the word problem."

"We do when we've got Cara Chadwick expecting to interview Beth Jackson."

"Ah. I see what you mean."

"Sit tight," Fin advised. "Promise nothing. I'll be there in just over an hour."

The first person he met upon entering the house was Beth. With her long dark hair hanging loose, dressed as usual in jeans and a sweater, she looked completely out of place in Lorelei Dakers's more-money-than-taste decor, like a real rose in a vase of artificial ones.

"How are you this morning?" he greeted her.

"Not happy," she said. Obviously in no mood for small talk either. "In fact, we'd like to go back to Last Reach."

"Okay," he said. "I'll get Paul to run you to the station."

"What?"

"King's Cross. I presume a train would be easier than flying."

"I thought you'd be angry," she said.

He smiled at her kindly. "Not a lot of point in you staying, if you're unhappy." She looked relieved, and he felt momentarily guilty, but there was a job to be done. "I hate to think that we've caused you any unhappiness," he said. "Because you're doing us such a great favour by being here." This was a calculated risk: on the one hand, it didn't really do to let people know you were depending on them, because that gave them

136

power over you, but on the other hand it might help to smooth the path. *Whatever it takes* was Fin's motto.

"I have to do what's best for my family," Beth said. "And we're obviously not wanted here. Lorelei — Mrs Dakers — wants us out. And I can't really blame her. It was all a big mistake."

"Let's sit down and talk about it." Fin gestured to one of the squashy armchairs which were upholstered with indecently soft leather in a colour he thought of as labial pink. Beth sat down and he sat opposite, at the same time glancing imperceptibly at his watch and calculating how much time he had to sort this out before he needed to call Cara Chadwick's producer. "I think I understand what the problem is," he said. Beth raised one eyebrow as if she didn't believe he could possibly understand anything about her life, and he had to admit to himself that he didn't. How could he really understand what it was like to be widowed and homeless and without prospects? Again he felt almost guilty for a moment, but reminded himself sternly of the task in hand.

"I have a proposal," he said. "Rather than living here, what about if we moved you to a flat, where you could live on your own as a family?"

Her eyes lit up. "Is it possible?"

"I'll do my best. I'm sure it's possible. I'll talk to Gareth about it now."

"Would this be in London?"

"Yes. A less salubrious area than this, I'm afraid."

"I don't care. I think I'd prefer that to living here, to be honest."

"Marvellous. But would you mind not mentioning this on *The Morning Show*? Until I've got it all sorted."

"*The Morning Show*?"

"It's a daytime TV thing."

"I know what it is . . . You mean I'm going to be on it?"

"Is that a problem?"

"It's terrifying," she said.

CHAPTER
TWENTY-ONE

It *was* terrifying and it was blinding. Hot and blinding, with lights shining in her eyes so she could barely see past them, just enough to make out lots of shadowy figures, scurrying around or leaning against things. She was terrified to move, because she was surrounded by wires — wires from the microphone clipped to her top, snaking down through her clothing to a battery pack on the back of the waistband of her trousers, so she couldn't lean back. Scared to move her feet because of the wires all over the floor.

Cara Chadwick was very pleasant. She'd popped in while Beth was having her make-up done (during which Beth had felt as though she was being submitted for the Clown Olympics, the girl was caking so much make-up on her face) and chatted away in a friendly manner to Beth, though she'd been a bit barbed with Fin, who'd accompanied Beth to the studio.

After she'd gone, and the make-up girl was done with clowning Beth up and had also left, Fin sat down beside her. He'd assigned himself to her for the day, it seemed, and she felt reassured to have him there. "How are you feeling?" he asked.

"Scared."

"Don't worry about it. There are just a few simple things to keep in mind," he said. "Number one, don't fidget. Keep your hands relaxed." His own hands dropped to a relaxed pose on his lap in demonstration. He had beautiful hands. "Then you'll look more sincere."

"But I *am* sincere!" she protested nervously. "I'm not one of your politicians, you know." The make-up on her face was so thick it began to itch, and she rubbed at her nose.

Fin leaned over to her. "Never, ever touch your nose on camera," he said, and gently patted a dab of powder on her face. "It makes you look nervous."

"I *am* nervous." For a second she felt his breath on her skin, and she was acutely aware of sitting so close to him, in a way that was almost more disturbing than the prospect of being on television.

He smiled gently at her as he sat back. "The thing is not to *look* nervous. Come on," he held his hand out to her and stood up. "Shoulders back, chin up. You're going to be fine."

Fin sat in *The Morning Show*'s green room, ignoring the world-famous actor and his entourage to his right and the star-struck victim for that day's makeover to his left, concentrating on the monitor, willing Beth to do well. And she did — she answered everything with that lovely direct honesty she had, her smile nervous but still radiant. If this woman ever decided to stand for Parliament, Fin thought, he'd be right there beside her. She was a natural.

CHAPTER
TWENTY-TWO

Beth was thrilled at the idea that they could move to a flat on their own. It wasn't that she was ungrateful for the chance Gareth Dakers had given them, and the (admittedly limited) hospitality they had been shown, but she wasn't comfortable being the house-guest of such weird people, and she knew her family weren't really welcome. Moving to another place was the best answer all round.

Of course it raised other questions, like how they were supposed to pay for it. Fin Lewis had said not to worry about rent, but Beth was determined that they would pay their own way, so she would have to think about getting a job quite quickly. There was also a school to find for Danny. Predictably enough, he was quite keen on the idea of never going back to school again, but he was only sixteen, and bright, and Beth wanted him to carry on with A levels and maybe university if it was possible. She would start to look into it as soon as they were settled into the new place.

It felt as if their life in London was about to really begin.

Beth staggered downstairs with Danny's suitcase. He was still in the bathroom doing whatever teenage boys do in there in the mornings (she tried not to think about that too hard). Fin was in the hallway, apparently looking for her. It was a pity he hadn't found her *before* there was a heavy suitcase to be carried rather than after, she thought.

"I've had the editor of the women's page of the *Evening Despatch* on the phone," he said. "She wants to know if you'd be interested in writing a column. Country girl in the big city sort of angle."

"What? I can't do that!" She laughed at the very idea of it.

"You can write, can't you?"

If he was implying that she was illiterate, she was naturally offended. "Of course I can! But I don't really have anything to say."

"You always seem to have plenty to say to *me*," he smiled. "But I could ghost-write it if you want me too."

"What? Wouldn't that be cheating?"

"Cheating?" he repeated, teasing. "Like liar, liar pants on fire sort of cheating?" He made her sound like a silly schoolgirl. She only realised afterwards that he'd done this deliberately: he knew exactly what buttons to press. And in her current situation the other big button to be pressed was the cash one. "They're offering to pay a hundred pounds for around five hundred words," he said, in a studiedly casual manner. "I can probably negotiate you a bit more."

"Blimey." That would be a start with the rent, at any rate, and she couldn't afford to turn the money down, whatever doubts she had about seeing herself as a newspaper columnist. "Okay," she said. "Tell them I'll have a go. If you wouldn't mind having a look to see if what I write is okay?"

"My pleasure," he said.

CHAPTER
TWENTY-THREE

The Jackson family stood on the pavement outside a dilapidated Victorian terraced house. There had been no offer of a lift: their arrival at this more humble dwelling was apparently intended to be as anonymous as possible, and the taxi which had brought them from the suburbs was now nosing its way up a narrow street congested by solid rows of parked cars on either side. Car horns blared impatiently. The pavement at their feet was strewn with litter.

"You're sure this is the right place?" Danny asked, perhaps voicing a glimmer of hope that there had been a mistake, and somewhere there would be another Dogwood Avenue waiting for them, one without such visual enhancements as a car with smashed-in windows and a poster about gun crime clinging to a graffiti'd and charred-looking lamppost.

But this *was* the right place, and although it looked a bit rough, Beth didn't feel any sense of disappointment. Quite the reverse: with the key in her hand, and only her family with her, she felt liberated. They had a place of their own, and that was far preferable to being the house-guests of the Dakers family. Beth picked up her suitcase, covered the length of the front garden path's cracked black and white tiles in two strides and unlocked the door.

The hallway was dark, with peeling-off wallpaper of an indeterminate colour, and it smelled damp and stale. They'd been told they'd be staying in the first floor flat, so Beth unlocked the yellowing white door in front of her, which opened immediately on to the staircase. Bill and Danny followed her up.

The flat itself was clean, sunny, quite pleasant if a little small, and furnished with old, threadbare furniture that looked like it had come from second-hand shops and car boot sales. Nothing matched. The bedrooms were hardly bigger than cupboards. It had been converted in such a way as to fit the maximum number of people into the minimum space. The sitting room, which overlooked the street, felt stuffy, so Beth threw open both the windows. Cool air and a great deal of noise from passing traffic gushed in. She could hear Danny elsewhere, laying claim to the room he wanted for his own.

She went to inspect the kitchen — always the heart of a house, in her opinion. Bill was already there (kitchens were his natural habitat too), and had put the kettle on. "It's not a bad little billet," he said, looking in the kitchen cupboards for cups. "Better than a lot of places I've stayed at."

"Fin Lewis said he stayed here himself a while back, so I knew it couldn't be too bad. It looks clean enough, but I won't be happy till I've gone over everything with bleach."

Bill frowned. "Can't you relax for a minute or two?"

Beth glanced out of the window at the scrub of back garden that they had no access to, which was overlooked by the back of an identical row of houses opposite. An aeroplane roared overhead. Well, this was certainly an improvement in some ways, but she didn't think she was ready to relax just yet.

There was a constant drone of traffic, even in the middle of the night as Beth lay awake in yet another strange bed, trying to make sense of the past few days. A police siren — or maybe an ambulance or fire engine, she couldn't tell — screamed along the road, and then a car with a radio louder than any radio had a right to be passed by, the deep bass notes producing a Doppler effect as it passed.

She was happy to be away from Dakers Acres, as Danny had rather spitefully taken to calling it. As she looked around the somewhat damp-looking walls of her new room, she knew that a lot of hopes were pinned on this unpromising home. Her greatest hope was that living here would bring Danny out of himself a bit more. Living at the lighthouse hadn't been good for him; it was too isolating. He'd been thirteen when his father died, and to say that he'd taken it hard would be an understatement. The word Beth always thought of was floundering — he seemed, for a while, totally lost, like they all were, but Danny had only partly come back. At some point since his father's death, almost when no one had been looking (probably *because* no one had been looking, she thought guiltily, she'd been too wrapped up in her own grief), her son had turned in on himself, folded up like a telescope, taken up smoking, and spent most of his time in his room listening to loud, angry-sounding music or out walking, probably still listening to loud, angry music on his walkman.

His musical tastes didn't bother Beth: she was part of the generation who'd come of age with the Sex Pistols so she was quite unshockable, but the sadness that hung about him bothered her very much. So she consoled herself that maybe this move to London would bring Danny out of himself a bit. She turned over and tried to sleep.

When she woke up and found herself in the strange room with floral wallpaper, Beth couldn't remember for a second how or why she was there. It was the wallpaper that did it: why did people bother with wallpaper? All those repeating patterns over and over again, Beth found it depressing. She'd always liked rooms painted plain white, and at the lighthouse she didn't even have any pictures on the walls apart from a couple of Danny's baby photos. But then she had a gorgeous view out of every window if she wanted something to look at.

She hauled herself out of bed and looked out of her new London window. The view was uninspiring: the top of a lean-to roof below, other roofs and chimneys, someone else's window opposite. Only just visible was a grubby-looking sycamore tree, now almost devoid of leaves, and she couldn't hear or see any birds.

Bill was already in the kitchen, which at least had a view across the garden.

"How did you sleep?" Beth asked him.

"The sleep of the just, as usual. What about you?"

"I don't have your lighthouse-keeper's adaptability to new sleeping arrangements, unfortunately."

"A nice cup of coffee will sort you out." He pushed a cup across the table to her.

She wrapped her fingers around it gratefully. "What are we doing here, Dad?" she sighed.

"Isn't it a bit late to be asking me that?"

"It all happened so fast."

"Aye, it did. It reminded me of the time I had to take over at Bishop's Rock when the PK came down with food poisoning." Beth had heard on many previous occasions the story of how the Principal Keeper had been winched across to the boat and at the last minute had thrown up all over the boat crew, and how her ever-sensitive father had almost lost his footing on the dog-steps he was laughing so hard, but she listened to it again anyway. "Eamon Bennett's missis said he stank of puke for the next month," Bill concluded finally, and stood up. "Anyway, I'm off to explore. It's great that we're close to a tube station. Can't stay cooped up in here when there's the whole of Londinium Town to explore, baby."

Baby? It was only after he'd gone that she realised he'd been wearing something that looked suspiciously like flared trousers. He'd timewarped back to the late sixties again.

148

Danny wandered into the kitchen soon after his grandfather had left. "Anything to eat?" he mumbled. Beth drew his attention to the loaf of bread and slab of butter on the worktop. He stared at them as if he was trying to make breakfast telepathically.

"Shall I make you some toast?" she offered at last, and he nodded gratefully and slumped into a chair, which he immediately rocked back on to the back legs.

"I wish you wouldn't abuse furniture like that. It isn't even our furniture," Beth muttered. She sliced the bread, which Jessie Wade had made for them the day before in the bread machine (this was an amazing thing — you simply threw the ingredients in, switched it on, and it did the kneading, proving and baking all by itself), and put the thick slabs under the grill. "Your grandad's gone out exploring," she said. "He's wearing flared trousers." Danny glanced quickly at her from under his fringe (which he was currently wearing at curtain length), and his grin was as cheeky and wide as when he'd been a little boy. "And he called me '*baby*.'" She took the toast from under the grill and buttered it. "Is there anything *you* want to do today?" she asked Danny, watching him sink his strong white teeth into the toast like it was his first meal in a month.

"I want to avoid Bill," he said. "If he's wearing flares."

"He looked like Dave Lee Travis *circa* 1975," she said, and the smile on Danny's face turned to mystification — having been born at the end of the eighties, as far as he was concerned Dave Lee Travis was literally prehistorical.

Their brief moment of connection apparently at an end, he shrugged. "Might watch telly."

"But we're properly in London at last! Don't you want to go out and have a look round?"

"Maybe later on."

"Well, I've got to go out shopping. We need all sorts of stuff. You could come with me?"

"Shopping? Nuh."

She hadn't expected him to agree to that: Danny hadn't been interested in shopping since the days when she could bribe him into co-operation with the promise of a Milky Bar.

As she stepped out on to the pavement, she wondered whether the offer of a Milky Bar might still do the trick — she suddenly felt so alone and detached from anything she knew that the company of her linguistically challenged but reassuringly tall son would have been most comforting. But by now he was slumped in front of some Japanese cartoon, and she was here in London all alone.

It had sounded so nice when Fin had given her the address: Dogwood Avenue. Images of a pretty, leafy lane had filled her mind, though now she'd seen it there was a lot more of the "dog" and less of the "wood" about it. Dogwood Avenue intersected at right angles with a much busier road, and Beth headed towards that. Faced with the reality of being alone in a big city for the first time in her life (that idea was so weird she kept turning it over in her head: in a big city for the first time in her life, and she was forty years old), she was somewhat nervous. She headed down the street, having a vague recollection that they'd passed a row of shops down that way when the taxi had brought them from the Dakers' the previous evening.

On the corner, however, her sense of direction deserted her. The street ahead was a solid mass of cars, louder than anything she'd ever heard, and chokingly smelly. She looked around, fighting back a desire to bolt back to the relative normality of the flat. A man was walking towards her, and she thought she'd ask him for directions.

"Awright, darlin'?" he said, which was friendly enough.

"I wonder if you could tell me if I'm going the right way for the shops?"

"Anything for a lovely lady." He moved a little bit too close to her, so she could smell his breath, which was like the smell of a wet dog. On second thoughts, a dog soaked in beer. He leaned in towards her until she could feel his horrible breath on her face.

"Don't worry," she said, stepping back. "I'll manage."

"No need to get uppity." Beth walked away at a brisk trot. Her armpits felt prickly and damp. Everything was too bright, too many colours, too crowded, it was all horrible.

But she needed to buy food, and she was determined not to go home empty-handed. Fortunately, just around the corner she came to the row of shops she'd remembered, the first one displaying fruits and vegetables on pallets at the front. At least the shop looked small enough to be manageable, even though inside it smelled of spices and incense, not like any grocery shop she had ever been into in Northlands. Potatoes, carrots, baked beans, biscuits and other familiar things jostled for space with things that were from a different world. Twisted root vegetables like deformed parsnips, blackened bananas, strips of dried meat hanging from hooks on the ceiling. She grabbed some milk from a chill cabinet, and noticed in front of this bowls of green and black olives, plump and slick with oil, along with cubes of a kind of cheese floating in oil, and vine leaves. She stooped to smell the exotic fragrances of olive oil and peppers and spices, lost for a few moments in this exotic wonderland of smells, until she realised someone was standing beside her and looked up. A young man of not much more than Danny's age was standing staring at her. He had tar-black hair and dark skin, and he was looking half bored, half menacing. Beth realised that he thought she was shoplifting.

"I'm sorry," she said, feeling like a total fool. "I was just smelling . . ." She realised how stupid that sounded and anyway, the young man had lost interest and had wandered off. Glancing up she caught sight of her image on a small black and white television mounted in a corner. She looked hunched and furtive.

Embarrassed, she continued with her shopping, managing to find everything she needed, adding on a whim a loaf of bread that was a huge, flat oval and smelled wonderful, and at the last minute going back and scooping up some of the shiny green olives into a small carton.

She put her basket on the counter in front of a man who was studying a newspaper written in a foreign language. He glanced quickly up at her from under greying, bushy eyebrows, and smiled. "It's a lovely day," he said, in an accent as thick as his eyebrows.

Beth looked out of the window, and for the first time realised the sun was shining. "Yes," she agreed, returning his smile. "It is."

It wasn't until she was halfway back to the flat that she realised that the paltry amount of shopping she'd bought had cost a small fortune.

CHAPTER
TWENTY-FOUR

They'd been in London for three days, and so far Beth had only ventured as far as the local shops, but even that short journey seemed fraught with difficulty. Generally people didn't smile or say hello like they did everywhere you went in Last Reach, or even in Boldwick, which was the nearest biggish place to it. People in London avoided looking at each other. It was almost an art form. When you were walking towards someone, you'd glance at them a couple of times when you were still quite a long way apart, but as soon as a person got within hailing distance, it was the habit to avert your gaze or affect a strong interest in a lamppost at the other side of the street. On a couple of occasions Beth had tried smiling and saying, "hello", and the response had been as if she'd said, "Watch out — I'm a nutter." It was only elderly people, who presumably came from an era when even Londoners were friendly, who returned her greeting.

She sat down in one of the scruffy armchairs, gazing at a patch of weak sunshine on the ugly orange-and-brown carpet, feeling bored and lonely. Danny and Bill were both out: Bill had taken to London with relish, and seemed to be trying to recapture the swinging sixties with all the enthusiasm of a geriatric Austin Powers. Danny had simply gone for a walk. This was something he was in the habit of doing at home, but while Beth had confidence that her son could keep himself safe on the coastal paths of Last Reach, it was different here: every time she heard the siren of an emergency vehicle (which was roughly every five minutes in this area) she felt a flutter of panic unless he was safely indoors.

She became aware of the soft thud of music playing in the flat downstairs. She hadn't met the neighbours yet, though she'd heard them coming and going. Quickly going to the kitchen and checking there was a plentiful supply of home-made cakes (she had little to do except bake and tidy up), she decided to go downstairs and invite the neighbours up for coffee.

She knocked on the door to the ground floor flat. There was no response, although the volume of the music decreased a touch. She knocked again, and this time a female voice called, "Who is it?"

"Beth Jackson. I live in the flat upstairs."

"Hang on." After much clanking and rattling, the door eventually opened, to reveal a young woman with a pretty, freckled face. She had extraordinarily shiny brown hair parted in the middle and hanging dead straight down past her shoulders. "Hi," she said, neither friendly nor unfriendly, but not opening the door wider than absolutely necessary.

"I just moved in," Beth said, "and I heard your music . . ."

"It's not loud."

"I know, sorry, I wasn't complaining. I wondered if you'd like to come up for coffee."

The woman looked at her as though she'd just suggested taking part in some nefarious activity.

"But if you're busy . . ." Beth said, not encouraged by the response, but then the other woman said,

"I don't drink coffee." Beth was about to turn away. "But I can bring some herbal tea bags up."

Beth grinned. "Okay. I'll put the kettle on."

A short time later she heard the young woman's footsteps on the stairs.

"Wow. It's nice up here," she said.

"Haven't you been up before?"

"Are you joking? The previous occupant wasn't exactly the coffee morning type."

"Was that Finian Lewis?"

"Tall bloke, always in a suit, don't know his name." She handed Beth two tea bags. "I thought you might fancy camomile as well. You look a bit stressed." She sat down at the kitchen table. "He was hardly ever here, mind. The bloke in the suit, I mean. And he didn't stay for long. We've had all sorts living up here, and none of them stay for long. I'm Carey, by the way."

"Nice to meet you," Beth said, settling down opposite her, with two mugs of camomile tea and a plate of flapjacks on the table in between them, which Carey proceeded to devour.

The downstairs neighbour looked to be in her mid twenties. She was astonishingly pretty in a retro, hippy kind of way. Beth wondered whether Bill was right and London really was in a time warp. Carey's clothes looked like something from the psychedelic era, a swirling paisley-patterned shirt and flared jeans. She had a narrow Celtic-style band tattooed on the ring finger of her left hand.

Beth pointed at it. "That's pretty," she said.

"Jon and I — Jon's my partner — we both got one. We don't believe in getting married, but it's a symbol that we're going to stay together."

"That's really nice."

"Are you married?"

Beth still wore her wedding and engagement rings, and without thinking about it she started to fiddle with them now. "I was," she said. "My husband died three years ago."

"Did you love him?"

"Yes, ever since we were children."

"In that case, I'm very sorry to hear that he died. What was his name?"

"Martin."

"How did he die?"

It crossed Beth's mind that Carey might be a little bit retarded: her questions were so direct, and death is a conversational subject that people normally turn away from as quickly as possible. "He was a fisherman," she said. "He worked on a trawler on the North Sea. There was a storm, and the boat went down. No one survived." Those were the bare facts, but between each word was a massive gulf of grief, for the Jacksons and the other families who'd been affected, and Beth hadn't even had the worst of it (though it felt like it to her). One woman had lost her husband and both her sons.

There was hardly a family in the area who weren't affected in some way by the tragedy.

"Must put you off fish," was Carey's comment, and Beth was so used to the platitudes that most people came out with, it made her glance up abruptly. But there was no malice at all in Carey's face, just honesty and warmth and humour, and Beth relaxed and allowed herself to smile.

"What do you do?" she asked Carey, to change the subject.

"As a job? I work in a garden centre, not far from here."

"A garden centre?" It didn't seem possible that there'd be such a thing in the middle of the city like this.

"It's not a very big place, only ten of us working there. We work a rota to cover the weekends. I'm working on Saturday, that's why I'm at home today."

"What about Jon? What does he do?"

"He works in a bike shop. 2 Wheels Good, 4 Wheels Bad, off Holloway Road."

"So that'll be his bike that's sometimes in the hallway."

"He can move it if it's in your way."

"No, it's fine," Beth reassured her. Why did Carey always assume she was being criticised? "I was wondering about getting a bike myself. I used to cycle everywhere when I was at home."

"Where was that?"

"Up in the north. By the sea."

"I'd love to live by the seaside. But you need to think carefully before you ride a bike in London. It's mayhem. Jon's, like, an expert, and he's been knocked off half a dozen times by idiot car drivers. If you want, I'll get him to give you some tips. He can maybe fix you up with a bike, too, if you're serious."

Now that Beth had thought of the plan, it sounded like a great idea. She could start to explore the area, and look for a job.

On the subject of which . . . "I don't suppose you know of any work going, do you?" she asked. "Maybe at the place where you work? I'm quite good with plants and stuff." The idea of working in a little oasis of green was very appealing.

"I'll ask my boss," Carey said. "There might be something going, to cover holidays and stuff. And I've got an address of an agency that I've sometimes got jobs through, I'll let you have that." She blew on her camomile tea. "So tell me about your family. Is that pretty boy with red hair your son?"

Beth felt ridiculously proud at hearing Danny described as a pretty boy. "Yes, that's Danny. He's sixteen."

"Cool. I'll have to introduce him to my cousin Eden; she's the same age. She stays with us quite often."

"Thanks, but I doubt he'd go for it."

"Why?" Carey asked. "Is he gay?"

Beth laughed. "No. At least, I don't think so. But he's a bit of a loner, keeps to his own company."

"Bit of a shy type, eh? Don't worry, Eden will have him out of his shell in no time." Beth doubted that

Eden would find it that easy, but she was very happy for her to try.

"So the other guy is your boyfriend?"

"Are you kidding? That's my father."

"Some women prefer an older man. So do you *have* a boyfriend?"

"No." Though Beth couldn't help an image of Harry flashing into her mind. He'd *almost* been a boyfriend. Almost a fiancé, even.

It occurred to her that maybe Carey had another cousin she wanted to hitch her up with. Maybe she had a cousin for each of them.

"You'll find someone," Carey said. "Jon laughs at me, because I'm quite practical otherwise, but it's just something I believe in. Romance."

"Do you believe everyone has a soul mate?" Beth asked.

She pondered. "Well, it might sound contradictory, but no, not really. I mean, in the sense that there's only one person for each of us. Because what if you never met them? Or what if they died, like your husband? Are you going to be on your own for the rest of your life?"

"I'm not on my own," Beth said.

"You are. Your eyes look lonely."

"This is mad. I only met you half an hour ago and we're talking about . . ."

"I know, I'm like that. Jon says I connect to people. My granny was psychic. I've inherited some of her gift. She had a tarot card reading business in Margate. Lovely woman, but lousy business sense. I mean, people mainly go to Margate to die, right? You don't

160

need your cards reading when you know pretty much what's going to be on them. If she'd relocated to Brighton like I told her she'd have been raking it in. There's a lot of very unstable personalities requiring guidance in Brighton."

"Do you believe in all that stuff, then?"

"Oh, definitely. I'm your standard new-age hippy, Jon says. Whereas he doesn't believe in anything he couldn't touch with his own fingertips. It's amazing we get on so well." She stood up. "Anyhow, I've got to go. Thanks for the flapjacks. You must come down and meet Jon later."

She clattered down the stairs in her clog-like shoes, and a moment later Beth heard her music start up again.

She picked up the plate and washed the few crumbs off it, feeling much happier now she'd made a friend in London.

CHAPTER
TWENTY-FIVE

The closest thing Lorelei Dakers had to a female friend was Paloma Percival, her nail technician. When Lorelei had been a hostess on the ratings-winning game show *Take It to the Limit* her hands had been on constant display, gesturing at the game board, caressing the prizes, steering the contestants around the set and so on. Having perfect fingernails was as important as having perfect teeth, and when you get into that sort of habit it's hard to break. Though not as hard to break as Lorelei's nails.

"Do you know," Paloma said, as she filed and buffed at the famous talons, "that as much research and development has gone into these nails as into the average fighter aircraft?"

"Really? Does that apply just to fighter aircraft, or commercial airliners too?"

"The military are always ahead on these things, aren't they?" Paloma put down her file and picked up a tiny bottle of oil, tipped it on to a cotton wool pad and commenced rubbing it in, buffing Lorelei's nails with the gentle brutality required to get the highest sheen. Paloma was a beautiful, elegant woman of half Mexican descent, who'd once done a spot of modelling herself but had given it up to devote herself to nails. "I was only yesterday reading in *Jane's Defence Weekly* . . ."

"In what?" Lorelei wanted to know. "What's wrong with *Hello!* or *OK?*" She didn't get her nails done in order to talk about armies and wars: it was meant to be an escape from all the nastiness of the world.

"I'm thinking of getting a gun," the nail technician announced. "Though *Jane's* doesn't really cater for the domestic user."

Lorelei involuntarily pulled her hand back. "Good grief! You're not serious?"

"Damn right I am." Paloma retrieved the hand and carried on buffing. "Where I live, you're not safe walking down the street. People would chop your arm off to get your mobile off of you. I like to do a bit of background research before I make a purchase, and sadly they don't do a magazine called *Which? Weapon*. You need a little infilling."

"What?"

"Here, on your index finger. I swear you have the fastest-growing nails of any of my clients." She reached into her enormous box of tools for the appropriate goop.

Lorelei couldn't shake the image of a manicurist with a gun. It was so . . . *American*. She wasn't at all keen on the idea of firearms being brought in to her house, and wondered about finding another nail expert. The problem was that Paloma was universally acknowledged as the best. Perhaps she could be dissuaded from the scheme. "Surely it's not that bad where you live? I thought it was quite gentrified these days?"

"Gentrified? Of course it is. Even the crack addicts wear Gucci. Get real, Lorelei, where I live the local comprehensive has turned one of its classrooms into a police station."

"Gosh. Well, why not move, then?"

"Can't afford to."

Lorelei pondered the economics of this. Based on what she was paying for this treatment, and how many sessions they had together a month, and how many clients Paloma had, she must be worth a fortune. House prices were ridiculous, but still . . . Though it was possible that Paloma was one of these people who was intrigued by the notion of gangster chic. It was all very alarming.

For some reason, this led Lorelei to think about Beth Jackson. It was true that Beth had taken unreasonable liberties with her kitchen, and had rather quickly become a tad too comfortable with Gareth for Lorelei's liking. But there was part of Lorelei (quite possibly the part that had until the age of fifteen been called Lorraine and had lived in a council flat and had a sister called Tracey) that rather missed Beth. She was so normal, and straightforward, and Lorelei could never in a million years have imagined her thinking about getting a gun. Or thinking about getting her nails professionally done, for that matter.

Lorelei sat looking glumly at her hands as Paloma painted her nails a predatory red, and suddenly felt very lonely.

CHAPTER
TWENTY-SIX

Her father had told Beth that when keepers were off on a tower lighthouse (the kind that sticks straight out of the sea without even rocks around it to walk out on) they'd do anything to keep busy. They got so bored that washing up became a jealously guarded prize task. She was beginning to feel like a lighthouse keeper herself — for want of anything else to do, she'd cleaned the flat from the ceiling to the floor then back up again.

So any diversion was welcome. The day after Beth had met Carey, Fin Lewis rang to say that a big, glossy women's magazine — the kind of magazine Beth had never bought but was very happy to receive second-hand from Linda — wanted to do an interview and a photo shoot.

"That's mad," Beth said. "How can I be of any interest to a glossy magazine? Just because I stayed a few nights in the home of a man who wants to be an MP."

"You've answered your own question," he said. "It's a good story for their readers. And you're very photogenic."

She laughed. "If you say so. But this flat certainly isn't."

"That doesn't matter: they want to photograph you in Gareth's house, with Lorelei. Country Girl and City Girl sort of thing. Is that okay?"

"It's okay with me — a bit weird, but if that's what they want to do . . . I can't imagine Lorelei is very pleased about it, though."

"Don't worry about her, she'll be fine. So will you do it?"

It was going to sound awful, but she had to ask. "Will we get paid?" She blushed at herself for sounding so money-grabbing, but cash was running out fast.

"Not this time, I'm afraid," he said. "But you would be doing us a huge favour."

"In that case I'll have to check my diary . . . only kidding. Yes, that's fine." She had to do whatever she could to repay them for giving her family a place to live.

"I'll come and pick you up."

This was an honour indeed, to have the great spin doctor himself offering to give her a lift rather than send round Gareth's secretary, Paul. Jessie Wade had told Beth that Lorelei had insisted that if Gareth absolutely had to have a secretary, it would have to be a male.

"Do they want Bill and Danny?"

"No," he said. "Just you."

Beth had absolutely nothing to wear for a glamorous photo shoot. It made her laugh at the mere thought of it — her, in a glossy magazine! That would be something to tell Linda when she rang her later. And maybe something to write about in her newspaper

166

column, which she hadn't even started yet. She'd been worrying about what to write about — her life seemed to be so dull she couldn't imagine anyone wanting to read about it. Maybe she could ask Fin about it.

After ten minutes of staring despondently at the meagre contents of her wardrobe, she decided to wear what she already had on anyway, which was a pale blue shirt and an averagely smart pair of trousers. They were clean and tidy and they'd have to do.

Bill came in while she was attacking her hair with a brush.

"Going somewhere nice?"

"I'm going to be photographed for a swanky magazine."

"Ooh la la. Get you, Jean Shrimpton. Proper media star. Well, have fun. I'm off out to the Tate Modern."

"Since when were you interested in art?"

"I'm interested in everything, baby. Complete Renaissance man, me." He bounced down the stairs.

Five minutes later Finian Lewis was at the door.

"Do I look okay?" Beth asked him, but his eyes already said that he approved.

"Perfect," he said, and she felt unexpectedly happy until he added, "Exactly the right unsophisticated, artless look."

Which was not the effect she'd been hoping to achieve. "Thanks," she said, slumping into the passenger seat of the Mercedes, which seemed to be the all-purpose Dakers family vehicle.

He drove like he did everything else, fast (as fast as the traffic allowed), skilful, totally aware but with concentration to spare for a hundred other things. He was quite intense.

"So how's it going?" he asked her. "Is the flat all right?"

"It's fine, thank you," she said. "I haven't ventured very far yet, but I'm going to start looking for a job. The girl downstairs is going to find out if there's anything going where she works."

"You don't need to pay rent, you know. Gareth isn't expecting you to."

"I know, but I want to. I've always been independent."

"Okay. I respect that." They were stuck in a traffic jam at some roadworks. "Good God, what a mess this city is in."

"Shame Gareth isn't standing to be an MP in this area, eh? Then he could get it sorted out."

"Oh, he'd love that. He's a city boy through and through, but when you're new into politics you have to take what you can get. Though I have to say, Northlands is a bit of a culture shock for him."

"I know how he feels, in reverse."

He looked at her. His eyes were deep grey, shot through with sapphire flecks. The car suddenly felt very small. "Do you miss Northlands?"

She considered how to answer. "Not as much as I expected to, to be honest," she said. "I mean, I miss living by the sea, and I miss the people, but it's so interesting here." As soon as she'd said it she felt as if she wanted to take it back. Oddly, it felt like she'd somehow betrayed Martin. She looked out of the car window at the bonnet-to-bumper cars, the boarded-up shop fronts and the houses with dirty net curtains hanging higgledy-piggledy, the people scurrying along the dog mess-strewn pavements through the usual November drizzle. How could she bear to be here when what she'd come from was open fields behind her, open sea in front of her, nothing but tranquillity and peace?

She realised that Fin was smiling at her. "I'm glad you don't find London too horrible," he said. "I would feel so . . . responsible."

"Oh, don't feel responsible for me. You've got enough on your plate being responsible for Gareth."

"You have a point there." The traffic started to move and he eased the car forward.

Encouraged by his response, she said, "How did you come to be doing this job, anyway? And why Gareth?"

He laughed. "That's the million-dollar question. You've seen him in action — what do you think?"

Beth recalled Gareth Dakers's performance at the meeting at Last Reach Community Centre, where he'd been plausible, engaging, and warm. "He's a pretty good performer."

"Exactly. But the thing with Gareth is that it's not all show. He really does care."

"Now you're spinning again."

"Why do you say that?"

"I've lived in that house, remember? As far as I can tell, Gareth is more interested in himself than anything else, certainly than the concerns of Northlands."

"I don't think that's true." He looked aghast. "God, you're not going to say that to the woman from the magazine, are you?"

"What would you do if I did?"

They'd left the congested streets and were now gliding along tree-bordered lanes, not far from Dakers Acres. He could tell she had no intention of saying any such thing about her benefactor and that she was teasing him and so he responded in kind. At least, she hoped that's what it was, because he said, "If you became a problem, I would be forced to take drastic action."

That sounded ominous, so she tried to keep the tone light. "Drastic action, eh? Sounds painful."

"Possibly, but it would hurt me more than it would hurt you," he said, and that stuck in Beth's mind in a way that would come back to haunt her later. "Anyway," he said, "it won't come to that." His voice made the statement sound like an incontrovertible command. It almost made her shiver. He turned the car smoothly into the Dakers' drive, pressing a small remote control that made the metal gates slide open just in time to admit the car without him having to slow down at all. The tyres crunched on gravel. He turned to her and smiled, his voice quite gentle again. "So how are Bill and Danny getting on?"

She tried to keep up with the change in gear of the conversation. "Bill is being a tourist. He's already done Trafalgar Square, St Paul's and the Tower of London; today he's doing art galleries. He wanted to revisit his hippy youth, so he went to Carnaby Street, but he said

170

it was full of tourists and all artificialised. Do you know there are shops there where you can buy Mod stuff, fishtail parkas, posters of the Who, racoon tails for your scooter and stuff like that? What's the point of that?"

"What else has London got to offer? It's a theme park for tourists. Why not trade on your strengths? London has been trading on its history for years, and history means the Beatles and the Who as much as Christopher Wren and Queen Victoria."

"And what about Northlands?" Beth said. "Are you as cynical about that as you are about London?"

"I don't really know Northlands yet," he said. "I'll let you know."

Lorelei was not pleased that the major attraction for *Today's Woman* magazine was evidently the lighthouse keeper's daughter, rather than herself or her home. Her lovely home, that she'd worked so hard to make as beautiful as possible, employing the best (at least, the most expensive) designers, sourcing the fabrics and furniture from as far afield as Sri Lanka and Clackmannanshire, and *Today's Woman* had never previously been near it. She felt decidedly disgruntled. And she knew who to blame — Fin Lewis, who was comfortably settled in Gareth's study, his ear as usual pressed to one of his endless supply of mobile phones.

It was time to put her foot down. She stepped smartly into the study, businesslike. "Can I have a word?" she hissed.

"I think I can spare a moment."

171

Lorelei resisted the strong urge to slap him. "What do you think you're playing at? How come we no sooner get rid of that Jackson brood than Beth is back again to be photographed here as if she owns the place?" Even as she was speaking, Beth was upstairs making free with the guest bathroom.

"But isn't that the point? As far as the press are concerned, she's still an honoured guest. You wouldn't like it if they accused Gareth of tokenism."

"But it *was* bloody tokenism! He didn't mean to invite them, you know he didn't."

"I know nothing of the sort." He spoke to her as if he was talking to the press. "But I'm glad I've seen you. We need to talk about you and Gareth moving to Northlands."

"Moving to Northlands? Over my dead body."

"He's up there now, meeting estate agents. You're due up there tomorrow. Didn't he tell you?"

"He didn't say anything about house hunting. As far as I know I'm off for a meet-and-greet with the constituency party. I am *not* moving to Northlands. I'd die of hypothermia!"

"It's not much colder than here."

"What about my yoga?"

"I've checked that out. There's a thriving yoga community just waiting to embrace you."

"*Ashtanga* yoga?"

"But of course."

"Pilates?"

"Ditto."

"Tae Bo?"

172

"Any time you want it. As well as Tai Chi, Tae Kwon Do, various forms of karate, judo, jujitsu and kung fu."

Lorelei marvelled at the oriental penetration of even the furthest outposts of the country, and marvelled even more at the way Fin always did his homework. But she had a trump card, and she produced it now. "Is there a flotation tank?"

Now she had him. "I'll have to check up on that . . . I didn't know you ever used a flotation tank?"

"I don't, but it's such a comfort to know it's there when you need it."

"Of course." He smiled his infuriatingly confident smile. "But property prices in Northlands are so cheap you could probably have one of your own installed."

If that was intended to mollify her it wasn't working. "I warn you, Fin, I'll be fighting this every step of the way."

Fin sighed deeply. "Lorelei, what is the point? Gareth wants to be an MP. I thought you wanted him to be an MP. You do, don't you?"

"I guess."

"So the way for him to become an MP is to be elected by the people of Northlands. Which means he has to be a whole lot more to them than the lord of the manor who just turns up to judge the village fête."

"Oh, God, they don't have one of those, do they?"

"I expect they have several, each replete with a carnival queen. You'd want to be around for those, surely."

She knew he meant that she would need to keep an eye on her famously errant husband, but he didn't have to say it.

For Lorelei, the thought of moving away from handy reach of the capital was like contemplating having a major body part removed. It absolutely wasn't on. Her entire social life, her whole support system, was based around London. If she was being honest, it was based around the Haven, and, more specifically, Dr Harrison Shah.

She thought about their lunch meeting the week before. He'd been charming, attentive, amusing — in short, the perfect lunch companion. They'd ordered a bottle of very good wine, but because he had patients to see that afternoon, he'd only had half a glass. Which had left the rest of it for Lorelei, and after he'd gone, she had another. That was the evening she came home and found her husband tête-à-tête with Beth Jackson.

Speaking of whom, Beth appeared in the doorway.

Lorelei adopted her very finest *Take It to the Limit* guest-greeting smile, as well trained and practised as a geisha. "Couldn't keep away, eh, Beth?"

Most gratifyingly, Beth Jackson looked embarrassed. She also looked annoyingly pretty, in that unstudied, artless way she had. It had taken Lorelei all morning to get ready, longer if you counted the manicure and hair appointments she'd had yesterday. She'd also had a small army of people cleaning and beautifying her home, and had spent a fortune on flowers, which adorned the top of every highly polished piece of reproduction antique furniture.

174

"I expect you're used to being photographed for glossy magazines," Beth said.

"Well ... not so much these days, but, yes, generally."

"I'm really nervous about it. I always come out in photographs with my mouth gaping open or my eyes shut or both, looking like I'm drunk."

There was some satisfaction to be had in that idea for Lorelei, who knew exactly how to behave in front of a camera: David Bailey himself had once asked if he could photograph her, but somehow it had never happened. It would be kind of nice if the photographs came out with the unutterably glamorous ex-TV personality looking fabulous in stark contrast to her idiot-faced northern lodger.

On the other hand, if Beth made a total cat's breakfast out of it, the chances were that the magazine's editor might decide not to use the pictures after all. They had plenty of other people they could use (which was the only reason why they hadn't been to Lorelei's home before, of course). Lorelei was painfully aware that this might be her only chance to have her beautiful house immortalised on glossy paper.

There was nothing for it: she was going to have to take Beth in hand.

"Would you have any objection to me doing something with your make-up and your hair?" she asked, couching her question unusually tactfully. Beth shook her head no. "And while I'm doing that, I could perhaps pass on some of the tips I've learned during my career." She led the way to the room she liked to describe as her "boudoir".

"You've got very nice skin, considering you've led a rural sort of life," Lorelei commented, smearing a touch of foundation into Beth's forehead. "Do you use a cream with an SPF?"

"I don't know. I don't think so."

"Well, you should start. You've been lucky so far, but it can't last. Factor fifteen at the very least."

"Okay."

Lorelei worked on in silence for a while, and eventually realised she wasn't hating this as much as she'd expected to. In a way, it was kind of fun. Living in an all-male household (she included Gareth, Fin and Paul, but didn't include Jessie Wade whose remit was so arcane as to have absolutely no interest at all) could be a bit dull, and now Paloma had apparently gone over to the dark side with her new interest in firearms, it was rather refreshing to have some non-mad female company.

"Dogwood Avenue is very nice," Beth commented. Lorelei hadn't seen the place, but knew the area it was in and doubted that "very nice" was an apt description. For this, she felt a little guilty. "It's not the kind of thing you're used to, of course," Beth went on.

"No indeed." Lorelei dotted a tiny dab of concealer under Beth's eyes, trying not to think about the flat on the thirteenth floor of a high rise in Camden where she'd spent her formative years. "Nor you, either. It

176

must have been fun living in a lighthouse. Don't all the beds have to be curved?"

Beth laughed, which produced friendly lines around her eyes. "We didn't actually live in the lighthouse tower," she said. "Our house was a cottage next to it. I don't think I'd really like to live in a tower."

No, you wouldn't, Lorelei thought, remembering all the times the lifts had been broken at Nickleby Heights, and her mother dragging her and Tracey and the week's shopping up thirteen flights of stairs.

Even Gareth didn't know about those days. She'd made up a whole history for herself, based a bit on her real life but with a large dollop of fiction, mainly inspired by the pre-Charles years of Diana Spencer. She had never, for example, worked in a kindergarten. But it did look nice on the CV.

Oddly, she began to feel that she might like to talk about her real life with someone one day. Not Mr Goldstein or anyone like that, certainly not Gareth, but someone like Beth Jackson, who seemed to accept everything quite happily. She supposed that was the advantage of a humble country existence — life was so much simpler.

Emerging from the study for a quick break, Fin was nothing less than gobsmacked to see the twin visions of Beth and Lorelei sweeping down the staircase as if they were old friends. Lorelei was actually laughing! And not in that snide, putting-down kind of way she normally employed, but laughing as if there was something genuinely humorous going on.

And Beth looked incredible. Fin had never seen her wearing make-up before, and had to assume that it was Lorelei's doing, but she'd done a great job, just enough to enhance Beth's luminous eyes and lovely skin.

"Ah — here's a *man*," Lorelei said at the sight of him, her usual acidity now back in place. "We'll get a man's opinion of how you look. Do you think you can manage that, Fin?"

"You look wonderful," he said to Beth.

She smiled at him and looked even more gorgeous.

"You can't believe a word he says, of course," Lorelei commented. "He's an accomplished twister of the truth."

"So if he's lying it means you didn't do a very good job with the make-up," Beth replied.

"So you think you look wonderful without make-up?" Fin asked, thinking privately that *he* did.

"No, quite the opposite. If I look nice it's *all* make-up, which is Lorelei's doing. If I look like Coco the clown, it's Lorelei's doing. That's all."

"You look beautiful, and it's *not* all Lorelei's doing," he said.

Which was probably more opinion than Lorelei had bargained on, because she ushered her protégée off to the sitting room with all possible speed.

CHAPTER
TWENTY-SEVEN

This was surreal, Beth thought: she'd spent yesterday being driven around in a very flash car by a handsome man, had her make-up done by a former game show hostess, been interviewed and had her photograph taken for a glossy magazine.

And today she was trying to get to grips with the London underground system, so she could get to a job interview to try and make enough money to support her family.

The sign on the front of the first train to arrive said it was going to Uxbridge. She hadn't heard of Uxbridge, so she let that one pass. The next one was going to Heathrow. Everyone had heard of Heathrow — wasn't it the busiest airport in Europe, or even the world? And Beth thought she'd like to visit it at some point, but not today, so she let that one go too. The one after that was also bound for Heathrow. Looking at the illuminated noticeboard it seemed that the one after that was destined for somewhere called Rayners Lane. **STAND BACK TRAIN APPROACHING** the display warned.

Beth stood back, the train approached like thunder on rails, and it was only then that she realised that she was the only person standing on the platform who didn't get on. Realisation dawned: either Rayners Lane was a hell of a popular place, or else there was a system to all this. There was a map of the underground on the wall and she studied it for a few moments and then felt like an absolute fool. It was plain as day — you got on the first train going in the right direction, and changed at one of the intersections. She glanced up at a CCTV camera which seemed to be pointing straight at her, and imagined someone watching it and laughing and saying, "Spot the tourist!"

Well, she wasn't a tourist. She was, for better or worse, a citizen of London, with a right to be here. It was with a mixed feeling of relief and triumph that she boarded the next train, and was hurtled into the blackness. Beth stared at her reflection in the dark of the window opposite, and hoped she looked present-able. Never having had to apply for a job in her life, she had no idea of what would be expected of her or what was going to happen.

Carey hadn't been very forthcoming with advice. "Dress up a bit," she'd said, "but not slaggy. Just be yourself."

So she'd chosen her only "posh" outfit, a bluey-grey skirt and jacket that she'd bought for the christening of Linda's daughter Cait. At the time she'd worried that it might be a bit showy, but Martin had loved it, and thought it looked really elegant. And Martin's approval was good enough for Beth, always. She sighed, remembering that sunny, breezy day. Martin and Kenny Morini cracking jokes about the vicar, who was so old he'd christened Martin too, so he was in a mood

180

to be indulgent if he overheard any of it; Linda fussing around with Cait's christening gown, hoping she wasn't going to scream which predictably she did. Martin and Beth were godparents, and when Beth was standing by the font holding the baby she looked up at Martin and he looked so handsome, she thought maybe it would be nice if they had another baby, too. Danny was already eleven, and showing every sign of becoming independent faster than anyone had a right to do.

But it never happened. They hadn't been conscious of trying, because Beth would have hated to turn into the sort of woman who's obsessed by having a baby, but each month she felt a little twinge of disappointment which she shrugged off by telling herself that it would happen next month. And then the months ran out, and Martin wasn't there any more, and Danny was always going to be an only child.

Beth thought for an awful moment that she was going to cry, right there in the tube train, and ruin her painstaking efforts with the mascara wand. It was odd, she hadn't cried much at the time when Martin's boat had been lost, but just lately any little thing had been setting her off.

To take her mind off things, she turned her attention to her fellow passengers, not one of whom was catching anyone else's eye. It was a version of that ignoring each other thing they did out in the street, only here even more elaborate because of the multiplication of eyes that you might possibly catch. Beth worked out that you could either look at a window where there was a gap between people, or at someone's knee — though you had to be careful it was a knee of the same gender and your gaze wasn't taken to be sexual — or at the advertisements over people's heads.

In Last Reach, the only comparable situation would be if you were on the bus to Boldwick. Then everyone would be talking to everyone else. "I told her, I said, 'You want to get that looked at.' But would she listen? Would she bugger. Now look at it: all inflamed and full of pus." That sort of thing. When you thought about it like that, maybe people in Northlands were a bit *too* friendly sometimes.

It was her stop: Covent Garden. She stood up, pulled at the hem of her jacket, and stepped off the tube, into central London for the very first time.

Beth had never seen so many people, or heard as much noise in her life. It seemed as if the whole world was standing in the street outside Covent Garden tube station, so many people she could barely get past them. Eventually with a lot of smiles and excuse-mes and sideways squeezing she managed it, and found herself in the middle of a crowd that seemed to know where it was going, borne along like a piece of driftwood. Everywhere there was noise. A young man was selling wooden whistles which, he claimed, made authentic bird noises. Not like any bird Beth had ever heard, but then there were a lot of exotic birds in the world, and from his tanned and casual appearance, maybe the young man was from somewhere like South Africa where the birds were more operatic than the ones she was used to. A gang of black-dyed teenagers

182

congregated on one pavement, surrounded by sheets of paper covered in what seemed to be tattoo designs. Surely they weren't planning to do real tattoos right there in the street? Wasn't that illegal? This place was mad. A shy-looking Japanese woman sitting on the floor selling bright beaded purses — and surely risking being trampled on — smiled up at Beth as she went past.

"Two for six pounds," the woman said.

"Can I just have one, please?" Beth pointed at a bright pink cat with a cluster of strawberries hanging over its ear. She'd send it to Linda's Cait as a birthday present.

Somehow making a purchase made her feel more confident, more a part of things. This only lasted until the first person muttered abusively at her for getting in the way. "Fuckin' tourists," they said as they shoved past.

"Excuse me" would have achieved the same result, Beth thought. She was very relieved when she got to the small black door marked Crispin Love Employment Agency.

She pressed a buzzer, and the door opened on a very narrow staircase, which got progressively more rickety as she ascended. At the very top, in what must have been the attic or perhaps the servants' quarters in days gone by, was an off-white door bearing again the name Crispin Love Employment Agency, underneath which someone had pinned a piece of paper bearing the slogan WORK FOR LOVE.

She'd pictured a "Crispin Love" as being someone with artistic hair and lace-trimmed cuffs, but he turned out to be a short, somewhat tubby man probably a couple of years younger than she was. His hair was dark and cropped close to his head, and he appeared to have no neck, his head attached straight to his shoulders with no intermediary. The room he showed her into was a tiny attic room with only a skylight window which was flecked with bird droppings. The air was fugged with tobacco smoke, which Crispin proceeded to augment further by lighting up another cigarette. He didn't offer one to Beth (she didn't smoke but felt it would have been polite of him to offer), or a cup of coffee, although he had one of those on his desk, too, in amongst a rubble of papers and files and an overflowing ashtray.

"So . . . Beth, is it? Short for Elizabeth?"

"I'm always called Beth."

"Okay. Beth. Tell me about your employment experience, Beth."

She told him about running the lighthouse bed and breakfast.

"You want to go in for catering, then?"

"I don't mind," she said. "I'll try my hand at anything."

"Are you computer literate?"

"I'm a bit rusty." This was a complete lie. Danny had a computer, but it was as much a mystery to Beth as most of the things he did. But she was fairly confident she could learn.

"Windows?"

This was safer ground. "I had to clean a lot of windows, on all the cottages and . . ."

184

His laugh was like a canary being minced. "Microsoft Office applications?"

"Sorry?" This wasn't going well.

"Do you drive?"

"No." He frowned. "Is that a problem?"

"Well, it helps if you've got your own transport."

"I'm planning to get a bike."

"I'll put 'no' then, shall I?" He was beginning to look a bit irritated now. "Look," he said, "I'll put you on the database, but to be honest I don't think we'll be much use to you. We're looking for a more contemporary skill-set, really." Carey hadn't mentioned anything about contemporary skill-sets, but Beth thought that was because Carey probably had one and assumed everyone else did too.

She was very depressed after that, and not even the fact that she managed to get back home without once getting lost on the underground cheered her up. She stopped off at a huge supermarket which was almost opposite the tube station. Even though she much preferred to do her shopping at the nice Turkish convenience store where she'd bought the olives on the first day in Dogwood Avenue, she'd quickly realised that everything there cost twice as much.

But even if she shopped at the cheapest supermarket, money was running out quickly. It was just as well that Beth was used to cooking from scratch and fruit and vegetables, flour and eggs were all more or less affordable. She had to walk quite briskly past the rows

185

and rows of more unusual and interesting goods, because she wouldn't have been able to afford them.

On the way back to the flat, she bumped into Carey, who was striding along in her usual bouncy way, unencumbered by the coat she was wearing, which looked as if it had been cut from lengths of Persian carpet. With her was her partner Jon, who was a very tall, very slender man with cinnamon-coloured skin, a boyish face and tufty, corkscrew hair.

"Hi Beth!" Carey greeted her. "How did the interview go?"

"Not too well." She told them how she was apparently too old and too skill-free to make any impact on the London job market.

"Oh, that's too bad," Carey said.

"What about that Christmas job you were talking about?" Jon reminded her.

"She wouldn't want to do that."

"I'll consider anything," Beth said.

"Are you sure about that? Even if it involves wearing green tights and a hat with a bell on it?" Jon said.

"Pardon?"

"Santa needs elves," Carey explained.

"That sounds quite sweet."

Jon laughed, a big, warm sound that he looked too skinny to be capable of producing. "Wait till you've been there half an hour," he said. "You'll be ready to kill."

"I could take you there tomorrow," Carey offered, shooting a disapproving glance at her partner. "I'll pop

186

in tonight and tell you more about it. Oh, and Eden's coming round tonight, I'll bring her up to meet Danny if you like."

CHAPTER
TWENTY-EIGHT

While Beth was trying to decide how to spend her money in the supermarket, Gareth Dakers was involved in spending decisions of his own. It had been hammered into him by Fin, with the relentlessness of Chinese water torture, that he had to buy a house in the constituency of Northlands, and Gareth had finally agreed.

"Nothing too flash," Fin had warned. It may just have been stereotyping, but Gareth always felt that his friend's Yorkshire accent was more prominent whenever he was talking about money. "You don't want to be looking like lord and lady of the manor."

"You still haven't got the hang of the present Mrs Dakers, have you?" Gareth had smiled.

Right now he was wondering if he had the hang of Lorelei himself yet. They were standing alone together in the empty hallway of a large, gloomy and very cold house perched on the edge of a moor just outside the Northlands market town of Boldwick.

"I knew you'd love it," he said to his wife, sounding anything but convinced.

"It's shit," she pouted. "I hate it."

"So you preferred the one by the sea?"

"In the sense that one could say one preferred rabies to anthrax."

"It wasn't that bad. Lovely view."

"If you like oil refineries."

"It is not an oil refinery. It's a petrochemical plant, and it's so far up the coast you could hardly see it from the house."

"But what happens on days when the wind's blowing from that direction?"

"Fin says . . ."

"Oh, stuff what Fin says!" Lorelei marched off in the direction of what was theoretically the lounge, leaving her husband standing there. He knew better than to follow her just yet.

Lorelei stood at the window, imagining whether it would look marginally better with some gorgeous satin ruched curtaining she'd seen in a magazine, but decided it would be pearls before swine to even contemplate wasting fabric in such a way. Beyond the window was a view of unremitting countryside, of the sort that people describe as austerely beautiful, a Brontë sort of landscape, and a huge quantity of sky. It was pants. She would die up here, without any kind of spiritual stimulation whatsoever. It simply wasn't on.

But Lorelei Dakers was made of sterner stuff, and she knew the best thing to do would be simply to agree with everything that was proposed, they could buy this wretched house (which probably cost the equivalent of what you'd pay for a caravan in London, after all) and then she'd find as many excuses as she needed to spend most of her time in London. She could perhaps turn up here to smile on election night, that should be enough.

She was also missing being flirted with by Dr Harrison Shah. She thought of his inky dark eyes, his fabulous smile and bone structure, the cute little wayward tuft of black hair that she always wanted to smooth down but hadn't dared — yet. It was an affair just waiting to happen, she was sure of it, but something was stopping her. It was sad, it was tragic, it was pathetic — but she loved her husband. If only he paid her more attention. She found herself looking back at Gareth, both in the sense of physically looking back at him in the doorway of the empty house — tall, elegant, eager, hopeful — and looking back at how they'd been when they first met.

Take It to the Limit had become one of the most popular shows on television. Its host, Pete Nixon, was one of the most highly paid presenters and most recognisable faces. Only slightly less famous were the Limit Lovelies who ushered the contestants around the studio, posed with the prizes and so on. For a job that a semi-trained rodent would have been able to do with its eyes shut, Lorelei was paid a massive amount of money. She loved the lifestyle that went with it, the parties and premieres, all the attention. This was what she'd worked so hard to achieve, but there was one thing missing.

That thing turned out to be Gareth Dakers.

She met him at a premiere, for the latest James Bond film. Her escort for the night had been a young man who was in a moderately popular Australian soap, but although he was friendly enough and most certainly a hunk, Lorelei had a strong suspicion he was gay. This was a depressingly regular occurrence in her life, and she was beginning to despair of ever meeting anyone who would be important to her, until the moment when Gareth Dakers placed an empty martini glass in her hand.

She looked at the glass, then at the rather dashing man who'd proffered it, a man whose face was so familiar from television but whom she'd never met before now, his eyes and lips smiling just for her.

"You've given me an empty glass," she said.

He sighed. "It was supposed to be a martini. Shaken, not stirred, in the James Bond tradition," he explained. "But I was so stirred and so shaken at the sight of your beauty that I spilled every drop on my way over here." She raised her eyebrows (she could still do that in those days) at him. What a line. "You don't believe me?" he said, and pointed to the carpet behind him. "There's the olive," he said, in time for her to see the small green orb being squelched beneath the kitten heel of a well-known actress.

She was instantly besotted. Although she was used to being surrounded by celebrities, there was something about Gareth Dakers . . . Possibly it was because he'd been born into a showbiz dynasty, the royal family of the variety show and the Christmas pantomime. He was the real thing.

From his side, she had no doubt that part of the attraction that she held for him was that she looked so good on his arm — a Limit Lovely was a bit of a catch

— but genuine love had quickly grown between them. Both born narcissists, they complemented and complimented each other like no one else had ever done.

Until the Windy Wendy episode. It was the cliché of it that Lorelei found so hard to forgive — a weather girl, for heaven's sake! It was all over the papers for a very long weekend, but as so often in these things it was Wendy herself who took most of the battering, as the cynical, immoral careerist who would break up a decent man's relationship for the sake of advancement. Gareth ended up in tears, begging Lorelei to forgive him. And she took him back, because she was less of herself without him.

When he said that he wanted to go into politics, Lorelei's first reaction had been that it would put less temptation in his way. Female MPs weren't generally known for their looks, after all. Though the fact that women found power so attractive was worrying; when you thought about all the truly hideous male MPs who'd had affairs it was clear that the position on its own was attraction enough for some types of women.

There was no arguing with Gareth on the issue, though. He was dead set on the idea of his next pantomime appearance being as a backbencher.

Things really started to turn pear-shaped, as far as Lorelei was concerned, when Gareth appointed Finian Lewis as his minder. One of his first pieces of advice was that Lorelei should give up her job.

Pete Nixon, her co-host on *Take It to the Limit*, had tried to persuade her not to leave the show.

"But it's hardly an appropriate job for a minister's wife," she said, gesturing at her sequin-encrusted dress which revealed rather more cleavage than was normally seen in the House of Commons. "You don't expect me to wear tit-tape for the Queen's Speech, surely?"

"It would perk the honourable members up, if nothing else," he said with a grin. "But seriously, you don't want to be a nice little MP's wife, darling, all those coffee mornings and charity do's."

"I'll cope."

"But how will you cope when his eye wanders again? And it will. I've seen his sort before." And had his heart broken by them, Lorelei knew.

He'd been right about Gareth's wandering tendency, but in a way, the Windy Wendy fiasco had brought them closer. It was this politics stuff that was driving them apart. Gareth seemed more interested in listening to Finian Lewis than to her, and this back-of-beyond she was supposed to live in was too horrible. But, as she looked up and saw Gareth walking towards her across the cold, bare room, she couldn't help thinking again of him at that premiere, holding out the empty martini glass. She made a mental note that it was time to shake Dr Harrison Shah right out of her mind.

"So shall I ring the estate agent?" he asked.

"Yes," she said. "You do that, and I'll get some designers up to give it the once-over."

He kissed her warmly.

CHAPTER
TWENTY-NINE

Imogen Callow-Creed slumped in her chair in the otherwise empty newsroom of the *Northlands Herald*. A copy of *Today's Woman* magazine was spread out in front of her, featuring a very phoney, arse-licking article about Lorelei Dakers and Beth Jackson from the Last Reach Point lighthouse. They were looking really pally, and the article was banging on about shopping trips and sightseeing together.

"How absolutely fabulous," Imogen said aloud, sniggering to herself, wondering which of the two women was Edina and which was Patsy. Actually, she'd have Beth down as more of a Saffy type — strait-laced and dull. Lovely looking, though.

Imogen wondered where Fin had been when these pictures were taken. Was he around? What did he think of Lorelei Dakers and Beth Jackson? Did he fancy either of them, she wondered? She didn't think he'd mess with Dakers's wife, he was far too professional for that. Which left the lovely lighthouse keeper's daughter. She suddenly felt certain that that was why he'd turned her down. There had to be another woman in the picture, and the woman in this picture in front of her was presumably she, Imogen thought, feeling her grip on syntax loosening as her irritation grew.

It wasn't only personal pride that was irritating Imogen: her professional pride was, she felt, also at stake. She'd been watching Dakers closely when he'd made the offer to the family to come and live with him, and there'd been real panic in his eyes — just for a second, but Imogen could swear it had been there. If only she could find out what had caused it, she'd really have a story.

Ideally she'd have liked to talk to someone in the lighthouse family, and get some nice insider juice. But her editor, Nigel "Regional" Packman, would never consent to her going off to London to follow up on something that was now deemed off the patch. What she needed was a mole, someone who could get right inside the lighthouse family.

Smiling to herself, she picked up the phone. "Oh, you're at home," she said to the person at the other end. "Do I take it that you're still what's known as 'resting'? In which case, I have a little job that might interest you."

CHAPTER
THIRTY

To Beth's extreme happiness and amazement, Carey was right: somehow her cousin Eden and Danny hit it off straight away.

Eden was nothing like Beth expected her to be. Probably because of her very hippy name, and her delightful sixties throwback of a cousin, Beth had pictured her as all sandals, braided hair and patchouli. But Eden was definitely a young woman of the noughties — trendily dressed in clothes you'd never see in Northlands but which were a routine sight on the streets of north London; she had large blue eyes, and light brown hair choppily cut around her face. But like Carey, she was sweet, genuine, and very direct.

Though with a mother's bias Beth thought Danny was the most handsome and perfect of boys, and Carey had described him as "the pretty boy with red hair", she was still surprised that the smart and streetwise Eden seemed to agree with them. Very quickly they started spending a lot of time together. Beth didn't think they were romantic, but they seemed to be becoming really good friends, and she was happy, and grateful.

For one thing, having a good friend of his own age was making Danny's transition from the small rural school he'd been attending to the massive inner city comprehensive a little easier. Beth and Bill had gone to visit the school, and had both been overwhelmed by its size, and by the loudness and apparent aggression of its pupils.

"We're just not used to seeing that many teenagers all in one place," Beth reasoned herself into calmness.

"I'm not used to hearing so much effing and blinding in one place," Bill observed.

Beth seriously expected Danny to hate it, and anticipated having to talk him into staying against protests that he would be happier leaving and finding a job, but to her surprise he seemed to settle in reasonably well.

In the meantime, Bill continued with his programme of cultural visits, which Beth occasionally accompanied him on. At first she found London terrifying: all those people, the crowds, and the traffic. It was so noisy! The tube totally bamboozled her, but she followed Bill, who seemed to know what he was doing, whether by memory or instinct wasn't clear.

Beth began to feel more at home as soon as she started her new job. True, she'd never pictured her future career path as including a spell as an elf in Santa's grotto at the Good Life Garden Centre, but stranger things had already happened.

It was still November, but Christmas was well under way in London, which was dressed up like a giant glittery ball. Moving to London hadn't stopped Beth thinking about Martin. She would never stop thinking about Martin: she thought about him every day, and still missed him. But it was all less raw than when they'd been at the lighthouse, and in a way moving south had helped her to realise that he was never coming back. But whenever she went out and "Jingle Bells" was playing in the shops and there was tinsel all over the place, she couldn't help but remember those Christmases when they were together. Like the Christmas when she was pregnant with Danny and couldn't even face the smell of a roast turkey dinner, never mind cook one or eat one. Bill was away staying with some of his old lighthouse friends, and Martin and Beth had nothing but Ritz crackers for Christmas lunch, because that's all she could face eating and he didn't want her to feel left out, so he had them too. Although he did eat the whole packet, and then later while she was supposed to be having a nap she heard him raiding the fridge.

You can think that you're managing quite well to cope with something, and then Christmas comes along. It's like one of those snow globe things, it shakes you up so all the parts of your life are like little flakes whirling through the water, where just before everything was settled. But Beth was learning to cope with these setbacks, and threw her energies into her job.

Santa's grotto turned out to be a huge operation: the children were marshalled in with expert speed and precision — the chief "loader" had worked for a spell on the huge London Eye, where they had to be extremely efficient in getting people in and out because the wheel never stops revolving. Neither did the turnstile of the grotto.

Santa's name, in this case, was Joe, and he was lovely — blue, twinkling eyes, calm, quiet manner, snow-white hair. The perfect picture-book Father Christmas. Carey told Beth that the garden centre had been thrilled to get him — apparently Joe was very much in demand, and had even been a Harrods Santa for several years before the tube journey got too much for him. There were six elves, working a rota system, so that three were on duty at any time. One was stationed at the entrance of the grotto, another at the exit, and one acted as chaperone and bodyguard to Santa himself. Beth's favourite job was the with-Santa one, because it was so sweet seeing the wonder in the children's eyes, and the pride on the faces of the parents. Though this wasn't always the case. Some of the kids, particularly the boys, could get a bit bolshy, try and pull Santa's beard, get a bit demanding if he demurred over whether he was going to be delivering the latest video game console or mobile phone on the 25th, some took absolute fright at the sight of him and had to be quickly given their "present from Santa" and ushered out. Others had tantrums and wouldn't leave, staging small, furious grotto sit-ins.

Her usual co-elves were a woman in her mid-forties called Barbara, who was a no-nonsense Liverpudlian, and a school-leaver called Ian, who'd trained with the St John's Ambulance service and had the added title of

Elf-and-Safety Elf. He was also tubby enough to look like a Santa-in-waiting.

To begin with, the weekday shift was fairly quiet, because the school holidays hadn't yet started. Most of the children who visited the grotto were pre-schoolers, who would generally react either of two ways — hysterics or dumbstruck. The biggest problem for Santa Joe was to try and work out their names. There were names from so many different countries, some of them completely exotic-sounding, and Joe had grown up in an era when most people were Mary or Annie or Bert or Fred. He did his best though, and when he couldn't even begin to work out what a child (or its parent) had just told him, he beamed widely and said, "Well, isn't that nice?"

There was a brief pause between children, when Joe could mop perspiration from under his beard, or have a quick snack. He was diabetic and needed constant supplies. During one of these lulls, Santa Joe asked Beth what she wanted for Christmas.

She didn't have to think about it. "If you were really Santa, and could do miracles . . ."

"That's not Santa you want, it's Jesus," he pointed out, rearranging his beard.

"Well, it sounds silly, but what I'd really like is one more conversation with Martin."

"That's your late husband?" She nodded. "What would you say to him?" Santa asked, looking at her kindly over the rims of his little round glasses.

"I'd tell him . . . oh, that I'm okay, and Danny's okay, and not to worry, and all that stuff."

200

"He already knows that."

"How do you know?"

"My dear, I *am* Father Christmas, after all."

CHAPTER
THIRTY-ONE

Beth was delighted to get a letter from Linda, the first post she'd had since moving to Dogwood Avenue.

Dear Beth,

Well, I wonder how you're all settling in. Imagine you living the high life in London, you'll be too good for us all soon. As soon as you get a chance write and let me know how it's all going. Do you get to see much of Gareth Dakers? I think he's really handsome, and Betty Cooper even has a picture of him on her fridge, next to one of Dale Winton. I tried telling her that Dale Winton wouldn't be interested in her, but she got quite narky and said even though she's sixty-two she still scrubs up well. I don't think she's heard of homosexuality so I didn't enlighten her.

Anyway, all's well at this end. We're up to our eyes trying to organise a birthday party for Cait. I'm sure we didn't have so many parties when we were five, but all her mates have had one so she has to do likewise. I've got Betty Cooper's niece Angela coming to do one of her turns. She's a leading light of the Northlands East Amateur

Theatrical Society (you remember, she was Julie Andrews in the NEATS production of *The Sound of Music* last year) and she does songs from the shows, magic tricks and face painting, all for a quite reasonable £20 plus lunch. Yours truly will be doing the catering, of course. We can save quite a bit of money by using stuff that's just past its sell-by date that we can't sell in the shop, Kenny says (he sends love, by the way).

Listen to me, going on about money! But you know what it's like.

I have to tell you, poor old Harry Rushton is going around with a face like a slapped bulldog. He's missing you, I reckon. He asked me for your new address — is it all right to tell him? Though you'd think being a policeman he'd have access to databases and stuff like that, but maybe they don't have them in Northlands. Everything I know about the police I get from *The Bill*, so I'm hardly an authority.

Best love,
Linda XX

She also included a front page from the *Northlands Herald*, dated from not long after the Jacksons had left. It featured a picture of the lighthouse, ghostly in fuzzy black and white, next to a photograph of the family and Gareth Dakers in the cosy sitting room in the principal keeper's cottage.

The headline was "Beacon of Hope For Lighthouse Family", and it retrod the old ground about how

Gareth Dakers had practically scooped them from the waves single-handedly. The article ended with more speculation about the possible golf course at Carver Bay, and how the coastline there had been reinforced, and that Gareth Dakers hadn't wanted to make a comment about that.

Beth was supposed to produce her second "Country Girl in the Big City" newspaper column, and she hadn't known what to write about, but now she did. She sat down and scribbled furiously.

When she'd finished, she thought for a second or two about ringing Fin to read it out to him before she sent it off, but had a feeling he wouldn't like it much and would want it changing to suit how he'd been portraying things so far. So she put it in an envelope, and posted it off to the newspaper's editor.

CHAPTER
THIRTY-TWO

"How the hell did this happen?" Gareth Dakers held up the *Evening Despatch*. The headline on page five read: "Why the Coast Means More Than Votes". "The woman is berserk!" he said. "Just because she has a nice arse doesn't give her the right to go talking out of it in print."

"There was always a danger that this would happen," Fin said, trying hard not to let Gareth's previous comment turn into a lingering mental image. "It was a bit of a gamble letting her write the column."

"Hindsight's a marvellous thing. Shame you didn't think about it before."

"I'm not sure why you're getting so worked up about it," Fin commented, his eyes scanning the page. "I mean, there's possibly a vague suspicion of ingratitude, in that she suggests you could be more involved in the coastal erosion situation rather than just plucking them out of it and carrying on regardless, but that's all really. She won't have written the headline. The rest is just ecology sort of stuff. Probably bore most people rigid, and the ones who'll bother to read it will know it all anyway and already have their minds made up."

"It makes me look bad," Gareth said, with just a suggestion of a pout. "You should have blocked it."

"I doubt I could reasonably have blocked it even if I'd wanted to."

"So what are you going to do about it? Can we get them to print a retraction?"

"Retracting what, exactly? It's hardly contentious stuff, Gareth. She hasn't libelled you or defamed your character, she's just putting forward a viewpoint, like any good constituent. Let it go is my advice." Fin tapped his pen against his teeth, thinking.

"That's a very irritating habit you have, you know."

"What?"

"That tapping thing with your pen."

"Sometimes I think we spend too much time together. Now — this is what we're going to do. I'm going to go and have a friendly chat with Mrs Jackson, mark her card so to speak, and you're going to go and meet with the local councillors and anyone who's involved in the Northlands coastal development scheme, and find out what's going on."

"What?" Gareth sounded alarmed. "I can't do that!"

"Why not?"

"Well . . . I've just got *back* from Northlands."

"That train ride is going to become your favourite waste of time over the next few months. I'll set up something balanced. We don't want to look as though we're favouring the people in the north of the constituency at the expense of those in the south, do we? Presumably the people in the south are pretty pleased that their bit of the coast is being protected.

206

Maybe I ought to get on to someone at the local university, they must have a tame boffin who could explain why the south is worth preserving and the north isn't."

"Is that really a good idea?"

"Yes, it is. I'll get it organised this afternoon. First I'm going over to the Jacksons." Gareth was wearing a face that mixed confusion and apprehension. Fin patted his forearm. "It's not the end of the world," he said. "You'll have to develop a thicker skin if you're going to be an MP."

CHAPTER
THIRTY-THREE

After a day spent in a fairy-lit grotto surrounded by screaming kids, and a bus journey that took for ever through the frosty London night (which she couldn't see anyway because the bus windows were so dirty), Beth was ready for a bath and a nice hot meal.

As she approached the flat on Dogwood Avenue it sounded as if there was a party going on in their living room. Even though the windows were closed she could still hear music blasting out halfway down the street, and inside the house it was deafening. As she climbed the stairs, she could smell cigarette smoke with a herbal tang to it. If it turned out to be what she thought it was, Danny was going to swing for it.

She stamped into the living room, getting ready to do her righteous mother routine, and preparing for the teenage backlash that would follow. But it wasn't Danny who was sprawled all over the sofa — it was Bill. And sitting opposite her father was another man. He was about thirty years old with longish, shaggy blond hair and a sweet, elfin face. He looked freshly bathed and was wearing a dressing gown that someone had given Danny for Christmas but which he'd never worn on the grounds that it was "naff". It was also very short. Beth had no idea how to take in the sight of a scantily clad man and her father apparently happily sharing a joint together.

"This is Tim Carter," her father said. "Tim, my beautiful daughter Beth."

"Ve'y please to mee' you," Tim slurred, attempting to stand up and thinking better of it, sinking back to the sofa but proffering his hand and smiling delightfully. "Sorry. I'm a l'il bit wrecked." She shook his hand, trying not to notice how skimpy the dressing gown was.

"I thought Tim could stay for a couple of days," Bill said. This was too much. Beth gave him a meaningful look and summoned him out into the hallway.

"Where on earth did you find *him*?" she hissed.

"He's been sleeping rough in that little park at the top of the road. You must have seen him," he said. She hadn't. "Don't look at me like that, Beth. What was I supposed to do? I couldn't leave him outside in that cold."

"But you don't know anything about him!"

"I know a great deal about him. We've talked for hours. He's a nice guy, on his uppers. All I'm doing is lending him a helping hand."

She sighed. "He could be an axe-wielding murderer for all you know! And you bring him in here where he could do God knows what to your daughter or grandson? You're off your head! And how do you think it looks, you sitting there with a nearly naked man?"

"Don't be so square, Beth."

"I'm not being square! *You're* being stupid and irresponsible. We don't know anything about him! I'm sorry, he'll have to go."

"He's totally stoned, you can't send him out in the cold now."

"And that's another thing! You're bringing drugs into the house too! What about Danny?"

"What *about* me?" Beth hadn't heard Danny come in, but he was coming up the stairs, closely followed by Eden, whose pretty cheeks were flushed with the cold.

"Your mother is objecting to my friends," Bill said, affecting the air of a man badly wronged.

Tim Carter appeared in the doorway, having apparently regained the use of his legs, which were very long, very white and very bare. "Shall I skin up another, Bill?" Eden and Danny both stared.

"Be right with you," Bill said, ushering him back into the sitting room and closing the door firmly behind him.

Danny looked at his mother. "Tell me I didn't see what I just saw," he said.

"You saw it all right." Eden's eyes were practically standing on stalks. "Your grandad's got himself a toy boy!" she said. "He is so *cool!*"

"He isn't a toy boy," Beth said, appalled at the very idea. "He's a homeless person. Apparently."

"So Bill thought he'd bring him here and let him wear my dressing gown?" How typical of Danny to finally decide to care about the hated dressing gown.

"That is so cool!" Eden repeated. "Though Bill's taste in music is very, very suspect." They could hear a long-forgotten anthem of the anti-Vietnam War protest days blasting out from the sitting room. Suspect, indeed.

"The problem with Grandad," Danny opined, "is that he isn't very streetwise."

"It's hard to be streetwise when you aren't even used to streets," Eden said. "But he ought to be a bit more circumspect about who he talks to." She was scarily sensible sometimes.

Danny was clearly bored with this topic already. "Anything to eat, Mum? We're starved."

"I don't know, I only just got in. Look, why don't you help yourselves to whatever you can find in the kitchen for now. I need to talk to your grandfather."

The "talk" turned out to be a raging argument. Beth ranted about strange men and drugs; Bill called her "unhip", "square" and various other anachronistic insults. Tim Carter sat silently, staring at them both out of huge, unblinking eyes. Eventually Beth said that she was very sorry, but Tim would have to go. To which Bill replied that if Tim was going, he was going too.

She thought he was bluffing — Bill might be stubborn, but was very fond of his home comforts — but not long after that, while Beth was in the kitchen making some belated preparations for a meal, she heard footsteps going down the stairs and the door slam. When she went to look in the sitting room, she found that Tim had gone, and her father had too.

CHAPTER
THIRTY-FOUR

Fin decided to take a chance on finding Beth at home. He always preferred to take people by surprise if possible. He took the tube: it was usually quicker than a cab at this time of day, he didn't have to talk to anyone en route and could use the time to catch up on reading. He enjoyed reading crime novels, trying to work out whodunit, or why, as soon as he possibly could, the remainder of the story being satisfactory only in vindicating what he already knew. If an author was clever enough to fox him (and still be plausible), they would earn Fin's undying respect and his readerly loyalties. Only a few had succeeded.

He took a seat opposite a pretty young woman with legs a mile long, who didn't exactly smile at him, but widened her eyes a fraction in an interested way and then settled down to trying to pretend she wasn't looking at him. She smiled at him for real when he stood up to give his seat to a woman holding a small baby. The chivalry thing never failed. He smiled back, and then immersed himself in his book. He wasn't interested in picking up girls on public transport, and was more cautious anyway after the Imogen episode. Still, he couldn't help one last glance back at the girl before he got off the train, and noticing that she was staring at him as he walked along the platform towards the exit. He grinned to himself.

Dogwood Avenue might be almost at the other end of the Piccadilly Line from his own home patch of Hammersmith (or Fulham borders, the estate agent had called it), but it was pretty similar in feel: noisy, dusty, filled with faces, languages and costumes from all corners of the world. The words multicultural and melting-pot sprang to mind as he steered around a group of men from Kosovo who were holding an impromptu meeting in the dead-centre of the pavement. Music blared out of the windows of passing cars, vibrating the shop windows, and a gang of loud schoolgirls pretended to collide with him and reeled away giggling. He instinctively felt in his pocket for his mobile phone: you had to always be aware of pickpockets.

It was about ten o'clock in the morning when he rang the Jacksons' doorbell. He wondered if the funny old dad would be wearing another comedy shirt.

Feet thudded down the stairs and the door opened. Beth was standing in the hall, wearing jeans and a T shirt, no make-up and her hair hanging loose around her shoulders, her eyes underlined with dark shadows. Like a witch-woman from the north, he thought. She looked as if she hadn't slept, and it was all somehow so intimate that for a second he had no recollection at all of why he was standing there.

She spoke first. "I thought you were Bill," she said.

"I hope this isn't an inconvenient time . . ."

"No, it's okay. Sorry, come in." She stepped back and allowed him to cross the threshold.

He followed her upstairs to the kitchen, and she gestured to him to sit down at the table. He looked around the spotlessly clean kitchen. Fin had been to the flat plenty of times before, had lived in it himself for a while, but today it looked totally unfamiliar: for the first time, it was homely. The difference amused him for a second, then he realised that Beth was looking seriously agitated.

"Are you okay?" he asked her. She hadn't sat down, but was looking out of the window in a distracted fashion.

She turned back to face him. "You're going to think I'm stupid," she said. "But it's my father. He's been out all night, and I'm really worried."

She looked about to cry, and like most men, Fin was helpless when faced with a crying woman, but he was also calm in a crisis and practical, he told himself. He stood up, propelled her gently to a chair and put the kettle on.

"So where do you think he might be?"

Beth told him about the row the previous day, and how Bill had stormed off afterwards. He hadn't phoned. "I know he's a grown man, and capable of looking after himself, but I fear for his good nature and gullibility. He's got this feeling that London's still in a summer of love haze when clearly everything's moved on and the world's harsher and more dangerous."

"You make it sound a lot more scary than it really is, you know."

214

"All I can think about is the size of this city. It's full of things I don't understand, and what you don't understand makes you afraid." She took the mug of tea that he handed to her and sipped from it without really noticing it was in her hands. "Our whole family was aware — more than most — of the risks in Last Reach: natural risks, like falling from a cliff into the sea, losing your footing. If you were the king of bad luck, you might get run over by the one bus a day. Here . . . well, anything could have happened, and it would be all my fault for making him so angry."

"You can provoke someone as much as you like," Fin said. "How they react is up to them."

"I guess. Doesn't feel that way, though." He sat down opposite her and she smiled at him finally. "Thanks for the tea," she said. "Did you come here for anything in particular?"

Now Fin had a problem. He could hardly say that he'd come to warn her against mouthing off in the *Evening Despatch*, not while she was in this state. "I was in the area, and thought I'd pop in to see if you were settling in okay," he lied.

"Under the circumstances, the answer would have to be I'm not," she said.

"He's probably crashed on a friend's floor, you know," Fin said.

"What friends? He hasn't got any friends. None with floors, at least."

"What do you mean by that?"

Beth explained to him about Tim Carter. "What do you think? Do you think I over-reacted?"

"Certainly not. You can't be too careful who you let into your home, and as you say, you've got your son to think about, not to mention Gareth's flat. I can't see him being too impressed that you're setting up a shelter for the homeless in his property."

"Charity doesn't begin in his home then," Beth said, and he wondered if she remembered that Gareth's charity was what had brought her here in the first place.

Fin was acutely aware that he had masses of work to do back in the office. But he couldn't leave Beth: she seemed too lonely and out of her depth, not self-possessed like she normally was.

"Should we ring the police?" she asked him.

Fin shook his head. "They wouldn't do anything. He's an adult, and he's been gone less than twenty-four hours."

"You think I'm being silly."

"I don't think you have any real reason to worry, but I certainly don't think you're being silly."

"I suppose I'm a bit overprotective," she said. "But Bill and Danny are all I've got. Look, you're probably busy, I shouldn't keep you. Thanks for letting me rant on."

"Any time," he said, then remembered that her ranting was exactly why he was here. He opened his mouth to say something about it, but she was looking at him in an odd way, as if she trusted him, like he really was being a help to her, and there was something about her face that made him feel a little bit softer than usual. This was unprecedented: when he was in work mode (and when wasn't he?), emotions weren't anywhere on

216

the agenda, he couldn't afford them to be. But there was something about Beth . . .

Then the phone rang.

"You didn't have to come with me, you know." In truth, Beth was highly embarrassed to have Fin involved in any of this at all, but she'd been in such a flap and not known what to do, and he'd called a cab and been so kind, and somehow he just came along too.

She wasn't exactly sure where they were going. Somewhere near Battersea Dogs' Home, she remembered the man on the phone saying, which seemed appropriate enough. Fin had gently taken the phone from her and taken all the details. Beth didn't know what to expect when they got there, and for that reason she was glad she had company.

Fin was reassuring. "It doesn't sound as though he's come to much harm," he said. "It's easy enough to get into trouble when you don't know your way around."

"If it was Danny, I could believe you. But this is my *father* we're talking about — a grown man! He should be at home doing the crossword and growing old gracefully, and instead I'm on my way to pick him up after a hard night clubbing, like some bloody teenager."

"Parents are designed to be embarrassing. You should meet *my* father."

This was the first time it had ever occurred to her that he had parents too, or even a real existence of his own outside of being the man who pulled Gareth Dakers's strings. "Your father can't be as bad as mine," she said, hoping for some extra information.

"Don't bet on it. Though if you asked him, I expect — no, I *know* — he would say that it's me who's the black sheep of the family."

"But you have such an interesting career! All this politics, and mingling with the rich and famous, and in and out of TV studios. He should be proud."

He didn't reply to this. Beth looked out of the window at London crawling by. The traffic was, as usual, practically at a standstill, although the taxi driver seemed to know a lot of short cuts.

She suddenly realised they were driving past the Houses of Parliament. "Wow! Look!" she said, like any excited tourist. "Big Ben!"

"A lot of people make that mistake," the taxi driver said. "Big Ben is actually the bell inside the tower. You can't see Big Ben from the outside."

"Pedant," Fin muttered, and grinned at Beth.

"Have you ever been inside?" she asked him, and the driver started to reply but Fin slid the glass between him and the back seat closed.

"Quite a few times," he said. "It's like a church inside. Well, outside too, I suppose. Very archaic looking — the MPs even have a place to hang their swords, though these days they're strongly discouraged from carrying one." He smiled. "You should put it on your list of places to visit."

"I will," she said. "I suppose you'll be in there all the time when Gareth gets elected."

"Oh, not me. My job is just to get him in there, then I guess I'll move on to something else."

218

They were crossing the river, and the view in both directions was beautiful. The Houses of Parliament, St Paul's, the enormous London Eye, with Battersea Power Station to the other side. Like a postcard.

"This is how I thought it would be," Beth said. "This is what you think of when people say London." He was smiling at her, in the way that people do at children while they're opening their Christmas presents, indulgent and pleased, as if the view was something he'd created himself, just for her. Beth remembered Martin looking at her like that, any time he did something especially nice. But there was really nothing else about Fin that reminded her of Martin. He was quite the opposite of him in almost every way.

He slid back the window between them and the driver. "Right just along here," he directed. "This is fine, thanks." They were apparently in the middle of nowhere, a row of warehouses set under railway arches, a seedy, deserted sort of area.

"Are you sure?" the driver wanted to know, addressing Beth. Perhaps he thought Fin was about to murder her.

"Sure," Fin said. He paid the driver, who went on his way. "Didn't think you'd want Mr Tourist Guide's input when we find your dad," he said.

"But how will we get home?"

"I've already called Paul. He's on his way."

They walked along a dirty and greasy pavement overhung by derelict-looking warehouses and some

219

boarded-up shops. It looked totally deserted, but no less threatening — Beth felt that at any moment someone could jump out at them from the shadows, demanding money or worse. She glanced at Fin. He was tall, but he didn't look particularly muscular, and she wondered how much use he'd be in case of attack. Though he had a confidence about him which was reassuring, a don't-mess-with-me way of walking that would deter anyone from picking a fight with him. She hoped that was the case, anyway.

A little further along the road there was a small greasy spoon café, and they went in. There was Bill, slumped over a table, apparently sound asleep. Beth rushed over to him. The proprietor wandered over, a huge man with a round belly, who would have been the right size and shape for a Santa Claus outfit although he was rather too menacing to have carried off the ho ho ho. "Does 'e belong to you?" he demanded. She nodded, and Fin steered the proprietor away again, while she concentrated on her father.

"What have you been up to?" she said, as he groggily opened his eyes.

"Oh, Beth, what are you doing here?"

"We came to get you, you prat," she said, not knowing whether to hug him or yell at him or what. He didn't seem to be hurt, anyway, which was a relief. "The person who rang said you'd been mugged."

"Well, not mugged, exactly. More ripped off, you might say."

"Ripped off?"

"Tried to score a bit of dope, and apparently asked the wrong people. Got into a bit of a ruck." He held up his right hand. The knuckles were grazed.

"You weren't fighting? What are you like? You're over sixty years old, for heaven's sake! What the hell are you doing in night clubs, trying to buy drugs and picking fights? You could have got yourself killed!"

"We were only having a good time."

"We?"

"Me and Tim. Where's Tim, by the way? He was here a minute ago."

"I might have known. Look, I told you Tim was trouble."

"You're really square, you know that?"

What was she going to do with this geriatric lager lout?

CHAPTER
THIRTY-FIVE

As the only female member of the *Northlands Herald*'s editorial team, Imogen had the privilege of having a tiny toilet cubicle for her very own use. It came in very handy when she had to make or receive phone calls she didn't want Nigel overhearing.

Sitting elegantly on the toilet seat, puffing at a cigarette to block out the smell of Toilet Duck, she said, "So what have you got?"

The man on the other end of the phone laughed. "Sore bloody feet and aching legs for one thing! Bill Turnbull is a hard man to keep up with. The other night I actually fell asleep in a club, and he was still dancing. Though he does complain a lot about the music. He's been trying to educate me about what he calls 'real' music, all these sixties guitar bands, and do you know *some* of them . . ."

Imogen cut in, impatiently, "But did you dig any dirt on Gareth Dakers? Has he been to visit? Do they talk about him?"

"I haven't actually seen him. They don't mention him much, either."

"But have you asked the grandad any actual questions about him?"

"Of course I have! I know my brief, Imogen. But I can't come across as too obvious, can I? I didn't find out much that would be any use to you, frankly. His wife spends all her time having beauty treatments and stuff, and they didn't get on very well with her to begin with. *He's* okay, from what I hear. The one they have most to do with is some guy called Finian Lewis. Do you know him?"

"Indeed I do. Dakers's press guy. Bit of a smart-arse." And the rest, she thought.

"That's the one. Well, between you and me, he seems to have taken a bit of a personal interest in the lighthouse family."

Imogen raised an eyebrow. "Really? That is interesting. If he's keeping tabs on them it only confirms my suspicion that they're involved in something more than meets the eye."

"Something?"

"Something to do with the coastal defences in Northlands. It's a vague hunch, but that's what I'd bet on. And I'm going to be the one to break the story."

"You're really serious about this journalism thing, aren't you?"

"You bet I am! What are you saying?"

Tim Carter paused a second or two before replying. "Imogen, you're my sister, I know exactly what you're like. And I've never known you to stick at something for longer than, what? Five weeks. That goes for jobs, taste in fashion, hairstyles, men. And whatever your latest fad is, Daddy bankrolls it for you."

"That's not fair," she pouted, and imagined her half-brother's face mirroring her own, the same pout, slightly exaggerated for comic effect. He was an actor, after all. "Okay," she admitted. "It was fair, up to a point. But not now. I really feel as if I can succeed at journalism — and I'm going to do it on my terms, and no more handouts from Daddy."

"Admirable. But speaking of handouts . . .?"

"You'll get your cheque, don't worry. As soon as you find me something really juicy."

CHAPTER
THIRTY-SIX

Lorelei was dearly hoping that her next meeting with Paloma Percival would be more relaxing than the last. No mention of guns, at least. She even thought about cancelling the appointment, but she was almost positive that the veneer on the nail of her left hand middle finger was coming away, and she'd been warned that if water got underneath the veneer then mildew could form. The thought of having mildewy fingernails made her feel so sick that she'd called Paloma for an emergency appointment.

The nail technician breezed in with her immense case of tools and potions, looking like a beautiful, exotic bird going on holiday. They settled down to business, at either side of a very pretty reproduction lady's writing desk that Lorelei one day planned to use to write her satirical columns on.

"You've been working too hard, darling," Paloma said. "These nails are designed to withstand practically everything. You haven't been *washing up*, have you?"

"Good God, no!" Lorelei was horrified.

"Gardening?"

"It's November," Lorelei pointed out, rather proud that she knew November was a bit of a lull in the gardening year. "I *have* been up north, though. Would that have made a difference? Change in climate, or water, or something?" She hoped Paloma would say that it did, then she could legitimately avoid Northlands on "medical advice".

Sadly not, though. "Shouldn't be a factor. Unless you've had your hands in detergents. You might be a little run-down, I suppose. The nails can be an early indicator of ill-health." She peered at Lorelei's nails as if they were crystal balls, even though none of the natural nail could be seen. "So what on earth were you doing in the north? One of these country house weekends, was it?"

"I wish. We were house-hunting in the constituency."

"You aren't moving, are you?" Paloma was distinctly unhappy at the thought that one of her best customers might be about to decamp to the regions.

"Officially, yes." Lorelei lowered her voice, even though they were alone in the house. "Though I'm going to do my damnedest to spend as little time there as possible."

"Quite right, too. There's an entire cosmetic and alternative therapy ecosystem down here depending on your continued presence."

Lorelei was pleased with the idea that so many people were depending on her. She couldn't help being a little wary of Paloma this morning, though, and finally had to ask her. "Did you . . . did you do what you were talking about?"

"What was that, then?"

"Get a . . . you know, a *gun*."

"Oh, that. Yes, I did, and I must say I feel much safer now. Though I draw the line at keeping it under my pillow. I have some friends who do that, you know, in case a masked intruder climbs through the window under cover of darkness and attempts to molest them. But I would be scared of it going off and shooting my head off. There'd be blood and goose down everywhere, ghastly mess."

Had Paloma always been unhinged, or had her madness only arrived when she became "tooled up"?

"So where do you keep it at night?"

"Oh, the old classic, bedside table drawer. It's within easy reach should the worst happen. Then for daytime use it simply pops into a handbag or a pocket." She made it sound like a handkerchief or a telescopic umbrella.

"But what if someone steals your handbag?" Lorelei asked, glancing warily at said item of luggage on the floor as if it might explode.

"Aha. Well, I have the solution to that, too. Allow me to demonstrate." Paloma picked the handbag up, gave the carrying strap a hard yank, and the bag started to screech like a derailed train.

Lorelei clamped her hands over her ears. "Turn it off, for heaven's sake!"

Paloma opened the bag, and rummaged inside for an off switch. The bag continued screeching, and her face lost its look of confidence. "I'm not exactly sure *how* to turn it off!" she bellowed at her cowering client.

"Get rid of it then!" Lorelei yelled, gesturing frantically at doors and windows. Paloma ran out of the room, clutching the bag to her abdomen like a fly-half intent on scoring a try, and the siren sound diminished until it reached a more acceptable level.

Paloma returned. "God, it's loud, isn't it?" she said cheerfully. The bag screeched to itself somewhere in the distance.

"Where did you put it?"

"In the small guest bathroom under a pile of towels. I must give the manufacturers a call and find out how to defuse it. You can see why I'm quite confident it won't get nicked, though. You can padlock it to table legs in restaurants too, if you want to. I don't do it myself, though, because I keep forgetting the combination."

Demonstration over, she sat back on her chair, picked up an emery board and reassumed her professional poise. "I'm surprised you don't have some security gadgets yourself, being a woman with such a high profile. Does Gareth carry a weapon?"

"No, he does not!"

"That does amaze me. I bet the Prime Minister packs a pistol. Or maybe not, actually, he's always got armed bodyguards around him, hasn't he? Did I ever tell you I went out with a bodyguard once? Gorgeous body, very fit. The relationship didn't go too well, though, sad to say. When he should have been gazing deep into my eyes he was scanning the exits. That's no way to woo a woman."

"Indeed not."

Lorelei thought that, if it had been her, the bodyguard would have had no option but to look at her. But then, Paloma may be beautiful but she didn't quite have Lorelei's — what was the word? — presence.

"So will you be getting a gun yourself?"

Good grief, the woman was obsessed! "I shouldn't think so," Lorelei replied. "I do martial arts."

This was true only in a strictly technical sense, and Paloma knew it. "Tai Chi is not going to save you if you're cornered in a dark alley by a gang of youths intent on rape."

"I'm very seldom to be found frequenting dark alleys," Lorelei said. "Not the kind favoured by youths intent on rape, anyway."

"Name me an alley that isn't reeking with criminality and I'll show you a corridor in the Vatican," Paloma said. "If you change your mind, and decide you want a weapon, just give me a shout. I've got contacts, if you know what I mean, and I could get you fixed up in no time. Unfortunately, it's not cheap."

"Money isn't a problem," Lorelei said defensively.

Badly needing to change the subject, she spotted the pile of magazines on the coffee table beside the sofa. She'd ordered extra copies of *Today's Woman*, because this was the edition that featured her and Beth in this very house.

"I must show you this, Paloma," she said, springing up from her seat and fetching a magazine.

Paloma looked at the four-page spread. "What a shame," she said.

"What?"

"You've got your hands completely hidden in this one." She pointed at a shot of Lorelei lounging on one of the pink sofas. "After I went to all that trouble."

"But they're not bad pictures, are they?" Lorelei said.

"Very nice," Paloma agreed. "Is this the lighthouse chick? Smiles a bit too much, doesn't she? Looks rather too eager to please, in my opinion."

Lorelei looked at the photographs of Beth, and remembered the fun they'd had doing her make-up, and how much they'd laughed.

"She's lovely," she said, and realised that it was probably the first time in her life she'd ever said anything nice about another woman. Particularly an attractive one.

CHAPTER
THIRTY-SEVEN

As the car slipped from motorway to A roads to B roads Fin felt himself shifting down several gears and his speedy city persona dropping away. It would be no use to him here anyway; it would only be antagonistic. He drove past bare fields and leafless trees, even a windmill standing like a cut-out against the cold blue sky, and none of it registered: he might as well have been driving past artificial, painted scenery or billboards. This was the landscape of his youth, and it was meaningless to him, he felt no sense of coming home. Quite the reverse in fact — London was where he felt most like himself, and was the place he would have called home had such a concept occurred to him.

He parked the car right outside the two-up-two-down terrace in which he'd been born. His parents didn't own a car, so the parking space was almost always free.

As he went inside (the door was never locked in the daytime), he smelled something delicious cooking. In the kitchen, his father was crouching in front of the oven, inspecting its contents. He straightened up when he heard the door open. "You came, then."

"I wouldn't miss Mum's birthday."

"You've missed loads of her birthdays." His father's voice was like Fin's, except that Fin managed to keep the Yorkshire accent subdued for most of the time, and in his father it was the dominant feature.

"Well, I wouldn't miss her sixtieth, then. It's a milestone, isn't it?"

"I doubt she thinks so. Another year closer to death's how she sees it."

"That's cheerful." And your words rather than Mum's, he thought. Miserable bugger.

"Did you bring her a present?"

"I wasn't sure what she'd like, so I thought I might take her shopping tomorrow."

"You're stopping, then?"

"Just for tonight. If that's okay."

"It's all the same to me. Your lord and master can spare you, can he?"

Fin chose to ignore this. "What are you cooking?"

"Swordfish. Never tried it before, and I know your mother's going to say it's too fancy, but I like trying new recipes out."

Cooking had been one of the hobbies his father had taken up when he'd lost his job as a miner. It was as if he'd chosen deliberately to take up something feminine as a way of emphasising the blow to his male ego. Even though he'd been in full employment practically ever since, he still referred to that time as "losing his job". When you were a miner, had been a miner since you were barely a grown man, and your father before you, and then the pits all closed down and there weren't any

232

miners any more, that sort of thing changed your outlook on everything.

His mother appeared in the doorway. "Finian! I thought I heard voices. What a lovely surprise!" She threw her arms around him and gave him a hug, then thrust him to arms' length to look at him. "Are you eating enough? You look pale."

"I'm fine," he said, wondering how old you had to get before this kind of fussing stopped.

"You're staying, I hope?"

"Just for tonight. I have to meet Gareth in Northlands tomorrow. Various Christmas things going on." He waited for his father to mutter something about him treating the place like a hotel, but he didn't, perhaps out of deference to his mother on this occasion.

The meal was strained, as these things usually were whenever Fin visited his parents. He was fairly close to his mother — in the sense that he knew that his presence meant a lot to her on her birthday anyway — but with his father, things were difficult to say the least.

"So how's the campaign going then?" his father asked him, in a voice dripping with sarcasm, which his mother caught and tried to deflect with "Finian hasn't come all the way up here to talk about work."

Fin replied, "It's going pretty well. Can't see we're going to have much trouble, anyway."

"Any old face can get into politics these days," his father grumbled. "Kids with the right degree from the right university and no life experience at all."

"That hardly applies to Gareth."

"And careerists only in it for themselves, I was going to add."

Fin caught the look on his mother's face, warning him not to rise to it, but he couldn't help himself. "What do you think, he's running for Parliament for the glory? Or the money?"

"People like that hate to be out of the limelight."

Couldn't really argue with that.

"You've got such a good brain," his father said, changing tack. "But you waste it putting your energy into idiots like that. If he gets elected, it'll be you who did it, not him, but you won't be by his side when he's in that division lobby, will you? He'll be on his own then, with his own sense of what's moral and what isn't, such as it is."

"He's not Jack the Ripper, you know. He's an ordinary man, with pretty much the same kind of morals as you or me."

"As you, maybe."

"Meaning?"

"Meaning, the way you can work for a party that betrayed your class and your heritage."

"I'm not working for a party. I'm working for one individual. And things have moved on since 1985, you know."

"Don't I bloody know it, and you'd know it too, if you hadn't ponced off to London first chance you had." He put down his knife, as if he was afraid he might use it as a weapon if he kept hold of it. "I've been a union man all my life, made more sacrifices than you'll ever know to help the lot of the working man."

234

"Oh, listen to yourself," Fin said, his voice now icy. "As I recall, it was Mum who made most of the sacrifices, while you and the brothers were manning the barricades."

"Women are part of the struggle, too," his mother reminded him.

The conversation grumbled on in this vein, until at last the meal was over. Fin volunteered to do the washing up. His mother, despite his father's protests that "the lad could do it himself" insisted on drying.

"Don't pay much attention to your dad," she said, when they were alone. "He's proud of you really. We both are."

Fin snorted. "That's pride, is it?"

"He's from a different world, love. You know what the miners' strike did to him. It changed everything."

"He's had nearly twenty years to get over that."

"But he's a union man. That's how he was raised. He looks at what you're doing, and it's not politics the same way he knows it."

"What good would it be trying to pretend that things were the same as before Thatcher? It'll never be like that again. And just because I'm not in a union and going on picket lines doesn't mean I've got no morals."

"I know you have morals, my love, but what worries me and your dad is where the morals come on your list. Some way under ambition and enjoying playing the game is how it looks from here. But you're a good man and you'll do the right thing in the end."

Fin smiled at her and handed her another plate to wipe. As he washed up he gazed out of the kitchen window and wondered why he bothered putting himself through this when elsewhere there was work to be done.

CHAPTER
THIRTY-EIGHT

While Beth was settling in to her new job, she didn't get to see much of Danny. They were both out all day and he was out most evenings — doing what, she wasn't sure. When their paths did cross, she took the opportunity to ask him about school.

"It's okay," he said.

"It must be a lot different to your old school," she said.

He shrugged. "Not really," he said. "I just keep my head down."

She asked him what he got up to in the evenings, and he just said, "You know . . . stuff." Beth wondered if "stuff" was a euphemism for something he shouldn't have been into, but she couldn't get a great deal more out of him than he'd been out with Eden doing "stuff".

Carey was reassuring on the subject. "Eden's a very sensible girl," she said. "She's lived in London all her life. She's savvy, she won't get into any trouble."

"Do you think they're — you know — a couple?"

Carey laughed. "Do you mean are they having sex? Who knows? Did you tell your family what you got up to when you were sixteen?"

"There wasn't anything much to tell. There wasn't anything to be getting up to where I used to live."

"There were boys, I bet."

"One boy. My husband."

"You were married when you were *sixteen*?"

"No, I mean he wasn't my husband then, he was my boyfriend."

"And were you having sex?"

Beth thought back. She couldn't remember exact dates: all she knew was that everything had happened in its right time. Usually Carey would have pressed a point like that, but she let it go this time with a tiny shrug. "Whatever. But Danny and Eden are really sensible. You don't need to worry."

"Then why won't he tell me where they go and what they do?"

"They're young." This was amusing coming from Carey, who wasn't that far into her twenties herself. "They need their secrets."

Beth still wasn't convinced. "Maybe I ought to ask Bill to have a man-to-man talk with him."

"Oh, that's a bright idea!" Carey said. "The one thing guaranteed to have him clam up tighter than a clam! And it should be Danny having a word with Bill, if you ask me."

She had a good point. Since the incident when Beth and Fin had had to pick him up after his disastrous night out. Bill had been a bit quiet and tended to stay at home more, and he hadn't brought any strange people home with him, but generally Carey was right that it was Bill who was the liability and not his grandson.

So Beth decided to relax and trust Danny to act responsibly. Then he performed a horrible act of self-mutilation.

She came in one day to find the bath was absolutely filthy. Not just the usual standard of filthy — a bit of soap scum, the occasional hair — that would normally have had her reaching for the bleach. This was absolutely disgusting, the bath tub circled with a thick ring of blue-black scum. There were further circles of frothy murk on the bathmat and across the floor. They led to Danny's room. She knocked sharply on his door.

"Go away!" he yelled.

"Danny, it's me. What's all this mess?"

"Oh, shit." There was a scrabbling sound, and after a moment or two the door opened. Her son stood there in just jeans, his head wrapped awkwardly in a filthy towel, his neck, bony shoulders and forehead stained with the same inky blue-black as the bath.

"Danny! What the hell have you done?"

The towel slid off, revealing his once beautiful reddy-brown hair now dyed an unconvincing black. While Beth should have been yelling at him and doing righteous maternal indignation (and at least getting him to clean up the bathroom) she did something else instead — she burst into tears.

It turned out to be far more effective than shouting. Danny looked mortified. "Mum! Don't cry. What's the matter?" Beth still blubbed. He was nearly blubbing now, too. "I'm sorry, Mum," he pleaded. "I'll clean it all up."

"Your hair!" she sniffed. "Your lovely red hair!" Exactly the same colour as Martin's had been, that was why she was crying. Every time something more of Martin was taken away, it felt as if he was slipping more and more into the past and soon there wouldn't be anything left of him.

A little while later, she'd calmed down, and she and Danny cleaned up together, like when he was a toddler and he'd spilled something or crayoned all over the kitchen table, and she would give him a cloth. He used to look so sweet, scrubbing away clumsily at the mess, clutching the cloth in his little fat fist. Beth would completely forget to be angry with him and they'd giggle together.

They mopped up the bathroom, she stuck the bath mat in the washing machine, and managed to get the worst of the dye off his skin with liberal amounts of the make-up removing cream that Lorelei had given her when she made her over for the magazine. His hair dried and looked sleek and glossy, though quite startling with his pale skin and sea-coloured eyes.

"So what's the deal?" Beth wanted to know. "Are you trying to look like Marilyn Manson?"

"What? Oh, yeah, I guess so."

"It's going to be very high-maintenance, you know. Your roots'll be through in no time." And hurrah for that, she thought.

240

"Just leave it, will you?" he said. Beth didn't know whether he liked his new hairdo or not, but it was obviously a touchy subject. He muttered something about meeting Eden, and left the house.

CHAPTER
THIRTY-NINE

There was work to be done in the offices of the *Northlands Herald*, only Imogen wasn't doing it, in the sense that she wasn't even thinking about the obituary of a local poet she was meant to be working on. She was using a quiet moment in the office to do some digging about Gareth Dakers. She was positive that there was more than altruism or a simple drive for publicity behind his offer to the lighthouse family. His reaction to Beth Jackson at the meeting had been knee-jerk and panicky. So whatever it was had something to do with the Last Reach lighthouse.

Tim wasn't getting very far. He seemed to have been spending all his time hanging around with Bill Turnbull and having a good time as far as Imogen could make out. He only reported nice things about Beth Jackson (Nigel Packman would have approved) and nothing at all about Gareth Dakers. He did tell her that Fin had mysteriously arrived with Beth to pick Bill up after a night on the town with Tim, which Imogen interpreted as meaning that Fin and Beth were spending time together independent of Dakers. She pulled a face at that idea.

Anyway, Tim had his orders — dig some dirt or the cash cow was going to run out of juice (glory be, those metaphors again). Meanwhile, there were the *Northlands Herald*'s archives to be combed through. Not a rich source of pickings if you wanted scandal and corruption, but there ought to be something there. She scanned through all the computer files. Hardly anything under Last Reach Point lighthouse, except the odd advertisement for the bed and breakfast offered there, and before that the tragedy which had claimed the life of Martin Jackson and the rest of the crew of the Jeannie-Beth.

Despite herself, Imogen couldn't help her eyes pricking with tears as she read how the boat had failed to arrive back in port at the expected time after a violent storm, and how lifeboats, and helicopters from the nearest RAF base, had joined in the search. How a few small pieces of wreckage had eventually come ashore, but no bodies were ever found. A photograph of Martin Jackson and the others who were missing: the picture was a little fuzzy, but she could see a look of Danny Jackson in his father's lively, handsome face. She almost felt sorry for Beth, until she remembered that she was comforting herself very well with Finian Lewis by the sound of things.

Imogen repeated her search of the computer archive, this time looking for Carver Bay. She found a short few lines about a bid to buy the land behind the bay at a knock-down price because of the coastal erosion. The prospective purchaser was a company called CWM. She looked this up on the companies register, and found that CWM was Colber Waste Management, director one Mick Colber.

A quick Google search for ["Mick Colber" "Gareth Dakers"] didn't just link them — it put them together at so many different parties and meetings that they were practically Siamese twins.

"Gotcha," she breathed.

CHAPTER
FORTY

It had been a normal morning at the grotto: Beth had had to mop up a small pool of wee generated by an over-excited child, had to deal diplomatically with several stroppy parents who thought the queue was too long, or the entrance charge too expensive. Some objected to the presents-from-Santa being gender differentiated ("How does Santa know that little Juliette wouldn't like a toy truck?" a particularly unpleasant specimen demanded to know, oblivious to little Juliette's protestations of "Wanna Barbie!"). Her co-elf Barbara almost sparked a race riot when one person asked if they had a "Santa of colour" and she said Santa's coat was bright red and how much more colour did they need.

Beth was chatting to Joe in the grotto during one of his biscuit breaks, when Barbara came in, all hustle and bustle and jingling from the bells on her shoes.

"We've got an odd one," she said.

"Odd in what way?" Joe asked, checking his beard for crumbs with a hand mirror.

"Probably a perv," she said. "This bloke out in the queue. No kids with him, looks completely out of place.

Will you come out, Beth? I might need reinforcements to deal with him."

Beth followed her out of the grotto and into the twilight world of the queue, which zigzagged back and forth like a queue in a big post office, except this one was overhung with a net of twinkling lights. Barbara was right: in the sea of tiny tots and their parents, Fin stood out a mile.

They sipped hot chocolate in the garden centre's café, which was under a canopy but otherwise outdoors, and therefore bracingly cold. Fin was wearing a heavy dark overcoat on top of his habitual suit.

"You don't trust me any more, do you?" Beth said to him. "You think I'm going to write all sorts of dangerous subversive stuff, and you want me to be 'on message'."

"How could you think that?" He blinked innocently at her, which didn't fool her for a second. "Okay, I'll admit you're half right," he said.

"Which half?"

"Well, all of it, really. I did come to talk about your next column, but that's only half the reason why I'm here."

"The other half being?"

"I've never had hot chocolate with an elf. I'm just disappointed that you're not wearing a hat with a bell on it."

"I left it in the grotto." Since the rest of her elf costume was covered by her coat, she could pretty much pass for a human being rather than one of

Santa's little helpers. "It wouldn't do for the children to spot an elf drinking cocoa with a mere human," she said.

"I'm *mere*, am I?"

"Possibly — but are you human?"

He grinned at her, and blew on his hot chocolate. She rummaged in her bag and passed over the piece of paper with the scribblings for her next newspaper column on it. This one was about her favourite Turkish convenience store, and how the proprietor was having a hard time staying in business. Beth thought it was a shame that little shops like that had to stay open for longer and longer hours to stay in business at all, and she tried to buy things there as often as she could.

Fin scanned the words. "Nothing too controversial here," he said. When he passed the piece of paper back to her she noticed again that he had very long, elegant fingers, which made her think of Martin's great shovel-like hands, all callused and rough. Which in turn made her wonder why, every time she noticed something about Fin, she immediately thought of Martin.

CHAPTER
FORTY-ONE

It was Paloma's gun that did it. It triggered a change of heart, Lorelei thought, marvelling again at her skill with a pun. Her only female friend turning into a gun-toting crazy woman just served to highlight her lack of friends and social isolation.

So she decided to take on Beth as a project. The big drawback to Beth, of course, was that she was a bit too good-looking, and therefore a bit of a risk factor where Gareth was concerned, but Lorelei had thought of a brilliant solution. The other risk factor to her marriage was the heinously attractive Dr Harrison Shah; if she set him up with Beth, that would remove two lots of temptation in one fell swoop, and she would be free to enjoy both of them as friends.

Beth had been wallowing in widow's weeds for too long. It was time for her to get back on the romance scene again, Lorelei informed her when they met for lunch. Beth had been ridiculously pleased to be invited for lunch, which was most gratifying. Lorelei was thrilled with the scheme already.

After listening to her whinge on about her wayward son, who had decided to dye his — let's face it —

ginger hair black (a decision Lorelei privately applauded), Lorelei introduced the topic of romance.

"I'm not interested in romance," Beth protested.

"Nonsense," Lorelei replied. "Every woman is interested in romance, and you're in your prime of blooming youth."

"I'm *forty*!"

"You're younger than Madonna and Sharon Stone, and just look at them. Not to mention Joanna Lumley, Tina Turner, Cher. There are ways of turning back time, and I know just the man who can do it, not that I think you need it yet. Eyebrow reshaping, yes, but not a face-lift."

"I'm not quite sure what you're talking about," Beth said.

"No matter. But you can't honestly be telling me that there hasn't been anyone since your husband?"

"No, no one. Although someone did ask me to marry him recently."

"What? Who?" Lorelei leaned forward, hungry for gossip.

"Oh, an old friend in Last Reach. Harry. He proposed to me, just before we moved down here."

"And you turned him down? Whatever for? What's he like?"

"He's a policeman."

"Never mind, you can't have everything. Do go on."

"He's kind, dependable, and quite handsome, really, in a Nordic sort of way."

"Blond and blue eyes? A little bit Björn Borg? Yum. So why did you turn him down?"

"Because I don't love him."

"Love? At *your* age?"

"What do you mean, at my age? You were just saying how young I am."

"You're old enough to be pragmatic, is what I mean. And when a dependable Viking asks for your hand it's churlish to refuse, I would have thought."

"But my husband, Martin — what I felt for him, well, it was huge. Loving Martin took up all the space in me."

"So logically, after his departure you should have been left with a vacuum, and nature abhors a vacuum."

"But that's not how I felt, or feel. I still feel full of love for Martin, whether he's here or not. Like whenever he went to sea, I didn't stop loving him just because he wasn't there. This isn't any different."

"You need to have a few sessions with my shrink, Mr Goldstein," was Lorelei's opinion. "Seems to me you're in denial. Goldstein'll help you move on."

"I don't want to move on," Beth said. She could be annoyingly stubborn sometimes.

Which all meant that Lorelei would have to be rather more subtle than usual in her matchmaking attempts. Anything too blatant would have Beth running a mile, she knew.

"Let's forget about men altogether, then," she smiled. "And do something purely for ourselves. You must join me at my health club. We'll have a pampering day: we can get those eyebrows of yours sorted out a bit . . ."

"Why do you keep going on about my eyebrows?"

250

"They're the frame to the eyes. Imagine a beautiful window with a grungy old pelmet."

"My eyebrows aren't grungy."

"No need to be embarrassed. They simply need a tiny bit of tidying up and your face will be quite perfect. It's called grooming, and if you're going to be in the media spotlight it's something you need to learn. Anyway, as I was saying, we'll spend a day at the Haven, and I promise you, you'll feel much better afterwards."

Beth thought that if she was going to spend a whole day at this Haven place Lorelei was so keen on, she'd better get a few supplies in to keep the family going in her absence, so she took herself off to the supermarket.

She was now pretty cool about supermarkets, but the first few times she'd visited one, it was as if she'd taken some kind of mind-altering drug that had stretched perspectives to a silly degree. The fruit and vegetable aisle on its own would have happily encompassed the very biggest food shop that Boldwick had to offer, and it made her feel very ignorant and provincial. She'd managed to get through forty years thinking onions were onions. Okay, she was aware of spring onions, and even red onions — from those magazines Linda gave her — but there were so many different kinds of onions in this supermarket that you could imagine universities dedicating entire departments to the classification and study of them. And she used to think bread was pretty much bread. In Linda's shop, it came in white or brown. In this one it came in white, brown, Best of

Both, granary, wholemeal, ciabatta, focaccia, bloomer, cholla, German rye, Danish rye, Polish rye, and one with linseeds in it that was supposed to help with the menopause.

She soon learned you had to deal with a supermarket like you'd skim-read a boring-but-useful book: dash through as fast as possible while taking care not to miss the bits of interest.

Even so, she always bought too much, and then regretted it when she had to lug it home. She was on her way back, loaded down with carrier bags, the wind (Force 5) against her, wishing she hadn't bought quite so many potatoes, when a voice behind her said, "Do you want some help with those bags?"

Beth turned round, and Tim Carter was standing behind her, bundled up in a grubby green parka which didn't prevent his waif-like face from looking pinched with cold. He smiled winningly.

"I'm fine, thanks," she said grimly, shifting the bags from one hand to the other and trying not to wince at the deep red lines scored across the insides of her fingers.

"Look, I'm sorry for what happened to Bill," he said. "It was all my fault, I should have been keeping an eye on him, he doesn't know his way around."

"But instead you just dumped him."

"I rang you first," he said. "I made sure he was okay. It would've made it look worse, me hanging around."

"So why are you back now?"

"This is my patch. It's the area I know best."

"And of course it has nothing to do with Bill?"

"He's a good bloke, your dad. I didn't mean any harm to him. We were just having a laugh. Is he at home?"

"I don't know," she said.

"Could I just pop in and say hello?"

"I'm a bit busy." She started to walk on. But Bill had been rather down since his escapade in Battersea. He'd stopped his jaunts around town, and even toned down his wardrobe somewhat. Beth weighed up whether Tim's presence would do more good than harm, and then handed him one of her carrier bags. The lightest one: he didn't look strong enough to carry any more. They walked back to Dogwood Avenue.

Tim and Bill greeted each other like long-lost friends, and Beth was completely won over. She was unprepared for the sheer niceness of Tim Carter, who very soon had her sitting listening to his life story.

He was orphaned at the age of eight (he said), no other family to look after him, in and out of foster care with a parade of nutters, left school without qualifications and by his own hard work (he emphasised this point) ended up as boss of his own wheelie-bin disinfecting company, which was doing okay until his local council gave up wheelie bins and reverted to black bags.

"I warned them the place would soon be infested with rats, but did they listen? Did they chuff. And the place is overrun now, rat capital of London."

Beth shuddered. She'd heard that in London you're never more than nine feet away from a rat, but it was something she tried not to think about. "So what did you do next?" she asked.

"I tried moving to the next borough where they still had wheelies. Trouble was, they also had the Dukes Boys."

"Who are the Dukes Boys?"

"Two of the hardest blokes in the whole of the wheelie-bin disinfecting game. It was their turf, you see, and there isn't room for more than one wheelie-sanitising outfit in an area."

Bill chipped in, "Tell her about your car."

"Woke up one morning, there was a bloody wheelie bin through the back window of my Astra," Tim said. "Didn't need to be Inspector Morse to work out who was behind that one. Anyway, one thing led to another, till I ended up homeless, jobless and living rough, begging for loose change. It's a comedown, believe me."

"That's terrible," Beth said.

"Stuff happens," he replied, draining his cup and placing it carefully on the floor. "Thanks very much for the tea," he said, aiming a smile that was as dazzling, in its own way, as Gareth Dakers's smile, at both Beth and her father. "But I don't want to be a bother to you. I'll be getting off."

"You don't need to rush off yet," Bill said. "You'll have to stay for some dinner at least."

"Well . . . if you're sure. Is that all right, Mrs Jackson?"

"Beth. Yes, I suppose so. I don't know what we're having though."

254

Tim ended up staying for dinner, then overnight, then he more or less moved in. He was so sweet, and got on with all of them so well, that Beth couldn't really object. But she had to make one condition. "No more dope smoking," she said, more to Bill than to Tim. "I don't want illegal drugs of any kind in here, is that understood?" They both nodded like naughty schoolboys.

CHAPTER
FORTY-TWO

Beth was getting used to things she'd never expected to have to deal with in her life, such as writing a weekly newspaper column, having her photograph taken, even a couple of times appearing on television, but nothing prepared her for the Haven. The word "plush" had been invented just to describe that place. It symbolised and defined the word like nothing she'd ever known before. Not that she had anything to compare it with: there isn't much that's plush about lighthouses.

The doors of the Haven were solid, heavy oak, but you hardly got a chance to find out before a uniformed lackey would sprint forward to hold them open for you. The carpets were softer and deeper than anything she'd ever seen. It was all designed to pamper and soothe and relax.

"I've put you down for a facial, a seaweed wrap and an eyebrow shaping," Lorelei said. She seemed obsessed with Beth's eyebrows. "And then we're having lunch with the most adorable cosmetic surgeon."

"Are we? Does he work here?"

"Occasionally. More often in a hospital, I believe, but certain procedures are carried out here. Much more civilised."

256

"I've never met a cosmetic surgeon before."

"You're in for a treat, then, dear, but first let's get you looking at the top of your game."

They spent the rest of the morning being ushered from one treatment to the next. Beth didn't fancy some of the more exotic-sounding things: there was no way she was going to submit herself to Intense Pulsed Light, no matter how many wrinkles it claimed to shift, and she declined the seaweed wrap, but a haircut and a swim in the spa pool sounded quite pleasant.

And after all that — lunch.

Now, was it her imagination, or was there some sexual chemistry between Lorelei and the cosmetic surgeon? Dr Harrison Shah was a very attractive man. He had beautiful almond-shaped eyes and a way of smiling that was similar to his namesake Harrison Ford — one side of his face smiled a bit more than the other and his face all crinkled up. It was very endearing. He was all charm, politeness and general loveliness. Beth could see why his patients flocked back for more of whatever he did: a man like that could make even being injected with paralysing toxins manageable. Not that it appealed to Beth, though: if this was intended as a way of getting new customers, she wasn't going to be wooed on to his treatment table by any amount of charm.

But there was definitely something between him and Lorelei. Though he was very attentive to Beth, his gorgeous asymmetrical smile was most usually directed at Lorelei. He was solicitous about everything from her choice of food to whether she'd experienced any tenderness after her last treatment (what treatment that might be was professionally skirted around). It might have been that he was merely concerned as a doctor to a patient. She was clearly a regular here and must spend a huge amount of money, so in a strictly business sense it was astute of him to be nice to her, but there was more to it than that, and she was responding. She kept trying to divert the conversation back to Beth, but very quickly it would slide back to something between the two of them and Beth was left feeling like a gooseberry.

As soon as he'd gone back to save the face of the next woman who was too rich to wrinkle, Lorelei said, "What do you think? Divine, isn't he?"

"Very nice," Beth said.

Lorelei beamed widely. "I knew you'd love him! We must get something organised — a little dinner party at home, perhaps. Give you two a chance to get to know each other."

"What?"

"Well, you said he's very nice."

"It doesn't mean I want to get to know him, not in the way you mean anyway. Is that what this has all been about? Are you matchmaking?"

Lorelei laughed her best tinkling, insincere laugh. "Not at all."

"Because you do realise he fancies you."

Did Lorelei blush? It was hard to tell under the perfectly applied foundation, but Beth suspected she did. "What makes you say that?" She looked as pleased as a teenage girl hearing that the class heart-throb fancies her.

"The way he looks at you. It's easy to see. He fancies you. And you," Beth didn't know whether she ought to say this but she'd always been one for speaking her mind, "fancy him."

"I do *not!*" Lorelei protested. Then a moment later she said, "Well, no, in fact I do fancy him. You'd have to be dead from the neck down to not fancy a man like that."

"Isn't it unethical, though? He's your doctor, after all."

"Don't think it matters with this kind of cosmetic thingy. But it's not as though anything's going to happen, anyway. It's just a bit of flirtation, which is marvellous for one's self-esteem."

"But what about Gareth?"

"What about him? It's not like he's never looked elsewhere."

Beth hadn't wanted to mention that, even though it was widely known about the weather girl and everything. "But isn't it . . . No, it's not my place to say."

Lorelei was looking a bit riled now. "No, go on, say your piece." Sometimes, when her guard was down, she could sound uncannily like Betty Cooper, doyenne of the Northlands Pig Farmers' Guild.

"Well, I think it's a shame, that's all. You're married — do your vows not mean anything to you? What about cleaving only unto him?"

"He's not been much of a cleaver himself, has he?" she said.

"So is this about revenge? Tit for tat?"

The other woman sighed. "It's about feeling attractive and noticed and interesting and important."

"To a man you're paying for whatever beauty treatments. He's *paid* to treat you like that, Lorelei, it's part of his job."

"And you're so worldly wise suddenly, are you?"

This wasn't turning out well at all. They were supposed to be spending the day being pampered, and instead they were squabbling like a couple of teenagers. Beth felt she got a lot more sense out of Carey, who was half her age, than Lorelei, who was old enough to know better but too vain to acknowledge it.

"I think I'd better go home," Beth said.

"Home? Back to my husband's flat, you mean. If we're talking about people being nice to you because it's their job."

Beth wished she could have thrown a handful of money down on the table like people do on TV, to pay for the day's "pampering", and make a stylish exit, but she knew there was nowhere near enough money in her purse to make a gesture like that. Anyway, she hated to walk out in the middle of an argument; it made it so awkward the next time you saw the person you were arguing with. And she felt sorry for Lorelei Dakers: despite all her money and her good looks, she wasn't at all a happy woman.

She took a deep breath. "I'm really grateful to you and your husband," she said. "I don't want to offend you." Lorelei's bottom lip stuck forward like a sulky child. Beth wondered if she'd had one of those lip-plumping injections she'd read about in the Haven's glossy brochure. "I think Gareth is a really nice man."

"Most women do," Lorelei said.

"But he's with you. That counts for a lot."

"Oh yes. The dutiful little woman on his arm routine counts for ever such a lot, career-wise."

"Is that all you think it is?"

Lorelei sighed. "No. I suppose not. There are plenty of high-profile examples who've traded in their wife for their fling, and the fling becomes the wife. But Gareth and I somehow stay together, not that he makes much effort."

"It seems to me that it's *you* who doesn't make much effort." Why did Beth have this tendency, whenever she got safely to the edge of the pond, to set straight off back to the thin ice again?

"Why do you say that? I'm always keeping myself nice for him, I make sure I'm looking my best."

"For what, though? You should be in Northlands with him, helping him to meet and greet, wowing the locals with your charm and beauty. You'd be such an asset to him up there."

"You've been spending too much time with Fin," Lorelei remarked.

Now it was Beth's turn to get defensive. "Why do you say that?"

Lorelei looked at her searchingly. "Aha!" she said. "I simply meant that you were beginning to talk like a damn spin doctor, but I see from your reaction that it goes a bit deeper than that."

"No, it doesn't. I just agree with him on that one thing."

"He is rather attractive, I suppose. In a vulpine sort of way."

"Why don't you like him?"

"Put simply? He's the competition. These days Gareth doesn't have another woman — at least none I know of — he has Finian bloody Lewis."

"He's helping him to get elected. You should be supportive."

"Beth, I've listened to plenty of advice from you today, and don't think I haven't been taking it in. Now let me give you some. Don't trust Finian Lewis one inch. He's a cold fish, completely career-minded. If he needs to be somewhere and you're in the way, if he can't get round you he'll go straight through you."

Beth remembered those words — briefly — when Fin rang that evening and asked her out.

CHAPTER
FORTY-THREE

Sometimes — most of the time, in fact — being a spin doctor was distinctly unglamorous. This was chiefly because the life of a wannabe politician is not a glamorous or exciting thing. Much of Gareth and Fin's time was spent schlepping between local radio stations giving soundbite comments, making appearances at WI meetings (plenty of scope for coming unstuck there, as Tony Blair had discovered, but Fin prepared Gareth's scripts carefully), photo opportunities wherever possible, fielding invitations from everyone ranging from the useful to the barmy nuisance. Anyone who ever had an issue was coming out of the woodwork and wanted their five minutes with the prospective MP.

Annoyingly, one of the issues that kept coming up was the coastal erosion. Fin had hoped that the lighthouse family might be the only people who actually cared about the cliffs crumbling into the sea, but it seemed not. A local ramblers' group was getting quite vocal on the subject, and the regional branch of the RSPB could prove to be a thorn in the side.

"I think you need to give some thought to the coastal erosion business," he said to Gareth, as they drove through an unpleasantly sleety morning to a Northlands primary school to watch a nativity play and present some prizes.

"I've talked to the local councillors," Gareth replied. "They seem persuaded that it's not worth the expense to do anything about the sea defences to the north of the coast, if that were possible anyway. And that university bod you dug up didn't have much to say."

"You're getting a lot of letters about it."

"I'm standing as Member of Parliament, not King bloody Canute. The sea's the sea. It's big. It does damage. It's probably global warming to blame, but I can't do much about that on my own either." He glanced at his right-hand man, who was looking stressed. "Don't worry, Fin, I'll make all the right noises, do some convincing clucking. But don't expect me to take it on as an issue, because there are more pressing issues in this constituency. Sometimes I think you spend too much time with Beth Jackson. She's like a one-woman lobbyist and she's certainly got *your* ear."

Fin sighed. "I thought inviting Beth and her family to stay with you would be like having a mini-focus group right there in the house. Seems a shame to ignore everything they say."

Gareth grinned. "It's hardly a representative focus group, though, is it? A widow, a sullen teenager and a pensioner who've lived in the back of beyond all their lives."

"The back of beyond being your future constituency," Fin reminded him. "Tell you what, why don't I knock up a questionnaire leaflet, and we'll do a bit of a

264

house-to-house and get some feedback about what people think."

"Fin, will you let this drop? That sounds like the biggest waste of time you could ever dream up."

"But it's something you're going to get asked about. It would be better to have a more positive position on it than 'I'm not King bloody Canute.' " He peered left and right at a totally anonymous junction. "Any idea which way we go now?"

"Isn't strategy *your* job?" Gareth's voice was sarcastic.

"I meant navigationally speaking. You must have got the lie of the land a bit while you were looking for houses." He made a decision based on instinct and turned left. "So how did you get on with the house-hunting, anyway?"

"We've made an offer on a crumbling heap on the edge of the moor. Rather grand, actually. One could imagine grouse shoots and that sort of thing."

"Very man of the people. Trust you not to go for an 'umble terraced dwelling. Does Lorelei like it?"

"Adores it. She couldn't wait to get back to London to start interviewing decorators and so on."

"Couldn't you have used someone local? It would look a lot better to be giving employment to people in the area. You still haven't got the hang of this, have you?"

Gareth gave him a look. "Can you really imagine my wife settling for whitewash and wood-chip, or whatever the local yokels can manage? A house like that demands skill and expertise. So she says, anyway."

"But if you'd used local decorators, that's another clump of the electorate you'd have reached without breaking sweat."

"I reckon I'm doing okay without having to get a gang of manual labourers on-side."

"A gang of manual labourers with wives, children, parents, friends, customers, drinking companions. You can't afford to alienate a single person."

"I'll mention it to Lorelei."

"And she ought to be here with you, Gareth."

"You know what she's like. She's even less suited to rural life than I am. She's used to having all the shops and everything."

An ominous-looking stretch of grey had appeared on the horizon.

"Oh my God — is that the sea? I think we've gone the wrong way," Fin said. "Have a look on the map, will you?" He shoved a road atlas at his passenger who peered at it cluelessly. A road sign was coming up, the first Fin had seen in some time. LAST REACH, it said. "Shit. Thought it was looking familiar."

"We're not meant to be in Last Reach," Gareth said helpfully.

"I know that." Fin slowed the car and was about to turn around, when he saw on the horizon a distant white tower. The Last Reach Point lighthouse, looking all at once like a dream castle, and like the most solid and permanent thing he could imagine. He kept driving towards it.

"Fin? Aren't we going the wrong way?"

"We've got enough time. I want to look at the lighthouse."

"Why?"

Fin didn't reply. He just kept driving towards it. The kiddies of St Catherine's RC Primary School's re-creation of the miracle of the first Christmas could wait.

The lighthouse looked ethereally beautiful with the wintry morning sun behind it, the paintwork gleaming white, the glass at the top of the tower sparkling, the grey sea glittering behind. Fin got out of the car and walked towards the gate that opened into a small courtyard area, enclosing the tower and three cottages, one of which had previously been Beth's home. The wind was cold and damp on his face, salty and uplifting. He saw that the gate was fastened shut with blue and white tape, the kind that the police use to cordon off murder scenes. It lent a sudden bleakness to the scene, as did the signs that had been put up on the sides of the buildings saying warning, danger, no access, no entry. It was a condemned place.

The sound of the sea urged itself on his ears, reminding him of childhood holidays at the seaside, where he would walk for miles by himself in the little waves and it felt as if he was all alone on the planet, just him and the sea. It made him feel like the smallest, most insignificant speck on the planet, though being tiny and insignificant was a comfortable feeling when you were next to the sea. He couldn't remember the last time he'd done that. More recently, visits to the coast had meant Spanish and more latterly French beaches, where the sea was less important than the nightlife, the girlfriend he was with or the tan he was trying to acquire.

But now it comforted and soothed him, somehow, and it made him sad that Beth had been forced to leave such a lovely place.

He heard the car door slam, and Gareth approaching. "What are you doing?" his boss complained. "We're going to be late for the school thing, and you're mooning about here."

"Why couldn't the council put some sea defences on this coastline?" Fin said, more to himself than to the other man. "Look at it. This shouldn't be allowed to disappear."

"It's not worth the money to shore up a coast that has nothing on it."

"But it does have something on it! It has this," he gestured up at the lighthouse.

"Fin, I don't even hear the Jackson family complaining about this any more. They seem quite happy to be living in civilisation. I can't quite see why you've suddenly got a bee in your bonnet about it. You're meant to be the cool customer, the shrewd analytical type."

"Doesn't mean that I have to stand aside and watch the good things in life being brushed aside," Fin said, and he wondered if he was really talking about the lighthouse, or about his own life.

"Nativity plays are one of the good things," Gareth said firmly. "All those adorable kiddies. So let's get

268

going." He turned back to the car, and after a last glance up at the lighthouse tower, Fin followed him.

A police car was coming down the track towards them, slightly faster than strictly necessary, Fin thought. The local constabulary playing at being macho, no doubt. The police car stopped in a position that would prevent their own car from leaving, as if it was the end of a high-speed car chase and they were trapped. A tall, uniformed officer climbed out of the driver's seat, settling a cap over his bright blond hair. "Can I ask what you're doing?" he asked, addressing Fin; Gareth was already in the car. "You're not exactly dressed for rambling."

Oh, well done, Sherlock. "And the presence of a car would indicate we aren't rambling," Fin said. "Officer . . .?"

"Sergeant Harry Rushton, Northlands East Division. So do you mind answering my question?"

"I was looking at the lighthouse."

"It's closed."

"I realise that. However, I didn't realise it was illegal to simply look at it."

"It's dangerous. We don't want people coming to any harm."

"How thoughtful. Now if you don't mind, we're late for an engagement."

The policeman looked at the car, and saw Gareth for the first time. "Mr Dakers," he said, nodding respectfully. Gareth returned the nod. Then Harry Rushton turned back to Fin and said, "Why didn't you say you were with Mr Dakers?"

269

"You didn't ask."

Fin waited for the policeman to indicate he was about to move his car, but he didn't, he stood there as if he wanted to say something. Gareth opened his window. "If you don't mind, officer, we do need to be going."

"Of course. Sorry. But I was wondering . . . How is Beth — Mrs Jackson — doing? Is she all right?"

"She's fine," Gareth said, and Fin, noticing the look on the policeman's face and the softness in his voice, thought: aha, there's some history between the two of them. He found he didn't like that idea.

"When you see her, will you pass on my regards? Tell her Harry's asking after her."

"Harry. Yes, will do," Gareth said. "Now, if you don't mind, we are on our way to a meeting. I don't suppose you know where St Catherine's RC Primary School can be found?"

"That's in Anford, about three miles back. I'll give you a police escort if you like."

"Good man. Splendid."

As the police car pulled away in front of them Gareth remarked, "Looks as though you've got some competition."

"What?"

"It seems you're not the only one interested in . . . the lighthouse."

CHAPTER
FORTY-FOUR

It had been a while since Beth last saw Fin. He and Gareth had been up in Northlands attending various functions, including school nativity plays, Lorelei had told her with only barely concealed derision. Beth wondered sentimentally whether one of the schools visited might have been the one that she and Martin, and then Danny, had gone to, and wondered if they were going anywhere near Last Reach, but apart from that she didn't really give it too much thought.

Though she did find herself thinking a lot about Fin. About how everyone said he was cold and conniving, but to her he'd been really kind, like when he'd arranged for them to move to Dogwood Avenue, and being so concerned and tactful when Bill went missing. He was a lot nicer than she'd expected him to be, and he was often on her mind.

Then, out of the blue, he rang her. "I've been visiting your lighthouse today," he said. Beth felt a little jump in her stomach, and didn't know whether it was because he'd mentioned the lighthouse or because of his voice which at that moment sounded like something sexy played by John Coltrane. "Beth? Are you still there?"

"Yes, sorry. So the lighthouse is still standing, is it?"

271

"It is. And being heavily defended by the local constabulary. Some sergeant called Harry. Who sends his regards."

There was what they call a pregnant pause, during which she realised he was waiting for more information on Harry, which she decided not to give him just now. Whether this was because of Lorelei's warning or loyalty to Harry she didn't know, but she kept quiet and eventually Fin said, "Gareth and I get back on Friday evening. I wondered if you would be free for dinner on Saturday."

What was this? Was he asking her out? Or was he just planning to grill her for more information about the constituency? Either way, she wished he'd built up to it more gradually, so she could have had a sensible response ready. What she ended up saying was, "I'm not doing anything else," which sounded horribly rude, particularly because the idea of being taken out to dinner by him was scary but very appealing.

He didn't seem to notice her brusqueness though, because he said, "Excellent. So where would you like to go? Name it, and I'll take you. Anywhere at all."

Beth didn't have to think for long. There was one place she'd always wanted to go, somewhere that to her represented the best, most glamorous and most magical aspect of London.

"I've always wanted to see Baker Street," she said.

A pause. "Sorry? What did you say?"

"Baker Street. It's in London."

"I know where it is, but I wasn't really aware of any particular restaurants . . ."

"I don't mean restaurants. I don't know about them. It's just that song, 'Baker Street', by Gerry Rafferty. It always sounds so . . . I don't know, haunting, sad, but in some kind of clean and renewed way. I always wanted to see it." Now he was laughing, and she felt angry and embarrassed. "There's no need to laugh," she said.

"I'm not laughing at you, really I'm not. It's just that I'd never thought of Baker Street like that. Are you sure that's where you want to go? I have to warn you it's perhaps not as magical as you're expecting."

She couldn't back down now. "Even so . . ." she said.

"Okay. Baker Street it is. I'll pick you up at seven-thirty."

CHAPTER
FORTY-FIVE

St Catherine's RC Primary School nativity play was a popular event that year. The audience included not only the adoring mummies, daddies and grandparents of the participating tots, the school staff and governors, but also their prospective parliamentary candidate. And wherever the prospective parliamentary candidate went, the press were not far behind. Including, on this occasion, Imogen Callow-Creed.

She made a bee-line for Fin. "We meet again," was her somewhat unoriginal opening line.

"Indeed."

"The campaign seems to be going well."

"Very well, thanks."

"Rumours are that the election is likely to be in May. What's your feeling about that?"

"I would think May is quite likely. That's what we're aiming towards anyway, but we'll be ready any time."

"Any chance of an interview with your man?"

"I wish you'd contacted me earlier," Fin said, his face doing a fairly good job of mock-regret. "We have to dash off as soon as this is over."

"What a pity," she said, her eyes cat-like. "Only I've been hearing some strange rumours about sea

274

defences, and your man's part in same. Wouldn't have minded a chat about that."

"Would you mind telling me what you've heard?" he asked.

She smiled at him, and pouted. She really did have a very beautiful mouth, Fin thought, and she knew it. "You don't play poker, do you, Mr Lewis? Otherwise you'd know it's best not reveal your hand too soon."

He laughed.

"What?" she said.

"You sound like a B-movie villain, that's all. You should try that line with a Russian accent; it'd be almost sexy."

He turned on his heels and rejoined Gareth, who was about to take his place in the audience for the nativity play.

The play was yawningly boring. The parents loved it, but if you had no particular emotional involvement with the tiny actors you were unlikely to be overly amused by the fluffed lines, the stubborn silences, the "donkey" that insisted on standing right in front of the crib until a teacher had to drag it to one side, and a Joseph who seemed to be suffering from an ongoing head-lice situation.

Fin's mind wasn't on the play, and nor was it on whatever Imogen was playing at. All he could think about was Beth, and her funny request to be taken to Baker Street. He feared she was going to be horribly disappointed. What was Baker Street, after all? Madame Tussaud's, the Planetarium, the usual raggle-taggle of shops selling tourist tat, American fast-food places, and a lot of traffic. Out of all the places she could have chosen, all the fancy restaurants, the beautiful backdrops of London (and it did have lots). He would take her to Baker Street, she'd see it was depressingly mundane, and he'd have trodden all over her dreams. He hated that idea.

He wished he was a film director. He could bring in scene artists to decorate the place, light it all very tastefully, perhaps add more trees, more birds, a rainbow overhead. Make it a proper setting for her. But he knew that life wasn't as magical as the movies. Hell, even the movies weren't as magical as the movies — he thought of *Singin' in the Rain*, and poor Gene Kelly having to dance through diluted milk with his raincoat and umbrella, because water didn't show up well enough on camera. What looked like the most joyous, romantic, carefree song and dance routine in reality had the stink of old cheese.

Well, he wasn't a film director, but he prided himself on being able to manufacture diamonds out of glass. Baker Street would be a challenge, but he'd find the best restaurant, make sure they got the best table in that restaurant (invoking Gareth's name if showbiz persuasion might help), the best food and wine brought to that table. He laughed at himself — he couldn't ever remember being so keen to impress a woman. But then, there'd never been a woman like Beth Jackson.

He realised the play was over, and the audience was starting to disperse. Back to work: Gareth posed for photos with the delighted parents, and also with the children for the benefit of the photographer Imogen had brought with her from the *Herald*.

Afterwards, Gareth and Fin were due to have lunch with the man who was going to be Gareth's election agent, Damien Kelly. Fin liked Damien — he was out of the same box as Fin himself, young, enthusiastic and prepared to do whatever it took.

They met at the Three Horseshoes. Damien had already occupied a table, and was halfway down his first pint when they arrived. He stood up to greet them, a stockily built figure of around five feet six, with lively black eyes and a quiff.

"How was the play?" he asked.

"You've got kids," Fin said. "I assume you know."

The other man grinned. "The wife normally goes to that sort of thing. I plead work commitments."

"Too bad it came under the remit of work commitments on this occasion," Gareth remarked. They ordered from the Three Horseshoes' limited menu of "plain but fair fayre" and Gareth went to the bar to obtain a pint of the local brew each for Fin and Damien, and a glass of red for himself.

While he was gone, Fin had the opportunity to mention what Imogen Callow-Creed had hinted at about having something on Gareth regarding the sea defences. He expected Damien to sweep it aside, but instead he said, "I was wanting to talk to you about that. You know what they're building at Carver Bay, don't you?" Fin shook his head. "A whopping great waste incinerator."

"A what? There'll be opposition to that, surely? I thought the majority of councils had moratoria on those things being built."

"Northlands isn't one of them. A planning application has been quietly making its way . . ."

"Quietly? How do you get something like that through quietly?"

Damien gave him a look like he'd always expected a soft southerner would lose his grip at some stage. "Oh, come on, there's ways and means."

"Not entirely legal ways and means, I take it."

"Who knows?"

"And what's this got to do with the sea defences?"

Damien finished his pint before answering. "There are two places the sea is seriously encroaching," he said. "Carver Bay and Last Reach Point. Trouble is, there was only the budget for one set of coastal defences."

"And the money went to Carver Bay, even though Last Reach was inhabited."

"Because Carver Bay is worth more money, because of this incinerator. It's simple economics."

"Shit." Fin knew exactly how this was going to appear. Moving the family out of the Last Reach Point lighthouse suddenly looked a whole lot more suspicious.

CHAPTER
FORTY-SIX

From housing a family of three, the flat at Dogwood Avenue had acquired a floating population of six or seven. Tim Carter had made himself pretty much at home, and Beth had to admit he was very charming company. He was always on hand to help out with any cooking or cleaning, and kept everyone amused with a stream of chatter about his adventures in the wheelie-bin disinfecting trade. Contrary to earlier indications, he was a positive influence on Bill; they still visited night clubs but were usually back at a more sensible hour, and they also spent a lot of time touring London's cultural sights.

Eden had been a semi-permanent fixture for some time, and she was constantly rushing up and down the stairs between the Jackson's flat and Carey's. She was such a sunny, friendly girl and Beth was so thankful Danny had met her.

Danny had brought other friends round, too: a nerdy youth with slightly protruding eyes who was known as Bugs, and a tall, slim and very beautiful Japanese boy with blue-black hair called Satoshi.

"He's gay," Tim whispered to Beth confidently after lunch on Saturday. Danny, Eden and Satoshi (Bugs had a bug and was at home, apparently) had eaten faster than Beth would have thought humanly possible and dashed off out somewhere. Tim was helping her wash up. "That Japanese boy. Gay as a daffodil," he opined.

"How do you know?"

"In my job you get used to spotting the signs."

"In the wheelie-bin business?"

"Erm, no, I meant when you're homeless."

Beth thought perhaps he'd had some bad experiences. He was very pretty himself: he could easily be a target for a more predatory sort of person. So she didn't say anything in case she opened old wounds.

"Have you ever thought Danny might be gay?" Tim asked, obviously not keen to let the subject of gayness drop.

"No." She turned the idea over in her head. "I'm quite certain he isn't. Why?"

He shrugged. "The way he started dyeing his hair and wearing make-up as soon as our Japanese friend came on the scene."

"Wearing make-up?" she echoed, feeling lost.

"Haven't you noticed? He washes it off before you see him, probably, but he's definitely been experimenting with a bit of eyeliner and pan-stick. It gets all over the towels."

"I thought that was Eden."

"She's far too fastidious to leave dirty marks on the towels. You don't notice much, do you?"

"Whereas you notice rather a lot."

"You have to observe people, in my job."

"Wheelie-bin cleansing?"

"Yes. I mean, it'd be boring otherwise, wouldn't it?"

"I guess."

"Anyway," he said, tossing the tea towel across the back of one of the chairs. "What are you going to wear for your big date with the spin doctor?"

"Now *you're* sounding gay," she teased him, to hide the fact that she was blushing at the mention of Fin. "Anyway, it isn't really a big date."

"Normally takes you out for dinner on a Saturday, does he?"

"No." She wished he hadn't said that; she was starting to feel nervous.

She had to admit to herself that she found Fin attractive. It was his aura of being in control, of power and capability. He was also very good-looking, in a completely different way to what she'd normally find appealing, a more polished, urban sort of attractiveness. Maybe that's all there was to it — he was different. Lorelei had advised her against trusting him, and Beth could see her point. She'd seen enough of the way he worked to know that he and the truth were more nodding acquaintances than friends, at least where work was concerned. But she believed that there was a sincerity about him when it came to personal relationships. It was his loyalty to Gareth, and even to Lorelei herself.

So she was looking forward to seeing him, and she was looking forward to being taken out and spoiled a bit. But what to wear? That was a problem. After much deliberation she chose a cherry-red top and a black skirt, and hoped she looked okay. Tim said he approved.

"You should wear red more often," he said. "It sets off your dark hair. And red is a very strong sexual signal."

"What?" Beth was mortified. Sexual signals were *not* what she was aiming to send. Not consciously, anyway.

"Baboons' bottoms, nipples, lips, red light districts. Red is sexy."

"Oh, heck. I'm going to get changed."

"You haven't got time. And you look great. Enjoy yourself."

Enjoy herself? Knowing she was dressed like a baboon's bottom? This date was a disaster before it even began.

Beth had told Fin she didn't want picking up, and that she'd meet him at Baker Street tube. She wanted to arrive there by herself.

She couldn't really explain how she felt about Baker Street. It was that song: it had planted a wistful and dreamy idea in her head that no amount of realism would shift. As far as she was concerned, Baker Street *was* London. She hadn't visited it yet because she'd been waiting for an occasion. Well, she reckoned that her first date with any man other than her husband in the whole of her life counted as an occasion.

She was surprised she didn't feel guilty or treacherous about Martin, but whenever she thought about him that day she felt only a peaceful sort of happiness. She'd always hated people telling her what

Martin "would have wanted", but that day she was confident that he would have wanted her to be happy, even though he may not have understood her on this particular day. His life had always been the sea and always would be the sea, and Baker Street would have held no interest for him.

Having all of these expectations ought to have meant she was setting herself up to be disappointed, but she believed that you find what you want to find.

Beth wanted to find magic, and that's what she got. When she emerged from the admittedly unexciting tube station, it had started to snow. White flakes spun their way out of a darkening sky, and in among the crowd of tourists and Christmas shoppers rushing home were faces lifted up in childlike wonder at the landscape-transforming thing that was happening.

And Fin. She spotted him before he saw her: he was standing in the entrance of the station, half turned to the outside and half to the direction from where Beth was approaching him, and his face wore an expression that she'd never seen on him before. He looked unguarded, and almost sweet. She didn't want to disturb him, but he turned round and saw her, and the expression on his face was all delight.

"It's snowing," he said.

"Told you Baker Street would be magical, didn't I?"

"You arranged it beautifully." He took her hand quite naturally, and led her out into the street, where traffic was already packed solid and due to get worse as the snow came down in a white cascade.

"Where are we going?" she asked him. She was acutely aware of her hand in his, and how intimate it felt.

"We're here," he said. "Baker Street. This is it." He studied her face. "You're not disappointed?" Snowflakes settled in his hair.

She looked around at the brightly lit shops and cafés, sniffing the smell of traffic and snow and perfume and damp coats, tasting snow on her lips.

"No," she said. "I'm not disappointed. It's as lovely as I expected."

Well, it was. That bubbly feeling, that mixture of half happy and half sad, it was exactly like the song, but she didn't think much of it was to do with the location but rather with her past and her strange present and what might happen in the future.

Fin was evidently not a man to be unprepared, and he told her he'd booked a table at a restaurant not far away. They walked along the street, through slushy puddles, talking occasionally but mostly not, which she was glad about because she wanted to savour everything.

Beth hadn't been to many restaurants in her life, and this one seemed dreadfully posh. A very smart-looking woman bustled over to them as soon as they appeared, and whisked away their coats and ushered them into a cosy corner. Beth sat facing into the room so she could look at everything. She felt sorry for Fin, whose view consisted just of her and a rather ugly abstract painting that was hanging on the wall behind her. He didn't seem to mind.

284

He was, as usual, wearing a suit and tie. She realised she'd never seen him without a suit; even when he was at Dakers Acres, prowling around like a panther with a mobile phone, he still wore a shirt and tie. She couldn't imagine how he would look in casual clothes, and thought that that was such a contrast to Martin, who'd only worn a suit for weddings, christenings and funerals. For Martin, a suit meant church.

She gave herself a little mental shake. She was going to have to try to stop thinking about Martin just for a while, especially comparing Fin with Martin, otherwise she wouldn't be giving Fin a chance, or giving herself a chance to get to know him.

They had some wine, which the waiter got Fin to taste before they were allowed to have a proper glassful. He looked ever so expert at it.

"Do you know a lot about wine?" she asked him.

"Not really. Enough to know if I like it and if it's drinkable."

"Do you ever tell them you don't like it and make them take it back?"

"It doesn't often happen, but I wouldn't hesitate if necessary."

She laughed. "That seems so rude!"

"Not at all. They expect it. You wouldn't eat a plate of food that was off, would you?"

"No, but I can tell if food is off. I wouldn't know if wine was. It would probably just be very posh wine, and meant to smell like that, and I'd make a fool of myself."

"And would you mind making a fool of yourself?"

"I think everybody does, don't they? Except not over important things, like Danny or Bill, I'd do anything for them and I wouldn't care if anyone laughed at me."

"I can't imagine anyone ever laughing at you," he said, and she found it so deeply unsettling sitting so close to him and being the entire focus of his attention that she had to faff with her napkin (or was it a serviette? She could never remember) until she could look at him again.

Even Beth could tell that the wine was lovely. It reminded her of Christmas and weddings and joyful celebrations, and when the food arrived that was lovely too, although it was arranged so artfully on the plate it was hard to tell exactly what it was meant to be. She loved looking around the very smart room, at the other people who were all well dressed and young and beautiful and sophisticated-looking. She ought to have felt out of place, but because she'd been to television studios and to the Haven with Lorelei, and she'd come to this restaurant with Fin, she felt quite relaxed. She couldn't believe how far she'd come.

She was so relaxed she even dared to ask Fin why he'd asked her out.

He looked surprised. "I don't think anyone's ever asked me that before."

"Everyone else is probably so pathetically grateful to get your attention that they didn't dare ask," she teased.

"I expect so," he smiled back. "So why the ingratitude from you?"

286

"I'm not ungrateful! I'm just curious. Is the plan to pump me for more information about the voting habits of the Northlanders?"

"I know more about that topic than I'll ever need," he said. "So you can step down from your role as part of Gareth Dakers's in-house focus group."

"So what's my role now?"

"Witty and amusing dinner companion."

"I'll never live up to that."

"You were doing okay until you started probing me as to my intentions. Isn't that supposed to be your father's job?"

"It would be, but he's gone to check out the Ministry of Sound."

"He's what?"

"Well, he's got this friend staying with us, Tim, and . . ."

"Hang on, is this the same Tim that Bill got into trouble with before? The homeless one?"

She nodded. "It's all sorted out now. He's really sweet, honestly. But he and Bill have this constant argument about whether the music of today is as good as the sixties, so Bill's gone to check it out."

"Bit old for that sort of thing, isn't he?"

"He says he's the same age as John Peel, so why not?"

"Fair point, and serves me right for my ageist attitude. I'm still a bit concerned about this Tim person, though. Maybe I should check him out for you."

"We don't need you to be concerned." She tried not to feel cross, but as usual the one thing that was guaranteed to disgruntle her was the thought that someone was trying to take over from her and be responsible for her family. She'd told him that Tim was okay, and that should have been enough.

A waitress popped up and asked them if they would like any dessert. Beth shook her head.

"Maybe in a little while," Fin said, and after the waitress had gone Beth glared at him.

"I said I didn't want any dessert!" It felt as if he really was trying to take over.

"Steady on," he said. "We might feel like coffee in a little while. I just didn't feel ready to leave yet. I was enjoying sitting here with you. Is that all right with you?"

"Sorry. I'm not doing very well at being a — what was it? — witty and amusing dinner companion, am I?"

"You're doing fine," he said. "It seems to be me who's getting it wrong somewhere."

He was getting it more right than he knew. She'd been aware for some time that she was growing to like him more and more. He was different, interesting; he seemed kind and caring but independent and exciting. He was very attractive, and his voice . . . well, it did wicked things to her insides. She couldn't quite work out why such a man would show an interest in her, when he must always be meeting much more suitable women. But the way he looked at her was starting to convince her that there was something happening for him, too.

They got home very late, by cab. Even fortified by the wine, all the way home Beth was in turmoil. She suddenly felt awkward, unsophisticated, and clumsy. She had no idea what was supposed to happen now, what the protocol was. She was forty years old, but less experienced than most teenagers. Romantically, the only man she'd ever known had been Martin, and she had no clue how to behave now or what Fin expected from her. His hand was lightly holding hers, as if they'd known each other for years, but she was aware of every millimetre of touching skin. She was tingling and almost giddy, it was stupid.

When the taxi stopped, he looked at her questioningly. Was this the end of the ride, or would he be needing the cab to get home?

"I'll make coffee," she said, hoping desperately that after screwing up all her courage to say that much he wasn't going to now say that he had to go home because he had an early start.

But he didn't. He paid the taxi driver, and followed her into the house.

It was all dark, and she wondered who was sleeping and who was out. They couldn't go into the living room because Tim would possibly be asleep in there, so they went into the kitchen, which was less risky anyway — no soft upholstery sitting there making suggestive invitations.

Fin sat down at the kitchen table. "It always seems odd being here," he said. "It's so much more homely than when I used to live here."

He used to live in this flat. The picture flashed into Beth's mind of Fin sleeping in her bed — it hadn't occurred to her before — and once she had the mental image of his bare limbs stretched out under her duvet, she couldn't get it to shift.

She turned to switch the kettle on, and began spooning coffee into cups. Her hands were trembling and, knowing he was watching her, the whole operation was trickier than it needed to be.

She heard his chair move, and then she felt him behind her, and his hands resting lightly on her hips.

"I'm making a mess of this coffee," she said.

"Forget the coffee," he murmured into her hair. She turned to face him, and he kissed her. She loved how warm and passionate he was, and felt her body responding immediately to him. She felt happy and desired and wanted him very much, but was too shy to take any initiative — afraid of rejection and almost more afraid of not being rejected and what that would mean and what would follow — but his kiss made her desperate for him to suggest they go to the bedroom, and she wondered if she dared to suggest it herself after all.

Then they heard the front door bang, and footsteps on the stairs. Beth pulled away. "That sounds like Danny," she said. Fin's arms were still around her waist, and hers were still around his neck, and he looked so outrageously beautiful she didn't want to let him go, but she did anyway, because a second later Danny walked in, followed by Eden, Satoshi and Bugs. All four of them instantly took in the situation: Danny's mother looking all flushed and dishevelled, in the company of a similarly flushed man and two cups surrounded by spilled Nescafé granules.

"We were going to make some toast," Danny said. His face was comically horrified.

"Sorry if we disturbed you," Eden said. The other two seemed oblivious to much except hunger, and sat themselves down at the table.

"You know where everything is," Beth said. "I'm just seeing Fin out." Fin gave her a look of quiet desperation that found an instant echo in her own heart, but she didn't know what else to do. They couldn't go to the bedroom now, knowing that her son and his friends would know exactly what was happening.

At the front door she said, "I'm really, really sorry about that."

He took her face in both his hands and said, "So am I. But I'll see you soon." They kissed again, cutting even that shorter than Beth would have liked because she had the idea four little heads might appear at an upstairs window at any moment. Fin went off towards the main road, to find a cab or catch a night bus, and she felt as if part of her went with him.

CHAPTER
FORTY-SEVEN

Beth dashed home from her stint at the garden centre, aching to her bones, looking forward to a long soak in the bath. She'd been no use to anyone all day at work, and had several times handed the wrong parcels to Santa Joe, which meant they had to spend quite a bit of time dealing with the cross parents of cross little boys who weren't pleased to receive a baby doll, and even crosser little girls whose idea of fun was not a plastic robot that transformed into a tank.

"Where's your head at today?" Joe asked her.

"Baker Street," she replied. Her mind was running through every second of her evening with Fin. She couldn't help wondering if he'd been put off by the sudden appearance of Danny and friends. He must have been able to have his pick of any number of young, available, baggage-free women — who was she kidding that he'd really want her, a middle-aged widow with a teenage son? But as she ran over the things he'd said and how it had felt to kiss him, she couldn't escape the thought that something lovely was happening.

Not so long before that she would never have dreamed that she could begin to feel this way about another man. She thought about Harry's proposal, and how at the time she'd felt so far from being able to contemplate being with any man except Martin. In London it was easier to feel that life might be about to move on than it had been in Last Reach. She was beginning to realise that for the last couple of years of her life at the lighthouse she'd been a bit like the Lady of Shalott, imprisoned in her tower.

She was just out of the bath and wrapped in her big towelling dressing gown, when the phone rang. Beth thought it was going to be Danny saying he was running so late he wouldn't be back at all (which was becoming increasingly, and disturbingly, common). Or maybe Fin, she thought with her stomach turning a flipover.

It was Harry Rushton. As if she'd produced him from thin air by thinking about him. When she heard his familiar voice, the northern dialect that she'd grown up amongst for most of her life, the same way of speaking Martin had (though it must be said Martin's language was apt to be rather more colourful than Harry's, but that's trawlermen for you), she surprised herself by feeling a pang of homesickness.

"How are you, Beth?" he asked. He sounded shy and awkward. Beth had hardly ever spoken to Harry on the phone, he always visited if he wanted to talk about something, and the unaccustomed medium made it all a bit difficult.

"I'm fine," she said.

"Really fine?"

"Yes, really."

"So you've settled in down there."

"Yes." It went on like this for a while, small talk. It struck her that it wasn't just that she wasn't used to talking to Harry on the phone. It was that she'd changed in the few weeks since she'd moved to London. The horizon seemed wider (ironic, this, since you hardly ever saw a horizon in London — you saw rooftops). Even though so much had happened to her, there wasn't much of it that she thought Harry would be interested in, so they didn't talk about anything of any consequence. They even talked about the weather. It had been pretty mild in Last Reach, apparently, no more storms, and no more wave damage to the cliffs by the lighthouse. Scant comfort, really.

But he did finally produce a big piece of news. "I thought you should know," he said, "there's been a planning application gone to the council to build a waste-processing plant at Carver Bay. It's going to be a massive thing, by all accounts; you'll be able to see it for miles. Belching out pollution and all that. Ruining the whole area down there."

"That's terrible."

"It gets worse. Rumours are that the company who are responsible have matched funding with the council to reinforce the sea defences at Carver Bay, which used up the whole of the sea defences budget. So that's why Carver Bay got the sea wall, and Last Reach didn't. There was no money left."

Beth's hand clutched the telephone tightly. It was as if the room around her had disappeared and she was standing again at the top of the Last Reach Point lighthouse, looking out to sea, and feeling dizzy from the height. "So they sacrificed our lighthouse to build a waste incinerator," she said slowly. She could hardly believe the unfairness, the sheer stupidity of it.

"I knew you'd be upset," Harry said.

"Upset? I'm angry, is what I am. I feel manipulated and taken for a fool. Harry, what can we do about it?"

"We? You mean you're still interested?" There was a smile in his voice. "I thought you were a Londoner now."

"I'll never be a Londoner," she said, feeling it was true at that moment but conveniently forgetting that most of the time she was bonding with her new home. "I care about Northlands as much as I ever did. So what *can* we do?"

"Well, what about lobbying our future MP for a start? You've got his ear."

"I hardly ever see him," Beth said. "He's always in the constituency."

"The constituency," he repeated. "Is that what we are to you now?"

"Sorry. That's how *they* talk about it, that's all. Look, I'll try to have a word with him, see if he can use his influence."

"That would be great." There was an awkward pause, then he said, "Might you be getting back up here for Christmas or New Year?"

"Don't think so," she said, feeling sad. "We thought about it, but it wouldn't be giving us a proper chance to make a life here if we came back so soon."

"Oh. How are Danny and Bill?"

"Bill is okay, I guess. It's all gone to his head a bit."
She skated over the drugs and the insalubrious
company he occasionally kept; those were not things to
be discussing with an officer of the law. "Danny has
dyed his hair black. It was a shock, but I'm getting used
to it. And he's got a girlfriend."

"Good for him. And what about you? Wowing the
local lads, I bet."

"No!" she laughed, mostly out of relief at the way
he'd phrased the question. She didn't think a date and
a kiss with Fin counted as wowing the local lads. Fin
wasn't even local, if she was being literal.

"I'm glad to hear that. There might be hope for me
yet."

What was she supposed to say to that? After a bit of
an uncomfortable silence she started telling him about
Eden, and about what it was really like on the set of
Cara Chadwick's show, and they laughed together and
it was nice.

"Don't forget to ask Dakers about the waste-
processing plant," he said before they said goodbye.

"I won't, I promise."

"And Beth . . . I'm always here if you need me."

She put the phone down and wandered into the living
room, where Bill and Tim were listening to Creedence
Clearwater Revival.

"This music's crap," Tim was saying.

"It sounds a lot better when you're stoned," Bill said,
and then seeing Beth added, "So I'm told, anyway. Are
you all right, daughter of mine? You look a bit peaky."

"It's love," Tim said.

"That was Harry Rushton on the phone," she said, ignoring Tim's comment and pushing his legs out of the way to make room for herself on the sofa.

"Beth's old flame," Bill said to Tim, winking.

"Will you two give it a *rest?*"

The unusual harshness of her tone wiped the smile off Bill's face. "Beth? What's wrong?"

She told them about the waste-incinerator plan for Carver Bay, and how that was the reason the sea defences hadn't happened at Last Reach.

"A bloody incinerator?" Bill said. "I knew it couldn't be a golf course. No wonder they kept it quiet." Beth had expected him to launch into one of his rants, but his face was just very depressed-looking, and almost tearful, which was far harder for her to cope with.

"Did Dakers know about this incinerator, do you think?" Tim asked.

Beth shrugged. "I wish I knew."

Standing with his back to the window of Gareth's room at the Three Horseshoes (which was twice the size of his own) Fin also wished he knew. He wished he knew where all these rumours about Dakers's involvement in Carver Bay were coming from. The man himself wasn't at all forthcoming.

"You don't really think I'd have anything to do with this?" he protested. "I'm a complete stranger to Northlands! The first time I ever saw the damn place was a few weeks ago when I came up on that train with you. How am I supposed to know anything about their wretched coastal defences?"

"I have no idea," Fin replied, "but they're getting this stuff from somewhere."

"Don't use your evil spin doctor voice on me, Fin. I've told you, I know nothing about it. It's just the opposition digging dirt, you know what it's like."

"Oh, I know what it's like, all right," Fin said. "And I know what *you're* like, and I have to say at the moment I don't entirely believe you."

Gareth was affronted. "Can I remind you who's paying your wages?" he said, coldly.

"Can I remind you what you're paying me those wages *for*," the other man said. "If shit is about to hit fans, I need to know the size, consistency and exact trajectory of said shit if I'm to stand any chance of intercepting it."

"Don't worry, Fin. It'll blow over."

Fin resisted the temptation to laugh at the image that comment produced. "It'll still leave one hell of a mess," he said.

CHAPTER
FORTY-EIGHT

The house on the moors was taking shape, under the guiding hand of Lorelei's chosen designer, Ossie Sailberth. Ossie and Lorelei had co-presented a pilot for a home makeover show several years previously. Ossie's undoubted talent as a designer was seriously undermined by his inability to read an autocue, learn the most basic of scripts or turn up to work either on time or sober, so the hoped-for series was never commissioned, and *Room at the Top: Lifting the Lid on Loft Conversion* never saw the light of day.

Still, Lorelei was used to showbiz types, and this time Ossie wouldn't be required to do any reading or anything much at all except stamp his eclectic vision on the house. He'd already given it a name — within minutes of walking through the front door he was calling it "Bleak House".

To mollify Fin, Gareth had prevailed upon his wife to use local artisans to do the actual work, so the house was filled with the cheerful sounds of a lot of Northlanders swearing, brewing up tea and grumbling over Ossie's esoteric choice of fixtures and fittings. Ossie himself flitted about like an exotic butterfly.

December was probably not the best time to try and get a house in the middle of nowhere redecorated. Bleak House was a long drive from Boldwick, perched on an exposed edge of a north-facing ridge and seemed designed to catch every draught that blew over the moors. Lorelei's first insistence was to have all of the windows replaced with something reliably double-glazed and weatherproof. Triple-glazed, if such a thing was possible.

"But, darling, period features!" Ossie moaned, picking with a nicely manicured fingernail (he was another of Paloma's clients) at the paint peeling off one of the loose-fitting sash windows. "I think you'd regret the loss of these," he said.

"Like I'd regret the loss of a verruca. They have to go. I want PVCu *everywhere*."

Ossie was horrified, but he knew better than to argue with Lorelei. "You're the boss," he replied. He gazed through the window at the landscape beyond. "It's particularly wuthering, isn't it?" he said. "I've never seen anything wuther quite as much in my life." He shuddered and strode off to yell at one of the "manual worker chappies".

Lorelei wrapped her coat more tightly round her and carried on looking out of the window. Gareth was due to pick her up soon to whisk her off to the relative comforts of the Three Horseshoes Hotel in Boldwick (relative comforts here meaning that it had hot water). Tomorrow they would be meeting the mayor of Boldwick for lunch and taking in a performance of *Jack and the Beanstalk* at the Boldwick Alhambra. Lorelei was rather looking forward to this latter event. Although it was bound to be dire, at least it had a whiff of showbiz about it.

When Gareth appeared he didn't look best pleased. In fact, his handsome face was decidedly glum. "What's up with you?" his wife asked him. "It's me who should have a face like a dead porcupine, being forced to spend the entire day without central heating or a home comfort of any description. Though I have to tell you, Ossie has some marvellous ideas . . ."

"Not now," he said, and closed the door of what was destined to be the dining room, so they couldn't be overheard by either Ossie or the workmen.

"Gareth, what is it?"

"The chickens," he said, "may be coming home to roost."

"What? You sound like someone in a Cold War thriller, darling."

"I'm in a spot of bother," he said, his face wearing that confessional look she knew so well. He sat down on an upturned crate.

Lorelei's heart dropped to her calfskin-leather boots. "You're not going to tell me you've done it again?"

He looked up at her. "Done what?"

"Another Windy Wendy." She could hardly say the words.

He sighed, and then a smile spread across his face. "No!" he said. "Nothing like that. It's something to do with the campaign." She kept her own relief in check while she waited for what he was going to say. "A while ago I made a couple of investments, and made quite a bit out of them."

"Which is good?" she prompted, wishing he would get to the point.

"Which *was* good. Until the same company I invested in decided to set up shop in Northlands."

"Don't see the problem."

"There might not have *been* a problem if I hadn't gone and invited the lighthouse family down to London."

"What? Explain this to me properly," she said, dusting off a crate of her own and sitting down.

"You remember Mick Colber? He came to that party we went to on the Thames that time."

"The one that the Duchess of . . ."

"No, the one Cara Chadwick had when her show moved from Manchester down to London."

"I remember Cara getting ridiculously drunk and disgracing herself as usual. I don't remember any — Mick Colber, was it?"

"Just as well, you don't remember actually. Anyway, I met him at that party, and he gave me a bit of investment advice, which turned out to be pretty sound."

"I hope it wasn't anything dodgy."

"Not at all — at least, I don't think so — he seemed to be doing very well for himself, anyway, and he knew what was what. And I needed a bit of extra money around that time."

"To buy off Windy Wendy."

He winced. "Exactly. Anyway, seems Colber's setting up shop in a bit of a venture in Northlands."

"Oh?" Lorelei perked up. If the sort of people who went to Cara Chadwick's parties and were well connected in business spheres were setting up shop in Northlands, maybe it wasn't going to turn out to be such a backwater after all.

"The thing is, it's not a very popular venture. I mean, it's a great money-making scheme, and very much needed, only it's one of those things people never want in their back yard, so to speak. It's a waste-treatment plant or something."

"It's not going to be near here, I hope?" Lorelei said, glancing quickly out of the darkening window as if a load of heavy machinery might have materialised there. She certainly didn't want it in *her* back yard.

"No, it's not here, it's at the coast."

"So what does this have to do with you, and with the Jacksons?"

He explained about Carver Bay and Last Reach Point.

After he'd finished, Lorelei was silent for a moment or two, and eventually she said,

"Darling . . . you're an idiot." Gareth looked stricken. "Does Fin know about this?"

Gareth shook his head. "Only you and I know. We've got to keep it to ourselves, because if it gets out, that's me finished in Northlands." He gestured at the shell of a house they were standing in. "And it would be the end of this. I suppose that would make you happy."

She leaned towards him and kissed his cheek. "It wouldn't make me happy at all," she said.

He was obviously upset, the poor lamb, and spent the rest of the day mooching about Bleak House, making a vain attempt to chat in a blokey fashion to the builders. He was even more useless at this than Ossie Sailberth, who, although he was irredeemably posh, at least could talk authoritatively about building materials and techniques. Gareth strove for a working men's club level of repartee, which produced only blank expressions from the skilled artisans who were busy replastering the kitchen. Gareth was useless without a script.

Left on her own, Lorelei found her thoughts turning to Beth, and what she would make of this story when it came out. She was bound to jump to the conclusion that Gareth had been entirely aware of this plan for Carver Bay all along. And she had that newspaper column and everything; she'd be bound to make a fuss. Worse still, she would think Lorelei had known all about it, too, and would hate her. Lorelei couldn't cope with that idea at all. She decided to give Beth a call.

CHAPTER
FORTY-NINE

"Say that again," Bill said.

Beth repeated what Lorelei had told her. "Gareth previously invested in the company that's developing Carver Bay."

"The bastard!" Bill said.

"Steady on." She'd known that Bill would jump to conclusions. "I said 'previously'. In other words, before this company even thought about Carver Bay. So it's nothing at all to do with him really."

"Except it's partly his money that's financing it," Tim pointed out.

Beth hadn't thought of it that way. "If you give someone money, it doesn't mean you have any say in what they might do with it in the future," she argued.

"But that's how it looks," Bill said.

They argued about it for some time, with Bill of the opinion that Gareth was in some way responsible for Carver Bay, even though Lorelei had said he knew nothing about it, and Beth believing it wasn't anything to do with him. At some point during the discussions, Tim said he had an appointment at the job centre and had to go.

"You're not very dressed up for the job centre," Beth said. She sometimes felt quite motherly towards Tim. "You should at least put a proper shirt on instead of that manky T shirt."

This was what Imogen had been waiting for. That one phone call made her little investment in Tim well worth the money.

"So he *is* in on it after all," she grinned. "Tim, you're a diamond. Anything else, you give me a call."

"I hate doing this," Tim said, his voice almost drowned out by the roar of traffic around the payphone he was calling from. "I feel like falling on my own sword."

"Plenty of time for all that Julius Caesar crap when you're a famous actor, lovey," she said.

"Julius Caesar didn't fall on his sword."

"There you go then. If he could cope with life's little trials, so can you."

CHAPTER
FIFTY

Fin had had a sleepless night. He'd laid in his bed at the Three Horseshoes Hotel, wishing that the election would be called, and he could hand responsibility for Gareth over to Damien Kelly, and get back to London and on to his next job.

London, of course, meant Beth. He realised for the first time that her face and her voice were always in his thoughts, even when he was working. No other woman had ever managed to bridge that divide he made between work life and personal life. Thinking about it rationally (which was the way of thinking that felt safest to him), she'd started off as work — she was linked to Gareth and to Northlands, after all. Following that line of thinking, perhaps it wasn't so significant after all, and perhaps he wasn't falling in love, with all the turmoil that would bring. Perhaps.

It was still dark, barely six o'clock in the morning, when his phone rang. He snaked his arm out from under the duvet. The Three Horseshoes central heating didn't come on for another half hour, and the room was chilly.

"Fin? It's Damien. Have you seen the *Herald* yet?"

"I'm still in bed," Fin mumbled, realising that now it was time to wake up there might finally have been a chance of falling asleep. "Why? What's up?"

"Only front page news about Gareth investing in this waste-incinerator company."

Even before he'd finished the sentence Fin was already getting dressed, as quickly as possible in the bitter air and juggling his phone from ear to ear as he demanded details.

"Oh shit," he said. "This is not good. I'm going to talk to him, Damien." He needed to know how much of this was true, and what else there might be, and decide what their line was going to be. "I'll call you back."

He strode out into the corridor, which ran for the length of three rooms and was carpeted in a nasty brown that was reminiscent of the carpet at Dogwood Avenue. Gareth's room was at the far end. Fin knocked sharply on the door, but there was no reply. He knocked again, more loudly, simultaneously punching out Gareth's mobile number on his own phone. Neither action produced any response. He made for the stairs.

The reception desk at this time of day was staffed by an elderly and rather overweight man who did word search puzzles and ate biscuits constantly. He looked up as Fin approached. "Early bird today, Mr Lewis."

"Morning, Pete. You haven't seen Mr Dakers up and about have you?"

Pete paused to brush some custard cream crumbs from the pages of his current puzzle book. "Hasn't been back all night," he said. "His key's still here."

308

The last thing he needed was to be starting rumours himself, so Fin did a good job of looking foolish and said, "Of course, he was away last night. I'm no use at all till I've had my first cup of coffee."

"Dining room's not open yet," Pete said helpfully. "But you've got tea and coffee making facilities in your room don't forget." The Three Horseshoes advertised this feature prominently and were clearly very proud of their mini-kettles and complimentary teabags.

Fin was about to ask if Pete had a copy of the *Herald* yet, but under the circumstances that wouldn't be the best plan, so he made an excuse about needing a breath of air, and walked out into the Boldwick morning, belatedly realising that a suit jacket was no insulation against the winter chill.

He hurried along the street which bore traces of mist making it look like it must have done in Victorian times. The sky was just beginning to lighten above the mist, and the air had that tingle of excitement about it that for most people would be to do with the approach of Christmas or remembered childhood Christmases, but Fin didn't have anything at all festive on his mind just then.

He grabbed a copy of the *Herald* at the nearest news stand, and read it as he walked back to the hotel. "Sources close to Gareth Dakers" had "confirmed" that he was an investor in CWM, the company who were seeking to build a "controversial" waste-disposal facility in Carver Bay. The byline was Imogen's, and she'd done her homework. There was background on this

CWM, comments from outraged environmental campaigners, and of course she didn't fail to mention the lighthouse family.

"Bugger, bollocks and shit," Fin muttered to himself.

He needed to speak to Gareth urgently. If they didn't act quickly, this story would get out of control, and the comments made by these "sources close to" would be fixed in the public consciousness as the truth. No doubt the opposition had their own people waiting to pounce on something like this. What he needed was to get Gareth's version of the story, agree on their line and put it out as quickly and as widely as possible.

First off, he needed Gareth. But when he got back to the Three Horseshoes, Gareth still wasn't there. Nor was he answering his mobile. Fin tried Lorelei's mobile, which was also switched off. He almost threw the phone down in frustration, but then it started ringing.

"Gareth?"

But it wasn't Gareth, it was Beth.

"What's going on?" she said. She did not sound pleased. "I got woken up by reporters ringing me about this business with Gareth and the waste plant in Carver Bay."

"That got around fast. What have you said?"

She paused, during which time he had a mad impulse to get on the first train for London just to see her, and forget all this Northlands crap. "I didn't say anything," she said. "But that was only because of not wanting to hurt Lorelei. There was plenty I could have said."

"Was there? Like what?"

"Well, it's all true, isn't it? About Gareth investing in this company that wants to build this great, ugly, dangerous thing and smother half of Northlands in pollution, not to mention paying the council so they reinforced the sea defences at Carver Bay and not Last Reach. And then he bought us off by bringing us down here."

Jesus. "You don't really believe all that, just from what these reporters said?"

"I didn't get it from them, I got it from the horse's mouth."

"Gareth?"

"Lorelei. She rang me."

He sat down at the small table that served as a desk in his hotel room, trying to get his head around everything. "Has Lorelei been talking to the press?"

"I don't think so. Why would she?"

"Well, how's all this getting to the *Northlands Herald* then? Unless . . ."

"Are you suggesting it was me?" She sounded seriously angry. "I just *told* you I haven't said anything to the press. I can't believe you would say that."

"Not necessarily you. What about Bill, or Danny . . ."

He didn't get to the end of his sentence, because Beth had hung up the phone. For a second he contemplated ringing her back, but his main priority now was to get hold of Gareth.

CHAPTER
FIFTY-ONE

Lorelei and Gareth had spent the night at Bleak House, their first night in their new home. There was no heating except an electric fan heater, which had whirred dustily all night, no bed apart from the newly fitted carpets, no bedding apart from their coats. This would normally have ruled out sleeping there just as surely as if someone had suggested camping in a minefield, as far as Lorelei was concerned, but the night had turned out to be blissful, almost as if they were newly weds. Better, in many ways: as their wedding had come hot on the heels of revelations about Gareth's former affair with Windy Wendy, it had had all the strained atmosphere of a shotgun job.

They'd sat in the gathering twilight in the room that was going to be their bedroom. Huge in size, it featured a massive picture window (double glazed, as per Lorelei's instructions and much to the horror of Ossie Sailberth) which looked west to the sun setting into an azure sky and disappearing behind the crags of the moor tops.

Lorelei looked at her husband's handsome face. He was looking older, she realised. The showbiz tan and gloss were going, and were being replaced by harder lines, a more stubborn set to the mouth. It was actually rather an improvement, she thought. It was so unfair that men could acquire these lines and look even better, whereas a woman had to have her regular Botox top-up or descend into a crow's feet nightmare.

Gareth sighed again. "The problem is, that it makes me realise how much I want to get into Parliament. It's been a dream for so long, and now I'm finally within a few months of it, and this happens. It's all I've ever wanted, to do some good in the world and give back to people all the good fortune I've been given, do my bit as it were."

She looked at him and couldn't help laughing. "Gareth! Sweetheart, this is me you're talking to, not a chuffing Dimbleby!"

"I'm serious, Lorelei." And she could see that he was.

"Oh, my poor darling," she murmured, and took his head between her hands and kissed his forehead. She loved it on the rare occasions when he actually asked her for help, and let her in on his private business. It was exactly the reason she hated Fin Lewis so much — he was too much in Gareth's confidence, making him more like a mistress than an employee sometimes.

Gareth kissed her warmly, and she felt a rush of love for him like she hadn't experienced in a long time.

"Let's stay here tonight," he said, his throat thick with emotion. "I just want to be away from telephones and microphones and bloody Fin."

"Amen to that," she said, loosening his tie.

CHAPTER
FIFTY-TWO

The press were ringing Dogwood Avenue all morning. Some of the journalists were people Beth vaguely knew or had talked to before, and they were apologetic but still wanting their two penn'orth, while some of the others were less polite, less caring about intruding on her personal life and her day.

Danny ambled out of his room. "We've got paparazzi," he said, like someone might say, "We've got mice."

"What?"

"There's a photographer lurking outside."

Beth went into the sitting room and peered through the net curtains, which were old and ugly, but now spotlessly clean. "I think one photographer is strictly speaking a paparazzo," she said, trying to be calm.

"There's another one behind the hedge."

She couldn't believe it. All of this nonsense had seemed to die away soon after they moved, and she'd thought they were on to a wave of what you might call normal existence.

"What do we do? I need to go out in a bit," Danny complained. "I don't want to get papped."

"With that hair they're going to think I have a reclusive rock star holed up here."

Danny laughed. "Rock star?" he mimicked. "Sometimes you sound so ancient, Mum."

"Well . . . I hate that hair dye. What was wrong with being a redhead?"

"It's part of my career strategy," he said, wandering off in search of breakfast.

She followed him into the kitchen. "What career strategy is this?"

"Never you mind," he said. "All will be revealed in the fullness of time. But I'm not ready for my public yet. Do you think I could go out through Carey and Jon's back door, and climb over some fences to the lane at the end to escape?"

"That's a fine idea. Then you'd get papped on your way to the police station when someone reports a strange-looking youth trespassing on their gardens."

"I don't look strange."

"No, you don't, son of mine. You look adorable."

"God's sake, Mother!"

"Is your grandad around?" she asked him, changing the subject.

"Haven't seen him." He poured cereal to the very brim of his bowl and poured apple juice over it — he was currently in a pseudo-vegan phase. Pseudo because it was very selective. "So what's all this press stuff about?"

She told him about the waste-treatment plant, and Gareth's part in it.

"So have you talked to Fin about it?" he asked.

315

Her heart flipped at the sound of his name, and sank at the thought of the phone conversation she'd had with him earlier. Danny gave her one of those knowing son-to-mother looks.

"I just rang him," she said. "He claims to know less than I do about it."

"Oh, I believe *that*," Danny said. "The man who knows everything about anybody before they even speak. Pigs might fly."

Beth didn't say anything. She felt so stupid, that she'd ever thought Fin could have any real feelings for her, or for anyone, come to that.

Danny munched cereal noisily for minute then said, "You really like Fin, don't you, Mum?"

She wondered what to say. Danny had been so tender and raw since his father's death, there had been times when she didn't know what to say for the best, because most of what she said seemed to make it worse, and he'd retreated into a ball of hurt that she couldn't reach. Since they'd moved to London, like Beth, he seemed to be feeling stronger, and was certainly more outgoing and confident-seeming, but she didn't know how he would take to the idea that she'd been having romantic feelings about another man. Would he think she was trying to replace his father? Because no one could replace Martin, not ever, and she wouldn't let them.

Anyway, that didn't matter any more, because nothing was ever going to happen with Finian bloody Lewis.

"I'm not interested in him at all," she said.

Danny gave her a quizzical look. "Didn't look like that the other night."

She blushed. "It didn't mean anything," she said. "Just your stupid old mother thinking she was young again, being duped by someone who specialises in bogus charm." She could have wept for how sad that sounded.

Someone suddenly started hammering at the door at the bottom of the stairs. "Beth! Come quick!" It was Carey. Beth ran down, closely followed by Danny. Carey was standing in the front hall, and through the frosted glass in the front door they could see several figures outside, and hear a bit of a commotion.

"What's going on?" Beth said.

"It's Bill," Carey replied. "I think he's just come back a bit the worse for wear and got into a fight with the photographer out there."

Beth groaned. "The idiot." She made for the front door, and as soon as she opened it, flash bulbs started going off in her face. This was ridiculous. Jon was there, holding one of Bill's arms, and Tim had the other. They propelled her father — who was looking sheepish — through the front door into the house. Someone pushed a microphone under Beth's nose. Had she any comment about the attack her father had launched on the innocent photographer? What comment did she have to make about being part of the cover-up in the Carver Bay development plans? And variations on these two themes.

She remembered Fin once telling her that saying "No comment" was more or less an admission of some sort of guilt as far as the press was concerned. His strategy, he'd told her, was always that the closest you could manage to honesty was the best policy. So she calmly said that they hadn't had any contact with Mr Dakers for several weeks, had been unaware of the Carver Bay project until yesterday, and didn't believe their move to London was in any way related. To the questions about her father she merely said that she was sure he didn't mean anything and it was stressful to have your privacy invaded.

Then she went back in, careful to double-lock the front door.

The door to Carey and Jon's flat was open, and she went in there. Bill was holding forth. "I just saw red," he said. "It's ridiculous, photographers laying siege to your own home."

"But we've had it before when we first moved here," Beth said, angry that he could have been so stupid. "You know they get bored and go on to somewhere else eventually. Except now what have you done? This is going to be all over the papers."

"Nothing happened," Bill said. "I took a swing at him, that's all. I missed."

"But I bet the other guy got a good shot of the swing."

"He didn't," Tim said. "I was in the way, I think. It should be okay."

"So what's all that about?" Bill asked, and Danny wasted no time in filling him in.

"Dakers is finished now," Jon said.

318

"You don't have to look so pleased about it," Beth said. "His career is probably ruined before it's begun."

"Don't see why you care," Jon said.

"Well, his wife is my friend, for a start."

"And his press bloke is your boyfriend," Carey added with her usual forthrightness. The look that Jon gave Beth indicated what he thought of such a relationship (that it didn't exist except in Carey's mind didn't seem to matter). "Put it this way," he said, and repeated what the journalists outside had asked, "How do you feel about being used to cover up Dakers's shady dealings?"

"How do you mean?"

"Well, it's obvious that when you started asking questions about the coastal defences, you were getting a bit close to what was going on with him and this waste plant. So he brought you and Bill and Danny down here to get you out of the way and shut you up. You're happy to let yourself be used like that, are you?"

Beth had long ago reconciled herself to the idea that they were just part of a publicity stunt. It had seemed a fair trade-off — Gareth got good press for his kind treatment of his future constituents, and the family got a place to live and the chance to make a new life for themselves. She'd even acquired a certain amount of fame herself, in a very low-key way. But the thought that they'd been used to cover up what amounted to Gareth Dakers selling off most of the Northlands coast (because one part had been spared to blight it with this plant, and the other — the part the lighthouse stood on — was being sacrificed altogether): that was too much to bear.

CHAPTER
FIFTY-THREE

Lorelei was in love. Twenty-four carat, highly polished, sparkling shiny in love. And the most remarkable and beautiful part of it was, she was in love with her own husband. In love with him like she'd never been before, not even when they'd first met.

It was partly this place, she thought, looking out of the car window at the mellow, misty moor gliding past. There was space to think out here, there was no competition from other women, everything was clear and real. She looked at Gareth, who was driving. The other thing was that he needed her, a bit like he'd needed her to cover for him after the Windy Wendy weather girl débâcle, but this time he'd come to her asking her advice. She knew how much he wanted to be an MP, and they both knew how much they were falling in love with Northlands and Bleak House — a house that was theirs rather than hers, as she'd always felt their home in London to be.

It could all have been quite lovely, if it wasn't for this business with Mick Colber threatening to destroy everything.

"I'd best get back to Boldwick," Gareth had said reluctantly, as they lay still curled up in their nest of coats, albeit slightly stiffly — neither of them was as young as they used to be.

"Do you have to?" She'd nuzzled at his neck, which smelled of the expensive cologne he liked.

"I'm afraid I do," he said. "I imagine Fin will be going apeshit by now."

She relished that image for a second and laughed. "Let him."

"It's not fair on him. I can't expect him to carry the can for me."

"Of course you can. That's exactly what you pay him for."

"I pay him to help me get elected. Not to bail me out of every single indiscretion I get myself into."

"If it becomes necessary," Lorelei said, "if you . . . decide not to stand at the election . . ."

"You mean if I'm deselected."

"I mean if you decide not to stand after all, we can still have Bleak House as a holiday home, can't we? I mean, the two of us, we'll always be able to find work, we've got contacts. Pete Nixon said he'd have me back on *Take It to the Limit* like a shot, and you had that offer from the shopping channel."

"I'm going to be the Member of Parliament for Northlands East," Gareth said. "That's all there is to it. It's the only show I'm interested in, and your part in it will be very much like your erstwhile role with Pete Nixon — gazing adoringly as you listen to the same speech for the umpteenth time, and leading the spontaneous applause. You're made for it."

He was avoiding the whole issue of deselection. He always reacted to problems by pretending they didn't exist. "You really want this, don't you?" she said. He nodded, and she had the feeling that he was too emotional to speak. She patted his upper arm gently. "Then I'm with you all the way."

CHAPTER
FIFTY-FOUR

Gareth finally appeared back in the hotel, with Lorelei in tow. Neither of them looked particularly well rested, but both had an absurd glow about them that Fin almost recognised with his heart but not, at that moment, with his head. He wasted no time in laying into Gareth for disappearing at such a crucial time and leaving him to deal with all the crap as best he could.

"Thank you, Fin. I knew you were the right man for the job."

"Bloody true I'm the right man, but *this* isn't the job. Covering for you while you disappear is *not* the job."

"We hadn't disappeared," Lorelei purred. "We were at our home in the constituency. Where did you expect us to be?"

"You were at Bleak House? But it isn't even furnished."

"Who needs furniture?" Lorelei responded. "And who needs telephones?"

Fin glared at her, and turned to Gareth without replying. "Well, now you *are* back, local radio wants a live interview for their lunchtime broadcast, and I would strongly suggest you come clean about your past associations with Mick Colber."

"What?"

"Don't play ignorant. I could kill you for this, Gareth. Now sit there and tell me every single detail, everything you know about Carver Bay."

The interview went well. Gareth stuck closely to the line he'd agreed with Fin about not meaning to deceive anyone, and not realising there was any connection between Mick Colber and the coastal development. He swore to Fin that this was the truth in any case, but Gareth's greatest skill was managing to sound sincere even when he had no idea what he was talking about, and he did it so well that Fin himself never quite knew what was real and what was artifice. He thought he was probably genuinely upset by this Colber business. After all, he'd never be so stupid as to get mixed up with something that could spell the end of his political career before it had even begun. Would he?

Always a belt-and-braces man (politically if not sartorially), Fin had also made sure that a couple of the local councillors had been named in dispatches. One of them made the mistake of showing up to be interviewed as well. He was a much less smooth operator than Gareth, and his self-contradicting and befuddlement on the issue of the sea defences took the heat from Fin's man very nicely, though Gareth was careful not to belittle or insult him at all, rather giving the impression of a concerned parent.

As they left the radio studio and stepped out into the usual Boldwick drizzle, Gareth said, "I think that went pretty well." Fin didn't say anything, didn't come back with the expected and looked-for encouragement and approval. "Fin?"

"Are you telling me the full truth about Colber? Because I've just gone right out on a limb for you. I've spent an entire morning basically telling lies to the press."

"I thought lies were your bread and butter."

"Lies get found out, and when they do, your credibility is shot. Yours and mine. I have to be a trusted source of information, otherwise no one will come to me when they want any information and no one will accept anything I give them. And you have to be the upstanding pillar of the community the electorate wants and needs you to be. A certain amount of sleaze is forgivable once you're in office, once you've got a track record and they can see how you perform and you've earned some loyalty, but not now, when it's as easy as making a tick in a box to choose someone with a blemish-free CV."

They walked together in silence through the murky streets.

"This place has a kind of baroque loveliness, doesn't it?" Gareth mused looking up at the stacked grey clouds massing over the tall grey buildings. "It's like Vienna in a perpetual thunderstorm."

"So *are* you telling me the truth about Colber?"

"Oh, for God's sake, I've told you, haven't I?"

Fin looked at Gareth hard. The man was such an actor it was hard to know what was going on inside him. "Okay, let's say I believe you and we're back to

325

square one. Now you have to convince the constituency party."

"What?"

"I had a phone call while you were doing your interview. You've been summoned to party HQ tomorrow morning."

"Oh shit."

"Indeed. So you'd better keep practising that innocent face, and have a bloody good outline of what your position is going to be about the waste-processing plant."

"And what's my position going to be?"

Fin sighed to the bottom of his lungs.

CHAPTER
FIFTY-FIVE

Beth wanted so much to trust Fin, but the bottom line was that he was paid to get Gareth elected and watch his back. This had been the first real test of Gareth, as far as she knew, and naturally Fin was going to do everything in his power to make sure it didn't do his boss any lasting damage. If that meant covering up any investments Gareth had made in the Carver Bay development, then he'd do it.

She was so angry with herself. She'd started to trust him, had found part of herself creeping out of its hiding place, like a creature in a rock pool, coming out to warm up in the sun. Her big mistake had been choosing a politician to fall for — because Fin was ten times more politician than Gareth. But she *had* fallen for him, and now she was going to have to learn what the world was like without him in it, because there was no way she could have him in her life now.

All day people were ringing them up — Harry and Linda rang from Last Reach, someone from the RSPB, people from villages near Carver Bay who were worried about what the waste-disposal plant would mean. Beth didn't know how most of them got her number, but it seemed as if she'd become some kind of focal point for people's anger about what was going on.

"I don't know what they all expect me to do about it," she said to Danny and Bill. "Who am I, just a lighthouse keeper's daughter who works part time as Santa's elf."

"They need someone to moan at," Bill said. "They ought to be moaning to Ted Bailiss and the rest of them on the council, I reckon."

"It's Lorelei I feel sorry for," she said.

Danny rolled his eyes. "For God's sake, Mother!" he said. "How can you feel sorry for any of them? We've been used to help cover up this scheme that's going to ruin huge chunks of Northlands, and our lighthouse is going to fall into the sea, all because of Gareth Dakers and his greed. What do you think pays for that huge house they live in, and this place here, and the one they've just bought in Northlands? They've got *everything*, and we've got nothing, and you're wasting your time feeling sorry for her. Have you got any idea what Dad would think of you?"

When a person who normally speaks as little as possible delivers a speech like that, you have to listen to them. Invoking Martin just added the finishing touch, as Danny had known it would.

"You're right," Beth said. "I'm not just Santa's elf. I can do something to help." She had some contacts, on radio and newspapers who would listen to her. She had her newspaper column, which, while it wasn't anything that was so widely read it was earth shattering, could still be a platform. She wasn't comfortable doing

328

anything that might hurt Lorelei, but on the other hand if Lorelei was prepared to support her husband while he made a mess of the Northlands coastline, then she'd already put herself on the opposing side.

So she made some calls.

That done, she thought she'd better talk to Danny, who'd clearly been angry with her. His door was slightly ajar, and she tapped on it.

"Who is it?"

"It's me. Can I come in?"

"No."

The bathroom door opened behind Beth and her father came out. "He's too secretive, that lad," he said, and as he passed Danny's door he mock-accidentally fell against it and it swung open. Beth wasn't prepared for the scene that confronted them: Satoshi, the Japanese boy, was sitting on the bed, in his underwear, his body as thin and pale as a plant that's been growing in the dark, and Danny was crouched over him, painting his lips dark crimson with a little brush.

"Mum!" Danny howled. He jumped up, leapt over to the door and slammed it hard in their faces. "I'm going to get a fucking bolt for this door!" they heard him yell.

Beth, appalled, looked at her father, who shrugged at her. "Weird," he said. "Best to leave them to it." They went into the kitchen. "I used to wear eyeliner when I was a mod," he said.

"You were never a mod!"

"I was. Mind you, your mother drew the line."

"Mum did your eyeliner for you?"

"No, I mean she drew the line at me getting a scooter. She thought it was completely impractical. I've always hankered after a Vespa. Might still get one."

"What did we just disturb?" she said. "Do you think I should have a talk with him?"

"He won't say anything," Bill said. "You know Danny, the more you push him, the faster he'll clam up. Just leave him."

"But . . ." She let the sentence tail off. It was too complicated, but she was seriously concerned. She was going to have to get Danny in a good mood, and find out what was going on. It had looked as if the pair of them were getting ready for some kind of drag queen show. At times like this she missed Martin so much, though she wondered if he would have known at all what to do — boys wearing make-up was not part of Martin's everyday experience. On the other hand, Beth knew that it would have upset and in some way disappointed Martin if Danny turned out to be gay, but also that he would have been on his son's side no matter what, and that's what Beth would do, too.

A moment later they heard the two boys come out of Danny's room. They appeared in the kitchen. Satoshi, she noticed, was now entirely make-up free, though even without any adornments his fantastic bone structure made him look almost too pretty to be a boy. She realised that, now Danny had dyed his hair, it was exactly the same colour as his Japanese friend's. She wondered if that had been the reason for it.

"We're off out," Danny said, and seemed to be waiting for his mother to start yelling at him or

330

something. He looked embarrassed but defensive, ready for a row.

"Okay," she said, not wanting to inflame things any further right now.

"I'll be back in time for dinner." This was Danny being conciliatory, and her part in the dance was to smile cheerfully and ask if Satoshi or Eden or anyone would be joining them.

"No," he said. "Just me."

Which meant that everything was all right for now.

CHAPTER
FIFTY-SIX

The following morning Gareth was summoned to meet with the constituency party. They were obviously not best pleased at the idea that their candidate was the centre of controversy even before the election began. Fin knew that they would be considering whether to deselect him now, so that a whiter-than-white alternative could be bedded in in time for the election. Fin had hinted to a couple of the more influential members that this would be sending out entirely wrong signals about their judgement in selecting him in the first place, and that their best bet would be to stick with him come what may.

Unfortunately, "come what may" cranked up another notch, with the publication in the *Herald* that morning of photographs of Gareth and Mick Colber enjoying a drink together — at a millennium party. Not as long ago as Gareth was claiming their association to have been.

"You are really trying my patience now," Fin told Gareth. They were in the car travelling through the gloomy Boldwick streets. Lorelei was driving, Gareth was in the passenger seat and Fin was in the back with a pile of newspapers. The saying is, "he had a face like thunder," even though thunder is, after all, a sound. In Fin's case the expression on his face was, as usual, fairly unreadable: it was his voice that was like thunder — not the bang-crashing sort, but that low, rumbling, threat-of-a-storm-on-the-horizon kind.

Enough to make Lorelei leap to her husband's defence. "There's no call to talk to him like that," she said. "He's employing *you*, remember."

"Not for much longer at this rate," Fin muttered.

"Meaning?"

"He's doing a good job to get himself deselected in," he looked at his watch, "about fifteen minutes' time."

"Will you both stop talking about me as if I wasn't here?" Gareth cut in. "And get a grip on yourself, Fin. Those pictures don't say anything. So we were at the same party. Liz Hurley was at that one, as I recall. Doesn't mean I've had close personal connections with her. Worse luck." Lorelei glared at him. "Keep your eye on the road, darling," he said.

Fin wasn't finished. "This time, Gareth, I don't believe you. And if I don't, no one else is going to. So you're going to go in there and come clean. And I mean *clean*. Tell them everything you know about Mick Colber, every single time you met him, show them every damn Christmas card he's ever sent you if necessary. And hope they decide to stick with the devil they know. Then grovellingly ask their permission to make the same statement to the press."

"Do I have to?"

"You can bet the opposition are lining their people up to talk to whoever will listen, so yes, you do have to. So I hope you've practised your speech."

"It's very well written, I have to give you that much, Fin."

"As long as you manage to make it sound as if it was written in blood you extracted painfully from your own heart," Fin replied.

The real star of the show was Lorelei. The meeting started with informal coffee, and she used this opportunity to work the room, concentrating, Fin noticed, on the men, who were all very susceptible to her charms. Like the other half of the perfect double-act they were, Gareth made sure that the women didn't go short of attention either. Fin hovered like an anxious parent at a school play, ready to smooth over any awkward gaps and difficult questions, his ears tuned to every conversation in the room at the same time.

Then the fourteen worthy Northlanders assembled behind a long oak table, looking like a modern-dress interpretation of the Last Supper. Fin and Lorelei took up seats at the rear of the room, and Gareth was positioned in the centre, facing the panel. The mood was serious now.

The worthies asked a few questions about Mick Colber, which Gareth answered candidly: yes, he did know Mick Colber, he'd been wrong-footed originally because he knew him as Michael, but subsequently it had been a mistake to deny all knowledge. No, he wasn't aware of the plans to build a waste-processing plant. No, he didn't have any particular standpoint about the plant as yet, he would have to look into the facts, but he believed that his job was to represent the feeling of his constituents so of course that would be taken into account along with the material details.

Fin realised, with a horror that flashed through him like cold water going down a plughole, that he still had Gareth's speech in his briefcase. It was going to look so obvious if he handed it to him now. Shit shit shit.

But Gareth was already speaking his lines, as if it was just occurring to him at that very moment. The well-minted words about Boldwick, making it healthy, happy, prosperous, the metaphor that Fin was so pleased with, about Northlands being the jewelled clasp that held the cloak of Britain together (he had in mind a Roman soldier or similar when he thought of this, and the area did have some Roman connections).

Then the chairman was smiling, making some comment to the effect that they looked forward to Gareth representing them for many years, and it seemed the crisis was over. For now.

CHAPTER
FIFTY-SEVEN

Beth decided to return to Last Reach.

Carey and Jon had given her a lot of books and leaflets about waste incinerators, and the more she read, the more disturbed she felt. This waste project would be a terrible thing for Northlands, one of the loveliest coastlines in the whole of Britain, if not the world. What was proposed was what was euphemistically termed an "Energy Recovery Facilitator" — which was an incinerator, to the English-speaking world. Beth was horrified to read that, in a report into a similar scheme, it had been estimated that over the life of the incinerator, the emissions of oxides of sulphur, nitrogen and particulates could be responsible for nine deaths, twelve hospital admissions and seven hundred visits to the doctor. Several local authorities had banned incineration. Unfortunately, Northlands wasn't one of them.

Carey and Jon had been interested in environmental stuff for years: they were boycotting more types of food than they would actually eat. They were always banging on about renewable energy sources and global warming and Beth had been generally sympathetic to what they said, but tended to glaze over when they got too earnest and pedantic. It didn't seem to make proper sense or relevance till it was about to happen in the area where she'd grown up.

On a rare moment at home alone with just Bill, she told him she was thinking of going back to Northlands.

"I might well come with you," he said. "This city is getting to be too much for an old bloke like me."

"What?" She didn't believe she'd just heard that.

"It's not the sixties any more, is it?" he said. "I can't keep up with all these new-fangled things the kids are into, music with no words, all these text messages and stuff, it makes me feel as if I'm from another planet. Which I am," he said. "I'm an ageing lighthouse keeper, and I should be keeping my light. I feel like I deserted it."

"There isn't anything you could have done to help the lighthouse," she said.

"But there is!" he said. "That's why *you're* going to Northlands, because you think there's something you can do. It might not save the Last Reach Point light, but it could help the area generally. I ought to come with you."

The thought of him going with her was reassuring, but there were other considerations. "I need you to look after Danny," she said.

"Danny's old enough to look after himself. He's old enough to get married, even."

"He's not old enough to buy a pint, or drive a car, or any amount of things that he might be getting into," she said. "You know as well as I do that there's something going on he's not telling us about, and one of us ought to be here just in case . . . well, I don't know what, but just in case. I'm going to be back as soon as I can, but I need you to promise to look after him. And," she added, "not to get into any more trouble with photographers."

He looked suitably contrite. "I'm amazed that never made it to the papers. Probably that Fin Lewis is keeping it in reserve, in case we start rattling Dakers's cage."

"Well we'll soon find out, because I guess I'm about to start rattling." Possibly running into Fin in Northlands was the part of the plan she was trying not to think about. Even though he'd apparently gone from friend to enemy so quickly, whenever she thought about him all she wanted was to lay her head on his shoulder and feel his arms around her. When she thought like that she would give herself a mental cold shower and tell herself that it was just that she'd been without male company for so long, that the first man who'd shown an interest in her was appearing to be infinitely more interesting than he really was.

"You'll be seeing Harry when you're up there, I expect," Bill said, in a studiedly offhand way reminding her that Fin *hadn't* been the first man to show an interest in her.

"Probably," she said. "I'm going to be staying at Linda's, so it's likely I'll be seeing everyone in the village at some point."

"You know what I mean," Bill said.

Whatever happened, her visit to Northlands was going to be very interesting.

338

CHAPTER
FIFTY-EIGHT

"I really don't think this is a great idea," Gareth grumbled, once again getting into the car. He seemed to spend his entire life in cars these days, flitting between one remote hamlet and the next, though he had to admit the spectacular scenery was often a compensation.

"Public opinion is firmly against this incinerator," Fin said. "There's going to be a protest at the council offices, and you're going along to lend them your support."

"But all this militant tree-hugging sort of thing really isn't me. And what about the people it might alienate?"

"Who's it going to alienate? Who in their right mind would want an incinerator building anywhere near them?"

"It's bringing a lot of money into the area, and jobs . . ."

"Not that many jobs. Mainly pollution, increased heavy traffic, a visually unpleasant plant, not to mention the money that's been diverted away from coastal defences in the north."

"By which you mean the lighthouse. I do wonder, my friend, if your attachment to Beth Jackson is preventing you from seeing this thing objectively."

"As your alleged attachment to Mick Colber may be preventing you. This is purely business. My job is to get you elected, and when you've done your damnedest to get the scheme overturned, you'll have proved yourself as one of them, and you'll walk straight into the House of Commons."

Gareth sighed. "Okay, then. Whatever it takes."

"Exactly. Whatever it takes."

Fin parked behind the council offices, which were housed in the kind of ugly, pompous Victorian public building that was a feature of the market town of Boldwick. They made their way round to the front of the building.

"One thing," Fin warned. "No placards. Make sure you don't stand in front of anyone else's banner, no SWP banners or paper sellers, no badges, nothing with words on that could be a hostage to fortune in the papers and on television later. I'll keep an eye on it for you, but be aware."

"I'll keep my back to the wall at all times."

"Oh, it already is."

Gareth grinned. "Fin! I do believe you're acquiring a sense of humour in your old age."

Fin scanned the scene in front of him. There was a small knot of people outside the town hall, a gaggle of the usual suspects: Greenpeace, Friends of the Earth, the ubiquitous Socialist Workers, only maybe a hundred people in all, hardly a massive turnout. There were only a couple of placards, and a banner made of a painted sheet which bore the legend: NO TO CARVER BAY INCINERATOR. It was to the point, at least. No press were in evidence yet, even though he'd alerted everyone to a photo opportunity. Glancing at his watch he saw that they still had fifteen minutes before the press were due to arrive. Excellent — it would give time to find a proper, noncompromising backdrop for Gareth.

They walked towards the protesters, a few of whom started to hoot and cheer at their approach.

And then Fin saw Beth.

CHAPTER
FIFTY-NINE

All the way up to Northlands in the train she'd wondered how she was going to feel when she got there. It had only been a couple of months since she'd left, but so much had happened in the meantime. She quite literally wasn't the same person who'd got on the train at Boldwick headed down to stay with her would-be MP and his wife.

She thought about that first day — how Lorelei had been so hostile under a veneer of pleasantness much thinner than the polish on her artificial fingernails. But when you got to know Lorelei, she was really quite nice. It was the life she led, all that showbiz flash and superficiality. Beth didn't think Lorelei really had any friends, and being married to Gareth, you could see why that would make someone a bit jealous and strange. Gareth was a born communicator, a born flirt, maybe a born philanderer. But Beth thought what Lorelei didn't realise about Gareth was that he really loved her — he was devoted to her, in his own way. They were an odd couple, in as much as they were both narcissistic and self-centred, but somehow they'd found soul mates in each other, the same as Martin and Beth had.

Before Beth left London, Bill had asked her if returning to Last Reach would be like returning to Martin, in some way. She'd tried to explain why that wasn't true. She'd never left Martin; she'd taken whatever was best about him along with her. He wasn't in Last Reach, or at the bottom of the North Sea, or in heaven; he was in Beth, and Danny, and he always would be. Bill had just smiled, that infuriatingly knowing smile he had sometimes.

So now Beth was standing in a freezing cold Boldwick gale (Force 8), which bore the smell of the sea and felt like home. She was outside the town hall, where she'd hardly ever been in her life even though she'd only lived a few miles away, demonstrating against the incinerator, which ironically had been the whole reason for moving to London, and for life getting better.

Linda was beside her — she'd persuaded Kenny to look after the shop. "It's time for women to get militant," she said. "I missed Greenham Common, I'm not missing this."

"You just want to spend all day gossiping with Beth," her husband had grumbled affectionately. "I bet you both end up in the shops before too long."

"Kenny Morini! As if!" Linda laughed. "Anyway, Beth wouldn't be impressed by our poor selection of Boldwick shops, when she's been used to the West End. She's all swanky now."

"I'm not!" Beth protested.

"No, love, you're not, and I'm very glad to see you aren't. Now, do you want to borrow a woolly hat?"

Beth was grateful for the woolly hat. Okay, so it didn't look particularly alluring, in fact it made her look as if she spent most of her time weaving baskets. But it was warm, and in Northlands warmth was the main thing. And it fitted in perfectly with the general look of the demo, such as it was. The hundred or so people gathered outside the town hall with banners and placards were dressed more for comfort than style, in layers of woollies and duffel coats and waxed jackets.

It wasn't a well-organised demonstration: no one seemed to have a clear idea of what they were meant to be doing, whether there was even a council meeting going on inside or not, what the point of it really was.

"Once any construction gets under way at Carver Bay it would be easy to blockade any work being done on the site," Beth said to Linda. "There's only one access road to Carver Bay, isn't there? If we could seal that off, no site traffic would be able to get in. It wouldn't take many people, we could do it in shifts."

"Ooh, get you, you've gone all militant!" Linda said. "We could use the bread delivery van!" A couple of other people had overheard this conversation, and were pitching in with ideas of their own. "We need a proper planning meeting," someone said. "Co-ordinated action." "A website," someone else added. It was all getting quite exciting, and Beth was wishing Carey and Jon were there. They had so much more experience of this kind of thing.

Then she saw Gareth, with Fin at his side. Her heart seemed to fly at her ribs.

"Oh no," she muttered.

344

"What?" Linda said, looking in the direction her friend was looking.

"It's . . . Gareth Dakers."

"Where? Do you think he's going to join the protest?"

Beth didn't know and almost didn't care. She was looking straight past Gareth at Fin, who'd seen her, too, and was looking — well, odd. Perhaps it was the woolly hat, she thought, but it would have looked far too obvious to take it off now, and who knew what her hair was looking like underneath? Good grief, she thought, when did I get so vain?

She hadn't told Linda anything about Fin. She'd *wanted* to, but wasn't sure how to express it, and now she was glad she hadn't. Things were going to be awkward enough, meeting him here in this crowd of people. Gareth hadn't seen her, and was beginning to work the edge of the crowd, who eagerly gathered around him.

Fin left him to it and walked straight towards Beth. "I didn't know you were coming," he said. His face was unreadable.

"I only came up yesterday," she said.

"So what's happening?"

She gestured around. "As you can see, we're protesting about the incinerator."

"So are we," he said, with a nod of his head toward Gareth, who'd managed to find a reporter to talk to.

"Gareth's protesting against an incinerator he's investing in," she said, trying to sound as sarcastic as possible.

"That's not true. Any previous associations with the same company were made in good faith and a very long time before he even thought about running for Parliament."

"Believe that if you like," she said. "I'm not sure I do."

He ignored this. "Where are you staying?"

Why did he need to know that? She wasn't going to reply, but Linda said, "She's staying with me."

Beth said, "This is Linda. My friend Linda Morini. This is Finian Lewis. He works for Mr Dakers."

"We've already met," Fin said. "You run the shop in Last Reach, don't you?" Linda looked absurdly pleased that he remembered, and Beth wanted to yell, he remembers everything! He keeps it all on file in case it ever comes in handy. But just then Gareth summoned Fin over to ask him something. Linda, watching him as he walked away, said, "I don't know about him working for Dakers, but he's working wonders for me. Ve-ery cute."

Whatever Beth had thought of Fin, the word "cute" had never come into it, and she laughed. "Oh, he might be good looking," she said, "but he's the sharpest tool in the box. Knows it too."

"Even better. I like my men intelligent."

"Like Kenny."

Linda laughed. "Mmm. Just like Kenny. Get him in the *Mastermind* chair answering questions about football and motor racing, and he's a match for anyone."

Beth tried very hard to stop herself, but couldn't help watching Fin, as he shepherded Gareth from one set of press people to the next, and couldn't help thinking of their lovely evening in Baker Street, and how she'd thought she was falling for him, and been almost convinced that he felt the same.

As if things weren't complicated enough, about five minutes later Harry Rushton appeared. He wasn't in uniform, and he was looking tall, blond and handsome in that strapping, Nordic way. Beth was surprised to see him. The odd thing was, he didn't look at all surprised to see *her*, almost as if he'd been tipped off. Forget "almost", she thought, as she looked at Linda's smug grin.

"Hi Beth," he said. "Linda said you would be here." She glared at Linda. Her coming up to Northlands was supposed to have been a secret. She was matchmaking again, obviously.

"Are you protesting?" Beth asked Harry.

"About you coming back? Of course not."

"About the incinerator."

"Oh." He looked embarrassed. "Yes, well, no, I mean, I wanted to find out more about it before I decide."

"There's not that much of a decision to be made," she said.

"She's gone all militant," Linda pointed out, helpfully. "She's been associating with environmental activists."

"Hardly associating," Beth said. "They're my downstairs neighbours."

"Are they here?" Harry asked. He probably wanted to suss her London contacts out.

Linda said, "*They're* not here, but guess who is?" She pointed to the other side of the road, where Gareth was busy talking into a TV camera. Beth couldn't see Fin.

"He's got a nerve," Harry said. "He's paying for it, and now he's protesting against it? What's that all about?"

"Have you ever thought that he might be telling the truth?" Beth said. "That he didn't know anything about Carver Bay?" Harry gave her a long, hard look, but not as long and hard as the one Linda was giving her.

"*You're* easily persuaded," she said. "Just a word from the right person."

"I'm not persuaded," Beth replied. "I was just floating it as a possibility."

She would have loved to talk to Fin some more, but the afternoon turned a bit mad. Fin was constantly with Gareth, keeping journalists sweet, talking away on that damn mobile phone or getting text messages on it, and Beth had a couple of interviews herself with local journalists. There wasn't a lot she could say, because the contract she had with the newspaper she wrote the column for was quite proscriptive about her dealing with other newspapers. She began to wonder if Fin had arranged it that way, because it was doing a wonderful job of keeping her quiet.

Then somehow the crowd was dispersing, without anything really being achieved, and Fin and Gareth had gone. Beth had expected Fin to come over to say

348

goodbye, but they just vanished. Linda and Beth took the phone numbers of a few people they'd been talking to, and promised they'd set up some kind of meeting as soon as they had any more information.

"Can I give you both a lift back to Last Reach?" Harry offered.

"You could drop Beth back," Linda said. "I've got my own car."

"It's okay," Beth said. "I'll go back with Linda."

"But didn't you say you wanted to take a look at the site at Carver Bay?" she said sweetly. "I would have loved to have gone, but it's time to pick Cait up from school, so I wouldn't be able to take you. I bet Harry would, though."

"It would be my pleasure," he said, just as if they'd arranged it between them. So Linda disappeared, too, leaving Beth alone with Harry for the first time since he'd proposed to her in the sitting-room at the lighthouse.

"I'm freezing," he said. "What about getting a drink and a bit of a warm before we brave Carver Bay? There's a coffee shop up the road here." It sounded like a good plan — Beth was freezing too — so she agreed.

They settled with two big mugs of tea and a plate of sandwiches in a pretty, traditional-style tea shop, the sort with tablecloths and waitresses in white aprons and tiered cake plates. It wasn't the kind of place Beth would have gone into when she was a resident of the area. "I feel like a tourist," she said. "I never thought that would be possible so soon."

"But you came back," he pointed out. "You still care about Northlands. You haven't abandoned us altogether."

"Of course I care," she said, then worried that he might misconstrue that added, "It's a very beautiful county. I hate to think of it being spoiled."

"Do you really think Dakers is involved in the Carver Bay plans?"

She shrugged. "He says he isn't," she said. "And I'm inclined to believe him." Or was she inclined to believe Fin, after all? She tried to support her argument with reasons, like it used to say on her A level exam papers, but the reasons she came up with weren't particularly convincing. "He might be a southerner, but he's not daft. Why get involved in something that would be so unpopular, and then try and get yourself elected in that seat?"

"Perhaps he didn't know that he would be having so much to do with Northlands. I get the impression it wasn't his first choice when he was looking for somewhere to represent."

Beth knew that was true, but that didn't mean that she thought Gareth had anything to do with Carver Bay, so she didn't say anything.

"You've had your hair cut," Harry said. Beth didn't think he'd notice — men don't generally, and it wasn't a drastic cut, anyway, just a bit of a tidy-up she'd had done on the day she spent with Lorelei at the Haven. And the woolly hat had completely disarranged it anyway. "You look lovely."

"Thank you."

"I've missed you a lot."

350

Beth could have killed Linda for this. She was almost sure it was a plot: Linda was hoping Harry and Beth would get together, then Beth would move back to Last Reach. Some shopkeepers just couldn't cope with losing customers. But what should Beth say to Harry? Should she tell him about Fin? Was there anything to say about Fin? So what she said was, "I think Bill's getting a bit homesick. He wanted to come up here with me, but I made him stay at home to keep an eye on Danny."

"At home?" he repeated, pointedly.

"Well, you know, where we're staying."

"Why does Danny need an eye keeping on him? Is he still moping about?"

"Quite the reverse, actually. He's been in a very chipper mood since we moved to Dogwood Avenue. But he's got some weird friends."

"Druggies?" The policeman side of him was all interested now.

Beth shook her head. "I don't think so." She didn't mention that it was Bill who'd had the problems with drugs — Harry would have been horrified. "But there's this Japanese boy who wears make-up and he seems to be getting Danny into it too, and Dan's dyed his hair black."

"Make-up? That's not right for boys. He'd never have been doing that if his dad was around."

"Well, we'll never know about that, will we?"

"Sorry, Beth, I didn't mean to upset you."

"I'm not upset," she said, realising with a gentle shock that it was true. "All I mean is, it's for the people who are still here to know what's best for Danny."

"Maybe I could come and visit," Harry suggested. "Put him straight on one or two things."

Beth smiled. Whatever Danny was doing, the thought of his policeman godfather turning up to "put him straight" wouldn't please him one bit. "If I need your help, I'll shout, don't worry," she said.

Her hand was resting on the table — she'd been fiddling with the spoon in the sugar bowl — and Harry put his own large, warm hand on hers. She looked into his eyes. They were blue like the sea, like home.

CHAPTER
SIXTY

Carver Bay was a ragged cove that looked as if a huge dragon roaring in from a north-easterly direction had taken a bite out of the coast. The land behind it was flat and grassy, and very exposed. Bitter wind whipped across it unchecked, and it wasn't useable for much apart from grazing sheep. The scent of the sea was strong, so fresh and cold it almost burned into Beth's lungs. That was the excuse she made to herself about the tight feeling in her throat, anyway.

Harry seemed to be waiting for her to speak, so she said, "It's incredible how different it is from the coastline at Last Reach. You wouldn't think the lighthouse was only a few miles that way." They both looked towards the north. The lighthouse wasn't visible, being obscured by the north headland of the bay, but in her imagination she could see it plainly. She hadn't been to visit it since she'd come back to Last Reach — she didn't know if she could cope with seeing it.

"This is a God-forsaken spot, isn't it?" Harry's hair was being whipped by the wind. He zipped his jacket right up to his chin and dug his hands deep into his pockets. Beth was glad she was still wearing Linda's woolly hat.

There was no clue that any work had started here at all, not a picket fence or a sign indicating any ownership. The land might just as well belong to the gulls that were squatting all around like dropped litter. Beth wasn't sure what she'd been expecting to find. All she'd wanted was to see the place that all the fuss was about, to try and get a feeling for what an incinerator would mean. A picture of the enormous, box-like construction loomed in her mind, squatting on this land like something from a malevolent planet.

"It makes me so angry," she said. "You ought to see London, Harry. Sometimes I walk down the road, and I think, under here was once all grass and trees. And now there's tarmac and concrete and bricks and more tarmac. People in London wouldn't believe a place could be as empty as this."

She didn't realise she was crying until Harry offered her his big, white handkerchief. Then he offered his arms, and she was happy to have their comforting shelter.

She cried for a little while and felt better, and pulled away from him. "Sorry about that," she said, and tried a tearful smile. "It's quite hard coming back here."

"Sounds as if it's hard for you staying in London."

"No," she said. "It isn't. That's not what I meant." She sighed. "Come on then, let's go back to Linda's. There isn't anything to see here, is there?"

"There's you," he said. "I could look at you for ever."

"Harry, will you stop it, please?"

But he wasn't so easily put off track — a technique that probably came in handy when he was interrogating

354

suspects. "We could be really happy, Beth," he said. "If Danny wants to stay down in London, he's a big boy, he could stay on by himself. You and me, we could get a little place — Bill could live with us if you want." He added, as an afterthought, "Maybe in an extension."

"It sounds . . . cosy," she said. "But I'm not sure I'm very good housewife material any more."

"You'd never be just a housewife to me," he said.

"I'm not sure I'd be good *wife* material, then. I've done that."

"We could live together instead, if you like. See how it works out. No pressure, Beth."

She smiled. "Not *much* pressure."

"It's all right for you to smile," he said. "I'm making myself look like a right prat here, aren't I?" He grinned, a rather sweet, boyish grin.

"No you aren't," she said.

"Is there anyone else? Is that it? Are you seeing someone in London?"

Beth thought about how to answer, and said, "There might have been . . . but it didn't work out."

"If he's fool enough to let you go, he doesn't deserve you."

"Thanks for that."

They stood in an awkward silence, about a metre apart, looking at the stupid gulls, and listening to the swooshing of the sea in the bay.

"You're right," Harry said eventually. "I should be getting you back to Linda's, so you can plan the next stage of your campaign." They waded across the hummocky grass towards where they'd left his car.

"Bear in mind if you do come down here to lie down in the road or something, we might be on different sides of the fence," he remarked.

Beth stopped and looked at him. "What do you mean?"

"Well, I'm a copper, aren't I? It's quite likely I'll be drafted in to keep any protesters out if it comes to it."

"But you disagree with the incinerator too!"

He shrugged. "It's my job. I'm not saying I'd take any pleasure in it, but the law's the law."

"Oh, good grief, you men always put your jobs first."

"Us men? I suppose you mean me and Martin."

And Fin. All men. Oh, for a man who'd put feelings before duty.

CHAPTER
SIXTY-ONE

Mick Colber didn't look like a happy man. A rich man, yes, a clever man, an ambitious man, but certainly not a happy one. And there were plenty of opportunities to judge, because he was all over the media. Turn on the TV news and he was there, head as bald as a baby's bottom and face as red as one with nappy rash. Open a newspaper and he was there. Switch on the radio and there was his voice, rasping and with a hint of a New Zealand accent. Fin wondered who was doing his PR: they were bloody good, whoever they were.

The message coming over loud and clear from Mr Mick Colber was the predictable one: What right did Gareth Dakers have to start leading protests against a company he'd already invested in? How could he possibly object to a waste incinerator when his money had already helped incinerators to be built elsewhere in the country? At this point in a TV news bulletin, a library picture of an incinerator would be shown, a huge, windowless box which oddly enough never looked operational, no billowing plumes of unpleasant smoke for the environmentalists to get worked up about.

"You need to get your money out of there asap," Fin told Gareth. "It's the only way to stay anywhere near the moral high ground."

"Don't think I can," Gareth muttered gloomily. "I've had my accountant on to it, but he thinks I'm contractually tied in."

"In that case, it's a massive uphill struggle."

Gareth just looked at him, like a child might look at a parent who has bought him the wrong brand of football boots. "You're not giving up, surely, Fin?"

Fin shrugged his shoulders. "You haven't made things easy for yourself. I told you at the beginning that I needed to know everything. If you'd only told me about this, we could have worked around it, no problem."

"But I forgot I even *had* money in Colber's bloody company. I didn't know anything about Carver Bay!"

"Who's going to believe you?" Fin said. "You might have to face the possibility that Northlands is over for you now."

"Surely not?"

"I hope not, but if it comes to it the best plan might be to stage a tactical retreat, in which you try and preserve as much dignity as possible, then with any luck you'll be considered for another seat in the next general election." He looked at Gareth's stricken face. "It's not the end of the world."

"It feels like it," Gareth replied. "We had our hearts set on Northlands."

"Did we?" Fin was puzzled. "Who's 'we'?"

358

"Lorelei and me." Fin was even more puzzled, until Gareth explained a little about what had happened at Bleak House. "Everything suddenly made sense," he said. "It seemed like the perfect arrangement: a lovely home up here, Lorelei happy, and trips down to London when the House was sitting. I could picture it. It would have been marvellous."

Fin wouldn't have been able to get his head round the idea of the metropolitan Dakers feeling at home on a moor in Northlands if he hadn't felt something similar when they'd visited the lighthouse. There was definitely something about this place that got into your heart, and that thought led him straight to Beth.

As they'd left the demonstration outside the town hall they'd driven past her in the market place. Fin almost didn't see her, because she was wearing that crazy woolly hat. Her cheeks had been flushed pink like roses on snow, and she looked so pretty he could hardly bear it. He was about to stop the car, he wanted to gather her in his arms and tell her he loved her, but then he realised she was deep in conversation with that policeman, Harry Rushton, whom all the villagers reckoned was going to marry her one day. That was the reason for the bloom in her cheeks. The car passed by, and Beth hadn't seen him.

CHAPTER
SIXTY-TWO

It was lovely staying with Linda. Beth enjoyed helping to get five-year-old Cait ready for school, tracking down her shoes, her swimming things, the picture she'd drawn for the teacher that she simply had to find and take to school that morning or she'd "die". She enjoyed the peacefulness when Cait's older brother Ant, who was the same age as Danny but totally unlike him (she hesitated to say it, but more "normal"), had taken Cait off to school, and Linda and Beth could sit in the kitchen and drink coffee and talk. The long-suffering Kenny had again been prevailed upon to look after the shop on his own.

"I don't see why you don't marry Harry," Linda remarked, blowing on her coffee. "Except that it rhymes, obviously. Marry Harry. Don't tarry. I always knew he'd carry . . ." she giggled, "carry a torch for you, that is."

"You're a crap poet," Beth said. "And an even worse matchmaker."

"But why not? Harry is eminently suitable."

"There's just a little matter of love."

"Love would grow. You're very fond of him."

360

"Yes," Beth said, "I am. And I'm fond of Kenny, but I wouldn't want to marry him."

"That's a silly comparison. Kenny's spoken for."

"Okay," Beth said, and took a deep breath, screwing up her courage. "I wasn't going to say anything, but there *was* someone in London."

"What? I don't believe you! You've kept this quiet!"

"I sort of told Harry."

"No! Poor Harry! And *imagine* him hearing the gossip before you've told me. I could kill you for this. Tell me all about it — I insist."

"There's nothing to tell, really," Beth said. "I had one date, with . . . someone I got to know while I was down there. And I thought something might be happening, but then it didn't."

"You'll see him when you go back though?"

"Probably not."

"Where do you know him from?"

"We kind of worked together. He helped me with the magazine column I write and stuff like that."

"Ooh! A writer! That sounds exciting."

Beth was happy to let Linda lead herself off the scent. She didn't want even her best friend to know how she felt about Fin. "But, anyhow, I don't think it was going anywhere. It's just that I started to feel with him as though I might be able to fall in love again one day."

"Wow. Good for you, girl!"

"Really?" Beth said. "You're not shocked?"

"Why would I be?"

"Well, you were a friend of Martin's, and I don't want people thinking I've forgotten about him."

Linda took her friend's hand. "Beth, this is me you're talking to. The person who held your hand every night after Danny had gone to bed and listened to you cry. I *know* how you feel about Martin. But you're only young, and you're lovely, and if there's a chance of happiness for you, you should take it."

Beth sighed. "I don't think there *is* a chance," she said. "Not this time." She tried to make her voice as perky as possible. "But that doesn't mean there never will be."

There was a time when she used to tell Linda everything, but there was no point now in telling her about Fin's fantastic smile, the way he'd looked at her as if she was the only person worth looking at in the whole world, the way his voice could make her feel hot and cold at the same time, like baked Alaska. No point saying she loved him.

CHAPTER
SIXTY-THREE

"What do you mean, you're bailing out on me?" Imogen had never heard such crap in her life.

"I'm not doing your dirty work for you any more," Tim said.

"But we're doing so well!" she protested. "We've got Dakers twisting in the wind over this Carver Bay thing. I *knew* he was up to no good, you could tell just from the look of him that there had to be more to it than simply wanting to be a good MP for Northlands."

"I wouldn't be able to give you anything else, anyway. The Jacksons never see Dakers any more. Mrs Dakers apparently thinks it was Beth who told you about Colber."

"It's an understandable assumption."

"But it's not fair! Beth is her friend! And Beth and Bill are *my* friends."

"Don't tell me, they took you in when you were down and out and destitute. Bet you haven't told them about your flat in Greenwich, have you? The one Daddy subsidises for you."

"Like he subsidises your sad journalist career."

"At least I'm doing something to improve myself," she hissed. "I've had offers already, which I'm considering, as they say. How many auditions have *you* been to recently?"

"I've got no idea why I ever agreed to this," Tim said. "But it's over, from this minute."

"And what will you do?"

"I don't know yet. Leave the Jacksons in peace, for one thing, but not until Beth gets back. I might tell Bill what's been going on first. It would make me feel better."

"And have him hate you? You wouldn't do that."

"Afraid they might find out you did all this because Dakers's spin doctor didn't want to shag you? Afraid *he* might find out he got to you so much?"

"Even if that was true, which it absolutely isn't — he's not *going* to find out, is he, because you say the Jacksons don't have anything to do with Dakers any more."

"With Dakers maybe not. But Beth Jackson and Finian Lewis were a bit closer than that."

Imogen didn't even try to pretend she wasn't interested in this. "Why do you say that? What's happened between them?"

"More than ever happened with you and him, anyway."

"Really. Well, have a happy retirement, Timothy darling. I have a political career to ruin."

Tim was stricken. "Imogen! Will you stop —"

But she'd already hung up.

CHAPTER
SIXTY-FOUR

Lorelei was feeling guilty as the stories about her husband and his connections with Mick Colber and the development at Carver Bay escalated. The people of Northlands seemed to be of the opinion that there was no smoke without fire (quite appropriate for an incinerator): even the proprietor of the Three Horseshoes was looking decidedly cool whenever they passed through the hotel's dining room or bar, despite all the money they'd brought to his wretched little hostelry.

The reason for her guilt was that she knew the story must have originally leaked somehow, and she had a horrible feeling that she was the source of the leak. She knew she ought to come clean about it — after all, it must have been Beth Jackson who'd gone to the newspapers, but it was Lorelei who'd supplied the information. She was horribly disappointed in Beth, but that was what happened when you trusted women as friends. They all went mad one way or another: just look at Paloma.

Now Fin was pacing around the room like some kind of pack animal — and no doubting who was the alpha male in this particular pack, damn him — and he was seriously talking about Gareth dropping his plans to stand as the MP for Northlands East.

He repeated what he'd said to Gareth earlier. "One route out of this is to make a tactical retreat now. If you stand down, there's the chance you'll be offered another seat in a year or two." Privately, Fin thought that this was the best option under the circumstances. Gareth and Northlands had been an uphill struggle to begin with, but with the biggest local newspaper against him, and all of this mud flying in his direction, it was going to be practically impossible now. The news from Damien Kelly was that the local party was sticking by Gareth but it was a seriously close thing, and he could never pretend to have their full support. Going into an election on that basis would be crazy.

Fin hated to admit defeat. It had never happened to him before, for one thing, and he did occasionally wonder how much of it was his fault. Perhaps if he hadn't got on the wrong side of Imogen Callow-Creed, she would never have pursued Gareth so single-mindedly. That had been a very bad misjudgement.

Lorelei was looking fierce. "Crock of shit," she said, in response to the idea of Gareth giving up the campaign. "If you'd spent as long as I have working with a pro like Pete Nixon, you'd know the motto should be never give up. I've seen Pete carry a show off triumphantly even after the autocue went down, the prize wheel jammed and one of the assistant floor managers was having a heart attack and being defibrillated just out of camera shot. That's the kind of professional *he* is, and that's the kind of professional

366

my husband is. The show must go on! We are not giving up Bleak House; we are not giving up Northlands. You're going to get out there and work your arse off and we're not giving up till we're Mr and Mrs Parliament, being introduced to the Queen and Black Rod and all those people."

Jesus, Fin thought, she's mutating into Christine Hamilton.

"But all the things Colber has been saying . . ." Gareth said.

"Aren't true," Lorelei reminded him.

"But they look true, which is the main thing," Fin pointed out.

"So what's he guilty of? Stupidity is all," she said.

"Thanks," her husband muttered.

Fin looked at Lorelei. The woman who'd moaned non-stop about having to spend any time at all in Northlands now seemed to be desperate to stay here. She'd even given up on those false fingernail things and was wearing normal, human fingernails, he noticed. And along with fingernails, she'd acquired backbone. Fin perked up. Perhaps it wasn't a lost cause, after all: with Lorelei's help, Gareth might still do it.

"Okay," he said. "We've tried working the problem. Now we'll try working the people who are *causing* the problem."

CHAPTER
SIXTY-FIVE

"You'd better look at this," Kenny said, holding up one of the more scurrilous tabloids. On an inside page was a photograph of Bill apparently throwing a punch at a photographer. The accompanying feature made a lot of how Bill had been drunk and aggressive — and that it hadn't been the first time. Somehow, they knew about the time when Beth had had to pick Bill up, drunk and disorderly, in Battersea (though Fin's part in this episode wasn't mentioned). It made Bill sound like an irredeemable old reprobate, rather than a silly old man who thought he was still in his twenties.

Beth wondered how the paper could have got that information. Surely even Bill wasn't daft enough to talk to a journalist about those things? She knew that Danny wouldn't have.

There was only one explanation: Fin had been with her when she went to pick Bill up. But she didn't know what he or Gareth could possibly gain from this — it was just nasty and vindictive.

"What are you going to do?" Kenny asked.

Linda replied for her — she was incandescent. "Sue the bastards, that's what!"

Beth sighed. "I'm not suing anybody. Nothing's changed," she said. "I'm going to go back to London, try and get more work at the garden centre or else find another job, and we'll have to look for somewhere to live."

"You don't have to go," Linda said.

"But Danny is so settled down there, and . . ." Beth looked at her friend, wondering if she might be offended, "Well, I was, too."

"I know what you mean," Linda said. "You look so much better since you've been away. Living at that lighthouse, it didn't allow you to ever stop grieving for Martin, did it?"

Beth shook her head. "And I think it was the same for Danny. But circumstances have changed in London. We're as stuffed there as we are here." She realised how dependent they'd been on Gareth Dakers. It wasn't much to show for a new life. Beth wasn't making enough money between her newspaper column and working at the garden centre to pay a proper rent on a place big enough to house her family, but she knew they couldn't be dependent on Gareth Dakers's charity. And now they were no use to him, she assumed that offer would also disappear.

"So have you thought maybe you've learned what you needed to learn from London," Linda said sagely. "I mean, you've learned to let the past go a little bit, and now you could live in Last Reach, or even Boldwick, if you're hankering after the bright lights," she paused so Beth could laugh at her joke, and then her face was serious. "But it wouldn't be the same, would it? Because you're not the same."

"You might be right," Beth said. "Moving back up here sounds like such a good idea, but I don't have any home or livelihood."

"Well, you've been writing for newspapers. Maybe they'd have a vacancy on the *Herald*."

"Oh, I can really see that happening!" Beth said.

"And you could screw Dakers for some compensation for the lighthouse, now the full story has come out."

"I don't want to have any more to do with Gareth Dakers."

"But if you could get some cash out of him?"

"Linda, I won't be bought by anyone."

"God, you're so proud sometimes," she said. "But why punish Bill and Danny because of your own stupid pride?" Beth could see on Linda's face that she was formulating a Theory. "Has this got something to do with the man in London you were telling me about?" Linda said. Beth shrugged. "It's Finian Lewis, isn't it?" she said. "I've been thinking and thinking, and I even thought for a minute it was Gareth Dakers himself, and I was gearing myself up for the full married-man speech, but it isn't, it's Finian Lewis."

"It *was*," Beth corrected her. "Not any more. I can't trust him."

"*Trust* him? What are you like, falling for a spin doctor of all people? Though, having seen him, I can entirely see your point of view. He's a very sexy man. But not really someone you could depend on."

"Thanks, Linda, I'd reached those conclusions by myself. So you see why I can't have anything else to do with Gareth Dakers. I've got to get my family right away from that lot."

"It's not going to be easy, if what you say about Danny is true. He won't take kindly to moving back up here. Could you leave him in London, do you think?"

Beth pondered. "Not right now," she said. "I don't know where he'd live, and he's been acting strangely, I don't think he's ready to be left to his own devices yet."

"Acting strangely how? All teenage boys act strangely."

"I think he might be gay," Beth said. "He's got this friend, this pretty Japanese boy, and they seem to spend their evenings dyeing each other's hair and putting make-up on each other."

"Wow! Certainly beats hiding porn mags under the carpet. That's what Ant does. He thinks I don't know, but some of those things are quite thick, and they make bumps in the carpet. You only notice when you Hoover."

"I'm worried that he might get into trouble. London's so new to him, and if he's, you know, exploring things, well, he might want his mother around."

"Or not," Linda commented.

That evening Bill rang, and the news from home was about as bad as Beth could have feared.

"I think Dan's started taking drugs," he said.

"What?" Beth was speechless with horror. Hair dye and make-up she could cope with, being gay she could cope with, but drugs? The thought of her little boy messing up his body with all kinds of poisons, mixing with drug dealers, was unthinkable. But maybe Bill was just being dramatic. "What makes you think he's taking drugs?" she asked.

"Well, Tim overheard him and Satoshi talking, something about drugs and needing to score."

Her mouth felt dry. "Did Tim say anything to them?"

"Well, you know Tim, he's on speaking terms with most drugs, so he was going to give them some advice about where to go, but he mentioned it to me first and I said he wasn't to do any such thing."

"Oh my God. I'm coming back." What had she done? In trying to make a better life for her son she'd only succeeded in putting him into the sort of danger that simply didn't exist in Last Reach. London had started to feel like home to them, but home was where you were protected and safe. She'd never forgive herself if anything happened to Danny.

CHAPTER
SIXTY-SIX

Whatever his faults, Fin wasn't a person who ever bore a grudge. Nor was he someone who would take sexual rejection personally (not that it had happened to him often), so he'd completely missed this element in Imogen's behaviour, and didn't realise how much of her wrath was directed at him rather than at Gareth or Beth.

It was the stories in the press about Beth that he couldn't take. Gareth, as a politician and a celebrity, was fair game and was used to it, but not Beth. Worse still, Fin knew she would think that he was somehow behind it. There was no use trying to persuade her otherwise: the best thing was to get it stopped.

He had dinner with Nigel Packman, the rotund editor of the *Northlands Herald*. Nigel's favourite words were "region" and "regional". It didn't surprise Fin to hear that Nigel prided himself in hardly having left the Northlands county boundaries in over fifteen years.

"I love Northlands," Nigel had stated as their main course had arrived. "It's like . . . food and drink to a native like me." Since food and drink seemed to be his other great passion, judging from the amount of both that he was putting away, this was a good analogy.

"How does it feel to have a southerner as a prospective MP?" Fin asked.

"I'll let you into a little secret," Packman said, leaning forward so that a roll of fat was nudging gently at the rim of his plate. "I'm originally from the south myself." Which Fin had already known. Slough, to be precise.

"It's amazing how the place gets into your blood so quickly," Fin said. "I've felt it myself." More the people than the place, to be precise, but it still counted. Sincerity was the main thing. "Your star reporter — Imogen, is it?"

"She's been giving you a bit of bother," Packman said. "The *Herald* isn't generally that kind of paper, but I believe in giving young people their head."

"Have you seen what she's been writing for other publications?"

"Can't say I have." Packman slurped on his wine. Fin produced a handful of cuttings from various papers and magazines, showing Bill's scrap with the photographer and hinting about various unwelcome goings-on at Dogwood Avenue.

Packman sniffed. "These don't have a byline. How do you know it's her?"

"Read them," Fin said. "They're her all right."

Packman's eyes skimmed across the columns, and he began to nod slowly. "You're right. This is her style. Didn't know she could be such a bitch."

374

"She's a bitch with a certain amount of flair," Fin had to acknowledge, "but a bitch, none the less. You realise she's using this to work her way into a job more . . . appropriate to her talents, don't you?"

"It happens. Talent like that was never going to hang round here for long. She never did properly bed down as a Northlander."

"Her departure will, I should imagine, leave you with a bit of a news vacuum."

"Oh no. We've always got plenty to say about the region."

"Then I have a story you might be interested in. Mick Colber is going to offer to pay to have the Last Reach Point lighthouse moved."

"Move it?" Packman echoed, shovelling *crème brûlée* into his mouth. "How do you mean?"

Fin explained that it might be possible to lift the entire tower on to hydraulic jacks and shift it backwards from the edge of the cliff, to a position where it would be safe for many years to come. "It's been done before," he added. "The Belle Toute lighthouse in Sussex, for example."

"Blimey," Packman said, mopping at his mouth with a napkin. "The lighthouse family must be pleased."

"They don't know yet. I thought this was exactly the sort of good news regional item that the *Herald* would be interested in breaking."

Packman's small eyes glittered with a journalistic fervour he hadn't felt in some time, but he had a question. "How come *you* know what Colber's up to?"

Fin raised his glass to his lips. "I don't," he said. "But it's my hunch that if you run this story, he won't be able to do anything else."

He wasn't interested in making Mick Colber look good, of course. Once it had been suggested and publicised, Colber wouldn't be able to reject the idea, as that would compound the PR damage he'd already suffered. As far as Gareth was concerned, that would take the heat out of the whole situation and it wouldn't be difficult to get his campaign back on track.

Just as importantly, he wanted his final task as Gareth Dakers's minder to be something that would make Beth happy. She'd given notice to Gareth that she'd be leaving Dogwood Avenue in a month. As far as Fin knew (and he hadn't spoken to her) she didn't have anywhere else to go. Probably she was going to move back up here anyway, and live with that policeman. At least if he gave her the lighthouse back, she wouldn't feel she had to live with the policeman unless she really loved him — Beth wasn't the sort of person to do something lightly.

He hated the idea that she would be moving back to Northlands exactly at the point where he would be moving back to London, because as soon as the election results were called his job was over. He may never see her again. But at least he'd know she was as happy as he could manage to make her.

CHAPTER
SIXTY-SEVEN

Coming back to London was like coming home. When had home shifted from north to south?

Beth even enjoyed the horrible tube ride from King's Cross, which as usual took almost as long as the train ride from Boldwick to London. She loved seeing all the differently coloured faces — even if they did all look pretty miserable — and hearing the mix of accents and languages.

She quickly filled Bill in on what had been happening in Northlands, and he told her that the newspapers had carried more smear stories about the family. There were hints that Bill had been frequenting insalubrious establishments, and also that Danny had transvestite tendencies.

"Oh my God," she said.

"I'm surprised at Finian Lewis."

"Maybe he's finally showing his true colours," Beth replied, ignoring the heavy feeling in her heart. "He doesn't care for anybody. It's all just a job."

"Even if he's that nasty, I would have thought he'd have more nous than try something as obvious as this, though," Bill said. "This'll surely backfire on Dakers. I know the people of Northlands, and they'll stand by their own rather than some flash-Harry from the south."

"Well, I hope they do," she said. "I'm surprised you aren't more angry about this — it's made you look a bit foolish."

He gave her one of his very cheeky, disarming grins. "Beth, I *am* a bit foolish. I'm a silly old man, and I don't mind admitting it."

"No, you're not," she said, and gave him a hug. "You're my dad and I love you."

"Then that's the only thing that's important," he said. "As long as none of this drives a wedge between you and me and Danny."

"Where *is* Danny?"

"At school, as far as I know."

"Oh. Something to be grateful for, at least. Any more developments?"

"Nothing I've noticed. I've been keeping an eye on him for signs of drug use. Tim was telling me how to spot if he's on anything. He's a virtual pharmacoepia, that guy."

"Is a virtual pharmacoepia what we really need around when we have a vulnerable young person in the house?"

Bill fixed her with one of his most liberal grandfather looks. "Since when did having too much information lead someone off the righteous path?"

"It depends what they do with the information," she said, which led her mind back to Fin again.

"Are you going to talk to Danny about the drugs?" Bill asked.

378

"No! He'd run a mile. I'm just going to be around. That's what he needs. I'll just keep an eye on him."

"I've been doing that."

"I know you have. And I've been running around the country as if I was a damn politician myself. I'm sorry."

"You've nothing to be sorry for," he said. "I'll put the kettle on again, and you can tell me all about what you've been up to."

CHAPTER
SIXTY-EIGHT

This, of all things, he had no need of, Fin thought as he turned the car off the M1 on to those familiar A and B roads. There were a thousand things he needed to be doing in Northlands and London, and here he was, somewhere in between, heading towards Sheffield again. And it wasn't even anyone's birthday this time.

His mother had been tearful on the phone. His father had had a stroke, she said. "Only a small one, nothing life-threatening, but you know your dad. He's taken it hard."

"He won't want me around," Fin said.

"That's not true," his mother said, but they both knew it was, so she said, "Anyway, I want you. I need you to come. Times like this you need your children around you."

And, as he was the only child, that meant him; so here he was. And if he stopped to really admit it to himself, he was terrified. Terrified of not seeing his father stamping around the kitchen like the righteous spirit of Arthur Scargill in oven mitts, terrified that instead of the angry, accusing ex-miner he might find someone drooling and dependent and finally beaten.

He was surprised when his father answered the door, and greeted him with a fairly typical, "Bloody hell. Two visits inside six months. We *are* honoured."

Fin chose his words carefully. "Mum said you hadn't been well."

"She fusses too much," his father said, though Fin's initial glance at him showed that he was moving a little cautiously, and that his eyes looked glassy and not as lively as usual.

"Where is she?"

"Popped out to the shops for something or other. Complan, probably. She keeps feeding me that bloody stuff like I was an invalid or something. Revolting." He nodded towards the kettle. "Stick the kettle on then," he said. "Mayas well make yourself useful now you're here. We'll have a cup of proper tea before the Complan Queen gets back." He sounded conspiratorial in this small defiance of his wife's attempts to feed him up, and Fin reflected that it was the first time he'd ever felt that he and his father were in the same team.

He filled the kettle while his father sank into an armchair that had been moved into the kitchen from the sitting room. He realised that being asked to make the tea was the greatest indicator that something really was wrong with his father: he wouldn't normally have surrendered kitchen duties to his son as lightly as this. Even now, he maintained a supervisory role. "Make sure you let that tea brew for at least three minutes," he said. "You make it like dish water."

"I'm used to teabags." He handed a mug of tea to his father, whose hand shook a little when he took it. "Are you okay with that?" Fin asked, and realised straight away he was supposed not to have noticed anything was wrong. He pulled a dining chair out from under the table and sat down. Father and son sat and sipped their tea in awkward and more or less unbroken silence for several minutes.

It occurred to Fin that this was one of those situations where suddenly being faced with the vulnerability and mortality of his formerly alarmingly powerful father was supposed to make him rethink his path in life. It was true that it had shaken him. He'd taken it for granted that his father would always be around to antagonise and belittle him at every opportunity. He was also smart enough to realise that a large percentage of what he himself was was a reaction to his father: to his politics, his working life, his whole attitude to the world.

But the truth was that Fin's world view was already wobbly enough as it was, largely thanks to Beth Jackson. She'd managed to find a way into his heart, boldly going where no woman had gone before even though she probably didn't realise it. Because of her, nothing he was doing for Gareth made as much sense at it previously would have. The fact that Gareth's head was being kept above water, politically speaking, was largely down to him, but it gave him no satisfaction as long as Beth saw him as the enemy.

He gave himself a mental shake: he was here to visit his father, not to think about his own problems. "So how are you feeling?" he asked.

"Useless," his father said. "I'm not supposed to do any gardening, or cooking — can't operate heavy machinery like a bloody food mixer even. How'm I supposed to feel?"

"You just need to rest, though," his son said. "Things'll get better, won't they?"

"As long as nothing else goes wrong in my head."

"You'll be all right."

"And you're the medical expert, are you?"

Fin fixed his grey eyes on his father's, realising with a jolt how similar they were to his own. "I'm only trying to show some concern."

"Too little, too late," his father muttered. Fin gave up, and a short while later he wandered out into the garden, and sat down on the blue-painted bench next to the greenhouse, still clutching his mug which was now practically empty.

The garden had always been neat and tidy with its carefully trimmed lawn and borders of all the usual kinds of garden flowers. He didn't know what they were called; though he did recognise foxgloves — or were they lupins? Anyway, it was a traditional sort of garden, not trendy or architectural or any of those things, no bamboo or exotic grasses. The garden of normal, working-class people. The garden he used to play in, though he couldn't really remember what the games had involved.

He would wait to see his mother, then make his excuses and leave. He was doing no good for his father, but he might be able to do some good somewhere else. Like London. Beth was in London. He could talk to her about the lighthouse, and finally do something that might make her life better.

His father shambled out of the house to join him, sitting heavily down on the bench at his side. "You're doing a good job in Northlands, I hear."

"What's this? Compliments?"

"No, lad, it's sarcasm. We've been reading about this waste-incinerator project, and how Dakers is really behind it."

"He isn't. You should know you can't believe what you read in the papers."

"I might have had a cerebrovascular accident, as they call it, but I'm not addled yet. There's no smoke without fire, and there wouldn't be so much activity going on to soil the reputation of this lighthouse family if there was nothing in it. I imagine you're behind that?"

Fin threw the tea slops from his cup out across the lawn in a fierce gesture. "It might disappoint you to learn that I'm not," he said.

"And pigs might fly."

"Think what you like. I would never do that."

"Never?"

"Okay, I admit, yes, I *would* do that. I *have* done that. But not this time."

"Why not?"

Fin took a deep breath. The smell of damp soil filled his nose. "Because I don't want to hurt the lighthouse family. I . . . care about what happens to them."

He expected his father to say something sarcastic or dismissive, like he had done every time Fin had

384

revealed what he was thinking, ever since he was a child. But this time his father sat in silence for some minutes and then said, "When you're deciding what to do, there's only one question that needs to be answered. It isn't how are you going to pay the bills, or what do your parents expect, or where is your career going, or any of that. It's: what's the most important thing in the world to you, right now?" His father's voice was unusually soft.

Fin didn't need to think about that. The answer had been creeping up on him for weeks now. The most important thing in the world to him was Beth.

CHAPTER
SIXTY-NINE

The most important thing to Beth for the last sixteen years had been Danny. He'd been the apple of her eye, the bane of her life, her biggest source of joy and worry in roughly equal measures.

At the moment, worry definitely had the upper hand. The hair dyeing and make-up had been one thing, the potential drug-taking quite another. Ever since she got back from Northlands her son had been acting in an odd, distracted way. It was a strange combination of a kind of suppressed excitement and the usual Danny apathy: he seemed to be in a constant state of tension.

They sat alone together in the kitchen. He'd been smoking again — she could smell it on his clothes. She glanced at his fingers to see if they were getting nicotine stained, and noticed traces of badly removed purple nail polish around the cuticles.

"What was in that parcel you got this morning?" she asked him. When he was a little boy, if any of their geographically distant relatives sent him a parcel for his birthday he'd come running into his parents' bedroom with it, eager to share the excitement of tearing the paper off. When a rather large package had arrived at

Dogwood Avenue that morning addressed to him, he'd taken it quickly into his room.

"It's thirty metres of gold lamé fabric," he said. "Since you asked."

"Not *really*?"

"Why not really? What am I supposed to be getting in the post that you would approve of? Porn? Anatomically accurate sex dolls?"

"I was just being interested," she said. "There's no need to be sarcastic and horrible."

"For God's sake," he muttered. "Look, you'll see for yourself soon enough, okay?"

"Gold lamé," she repeated. "Is it for a drag act or something?"

"Oh, yeah, bullseye, Mother."

"I wish you'd take this seriously," she said.

"Why? It's not serious. How people dress isn't serious, even if I *was* in a drag act. And you've never seen me in a dress, have you?"

"No, but I've seen you dyeing your hair, and you've got nail varnish on your fingers, and you and Satoshi wear make-up."

"Mum! Remind me where you were in the early eighties."

"I was at home at the lighthouse."

"But you had a television, right?"

"Yes."

"So I'm sure you've seen men in make-up before."

"But . . ."

"I'm going out," he said, and stumped out of the room.

Oh, very well played, she thought. She hadn't even managed to talk to him about the smoking, never mind the drugs.

She did mention her worries to Tim though. The "human pharmacoepia" was not very reassuring. "If it's drugs, it's some very weird shit," was his assessment.

Later the same day she made, as they say in the tabloids, a shocking discovery. While she was tidying the sitting room she picked up a piece of paper Danny had been doodling on. In amongst images of brooding dark-eyed men (who looked suspiciously oriental to Beth, and she wondered again about his feelings for Satoshi) he'd written a confused jumble of a message in which he said he wished everybody would leave him alone, and that people were always ringing him but when he picked the phone up there wasn't anyone at the other end. This was written in thick black script, with the words written over and over so it resembled a piece of very gothic knitting.

Beth showed the paper to her father. "That's not good," he said. "I'm no psychiatrist, but I would say that's showing disturbing signs of paranoid schizophrenia."

"Oh, come on," she said. "That's a bit extreme." But she was worried. Thinking imaginary people were ringing you and then hanging up did indeed sound paranoid, and the dark scribblings didn't look like the work of a happy mind. "What are we going to do?" she said. "Should I go and talk to his teacher at the school?"

Bill thought that was a good idea. "But talk to Dan first," he said.

"I knew we shouldn't have come to London," she fretted.

"You don't mean that. You're just feeling guilty because you like it here."

"But maybe he can't cope with city life. Linda keeps telling me I should go back up north. It might be best for Danny too. I just wish we could go back to the lighthouse."

CHAPTER
SEVENTY

It was pouring with rain, dark and miserable; the rain was like a solid curtain of water. Beth looked outside and the road was awash, with cars slooshing through it making a wave behind them. Bits of litter and dead leaves swept along the gutters. The few people who were out clutched desperately at umbrellas, but still looked soaked through and perfectly miserable.

Beth was alone in the flat. Tim had announced that he was leaving the next day. He'd found a place with a friend in Greenwich and would be moving there. He thanked Beth for her kindness and gave her a pretty little houseplant as a parting gift. Bill had taken him out for a farewell drink.

Danny had gone out not long after them, clutching the parcel which had arrived that morning. Beth hadn't had time to talk to him about the worrying scribblings on the piece of paper — she had to find a way to broach it without antagonising him further.

She sat by the gas fire with a book open on her lap, not reading but listening to the rain and the wind howling in the chimney, and worrying about Danny, and where they were going to live. It was a different location but still the same old set of problems as when they were at the lighthouse. And in the only corner of her mind that wasn't occupied by worrying, a corner she kept wrapped up and only opened cautiously in moments like this when she was alone, she thought about Fin, and wondered what he was doing. Was he still in Northlands?

The creaky doorbell rang twice.

Beth didn't open the door to just anyone any more. She'd opened it once too often only to find journalists and photographers camped there. So instead of going downstairs, she went to the small window which was right above the door and peered through the net curtain. It was pouring with rain, and getting dark, and she couldn't see anyone. She wished they'd had an entryphone put in, as Fin had suggested ages ago, but as it was she had to make do with the low-tech version: she opened the casement window a fraction and looked out, the rain immediately lashing at her face.

As if she'd imagined him into reality, Fin was standing below, looking up at her, rain splashing his face, his hair as wet and sleek as an otter's pelt. For more than a few seconds she contemplated the possibility of shutting the window and ignoring him. But only for a few seconds, because then she was running down the stairs and opening the door.

He smiled at her, somewhat shyly, she thought.

"You're soaked," she said. She wondered what had happened to make him come to see her in a storm like this. It must be pretty important, whatever it was.

"Could I come in?"

Should she leave him here to drown or be kind and let him in? She didn't even think about that for more than a fraction of a second. She led the way upstairs to the flat, and brought him a towel from the bathroom. He dried his hair vigorously, so it stood up in fluffy spikes, a hedgehog now rather than an otter.

"I didn't expect to see you," was all she could think of to say, because she'd been thinking about him so much, with such a mixture of feelings, that having him standing here now in her hallway, with his hair all fluffy and standing on end, looking damp and downright beautiful, she couldn't think straight.

He handed the towel back to her. "I came to tell you . . ."

"I'm not sure I want to hear anything you have to tell me," she said, going to throw the towel into the laundry basket in the bathroom.

There was such a long pause that she turned back to look at him; she could almost have thought he'd gone, crept away downstairs, and she had to acknowledge that if he had, she'd have been disappointed. But he was still standing there and looking at her with that same almost shy expression.

"I didn't come to make any excuses," he said. "All I've been doing is my job."

"Some job. Dragging me and my family through the dirt is all part of the job, is it?"

"What?"

"You told the newspapers about the time we had to pick Bill up in Battersea."

392

He looked quite genuinely aggrieved. "Beth, I swear I didn't. I wouldn't do that."

Beth wanted to believe him, but how can you believe a person whose job it is to school other people in the arts of presentation and manipulation? Linda was right — out of all the people in the world she could have fallen in love with, she'd picked the worst.

His arms were by his sides, his hands relaxed. *Don't fidget,* he'd told her the first time she was on television, on Cara Chadwick's show. *Keep your hands relaxed. Then you'll look more sincere.* Was he following his own advice now, trying to look sincere? How could she tell what was an act with him and what was real?

Then a trickle of water found its way from his hair and began to course down the side of his nose. He rubbed it away, and somehow with that tiny, unconscious gesture, she suddenly believed him.

"Never touch your nose on camera," she reminded him of his own advice. "It makes you look as if you're uncomfortable."

"I *am* uncomfortable. I've never been more uncomfortable in my life." He smiled again. "And I'm very wet. I'm dripping on your carpet."

"By rights I shouldn't care if you get pneumonia."

"By rights you shouldn't."

But she did. "You said you came to tell me something," she said.

"Yes, I . . ."

She interrupted him, hearing a commotion in the hallway downstairs. "What's all that noise?"

The door at the bottom of the stairs banged open, there was a sound of hilarious giggling, and she looked away from Fin to the stairwell in time to see Bryan Ferry and Roxy Music walk into the flat.

CHAPTER
SEVENTY-ONE

Bryan Ferry had jet black hair in a louche, greased-back style, a stray lock of it hanging fetchingly over his turquoise eyes, which were underlined with black. He was wearing a suit that was almost teddy-boy in style, cut long and boxy and made of sparkling gold lamé. The two members of Roxy Music were similarly attired. Beth couldn't help noticing that one of them had an oriental look. The supermodel Jerry Hall was right behind them, poured into a shimmering red dress, long blonde hair swept low over one eye. She was doing most of the giggling.

The Geordie hit-maker tossed back his oiled lock of hair and glared at Fin. "What's *he* doing here?" he wanted to know, squaring up his padded shoulders.

Beth wasn't able to reply to that, because she didn't actually know what Fin was doing there, other than dripping on the hall carpet. She wondered how Roxy Music managed to still be dry. Everyone stood looking at each other.

Jerry Hall finally broke the silence. "So what do you think?" she said. "Are you impressed?" She wiggled her hips to show off her figure-clinging dress.

Beth looked at the supermodel, better known to her as Eden, and at Bugs and Satoshi whom she took to be to be Brian Eno and Andy Mackay respectively. And at Bryan Ferry, her own beautiful son.

"Are you going to a fancy dress party?" she asked, at which Danny rolled his eyes to heaven, but she didn't care at that moment if he thought she was being naff — she was just so relieved that the make-up and the hair and the gold lamé had a relatively harmless explanation.

"Do you do the music or just the look?" Fin asked.

Danny looked as though he was inclined to ignore him, but pride overcame cussedness and he said, "Of *course* we do the music."

"Do you?" Beth said. She didn't think she'd heard Danny sing since he was about five.

Eden twirled a finger in her silky blonde wig and said, "He's a genius. When he sings, he *is* Bryan Ferry."

"Is he? Why?" Beth knew she was sounding as stupid as she felt.

"We're a Roxy Music tribute band," Satoshi said.

"And we're a bit hungry. Anything to eat, Mrs Jackson?" Bugs added.

"Yes — no — I mean, explain this to me properly, Danny."

"Like Satoshi just said. We've been practising for ages. We've got a gig at the college on Saturday."

"Why didn't you tell me?" Beth asked.

"Mum! How embarrassing would *that* have been?"

"Well, I have to say I'm pretty relieved. I thought you were rehearsing to be in a drag act." Danny received this revelation with a very deep blush, and the others had hysterics.

During all this, Fin stayed in the background. Beth was constantly aware of him, like hot sunshine on her skin.

But for now, Danny was holding court. Beth was amazed: somehow, in the guise of Bryan Ferry, Danny was more confident, a bit taller in his creeper soles, more relaxed looking. The others even persuaded him to sing a few notes. He'd got that distinctive Bryan Ferry warble off perfectly and, more than that, as soon as he started singing he seemed to *become* Bryan Ferry — stylish, languid, sexy even (Beth felt strange to be applying the word "sexy" to her own son — but Jerry Hall was clearly impressed with him).

The excerpt he sang, from "Street Life", made his mother realise with a mixture of embarrassment and relief that the notes Danny had been scribbling about people ringing on the telephone were lines from the song. So he wasn't planning to be a drag act and he wasn't suicidal. A double result. She wanted to hug him but didn't want to crumple his suit.

CHAPTER
SEVENTY-TWO

Carey and Jon appeared while all this was going on, and admitted to Beth that they'd known about this Roxy Music thing for some time. Carey had even helped Eden to make the costumes. Carey raised her eyebrow very subtly at Beth when she realised Fin was there, but no facial gesture had been invented to allow Beth to relay any kind of response to her so she just smiled, while fervently wishing everyone would go away.

The party was not yet complete, of course. More footsteps on the stairs announced the arrival of Bill and Tim, who was looking a bit pale and sheepish, Beth thought. It was probably the end of a long night of drinking. Bill was introduced to Roxy Music. "Bloody hell," he said. "Why didn't you tell us? We've been thinking all sorts. This is brilliant!"

Then he noticed Fin. "Come to dig up some more dirt?" he said. "Haven't you had enough out of this family?"

Fin stood up from the chair in the corner where he'd been sitting. He had quite an audience: a lighthouse keeper and his beautiful daughter, a hippy and her eco-warrior partner, three members of a glam rock band and a supermodel, and a wheelie-bin cleanser fallen on hard times. There was a long, not altogether comfortable, pause.

Fin spoke directly to Beth as if there was no one else there. "Beth," he said, "I came to tell you about the lighthouse . . ."

Bill interrupted him. "Don't think you can walk in here and come out with a load of spin doctor flannel. By rights I ought to throw you down those stairs on your arse."

"In a minute," Fin said, "you can do whatever you want. I just want to say to Beth . . ." She realised his eyes had been on her the whole time. "This wasn't what I came to say, but it's the only thing I *do* want to say, and I wish I could say it more privately but — I love you."

Eden, Carey and Satoshi clapped their hands, Danny, Bill and Jon looked annoyed, Bugs looked puzzled and Tim looked as if he might be about to pass out. And as for Beth, she felt such a rush of emotions, like all the feelings of the last few months had massed together and hit her from all sides like a rip tide, and when that had ebbed everything seemed to have changed colour.

"I love you, too," she said to him, the words escaping before she'd even consciously thought about it.

Eden and Carey said, "Ahhhhh," and there were a couple of mutters and tutting noises from the others, but all Beth was really aware of was that Fin was smiling at her, and, quite unexpectedly, Danny was smiling too. Everything was going to be all right.

Not quite all right. Her father went ballistic. He was so angry she didn't think even he knew whether he was angry with her, or Fin, or himself, or Gareth or everybody.

Danny and his friends, led by Eden, all retreated diplomatically to Carey's flat with Jon and Carey, which left only Fin and Beth, and Bill and Tim.

Bill was in full rant mode, blaming Fin for everything from the dodgy state of the cliff at Last Reach practically to Martin's death.

"And you can keep the hell away from my daughter!" he finished, which made Beth want to laugh because it made him sound like John Wayne. She didn't think laughing at this point would be the most diplomatic thing to do, even though her heart felt very bubbly and she wanted to laugh at everything.

Fin was looking, for once in his life, lost for words, and Beth couldn't think of anything to say either, because in her head she agreed with everything her father had just said. It was her heart that rebelled.

Then Tim, who'd been standing by quietly, spoke up. "You've got it wrong, Bill," he said. "Fin didn't give those stories to the papers." To Fin he said, "And Beth didn't give the *Northlands Herald* the original story about Dakers and Colber."

"Not that it's anything to do with you," Fin said.

"But it is." Tim's handsome cheeks were flushed deep red. "My surname isn't actually Carter, it's Callow. Imogen Callow-Creed is my half-sister."

400

CHAPTER
SEVENTY-THREE

The sun sparkled on an almost-flat sea, the smell of warm grass mingling with the salty air. The sound of waves lapping gently at the foot of the cliff was as hypnotic as the lazy buzzing of bees.

Beth lay back on the short, scrubby grass, one arm across her forehead to shield her eyes from the glare of the spring sunshine, and looked at the lighthouse tower above her, enormous and looming from this perspective. "I wonder how long it'll last?" she said quietly.

"Hmm? How long what'll last?" Fin asked, looking down at her from his position propped up on his elbows. He was wearing an open-necked shirt and jeans — no need for a suit and tie now he was no longer a spin doctor.

"The lighthouse. I wonder how long it'll be before it falls into the sea."

"It might be years, according to that structural engineer I talked to. Depends on the weather." His face was concerned, worrying that she might have regrets. "You could have taken up Colber's offer to have it moved back, you know."

"That would have looked like accepting a bribe, like I was agreeing to the incinerator being built."

Fin smiled. "Colber reckoned without Gareth, though. He's done even better than I thought he would, I have to admit." Beth had to agree. Gareth and Lorelei had thrown all their energies into protesting against the waste-disposal project, and had swayed the local council into refusing the planning application. Colber was livid, of course, but there wasn't much he could do.

And the lighthouse was still standing. Maybe some money would be found to shore up the sea defences at Last Reach, and maybe it wouldn't. Beth would be sad if the lighthouse was to crumble into the sea, but it wouldn't be the worst thing that could happen.

People were more important than buildings. People like Danny, happy now he was settled in school, and doing quite well as Bryan Ferry. And Bill, currently touring manned lighthouses on the South American west coast with the now-forgiven Tim Callow, partly for fun and partly to make a documentary for Channel 4. Moving to London had done all of them a favour, but when she looked at Fin, Beth thought she was luckiest of all.

"It wouldn't be the end of the world if the lighthouse wasn't here any more," she said. "Things have to take their natural course. Nothing's permanent, we just have to enjoy what we have while we can."

Fin smiled at her, a smile full of affection. "You know what I love most about you?" he said, "When I look at you. I know exactly how you're feeling. In your eyes I can see straight to your heart."

And in his eyes she could see he meant it.

★ ★ ★

402

Holidays in Northlands were all very well; they soon had to return to London. There was a lot to do there: Danny and the band were playing in a seventies revival show in Hoxton, the garden centre had offered Beth full-time work now that spring had arrived, and Fin was starting his new job, as press officer to a health charity. An appointment which had finally earned him the approval of his father, as had his relationship with Beth.

Gareth invited them to the House to listen to his maiden speech, which was going to be about toxic emissions from waste plants, a subject about which he'd become very well informed recently.

Fin and Beth sat with Lorelei in the Strangers' Gallery, looking down on a large quantity of empty green leather benches. This was a surprise to Beth — she'd expected the House to be packed, like it is at Prime Minister's Questions, but it was five p.m. and it looked as though most of the honourable members had gone off for a spot of tea. When the Speaker called Gareth, he stood up from his position on the second-to-back row, and gave a brief, witty and to-the-point speech with his usual conviction. It seemed to go down well, and he sat back down looking relieved that he'd carried it off. When someone from the opposition benches had stood up to reply, Gareth looked up at the Gallery and gave them a quick smile.

Fin leaned towards Beth. "That's the last speech I'll ever help him with," he whispered. "He's on his own now."

Well, not quite on his own: Lorelei was smiling fit to burst with pride.

Also available in ISIS Large Print:

The Starter Marriage

Kate Harrison

A bitter-sweet comedy about marriage, mistakes and moving on . . .

"A funny, engaging and bitter-sweet read about life after the supposedly happy ending. Brilliant." **Mike Gayle**

"A slick, bitter-sweet comedy" **Mail on Sunday**

Known to all her friends as "Tip Top Tess" because of her dogged pursuit of the perfect home, the perfect marriage and the perfect career, she's now in the biggest mess of her life. And it's all because Barney has walked out.

But there's a life raft on the horizon: The Divorce Survival Class. It may be uncomfortable, overcrowded and nearly sinking under the weight of excess baggage, but it's a boot-camp for the broken-hearted. Over eight weeks, Tess and her battle-weary classmates will lay bare the darkest secrets of their failed marriages — from the thrills of a threesome to the monotony of monogamy. And course leader William will turn their lives around in truly spectacular style . . .

ISBN 0-7531-7483-9 (hb)
ISBN 0-7531-7484-7 (pb)

The Rock Orchard

Paula Wall

"Authentic, romantic and beautifully told, this is a story to treasure" **Adriana Trigiani**

Lacking much in the way of distraction, the townsfolk of Leaper's Fork, Tennessee, have little else to preoccupy themselves with beyond each other. Foremost among the town's oddballs are the Belle women, five generations of floozies who have managed to amass one of the largest fortunes in the region without needing to stoop to marriage.

Musette, the matriarch of the clan, still presides in the form of a nude statue sitting atop her grave. Her granddaughter Charlotte, technically a spinster, is a hardhearted businesswoman who made a rare indulgence into sentimentality by adopting her niece, Angela. As feral as a wildcat, the slatternly Angela has an innate gift for striking men dumb with desire. Her latest victim is Dr Adam Montgomery who moves in next door with his Yankee fiancée. With seduction in the graveyard and unexpected sexual awakening, it seems that the whole balance of the town has begun to shift . . .

ISBN 0-7531-7447-2 (hb)
ISBN 0-7531-7448-0 (pb)

Beyond Indigo

Preethi Nair

Nina knows there's more to life than black and white . . .

Nina's lost her job, boyfriend and faith in her guru in the space of 24 hours. Unable to tell her parents what has happened, she puts on a suit every day and pretends to go to work.

What she's really doing is escaping to a studio, where she begins to paint for the first time in years. But when her work is spotted by a top gallery owner, she cannot admit she is the painter and pretends to be the agent instead. Meanwhile at home, she's agreed to an arranged marriage to keep the peace. There are too many layers of pretence and something has to give way — but at what cost to Nina?

ISBN 0-7531-7351-4 (hb)
ISBN 0-7531-7352-2 (pb)

The Making of Henry

Howard Jacobson

"It's powerful, bang to rights, monstrously funny"
Independent

Out of the blue, Henry Nagel receives a solicitor's letter telling him he has inherited a sumptuous apartment in St John's Wood. Divine intervention? Or his late father's love nest? Henry doesn't know, but he is glad to escape his solitary life in the North.

Henry's new life is full of surprises as he finds himself making friends with his neighbour (and his dog) and falling in love with a waitress. Yet even as this unfolds, Henry cannot stop obsessing about his past life, envying his childhood friend turned Hollywood star and talking to his dead father.

Eventually Henry realises that, despite his reservations, his new life might just be the making of him.

ISBN 0-7531-7313-1 (hb)
ISBN 0-7531-7314-X (pb)

Change of Heart

Barbara Anderson

A glittering jewel of a book, an audacious mixture of comic invention and human insight that is Barbara Anderson at her very best.

Oliver Gurth Perkins is seventy-five, and the darkest cloud on his horizon is that the local bookshop no longer stocks paperbacks of the Times cryptic crosswords.

He has an easy companionship with his wife; his dental practice is undemanding; his son is a decent enough sort; and his granddaughter who comes for the school holidays is his delight. But when a minor heart episode convinces Oliver that it's time for him to take more interest in the lives of others, further shocks are in store . . .

Change of Heart traces Olly's passage from the desolation of his first realisation that his wife, Hester, is quite happy with the way things are, to his happy embrace of an extended family life.

ISBN 0-7531-7283-6 (hb)
ISBN 0-7531-7284-4 (pb)